THE
Artist

THE Artist

By:

MICHELLE WALLACE CAMPANELLI

ARPress
ILLUMINATING IDEAS
EMPOWERING VOICES

ARPress
45 Dan Road Suite 5
Canton MA 02021

Hotline: 1(888) 821-0229
Fax: 1(508) 545-7580

Ordering Information:
Quantity sales. Special discounts are available on quantity purchases by corporations, associations, and others. For details, contact the publisher at the address above.

Printed in the United States of America.

ISBN-13: Softcover   979-8-89330-179-3
                eBook   979-8-89330-180-9
                Hardcover   979-8-89330-181-6
Library of Congress Control Number: 2024902604

DEDICATION

This book is dedicated to my Great Aunt Barbara Lossman, a brilliant painter who was the must for this fiction novel.

I'd also like to thank my late husband Louis V. Campanelli, my wonderful mother and personal editor, Fontaine M. Wallace, Grandfather Tom & Margaret, Grandpa Jim & Lauretta, Dawn, Melisa & Dick, Colette.

David & Greg, Steve & Heather Sigety, and all those in the Wallace & Campanelli family. To God be the glory!

To those with great talent who also have inspired mine: Voice Teacher Sherry Maclean, Director of the Space Coast Symphony Orchestra Aaron Collins, SCSO Chorus Members, Brevard Community College Music Directors of Brevard Corale Jim Boyle, Jean Black & BCC Community Chorus Director Robert Lamb, Mark Brasel from The Zone Studio, Vin, HNJ Player Directors and St. Mark's UMC Shekinah & HNJ Players Theater, St. Marks United Methodist Church Choir & Directors, the Florida rock band members of Black Widow, Nameless & Bad Asspex with special loving memory given in honor of Kristen Pepper Kirschten, bass player.

We are the clay, you are the potter;
We are all the work of His hand.
-Isaiah 64:8

CONTENTS

CHAPTER 1

Stuck inside a four-door sedan for the past twenty hours, Mia was tired of looking at all the trees in Michigan. Although this landscape was so different than her Florida beachside community, Mia just wanted to arrive at "Birds Nesting," her great aunt's family estate, as soon as possible.

She had never been to "Birds Nesting" before, nor had she ever met her great aunt, the youngest sister of her grandmother Marlana. Word had come that this aunt had a terrible fall and was bedridden; her prognosis wasn't good. The phone call where her aunt begged her to come shook Mia to the core.

Meeting her aunt now seemed like bad timing. She was in line to inherit the estate and to many relatives it might appear she was going to visit the estate and see if it was a place she wanted. Mia hated that thought. She was quite happy living in the warmth of the Florida sun and she cared for her aunt.

Her younger cousin Nathan drove. They had been close growing up, but Nathan had moved away years before and now they were like strangers. Next to him sat his wife, Toby, a red-haired, slender woman wearing a very tight dress.

Beside her, his massive hand engulfing hers, sat her husband Gus, a big, lofty Italian. Near six feet in height, shaven headed with deep features, a Roman nose and dark, dangerous eyes, no one messed with Gus.

Mia admitted they probably should not be stuck in a car for over twenty hours, but circumstances forced the situation. She was happy living in Florida. Writing was her passion, and her home state offered the slow relaxing atmosphere she needed to create. Nothing moved quickly in her beachside resort town and that was just how she liked it.

As she stared at the miles upon miles of maples and birch trees, she wondered when the next time would be that she could see a palm tree.

"Don't you think all these trees would be beautiful in the fall?" Nathan asked, lowering the radio. "All these trees."

"Yes," Mia agreed as the car passed a sign for Bear Lake.

The car made a quick turn into the parking lot of a bar whose sign read, "Home of Bear-sized Burgers." Toby got out of the car, and Mia didn't need to ask why. They were lost again. Mia was grateful she was traveling with Toby, because she would ask for directions.

"Should we worry about her walking into a bar dressed like that?" Nathan said. "Maybe I should go with her."

"If you think it's best." Mia smiled. "How far away do you think we are?"

"Maybe fifteen minutes according to this map. It shows a side road and I want to know if it's on the right or left," Nathan said.

Toby got back into the car, grinning. "The very ugly, toothless man behind the bar told me the road was on the left side near the lake."

"Big burgers here, huh?" Gus asked. "I could use one."

"Wait until we get to your Aunt Barb's." Nathan shot Gus a stern look. "We're almost there."

Mia closed her eyes, praying Gus wouldn't snap back. He simply leaned over and whispered in her ear, "I really love you, just so you know that."

The sedan backed out of the parking lot and went through a dirt road between thickly wooded birch and purple-flowered crab-apple trees. One last left and in front of them was a large wooden gate and a high iron fence. Two dogs rushed from the house to greet them. One was a giant Collie with long golden and white hair; the other a terrier mix, white as a ghost with big happy eyes. Both barked and wagged their tails wildly.

Nathan parked the car beside the wooden sign which read "Birds Nesting." He removed the key and unlocked the doors. "We're here, finally."

Mia exited the car, her jaw dropping at the sight of the expansive estate in front of her. The home was huge and breathtakingly beautiful, right on the lake, and the water seemed to go on forever. The house was painted a light green with big red window sills and ivy crawling up the sides. In the front yard sat a large birdbath with the statue of an angel pouring water.

"This is incredible," Mia said.

"Worth more than a million," Nathan mumbled. "It should be." Gus unfurled out of the car. "This is a huge place."

"Wow." Toby got out and unlatched the gate. She walked in and Mia wondered if they should follow, with the dogs barking. Immediately the dogs jumped up on Toby, licking her make-up covered face.

Mia's worries about the dogs quickly subsided as they entered through the gate and up the long drive to the bright red door.

"Who wants to knock?" Gus asked.

Mia's heart began to pound. *What if she looks just like my Grandmother?* She missed her grandmother almost daily and to see someone the same age, bedridden, who even looked like her might be too taxing on Mia's emotions.

"I'll do it." Nathan pounded on the door.

They waited a moment before the door opened and a thin blonde with a brilliant smile on her face answered. "Hi, I'm DeeDee, the caregiver. You must be Barb's family from Florida. We've been expecting you."

Mia smiled and slowly walked in. The house was very dark inside until she entered the main living quarters. There was a bed facing an enormous window that made up an entire wall of the room. With her aunt confined to bed, it was obvious the furniture had been moved to accommodate her looking out onto the water.

Mia couldn't believe the view. For miles, the water drifted slowly past. A tall birdhouse hung near the window where little chickadees sat on their perches, one of six small feeders throughout the large backyard that curled into a beach.

Her aunt was just like her. They both loved birds. Mia immediately smiled and walked over to her aunt. Even in her seventies, Aunt Barb was very attractive. Her gray hair was curly, her eyes light-colored like Mia's. Near the bedside was a picture of Barbara in her twenties and Mia realized not only did Aunt Barb remind her of her grandmother but also of herself.

Nathan came around her. "Hi, Barbara. It's wonderful to finally meet you."

The woman's eyes filled with tears. "Come closer so I can see you."

He rushed forward and kissed her cheek. "I've heard so much from my mother."

"Oh, I'd know you anywhere," she said kindly. "You look just like your father. Where's Mia?"

"Right here." Mia took a step closer. "Is your husband here?" she asked.

"Hi, Aunt Barbara," Gus said with his Italian accent. "Nice to meet ya'."

"And this is Toby," Nathan interrupted. "My wife of two years."

"I've heard all about your wedding," Aunt Barbara said. "Only good things except for the cake. I heard it was lemon instead of white."

Toby's half smile telegraphed her displeasure. "Oh, I know the person who complained about the cake."

"Come and sit down and let's talk," Aunt Barbara said, tears running down her cheeks. "You have no idea how long I've wanted to meet all of you."

Mia wondered why Barbara wasn't moving to wipe her tears, and then she realized her Aunt couldn't. A sudden horrible feeling crawled up her spine. Her Aunt had been through hell and yet she lay here so happy to see them.

"I love you all so much," Aunt Barbara said. "I've heard about you so much I feel like I know you."

Mia could tell that Aunt Barbara's affection was genuine; she wasn't putting on airs or waving property in their faces. She simply cared for them and was genuinely pleased they came.

"Do you mind if I take pictures of all of us together?" Nathan asked.

"Oh, not today, dears; my hair isn't done," Aunt Barbara said. "Besides, I don't want to be remembered like this." Nathan took a step back. Mia was surprised how that sudden honesty affected her cousin. He, too, was moved, seeing her in this state.

"How about I take pictures of your paintings and your trees then?" he asked.

"Of course, you might even see a robin. There are many bird nests close by." Mia sat down in a chair beside the bed. She stared at Aunt Barbara for a few minutes, moved that she was so happy to see them. She regretted not sending more gifts, cards and things through the years. Mia should have called her more often and would have if she knew how much it meant to her.

Nathan and Toby walked out the door and Gus followed. The two dogs sat at Mia's feet. She ignored her allergies and began to pet the white terrier. "Looks like you made a new friend." Aunt Barbara giggled. "That's Lacy."

"And the Collie?"

"Her name is Mango."

"You have very friendly dogs."

"Animals have always brought me such joy. They never seemed to mind my being in bed so much."

"So, it wasn't the car accident that made you bedridden, Aunt Barbara?"

"I have muscular dystrophy."

Mia had heard that she had an illness, but now she had a name for it. "That must have been hard on you."

"It's worse now, because I can no longer paint. I still hope after my bones heal from the fall I'll be able to raise a paintbrush again. Take a look around. I did all these paintings except for the ones in the hallway. There are a few there from my art teacher."

Mia rose and walked around the room. One painting was of a boy in a rowboat fishing near a dockside village. Every inch looked like a photo—it was so clear and perfectly proportioned. Another was a fall landscape, as if you were looking out your window at every perfect falling leaf. Mia could hardly believe how talented an artist her aunt was. She was as good as the painters she had seen at the famous Cleveland Art Museum years ago.

"Pick one," her aunt said.

"You can't be serious." Mia gasped.

"Be careful which one you pick. With every painting comes a story you'll have to hear."

Mia sensed this was a golden opportunity. She decided to pick the most unusual painting and learn exactly who her aunt really was. Were they kindred spirits with windows to the soul? Aunt Barbara's paintings seemed a part of her, just like Mia's books were a part of Mia.

Although their crafts were different: Barbara the painter, Mia the writer—Mia knew an artist heart was the same.

One can get to know the other, just by studying the other's passion. Even though they had spent their lives apart, they would get to know each other by their art. After all, Mia decided, there is no better way to get to know an artist.

CHAPTER 2

Mia walked down the next hallway. She didn't want to hear any lectures on why she still should write or how much she had done. "My ex-husband, Mathew, that New York Literary Agent, told the world before he divorced me that my written works were a joke and without him, my novels would never make money. On public television, he actually shrugged his shoulders when the newscaster asked him if I had any talent. For years after, Aunt Barbara, I struggled not to believe him. I cared too much what he thought."

"Then you married Gus."

"Yes, and he is the perfect husband. I love him!"

The hallway was lined with more paintings, changing the direction of her thoughts. One was of a bucket of apples spilled over. They looked so good she wanted to taste them. Beside it was another of a collie that looked exactly like Mango. The dog's happy disposition had been captured perfectly. On the final wall, Mia noticed a landscape different than anything she'd ever seen before. The trees were tall and slender, the dirt below brown and slightly hilly, and it was a watercolor, not an oil.

"Auntie, did you do this landscape at the end of the hall?"

"You can tell I didn't paint that one because the strokes are different, right?" Aunt Barbara chuckled. "You'd be right. That one was painted by my art teacher."

Just then Nathan, Gus and Toby hurried into the living room.

"We took some great pictures, Aunt Barbara," Nathan announced. "We got some really nice ones of the house and the birdhouses from the beach."

"How nice." She smiled.

Mia walked back and Gus quickly asked her, "What were you doing? You okay?"

"Looking at her paintings and talking." "

You're quite a painter," Toby praised.

"So do you like the landscape watercolor?" Aunt Barbara asked Mia.

"Yes." She didn't lie.

"It's yours. I call this painting *For Loren*."

"*For Loren*?" Gus raised a brow. "After a friend of yours?"

"Something like that." Aunt Barbara's eyes turned to the ceiling. "Come, all of you, sit. I want you all to know this."

"Is Loren a man or a woman?" Toby asked.

"Loren was a man," Aunt Barbara said, "and a very handsome one at that. Since you've decided on *Loren's* painting, my gift to you is more than the artwork but to learn of Loren and why that landscape was painted in honor of him."

Mia sat next to her aunt's bedside. Gus sat down beside her. At her feet, Toby and Nathan pulled together two chairs and put down their cameras. They leaned in and listened as Aunt Barbara began telling her tale.

CHAPTER 3

"This story is very close to my heart," Aunt Barbara said. "It starts all the way back in 1941 when I met Loren."

"Telling this won't upset you, will it?" Toby asked.

"It's important that you all know the history behind this painting. It will mean more to you then. Take it from the hall and bring it in."

Mia hurried down the hall, removed the landscape from the wall and held it out for all surrounding Aunt Barbara's bed to see.

"Incredible," Toby said. "Is that France or perhaps Italy? What kind of trees are these? They are pointed straight up!"

"You're getting ahead of yourself, dear."

Mia walked closer to Aunt Barbara's bedside table and leaned the painting against the wall so everyone in the room could better view it. The moment her aunt's head turned to the picture, a light shone in her eyes, a brief moment of happiness which turned to pain.

"I haven't been able to walk down that hall for many years." She gulped. "It's good to see that painting, again, and even better to know that others will enjoy it long after I'm gone."

"Don't talk that way," Gus said. "You'll be here next year when we come to visit."

"I pray so, but the Lord may have other plans for me."

"Are you sure you're up to talking about this?" Nathan asked.

"There will be no better time."

Gus rose. "Can I get you a glass of water then?"

"Oh, there's pop in the fridge," Aunt Barbara said. "Bring some soda for everyone, dear."

Mia stared at the painting, her eyes focusing on the unusual looking dark green trees.

"Those trees point toward heaven," Aunt Barbara said.

"Can you at least tell me where this painting is from?"

"I will get to that," Aunt Barbara said. The only movement was her eyes and the sides of her mouth. "These facts are worth waiting for."

"I want to know all about Loren," Mia admitted. "How handsome was he?"

"Loren was the most handsome man the world has ever seen."

Mia gasped. "Wow!"

"I'll get to our story as soon as Gus comes back."

Gus returned and handed out soda cans for everyone. Next to Aunt Barbara, he raised a can with a straw in it. "Would you like a sip, Aunt Barbara?"

"In a few minutes, Gus. Please sit and listen," she said. "All of you listen."

* * * *

1941

Barbara grabbed her art textbook and hurried into the small wooden classroom. This senior classroom was full of students and only one seat remained—the desk right in front of the teacher. Barb rolled her eyes, completely disappointed. In this seat, the teacher would be able to see everything she scribbled, even notes to her friends.

Slowly, she plopped down. Beside her was a blond boy who she had seen before in her Math class.

He grunted at her as she sat. "Got a pencil?"

She didn't have an extra, but she stuck a hand in the pocket of her long skirt and pulled out a penny. "Here you go."

"Swell." He snatched it and rushed for the door, presumably to go to the school store at the end of the hall. The door opened before he got there, and a woman entered. She had dark hair with white streaks. Thin, she wore unusual-shaped glasses above a big smile that revealed sparkling teeth.

Barb admired her dress and the silver necklace around her neck. It sparkled as she walked to the chalkboard, picked up a piece of chalk, and began to write her name—an unusual one.

"My name is Mrs. Aleavia Kays."

The teacher turned around, put the chalk in the slot next to the chalkboard, and spoke in a clear tone, "Good morning, students."

"Good morning, Mrs. Kays," they responded in unison.

"Welcome to Maple High's Senior Art Class. Many of you have never studied art before, but before long I will have you all learning about our great American painters. You will also learn the basics of sculpting, sketching and watercolor."

Barb's heart began to pound. She had seen many paintings hung up in her father's grocery store on Hill Road. Mostly fruit and vegetables, the artworks were donated by a friend of his. Barbara thought if she could do some, too, her father would display them in his store for all in their Maple, Michigan town to see.

The boy who had sat next to her was now running back to his seat, catching the teacher's attention for a moment. In his hands was a pencil— still with the price tag of one penny dangling from the top.

"You won't need supplies here," Mrs. Kays announced. "We have them donated by Maple's museum director. At the end of the year, we will all be going on a field trip to thank Mr. Morten."

Barbara had always wanted to go inside the museum, but it cost almost a quarter to enter. Finally, she would be able to see all those paintings her father's friends talked about. She heard there was even one of a nude man among them. Her cheeks suddenly blushed.

"And what is your name?" Mrs Kays leaned over her desk.

Barbara started in surprise, and spat out, "I'm Barbara Larson, Ma'am."

"Well, Barbara, you got the lucky desk, I see. Whoever sits in this front desk every year is in charge of handing out supplies and for helping me put them away after class."

Barb's face dropped. "Oh."

Mrs. Kays laughed. "It's not that bad, dear. It's extra credit."

A hand shot up in the back of the class. A red-haired girl with big green eyes and lots of freckles asked, "Mrs. Kays, Mrs. Kays?"

"Yes?" She pointed to her.

"Will we be able to see that big naked man picture at the museum? He's the cat's meow!"

All the girls quickly giggled across the classroom. Mrs. Kays removed her glasses and they hung around her neck from the silver chain Barb had first thought was a necklace.

"I heard that he's very well endowed." The girls suddenly exploded in a fit of laughter. "And he doesn't have a head. One time, my mother and I went into the museum, and she told me she'd like to find a new husband like that. Heebie Jeebies!"

The classroom burst into laughter.

"Brainchild," Mrs. Kays said, "there is a time and place for everything and now is not the time for jokes. Art is serious business. If all goes well, we will be in charge of decorating the backdrop for the school play this year, which is Romeo and Juliet."

The snickers disbursed and Barb prided herself that she was the only student who hadn't laughed. She noticed Mrs. Kays glance at her. Barbara suddenly realized having this seat meant she would have to lead by example. She would be directly under the teacher's nose. Perhaps that wouldn't be so bad if she learned how to paint.

Once, Barb had sketched their dog, Teeth. She made his mouth look vicious as if he were snarling, like when he scared all the ducks away from around the pond in their backyard. Her father had said, "Teeth never looked better."

"Everyone, please turn to page one in the senior art book," Mrs. Kays said.

"Mrs. Kays, I left mine at home," a girl shouted.

"Go get it, then," Mrs. Kays said.

Barbara opened her book and saw a painting of a schoolteacher in front of a classroom. She couldn't believe it; it was Mrs. Kays. She gasped when she recognized her and looked up. "This spiffy painting is you!"

"That's right. My portrait is the very first painting in the book. Right in this classroom, I had the honor of posing for the painter who was interviewed in this textbook as being one of the greatest painters in the world. He made my image immortal. My portrait as an Art Teacher will remain long after I leave earth. Who would like to read the first lesson on art on page two?"

Barbara stared at the painting in her textbook, noticing how closely the brush strokes resembled her teacher's every feature. The artist even captured the small birthmark on the side of Mrs. Kays' temple. She decided then, to show her father the portrait when she got home. He would be interested that her teacher posed for this portrait.

Mrs. Aleavia Kays was famous!

CHAPTER 4

"**S**o that's how you met your art teacher?" Mia asked.

Aunt Barbara smiled. "We spent many years together. I took beginning through advanced art with her. I loved every day being in her classroom. At first, I didn't like having that seat, but by the end of the year I woke up an hour early just to make sure I got that seat."

Gus laughed. "So, you became the teacher's pet?"

"I was her helper and enjoyed every minute of it," she explained. "By the third year, my father had one of my paintings in every part of his store."

"Does that explain that apple one?" Toby glanced over to above the fireplace.

"I don't have those anymore."

"How sad." Mia gasped. "You don't have all of your paintings?"

"I'll explain what happened to those. Now let me get back to my story. In the last year I was at Maple Hill, I was asked an honor you would not believe."

* * * *

"Barb, may I see you after class?" Mrs. Kays asked.

Barbara flipped back her hair. "I'm sorry, but I have a date."

"Any type of Drugstore Cowboy can wait until after we speak," the teacher said, her tone cold.

The class quieted and Barb worried that she had done something to upset her teacher. Throughout the class she remained silent, thumbing through the art book, reading up on early Renaissance sculptors—the reading assignment on the board.

When the nurse entered the hallway and rang the big cowbell, all the students rushed up and out the door. Barb remained seated, continuing to finish the page she was on.

"We need to talk," Mrs. Kays said.

"Horsefeathers." Barb shut the book. "Am I in trouble?"

"I want to ask you a favor."

Barb's worried expression turned to a smile. "Sure, anything."

"You know how I ask the class to paint the backdrop for the school play every year. Well, this year, the principal has decided the freshmen deserve to have their own talent show. At first, they were going to just stand in front of the curtain, but that made me wonder how it would be if you painted something for them to stand in front of—violins, guitars, anything having to do with music. You could even sign the bottom to show off your own talent. There will be other paintings displayed in the theater for everyone to look at, but I wanted you to have this special honor."

"I've never done something that big before on my own."

"I know." Mrs. Kays nodded. "It will be quite an extensive project that could take you the rest of the year to complete. Out of my students, you were the one I thought to ask."

Pride welled up inside her. Barb couldn't turn her down—nor did she want to. She envisioned guitars with giant notes cascading down.

"The sign-up chart is right here." Mrs. Kays showed her a sheet of paper.

"Are you pulling my leg? You want me to do it all? I'm not sure I know exactly what to paint."

"You have the moxie. What do you think would look appropriate?"

Barb thought for a moment, visions of instruments dancing in her head. She wanted to paint exactly what she saw in her head. "I have some ideas but I'm not sure I can do them."

"What are they?"

"A guitar with notes coming down; that's what I thought of first. Then, I guess, some of the cheerleaders will be dancing, so I could put a dancer in the center with Maple High in big letters right above her head."

"That's the bee's knees!" the teacher praised. "That sounds perfect. Anything else?"

"Someone is bound to do a magic trick, so I could put a wand pointing at a big trumpet with a bunny coming out!"

"Interesting."

"You don't like that last idea." Barb suddenly worried she wouldn't be able to do it if her teacher didn't approve.

"On my back porch I have every supply you can think of. Come to my house on Saturdays and I'll oversee the backdrop. Does that sound good to you?"

"You won't paint on it though, right?" Barb questioned. "I want to be the only artist, not like with the school plays. It will be mine?"

"Absolutely, we just can't have anything too bazaar or Mr. Renolds won't let you put it behind the talent show participants. What do you say?"

"Hot dog!" Barb couldn't stop herself. She stood, rushed over to the desk and gave Mrs. Kays a big embrace. When she pulled away, she noticed there were tears in her teacher's eyes. "Did I say something to upset you?"

"No." Mrs. Kays wiped her eyes. "I just love to see this kind of enthusiasm in my students. You have a very unique style and I think with enough concentration you could become one of the greatest artists of our day."

Barb gazed up at her, bewildered.

"I mean it, Dear. I wouldn't ask you if I didn't think you would do an incredible piece. This is an opportunity to be a real high pillow. Every person in this town will be coming to this shindig. Your name will be behind every student and if this backdrop really stands out, it could be the beginning of a career for you. Even if you don't start on portraits right away, you could do advertisement signs for the shops. This could turn out to be a beginning. Please don't take this lightly. I want what's best for you.

"You're my favorite teacher."

"That's only because I teach the subject you love most. You're no flub the dub." Mrs. Kays wiped her eyes again. "I know you will put every effort into this, and I just want you to realize how important a project this is."

"I won't let you down."

"I know." Mrs. Kays suddenly grinned. "Every time I see one of your paintings, I get goose bumps."

"They're that bad?"

Mrs. Kays rose and opened her top desk drawer. She pulled out a pile of paintings done on newspaper. On top was a picture of Teeth, Barb's dog. The dog's tongue was hanging to the side and his fur was dirty on one side of the face. "You see how you painted him with soot on his cheek and the tongue too far right."

"I didn't do good?"

"No, you painted him divine. All the other students painted their dogs to look like showcase animals, but not you. You paint what you see. You captured this dog's spirit. It makes the person looking at it wonder how that dog got so dirty."

"From my pond—he chases the ducks around it and never catches them. He lands on his head, and then he gets so tired, he pants. His tongue drools, but I didn't put that in."

"You put in enough." Mrs. Kays took her by the wrists. "You painted the perfect picture; you captured the life of this dog. I imagine him to be a happy dog and one that is so loved. I got that from your painting. You have something special in these hands; now is your chance to show this town."

"I won't let you down."

"You haven't yet." Mrs. Kays released her grasp and said, "Now go ask your father if it is okay. He's welcome to come along on Saturdays with you and your mother too. We can have sandwiches and hokey-pokey candy while you paint."

"Okay, but he's a real crab patch."

CHAPTER 5

Barbara was nervous as she knocked on the door. When Mrs. Kays answered, she put on a smile, trying to veil her trembling emotions. With a few days to think about it, Barb finally realized just how important this painting would be.

"Hi, Barb, come on in." Mrs. Kays smiled.

She noticed how her teacher's hair was down, covered by a white babushka, not in her usual styled bun. How long Mrs. Kays' hair was! Instead of a fancy dress, she was in a swing skirt and blouse that wasn't tucked in.

"Please excuse my attire. I am not a glamour puss at home."

"I just put it on." Barb pointed to her cotton top. "It was in my junk drawer at home so if I spill paint on it, it doesn't matter."

"Good." Mrs. Kays led her inside.

The moment Barb came into the living room, she gasped. Painting after painting lined the room, more hung down the hallway and back into what appeared to be a very large kitchen. To the right was a doorway, which Barb guessed was either a bedroom or a bathroom.

Her eyes trailed up and down the walls; she wanted to spy every canvas, every awesome work of art. A few were portraits. One of an older woman wearing a black dress with a white collar, was especially fine.

"That's my grandmother," Mrs. Kays said. "She didn't like sitting for that."

"She didn't?"

"I don't mean to be a scuttle butt about my family. Over time you'll learn everyone would love to be in a painting, but no one wants to put in the effort to sit, sometimes for twelve to twenty-four hours, while it is being done."

"Why don't you just use photos?"

"That's too modern." Mrs. Kays smiled. "It gripes your cookies?"

"It's better to see the person. That way you know exactly the way the light shimmers off their features."

Barb examined more paintings but quickly felt a hand on her shoulder. It was tugging her down the hallway. Although she wanted to stay and look over every piece of art, she knew she wouldn't be painting inside the house. "I've set up a large picnic table. There will be four panels to the backdrop, so decide what you want featured on each."

Barb gazed at the large canvas already covering the wooden table. It wasn't blank newsprint like in school. This was enormous. Four of these panels would make up almost a whole wall. It would span the entire stage even with the curtains opened. Turning her head to the right, she noticed how the porch was filled with boxes of art supplies. There were jars of every color in the boxes. To the left of the table, on a cement wall, sat a vase full of brushes of every size.

"I hope this gets your approval." Mrs. Kays laughed.

Her teacher had gone out of her way to make sure Barb had every supply she would need. Her father, who owned a grocery store, couldn't have afforded all of these supplies, what with wartime rationing affecting his inventory.

"Yes, thank you so much!" Barb praised. "So, you have four of these for me to paint on?"

"It will become a very extensive project, probably taking you every Saturday until the talent show in eight weeks. Do you think you can handle it?" Barbara pulled out her sketchbook and sat at the picnic table. Mrs. Kays stood behind her.

"You know in class how you always tell us to kind of sketch out what we might want to paint, to see if it will be worth doing?" Barbara opened her book. On a sheet of paper sat the portrait of a violinist, one string popping up from his violin as the eyes of the player bulged in shock. "What do you think?"

Mrs. Kays stared at it a moment and then nodded. "I don't want to give you any opinions on this. I've decided."

"What?"

"In class I often would guide you to what I feel would make your painting more enjoyable for the masses, but not this time. This will be completely yours. I don't want you to even ask for help unless you have a problem finding something you need. For the most part, I will probably just forget you're here. I'll be inside cleaning, although sometimes on Saturday afternoons I like to sit in that rocking chair in the back of the porch and read."

"That won't disturb me one bit."

Suddenly a loud noise began coming from above. Barb knew what it was, but she hadn't seen one in quite some time. She rushed to the screening and peered up. "Is that a plane? There are planes on this side of town?"

"Yes, I hope that won't bother you too much. My son is a crop duster for the Ronin Farms. He gets paid every week for one field or another. Then on Sundays he flies to transport the corn and tomatoes to Westport for Monday's market."

"You have a son?" Barb gasped. "I didn't know you were married."

"Funny that would surprise you more than the fact my son's a pilot." She laughed. "His name is Loren and he just turned twenty last week. He's a bit of a lamb pie. Right now, he's landing and he'll be in sometime this afternoon. Saturday is his short day, so I'll be sure to mention not to come out onto the porch while you are working."

Barbara watched the plane lowering in the sky. Just at the tree line it vanished, and she guessed he was landing near the pond. How many times had she seen that red plane with white wings while she went fishing with her father? Now she could tell him where the plane came from, and that it was her teacher's son's. "So how long have you been married?"

"I am a widow," Mrs. Kays said. "My husband died last year."

Barbara hadn't known. Then she recalled all those days last year Mrs. Kays missed and had been told there was a death in the family. Even after she returned, she hardly spoke about anything but paintings for over a month. Barb had thought she was mad at her for a while and now she knew what had happened. "I'm so sorry."

"We had a good marriage while it lasted."

"Are you lonely?" Barbara asked, but before the last word came out she realized it was too personal a question.

Mrs. Kays smiled. "I was for a while, but now, not so much."

"My uncle isn't married anymore. My aunt left him for a bartender in Flagstone. If you want, I could mention you to him and see…"

"I'm already dating someone or as you teenagers call it, 'rationed.'"

"Who?" Barbara wanted to know. There weren't many single men that age in Maple, other than her uncle who, she had to admit, drank a little too much on the weekends.

"You'll see soon enough. He's very handsome though, a real sheik. I think you'll like him. We might get married someday if Loren takes a liking to him. Right now, he's kind of bitter about his father."

"I can understand that" Barbara said, closing her notebook.

Mrs. Kays put her hand on the canvas. "Now, no more. Get your boots on. This isn't going to be easy."

Barbara stared at the blank canvas. A queasy feeling came over her and settled in her stomach. Her hands began to shake for a moment, and she had to exhale from nerves, then took a deep breath.

"There's nothing more frightening than when it's blank, is there?"

Her teacher seemed to know her better than anyone. She looked up and said, "What if I paint three sides and fail at the fourth?"

"You won't."

"I've never done anything this big before."

"No different, only the scale." She patted Barb's head. A door slam echoed from the front of the house. Barbara jumped at the unexpected noise.

Mrs. Kays grinned. "Please, excuse me. Loren is home and I want to get some lunch on the table for him."

"Swell," Barbara said, nervously, contemplating what she should paint on this piece—the violin or the dancer. No, the dancer should be in the center.

The back door slid open to reveal a man standing behind it. He was about six feet tall and two across with those muscled shoulders. His frame was large but not as big as the grin splitting his face. His hair was dusty blond and hung in waves around his stunning dark features. His brilliant blue gaze lowered and rested right on Barbara's face.

Barbara could barely breathe. She hadn't seen a man so stunning ever before. He looked nothing like Mrs. Kays except maybe a little around the long nose. He was muscular and broad.

"Hi," he said to her, then immediately turned to his mother. "I picked up some sandwiches at the diner for us. I didn't know we had company, though."

"I already ate," Barbara said; her tongue lodged in her throat. She couldn't believe how much it sounded like a stammer.

Mrs. Kays wrapped an arm around him. "Barbara, this is my son, Loren. Loren, this is one of my students, Barbara Larson."

"Oh, yeah, my mom talks about you a lot." He turned and walked away.

Barbara half-thought he was rude but didn't seem to mind one bit as he turned. She got to see how attractive he looked on the reverse side.

Mrs. Kays must have noticed her staring because she grabbed Barbara's head and turned it back toward the canvas. "That will be enough distractions today."

"Yes, Mrs. Kays." Barbara blushed.

Mrs. Kays began to head after her son, but before she slid the door shut, she whispered. "Good luck."

CHAPTER 6

"What a Drooly." Barb stared at the blank canvas for quite some time. She tried to focus on what she needed to paint, but her mind kept drifting back to the young flyboy she had just met. How exciting to be in a plane!

She wondered if he would offer to give her a ride someday. That wasn't all she wanted, she realized, blushing. Loren was about the most gorgeous man she had ever seen.

What made him the most striking was his eyes. What a shade of blue they were! It was like staring into the still waters of a creek—the palest shade of blue on a warm summer's day.

He would be her inspiration.

The dancer in the middle of the panel would have eyes that color, piercing right back at the audience. No one would ever be able to forget that color. She would give the dancer hair his shade of blond, too, but instead of slight waves, the hair would be whipping about as if turning.

This was good.

Barb quickly made up her mind to begin on the dancer first, the face and the hair. They must appear at the bottom, because all four pieces would connect with the dancer. After the spinner was created, the rest of each side would contain some sort of instrument being played and perhaps in the far-right hands applauding.

Oh yes, there needed to be clapping in this painting.

Barbara reached for a brush, grabbed for the black paint container, and began to outline the head of the dancer. As she worked, she pictured

Loren's face. She couldn't give the dancer the same features; they were far too masculine for any ballerina, but she would give her the same eyes.

Her heart began to pound.

A few times she had to tell herself to slow down and take a deep breath. This was so exciting. Passion was flowing through her fingers right onto the canvas. She felt as if nothing could stop this from being the most incredible masterpiece.

Then the door slid open.

Barb heard it but didn't turn her head. She figured it was Mrs. Kays again just checking on her. Sure enough, she heard the door shut again. A few seconds passed and then Barb felt warm breath falling down against the back of her neck.

Goosebumps rose down her arms. Her stomach went into knots as she slowly glanced back over her shoulder to see his stunning eyes nearly inches away from her.

"Looks dreamy," Loren said. Barbara was speechless.

His big eyes blinked, and she was drawn into that magnificent color. He gazed back into hers and for a second, she didn't mind.

Then being so close to him, gazing back, made her tremble. Barb forced herself to look back down at the canvas. "I've started on a dancer. Maple High has a very good squad and several of them have already signed up for the show."

"I thought an Able Grable like you didn't like cheerleaders."

"What do you mean, Able Grable like me?" She raised her chin and turned around to face him.

"You know, artistic whistle bait."

"Is that what I am?"

"You're a painter," he said, glancing down to the outline of the dancer's head and hair. One arm was reaching up with fingers curled back. "You're also without a doubt as beautiful as Betty Grable."

She smiled. "I've just begun the painting."

"How long are you going to be coming to my house?"

"Does it matter?"

"Of course, it does. So, how long?"

She wondered if it bothered him. "Until I'm done. Your mother said I could use her supplies."

"Oh."

"Is that a problem for you?"

"Doesn't your father's store on Hammel Street have art supplies?"

He knew who her father was! She was amazed, wondering how he did. Then he had seen her work! She hoped he'd seen the one she did in the produce aisle of all the different fruits in baskets.

"Actually," she said, "my father doesn't carry art supplies, but he does have paper and pencils."

"I thought that's where you got the stuff to paint all those pictures." He grinned. "You know which is my favorite?"

"The fruit?"

"No." He chuckled.

She liked his laugh. It was deep and sultry, but she didn't like him snickering at one of her best works. "Is there something wrong with the fruit? Most of his patrons think that's my best painting!"

"I like the one over the butcher's station. It's smooth."

"The cow!" She suddenly pictured the portrait of Old Betty. It was the oldest living cow in the county and had the biggest eyelashes. Barbara giggled. "You liked Old Bet. That is a different kind of pin-up girl."

"You painted her so cute that your father admitted to me he's lost money selling beef."

"You're pulling my leg."

"No, I told him I thought it was swell and he told me. He didn't know I was the son of your teacher, or I doubt he would have made such a comment." His jawline lifted to show off his brilliant smile. "I think your father even takes it down on the days you're not going to be there, because I went once for some sliced ham, and I didn't see it."

"Cast a kitten!" Barb rose, angry. "My father wouldn't take down one of my pictures."

"Well, you have to admit painting the cutest cow in town above where people go to butcher them probably wasn't the greatest idea, a real humdinger."

"Take that back." She tightened her right hand into a fist.

"What's eating you?" He tilted his head.

"Take it back!"

"If you punch me, I'll just make you kiss me to make me better."

"You're kidding." Her hand dropped, her cheeks turned a crimson shade and she quickly sat back down.

"I never kid about having a smooch with my dream girl."

Barb didn't know what to say. She stood there for quite some time, not knowing what word should come out of her mouth and, fearing she'd say the wrong thing, said nothing.

"I'll let you get back to business." He chuckled, making his way to the door.

"It's not true about my father," she shouted back. "He wouldn't remove any one of my paintings."

"Is that what's bothering you?"

"It isn't true."

"Why don't you stop by the store today when he doesn't know you're coming?" he suggested over his shoulder, then shut the door behind him.

Barbara was half-thrilled and angry all at the same time. Her father wouldn't do such a thing. He had told her he liked the Old Betty picture. That cow was a fine animal, and it was so cute! Everyone loved

Old Betty. She won every year at the fair for the most adorable cow! Five years in a row she got first place. It was because of her unusually long lashes and Barb painted them true to size!

For an hour, Barb painted the outline, then she packed up and began heading out of the porch. She started walking toward her father's store. He was supposed to pick her up in his Chevy Coupe after work, but she wouldn't wait one more minute. She wanted to see for herself if that painting was hanging.

Besides, it kept her from pondering about Loren.

CHAPTER 7

Barbara walked down a few side streets and hurried into the back street of her father's grocery store. To walk in the front would give anyone enough time to re-hang the painting over the butcher's stand, so she figured walking in the back she would be below Old Betty within five seconds. There would be no time for her father to explain and she would need an explanation.

"Barb!" she heard a voice calling from behind.

She turned and couldn't believe Loren was standing behind her. "Are you following me?"

"I shouldn't have told you. Wait!" he said, grabbing her arm to keep her from hurrying in the back door.

"I want to see with my own eyes if he takes down my painting."

"Think of this from his point of view. It isn't an insult to you or what you do. It's just no one wants to look at a cute cow before they order one to be cut up."

"That's no excuse," Barbara said, now believing him. She rushed past him and entered the store. She went through the freezers. No one was there, and when she walked through the curtain, she simply looked above the butcher handing a woman thinly sliced roast beef.

There was no picture.

She glanced around the store and saw others removed as well. The only picture still hanging was that above the produce department. Even the simple portrait of a milk glass was gone. The air escaped her lungs.

A hand touched her shoulder. "Come on. Let's split. Let's go before your father knows you're here."

"Why?" Tears stung her eyes. "Why would my father remove them?"

"Patrons complained," Loren said. "One said that the milk jug looked as if the milk would fall right on your head. And the cow I explained. But your father talked to my mother. He told her he knows how talented you are. Listen, it's not what you think."

Barbara wiped her cheeks. A short man with balding hair came around the corner, holding a box of cans. He nearly dropped them when he saw her. The blank expression on his face clearly changed to one of shock and horror.

He didn't say a thing.

She walked away, wiping her eyes; Loren followed her out the back. As soon as she walked into the sunlight, she dropped to sit on the ground, crying. "Didn't he know how much that meant to me? I worked all year on those for him! I even asked your mother for help."

Loren sat down beside her just as the back door opened and Mr. Larson walked out. He straightened when he saw how upset she was. She peered up through the sunshine at the dark outline.

Her father said, "I just didn't know how to tell you."

"You couldn't tell me you didn't like them!" she shouted back. "How could you?"

Her father turned. "Don't mouth off to me." And he walked back into the store.

"What a chump," Loren said.

"That's my father you're talking about."

"So what," Loren said and shook his head. "You sit here crying your eyes out and all he says is, 'I just didn't know how to tell you.' What a brush off! He didn't even apologize."

"They weren't good enough."

"That's baloney!" Loren took her face by the chin. "Don't let my mother ever hear you talk like that either. You are her best student. She may not tell you, but I will. She even told me once you have magic in your fingers."

Barbara sniffled and wiped her eyes.

"You can't spend your life worrying about a Fuddy Duddy who doesn't believe in you. No matter what you want to do, there're always going to be people who don't approve or laugh at you and call you small. When I told my father I wanted to be a flyboy, he grounded me for a month and said it was for fools. 'If God had wanted you to fly, he would have given you wings,' as if it were 1904 instead of 1944. But you know what? I snuck off and learned how anyway. Not long after, my father died and if I hadn't learned how to fly, we wouldn't have made it on Mom's salary alone!"

"How did your dad die?"

"I can't talk about it. That's not why I came after you anyway. I just got worried that when you saw it you'd be upset and I shouldn't have even told you at all. I guess I just wanted you to know the truth."

"That my father thinks I'm talentless."

"Don't think that way. That's your whole problem here. Instead of telling yourself 'even my father thinks I can't do it,' think this way. 'He's just one more fathead I'm going to prove wrong.'"

"It's so easy for you." Barbara smiled, forgetting for the moment, her disappointment and relishing the ice blue in his eyes. "He isn't your father."

"No, you're right. Maybe the whole world doesn't feel like it's against me at the moment, but as long as you're blue, I'm blue." He pulled a handkerchief from his pocket and wiped her eyes.

"Why do you say that?"

"To see you cry rips me apart."

"You hardly even know me!"

"That's kind of funny, because I feel I know you better than anyone else. Mom would come home every weekend, show me your homework assignments, and point out what she liked most. She'd say things like, 'You see this, Loren, this big smile she painted; she made one of the teeth bad because not only was it correct, she made it appealing.'"

"I don't understand."

"I know you because in every one of your paintings I see a little more of what's in your heart. Sometimes I see sadness and it makes me sad. Other times I felt happy when I saw one of your paintings. It doesn't matter to me if your father hates them because you are so good; he's a fool not to agree with me."

Barbara couldn't believe what was coming out of his mouth. It almost sounded as if this incredible-looking guy, the most beautiful man she'd ever seen, cared for her. How could that be? How could anyone feel so much just by looking at her work? "Your words move me. I don't think I'll ever forget them."

"Not even when you're old and gray?" He laughed.

"No, not even then." "You have more talent in your hands than most people have in their whole bodies. Your soul comes out on that canvas. And you know what I see when I look at it?" Loren leaned down and his lips gently touched hers.

Barbara couldn't fathom he was kissing her. Her heart skipped a beat as she felt how soft his full lips were against hers. Nervous, she backed away, but her eyes quickly opened to look deeply into his.

"Come to dinner with me tomorrow night."

"I'm not allowed to date until I graduate."

"You're eighteen, right?"

"Yes, how did you know?"

"That's one of the first questions I asked Mother after I saw you today. You see, I knew I loved the heart of the girl who had such a claim to fame in her fingers. I just didn't realize I loved what she looked like, too."

Barbara had never felt so moved. She hardly remembered that her father had insulted her by taking her work off those walls. She stood to her feet and smiled. Loren heaved himself up to stand beside her.

"I'll see you tonight instead," she said. "I'll tell my father I've got to finish more of the backdrop."

"That's lying." He cocked his head.

"Everyone lies at one time or another." She winked. "Just try not to lie about the big stuff."

"Then I adore you," he said, walking away. "Now is that a lie?" She giggled.

"Never lie about the big stuff," he echoed then he clasped her hand and walked her back to her house three blocks down Main Street.

CHAPTER 8

She snuck out.

Forgot something at my teacher's house and I was invited to dinner.

She left the words written on a note on the table. Her father hadn't come home yet, and she didn't mind.

Dressed in a knee-length white dress and a small white and red hat, Barbara looked up at the sky as she began to walk down the street. She had planned to wear this ensemble on Easter, but tonight, dressing up seemed a must.

The sky was full of a big moon and brilliant, sparkling stars that seemed alive as they glittered. The night air was cool, and she tightened her headscarf before it blew off into the grass. Under her arm, she clutched a purse that matched her hat perfectly and the color of her wooden platform shoes.

This was not like her.

She didn't usually care about dress, shoes, or if everything matched. Tonight, she did. Barb wanted to take Loren's breath away. She wanted his heart to pound as hard as hers did when they kissed earlier.

One thing she liked about him was how much he appreciated her paintings. It's not every day that a painter finds one who loves their art. He did. That was all she needed to know to figure out that he meant something to her.

When she walked around the corner, a car honked. With its headlights partially painted over per blackout laws, Barb hadn't seen it, and she realized she had almost stepped off the sidewalk and in front of it. She shouldn't stare at the sky as she walked. Dangerous, but what fun!

Imagine a world so big that one cannot see the end. How divine! She surely should paint the sky and remember how she felt when she was walking back to Mrs. Kays' house to see the man she wanted to marry. Marry!

A giggle escaped her lips. How ahead of herself she was getting. Besides, he wasn't marriage material. A pilot. A daredevil! He was a man most women would think a dangerous risk taker. With the war going on, he was lucky he hadn't been drafted.

Barb put her gloved hand to her lips, trying not to smile. Was she really this happy? Is this what it was like to be in love? When she moved across the street, her eyes drew to who was across it.

There he was, standing on the corner. Dressed in a zoot suit and wearing a dark, red-colored tie. Loren was waiting for her. His eyes were on her, and her knees weakened. She slowed her pace as a smile crossed his lips. His hand lifted and she took it.

"Nice hat," he said, "very swanky."

"My mother bought it for me for Easter and I said it was too hotsy-totsy to wear to church."

"So, you wore something so spiffy for me?" She nodded yes, her eyes squinting in joy.

"You are the most adorable dame I've ever seen. I watched you walk down the street, and I sure am stuck. Don't you know to look where you're walking? You almost got run over by a Cadillac."

"I was looking at the sky."

"I saw." He glanced up. She regretted telling him so that his eyes were no longer on her.

"And what's in the sky that you must risk your life?" Before she could answer, he did for her. "Never mind, I know."

"You do?"

"Yes, probably the same thing as why I fly." He clasped an arm around her shoulder and began leading her around the bend. "You find beauty in the openness, right?"

"Actually, I was thinking I wish I could capture this feeling."

"And what feeling is that?"

She couldn't explain it; instead, she glanced at him and tried to calm the beating of her heart. Nor could she stop worrying about how sweaty her palm was getting in his hand. How embarrassing!

"Here we are," he said, opening a door which read, "Seafood."

"Seafood?" she asked.

"Yes, don't you like fish?"

"I honestly haven't tried it." She grabbed her hat again as the wind tickled her hair. "My father only eats beef and chicken."

"You mean to tell me your family owns a grocery store and you've never had seafood in your life?"

"That's right." She smiled then walked in. She noticed the "Seat yourself please," sign, moved past it and let him guide her to a booth. All the other tables were full and most of the patrons were looking at her.

Loren sat down opposite her and didn't speak as Barb slowly removed her gloves and placed them on her seat. Menus were placed in front of them as glasses of water were filled and on the table.

Barbara picked up the menu and began to read, *Mullet, Cod, Lobster, Mahi Mahi, Tuna steak.* She thought it over and since the Tuna had the word Steak after it, she guessed she would like that best.

The waitress came back and asked, "Have you both decided?" Barbara looked up from under her hat.

The woman's smile dropped. "My, my, aren't you a pretty one?"

"She is," Loren said. "I'll have the Lobster and can you bring me some cutters, please?"

"Of course," she said and nodded. "And, you, Miss?"

"I'll have the Tuna Steak."

"Baked potato or rice with that, Miss?"

"Rice."

"I'm surprised you didn't try the lobster. My last three dates all got that."

"That was the most expensive item on the menu," she said. "My mother taught me better than that. Besides, I'm not sure I'd even like it."

"Well, how do you know if you don't try?" he asked.

"That's true, but I'll start with Tuna Steak and work my way up." For some reason that sounded almost like a come on. How unlady like! *Oh my goodness!* She blushed.

"You are unique," he said. "I've never met anyone as fascinating."

"Thank you."

For quite some time, they sat staring at one another. Barbara normally would have felt worried about starting conversation, but with him, for some reason she didn't feel worried about it.

When their meal arrived, Loren picked up a nutcracker and began to crack open the very red lobster sitting on his plate. Barbara couldn't believe what it looked like. It could have crawled off its plate. Gazing at it bothered her. She squinted her nose and turned away to look at her own dinner.

"Heebie-Jeebies," she mumbled.

The rice looked good, but the fish looked nothing like beef. She picked up her fork and decided to try it. She took a big bite and began to chew. At first the taste shocked her senses and then she realized just how good this fish was! "This is swell," she said.

"I'm glad you like it."

She took several more bites and continued to gulp it down. "Slow down," he said and laughed. "I guess you do like it."

Suddenly she felt hot. Her throat seemed to feel as if it was swelling. She coughed and then felt her heart pounding like a drum. She gasped.

"Are you okay? Are you choking?" He jumped up to her side.

"Um, I feel like I did when I got stung by that wasp when I was twelve. It's hard to…" She gasped again.

The waitress came over. "She's turning beet red. I'll call for the doctor."

"I don't feel well," she said, as her insides curled up in a tight knot.

Loren wrapped his arm around her. "Let's get you to a doctor! I think I just figured out why your father doesn't eat fish. You wouldn't happen to think he might have been allergic to it, would you?"

"I don't know. Am I?"

"I think so!"

"This isn't funny," she said, touching her puffy lip.

"No, it's not," he agreed.

"The doctor is on his way," the waitress said as she came back over. "He'll take you to the hospital."

"Hospital!" Barbara gasped. "I've never been there before. I don't have any money on me."

"I have plenty to barter if necessary. I'll be right with you. I'll handle everything," Loren said and grimaced. "Just close your eyes and put your head on my shoulder. You'll be fine. You'll be just fine. I promise. You'll be okay."

When she did, her hat came clear off. She didn't care. Her heart was pounding so fast she could barely breathe now. She felt something on her arm and noticed someone giving her a shot. She didn't have the strength to ask what it was.

Chapter 9

When Barbara woke, she felt relaxed; so different than before she passed out. Her heartbeat in perfect rhythm. She no longer felt flushed and short of breath. It was as if she'd awakened from a nightmare.

She glanced around the bright room and quickly realized she was in Maple Hill's Bayside Hospital. A song, "A-tisket, A-tasket" being sung by Ella Fitzgerald was playing softly from the hallway.

The room was dark. There was only one small window overlooking the sailboats and fishermen near the shore wearing Mae West jackets. A hand quickly reached over her head and the overhead light went on. Standing beside her bed was her father, leaning over her, his eyes filled with worry. Her mother, short and pudgy with her hair in a bob, was holding her hand on the opposite side of the bed.

"Hi," her mother's voice squeaked. "How are you feeling?"

"Peachy," Barbara replied.

"You gave us such a fright," her father said. "They are going to keep you the rest of the night, but they think you'll be able to leave in the morning."

Barbara then remembered what happened. She had been having the time of her life, eating dinner with Loren, when she got ill. She glanced around the room and saw he wasn't there. Barbara realized she probably scared him off and would never see him again. That hurt covered her fear. Wanting to talk to him, she tried to sit up.

Her father immediately put a hand on her shoulder and pushed her back. "I'm paying a lot of money for you to stay in this bed, so rest up."

He almost sounded angry that she was sick. "Sorry," she said.

"How are you feeling now?" her mother asked, tightening the grip on her hand.

"I feel almost normal, just tired, like I ran a mile."

"You'll be better by morning," her mother comforted, sitting on the edge of the bed. "We were so worried. When we got the call from Loren we rushed right over and you were almost turning blue."

She wished she didn't know that. How wonderful of Loren to ring her parents and be so responsible. Yet, that might have been it for them. Men don't like weak women.

"Why were you eating fish?" her father asked. "Tuna of all things!"

"Am I allergic to it?" she finally asked.

"I am allergic to seafood, all kinds," her father said. "I must have mentioned it a thousand times. You should realize if I am, you could be, too! I would have told you not to even try it. It runs in the family."

He was making her feel like a Dumb Dora.

"Well, if she didn't know, she isn't at fault," came a voice moving in.

Barbara turned her head and saw Loren standing beside his mother, her teacher. Aleavia Kays hurried across the floor and kissed her forehead. She then backed away and the tension could have been cut with a knife.

"This is the young man who took you to the store today," her father recalled. "And why didn't you ask me if you could take my daughter out for dinner?"

"I apologize, sir," Loren said. He looked like he might bow.

"It's my fault," Mrs. Kays cut in. "She was coming over to gather some things she left at my house, and I asked them to pick up something at the grocery store for us. It was a simple mistake. My son loves seafood, and we cook it often at our house. We had no idea that she might be allergic, or we would not have fed it to her."

"So, you were there, too?" her father asked Mrs. Kays. "It wasn't a date then?"

"Of course not!" the teacher said. "It was dinner time, and we were all hungry. I was there too."

Barbara couldn't believe she was lying to her father. Mrs. Kays probably didn't even know about their date and even if she did, she certainly wouldn't have been accompanying them.

"I see," her father said. "Then it was a mistake that won't happen again."

Mrs. Kays gasped. "We wouldn't have even walked into that restaurant had we known. I was trying to congratulate her on doing so well painting today."

"I found it odd that she had never eaten there," Loren said. "We should have thought better of it, Mother."

"Indeed." Her father grabbed his coat off the chair. "Come, dear, let's leave them to her for a moment and get some coffee." As he walked to the door, he said, "I want to make myself very clear. My daughter is not allowed to date, especially someone who is as old as this young man."

"I'm only a few years older," Loren said. "So, you want to date my daughter?"

"With all due respect, any man with half a brain would. Your daughter is quite beautiful. She looks like her mother. Barbara is smart and very polite. She's a good girl, sir."

Her father preened. "Yes, she is. Don't think I don't know who you are. Your father and I go way back. We used to play on the Maple Hill Football team. He was nothing but trouble, son. You'd best not be anything like him."

Loren's eyes narrowed. His hands curled into fists.

Mrs. Kays put her arm around Loren and said, "You needn't worry about my son," as she guided Loren toward the door.

Loren snapped back at Barbara's father, "I like your daughter, Sir, or I would have knocked your block off for talking that way about Dad."

"Please, son."

"Mom, he treats Barbara so disrespectfully. I told you how he removed her paintings."

"This is between them," Mrs. Kays said. "Besides, you won't be here much longer." Loren immediately turned and saw Barbara near tears.

"What do you mean he won't be here much longer?" Barbara asked Mrs. Kays.

"My son didn't tell you?" Mrs. Kays turned to him. "How could you not!"

"I was going to, at dinner, but then she almost died on me. I didn't think that was the time and neither is this." Loren walked out.

"Loren!" Barbara called out, sitting up. When he didn't return, she looked up at her teacher. "What did you mean?"

"It isn't my place."

"Yes, it is," Barbara said. "Your son is leaving somewhere?"

"My son was drafted, dear. He leaves for basic training next week."

Barbara felt worse than when she had eaten the fish. She leaned back onto her pillow and tried to fight the tears. She didn't know why this news hit her so hard; she barely knew him.

Yet, she somehow couldn't picture life without him either. That's the last thing she remembered.

CHAPTER 10

It didn't take long to recover. A few days and Barbara felt fine physically, but sadness had entered her world. She couldn't believe Loren didn't mention he was leaving for the war.

A part of her envied his strength and courage. The war had drafted many of the college boys and with them had come word of many victories along the way. The front lines were also full of deaths, especially those of the parachuting bloomer boys. Several enemy eggs took out some planes, too, a B-17 Fortress, B-24 Liberator and Hellcat, and a Grumman F6F. Then word came of a few WACS deaths; that terrorized all the mothers and fathers of the boys and GI Janes gone.

How young they were. Loren was only a few years older and now he would be risking his life in a war no one had expected to last this long. Too many gone, and the wives and families left to struggle.

Barbara now understood what it felt like to have a loved one leaving. Her heart mourned what could have been. In school, she smiled at Mrs. Kays but didn't stay after class. She was hurt that Mrs. Kays hadn't let her know sooner that Loren had been drafted.

She liked him.

So casual a word for how she truly felt about him—like. *Too weak a word,* she thought as she walked back to her teacher's house. She regretted now taking on the assignment that would bring her back there.

She wanted to avoid Loren altogether. Perhaps he wouldn't be there. Did she mean that?

Barbara knocked on the wooden door; her teacher opened it and said, "Go around back. I unlocked the porch," and shut it between them.

Obviously, the teacher was upset with her too. Mrs. Kays seemed cold at the sight of her. She, too, must wish she hadn't offered Barbara the opportunity to paint the backdrop for the school talent show.

It was an honor, Barbara reminded herself as she slowly went into the porch. She shouldn't be angry but pleased she would get such exposure, even if her heart had broken.

She sat on the bench before her painting. The dancer's head and arm was near completion. Now she would capture the color of the hair, blond, like Loren's.

Perhaps she should paint the locks brown.

Before deciding, she began to paint the background color in the corner, pale bronze. How perfect a shade to highlight the dancer—like she was dancing on gold.

For about an hour, she worked on the corner until she heard the screen door open. Turning, she hoped to see Loren, but instead found Mrs. Kays with a pitcher and glass of lemonade.

"It's shaping up wonderfully."

"Do you like the background?" Barbara questioned.

"Yes, very much so, I admire how you are highlighting it against the brown of the violin."

"I'll paint that next."

"And what of the dancer?" Mrs. Kays asked. "You were almost done except for the hair. What eyes she has! Such an incredible shade of blue."

Barbara's gaze lowered as she recalled why she painted that particular shade of blue. It matched Loren's eyes. What incredible eyes he had!

"Are you all right?" Mrs. Kays asked. "You've been acting upset for quite some time now."

"You lied to my father."

"Yes, to protect my son. Your father can be somewhat of a burden."

"I know. No, I'm not angry with anyone."

"Hurt perhaps?" Barbara didn't answer. "You're upset I didn't tell you my son was leaving for the Army Air Corps?"

Instead of answering, she returned to the painting. "I must get back to this. I feel inspired today."

"You indeed need space to finish such a project." Mrs. Kays slowly turned and walked away.

Barbara blinked to battle her stinging eyes. She wanted to ask why she hadn't been told that Loren was putting himself into such danger. Without turning away from the backdrop, she asked, "Why didn't you tell me?"

"This is a good war. A noble cause to free the world of Hitler's reign. However, it's hard for me to admit even to myself that he's going. He's my only son. My only family, other than you. That's how I feel about you, too. I'm sorry. I didn't know how you felt about him until I saw the look in your eyes when I mentioned he was leaving."

Barbara couldn't admit that she did. She simply forced a smile. "I see."

"I didn't even realize you'd be hurt."

"I know." Her smile turned genuine. "You have a very fine son."

Mrs. Kays admitted, "He's a very handsome fellow with the biggest heart; any girl would be lucky to date him."

Barbara nodded.

"I told him to eat lunch in town today so you wouldn't have to see him," Mrs. Kays informed. "It's better; so when he goes, it will not hurt worse."

Barbara wished she hadn't done that. Even as angry as she was, she wanted to see him. Talk with him. She gripped her paint brush and turned around, fighting back her tears.

"If it makes you feel better, he was quite angry I asked him."

"No bother." Barbara sniffled. "Please don't do that on my account. I'm fine now. I see it wasn't going anywhere, and I have no more feelings." She returned to the backdrop, brush in hand.

"Very well," Mrs. Kays said to her back. "Then next Saturday I'll tell him he can be here. However, I'm not sure that he will now that I no longer approve of your friendship."

"Am I not good enough for your son to be his friend?" Barbara inquired, turning around, feeling sudden betrayal.

Mrs. Kays must have seen her tears, because she gulped and backed away. "Oh, dear, if I could pick a girl for him it would be you! Please don't think that way. I didn't mean for it to sound like that. It is nothing against you, only I know how your father is. He would not approve."

Barbara swiped a hand at her eyes. "Indeed. There has been too much dishonesty. You should have told me he was leaving. If you had, I would have never gone out to dinner with him."

"I thought you would be friends. He's about your age."

"You didn't even think I might want him for more," Barbara questioned.

"One date and you think you are in love." Mrs. Kays grinned. "You are so young. I should have realized."

Barbara was offended. Neither of their parents believed they would have been more than friends. They simply put a stop to even the possibility before she and Loren could explore their options. But there were no options.

Loren was leaving.

"Please tell Loren I am his friend. There is no need for him to stay away from his own house as I paint."

"Then you will give up on the idea of there being more."

"The war decided that for me," Barbara said, but even as she said it her heart didn't believe that this was all for them. She didn't want to believe it.

CHAPTER 11

*B*arbara finished for the day. Her fingers ached from holding the brush so tightly. As she washed her brush, she admired what she had completed. One panel was near completion. A violin with notes was being played on the left side; the dancer's head and arm pointed up were on the right and in the corner were the words "Maple Hill."

The words themselves were painted in maple leaves, something Barbara thought was quite appropriate. Even though she was disturbed by her teacher and how she no longer approved of Loren's and her friendship, Barbara still appreciated being asked to paint the backdrop. She painted the leaves in honor of Aleavia. The name always sounded similar to "leaf" to her.

They were her muses, Aleavia and her son, Loren Kays.

What a tribute to them, the leaves for the mother, the eyes the color of her son's. They may never know she used them this way. Would they even appreciate it?

As Barbara traveled down the path to her house, she saw a brown bunny with big ears chewing some grass on the side of the road. It stood completely still until she passed. How unusual. When she turned to spy it again, it hopped off quickly, as if she were a cat.

A giant crow sat on a fence and squawked. In her mind's eye, she saw how this would make the perfect canvas, a bunny below a fence with a crow sitting above. How often this happened to her, wanting to capture daily events.

After she turned around the bend, Barbara sat beneath a giant purple crab apple tree. She leaned back against the trunk. The sun was setting in the west and she figured it would be best to wait until after dinner time to return home. She didn't want to eat with her family.

She had yet to forgive her father for taking down her pictures.

The crow flew to a branch above her head. Barbara glanced up and made the most amazing discovery. There were carved names in the tree, many of them initials of lovers she didn't know.

How romantic! She suddenly wished she had a knife to carve Loren's name into the tree and place her name below.

"That's my dad's," a voice came from behind the tree. She started in shock until she saw the face.

"Loren!"

"Right here." He pointed to the tree. "AD loves GK, that's Aleavia Dakota loves Garrett Kays. My father carved that when they were dating. He took my mom here and showed her and then asked her to be his wife."

"Sweet." Barbara caught her breath.

"I'm sorry I wasn't at the house today. My mother forbade it," Loren explained.

"I heard."

"She told you?"

"She informed me she no longer approves of our being friends."

"How nice of her." She could hear the sneer in his voice. "Isn't it wonderful how our parents reacted to our dating? You'd think we started the war."

She grinned since he admitted they were dating. "True. They all seemed to overreact."

"You did almost die."

"From the fish, not the company."

Their eyes met and lingered. She couldn't get over the color of his eyes or the way he looked at her. No man had ever stared at her so openly before.

"You are too charming a rogue."

"Charming?" He chuckled. "No one has ever called me that before. You're the real bombshell."

He moved in and took her in his arms. His lips came down and touched hers for a moment. When he stepped back, Barbara sighed.

"How about dinner again?" he asked.

"Do you think I'll survive?"

"Stop joking about that. I suggest nothing from the sea."

"How about burgers?"

"You must be joking." He shook his head. "You deserve a steak after all you've been through. You bring your ration book and I'll pay."

"I don't need you to spend money on me. A burger is fine."

Loren wrapped an arm around her and led her to the path. They walked together for several feet before he said, "Not even my mother will stop me from sharing a cow with you. Better than a chug-a-lug."

She burst out laughing. "See what I mean. Charming."

Together they went to the Burger Barn, a small diner near the path. Around the back, there were benches and tables set up for anyone to eat burgers cooked over a grill. For one dollar it was served with a giant milkshake or a root beer float. Loren paid for two burgers and milkshakes and carried them outside to the farthest bench. Barbara followed him and sat down. He handed her a plate.

"You seem happy with burgers after all." She glanced over at him, noticing how big a bite he was taking.

"These are good."

"The finest in town, for only a clam."

"I'm glad you're happy again."

"You make me that way."

"I thought my last days would be rough, but I can't stop thinking about you. Do you realize I haven't thought about leaving for almost four days? All I could think about was if you're okay, if you're upset with me, and when I was going to see you again."

She took a bite of her burger and relished the juicy flavor. They were the largest burgers in town, nearly eight ounces. Her father always saved his leanest, freshest cuts for Maybell, the owner. She wanted to tell him all her father's secrets of who got the best cuts of beef or chicken. Maybell was one of his favorite clients, along with Catherine Grettis, owner of the Flavors Restaurant on the Westside. She got the largest chickens, even during rationed times.

"Is it the same for you, or is this just hopeful thinking on my part that you'll keep writing me and maybe when I get back we can be together again when I return from the war?" He then stopped himself from eating. "Although, that isn't fair of me to ask you to wait like all those other chumps do to their girls, is it?"

"No, it isn't."

They finished eating and Loren was silent for quite some time. Then, after returning their food baskets, he said, "You're right. It isn't fair. But I want you to know, I'm going to write you. Even if we'll only be friends and you date others while I'm gone."

"You'll write?"

"Every day I can. Would that be all right, or do you think your father will toss out my letters?"

"I'll tell him not to." Her lips curled, fighting back a grin of happiness. "It can never hurt having friends."

"You mean more to me than my buddy, Randy." Loren kissed her lips again and leaned in. "I don't do that with him. I think he'd box my ears."

Overwhelmed, she chuckled.

"Then it's settled. We'll write each other. If you date any other chump while I'm gone I won't hold it against you because I might not come back. However, I ask only one thing with these chumps."

"What is it?"

"Promise when I return, you'll date me again."

"What if I'm married by then?"

"Write me before marrying someone else first. Promise me." He kissed her lips. "That will at least give me hope that when I return you'll be my girl."

"I promise."

"I'm going to hold you to this. You can date others, but when I return you date only me. If you marry, tell me first so I can go AWOL and kick him straight in the ass away."

She laughed so hard her sides hurt.

"Promise me, Barbara?"

Still laughing, she agreed. "I promise."

CHAPTER 12

The week flew by so fast Barbara could barely fathom this would be the last time she would see Loren until the end of basic training. Then he could return for one week before being deployed to whichever base he would be stationed at overseas.

Her life had changed so much.

Just two weeks ago, she hadn't even known Loren, but now her entire life revolved around him. This morning would be the last time she would be able to kiss him for six weeks!

On a bus to travel to Ohio for basic training this morning!

Saying goodbye to him would bring her such pain Barbara wasn't even sure she could do it. She dressed in a sundress and put on her Easter hat. She put on a pair of red gloves and slipped into a pair of matching shoes.

She walked to his house and knocked on the door.

No answer came. She couldn't believe it! Barbara repeated knocking and when the door didn't move, she realized he was no longer here. Where was he? Loren had told her he was leaving by nine.

Pivoting, she noticed a man walking a dog down the street. She rushed over to him as the dog barked at her angrily. "Excuse me, Sir?"

"Yes?" His elderly eyes widened. "Are you all right?"

"Have you the time?"

He glanced at his watch while continuing to walk. "Quarter to ten."

"Ten!" She gasped. "Already?"

"Time flies." He trotted off, the boxer pulling him down the street.

She hadn't known how late it was and now she might miss Loren's bus! Quickly, Barbara pulled off her heels and ran for the bus station three blocks away. His bus was scheduled to leave at ten.

When she came to the station, she saw Aleavia waving goodbye with a handkerchief, to a bus that was leaving.

She had missed him! Barbara rushed through the crowd and stood by his mother, gasping for air, waving with her. From the back window, Loren waved to her, standing.

"There he goes." Aleavia's voice was thick with tears.

The Ford Model 19-B, ODT bus was halfway down the street, when suddenly it stopped at a corner stop sign. A couple began to head across in front of the bus to the other side of the road. Without thinking, Barbara ran for it. Her hat flew off and tears were streaming down her face. How much she wanted to kiss him goodbye. She ran faster and then the bus stopped again.

Wham! Her body pounded against the back of the bus, knocking her off her feet. Her head snapped to the dirt as pain seared down her right leg, which had hit the bus first.

"She's hurt," a voice cried out from the street. Loren raised the bus window.

"Barbara!"

The bus engine cut off and the door opened. Loren ran to the back of the bus and wrapped his arms around her. "You are the most accident-prone person I have ever met," he said. "First seafood and now you run into a bus."

She smiled as tears fell. The pain from her leg hurt her to the point she knew it must be broken.

"Are you hurt?"

"A little," she admitted.

"Where?"

"My leg," she said.

He felt down her leg and grinned. "Doesn't feel broken here. You just took a very bad hit."

"Barbara, of all the crazy things," Aleavia said, bending down beside her.

"I'm sorry I was late." Barbara ignored her and turned back to Loren. "I didn't realize what time it was."

"I figured that." He started helping her up.

Barbara leaned on him until she noticed her leg could take her weight. She took a step and felt the stiffness setting in. "That is really going to hurt."

"Mom, take her to the hospital."

"Again?" Mrs. Kays gasped.

"There's no need." Barbara took a few steps. "I'm all right. See?" She ignored the pain. "Forget about it." Then she moved in and kissed his lips right in front of his mother.

Loren's arms wrapped around her and he kissed her back. When she backed away, she heard the applause of the crowd that was now surrounding them.

"I'll see you when you're done with boot camp," Barbara said against his lips, then let him go.

"Come on now. Leave the Lamb pie," the bus driver said to Loren, tipping his hat. "I have a schedule to keep."

Loren hugged his mother one more time and said, "Keep an eye on her."

"That will be easy enough." Mrs. Kays embraced him, tears coming to her eyes. "Please be safe."

"I'll write, Mother. Be sure Barbara gets my letters, too."

"I will." She grinned.

Mrs. Kays released her son and stepped next to Barbara. He kissed Barbara one last time, looked deeply into her eyes and said, "I love you."

Barbara couldn't believe her ears. She wanted to say it back, but her shock kept her from speaking.

Loren walked around the bus. Its engine started and the giant vehicle belched some smoke and took off as Loren headed back to his seat.

"I thought you two decided to only be friends."

"We are," Barbara said, hobbling. "Friends love one another."

"They don't kiss like that." Mrs. Kays raised a brow. "I'm not sure I like this. Now he's got me giving you his letters when he mails them."

Barbara knew that was the only way she could read them. He couldn't dare send them to her house. "Thank you."

"No, thank you. If it wasn't for you, he probably wouldn't write me at all. Now at least I'll know how he is. I'm worried sick about him. I heard they don't treat the boys nicely at that camp."

"He'll do just fine," Barbara said, her teeth gritted.

"You're hurt, aren't you?"

"I'll be good as new soon."

Mrs. Kays leaned over. "Come on, we'll go to the hospital again. Just don't tell your father. I'll pay for the checkup. I want to make sure it isn't broken."

"Thanks." Barbara bent down and picked her hat up off the street, hobbling all the way to Mrs. Kays' Model T Ford.

CHAPTER 13

Packed auditorium.

When Barbara walked in she noted how many people had turned up for the talent show. She glanced up at the curtains and they were still closed. No one had seen her masterpiece yet.

She couldn't wait.

Her parents sat in the front row. Taking the aisle, she moved past many familiar classmates and their parents seated next to them. She scanned the room, looking for Mrs. Kays.

This was her moment, too.

For five weeks, Barbara had been going to her house on Saturdays to paint the backdrop. If it wasn't for Mrs. Kays suggesting she do it, Barbara wouldn't have had the courage or been so bold as to paint and capture anything so large.

"You look like you've got butterflies in your stomach," her mother said in her ear. "Don't worry about a thing. It will be just fine; you're in-like- Flynn."

"I hope so," Barbara said. "I sure have a bad case of the heebie-jeebies."

Mrs. Kays suddenly appeared, coming out between the two curtains to stand behind a lectern at one side of the stage. She glanced down to the crowd and nodded to a few of her students, including Barbara.

"Good evening. Thank you all for coming to Maple High's Talent Contest. Our students are very talented and tonight will be one of our greatest shows ever. All of you will soon be dazzled by musicians, dancers, artists, and scenes acted out by Mr. Cameron's best drama students. We have sports stars who will be receiving awards and two magicians who will surprise us all with their illusionary skills. After the show, please go to the cafeteria where you will see some fine paintings and sculptures as you have snacks and drinks. Let's begin with our first dancer, Darla Miller. A ballerina's rendition of *The Nutcracker*."

The curtains opened as the crowd applauded.

There it was—her backdrop. A masterpiece of brilliant colors and shadings and in bright letters, "Maple Hill's Talent Show." She expected everyone to gasp at the sight of it. Barbara looked around and noticed no one was looking at her painting. The crowd seemed transfixed upon the beautiful blonde gracefully pirouetting across the floor. The music began and Darla began.

She was mesmerizing. She jumped up in perfect rhythm to music that reminded her of Christmas. No one was noticing the backdrop. In the bottom corner, underneath the drama masks she had painted in silver and greenish tones, her name was too small to read from the audience.

Barbara was crushed.

When the music ended, applause rang out. Another teacher walked to the lectern and announced that the drama students would be doing a rendition of *A Midsummer Night's Dream*.

The night went on, talent after more talent. When Barbara first walked in, she had felt such pride. Now, as she watched the crowd gasping at a student dressed as William Shakespeare's character Puck, she realized how small a part she was playing in all of this.

No one would even remember her work.

Her mother, her father, no one leaned in to tell her how fine a job she did, that her painting was a star all its own. Did no one appreciate her gift to this show?

As the night wore on, the smile she had plastered on turned to a blank stare. The magician who pulled a guinea pig out of a big black hat got more attention for that simple trick than her painting, which had taken her six weeks to complete.

When the last violinist had played, Mrs. Kays regained the lectern. "Thank you all for coming. And last, I would like to call your attention to this fine backdrop, painted by one single student of mine. Barbara Larson, please stand and take a bow."

Barbara gasped.

"Come on, Barbara. Stand up." Mrs. Kays waved to her.

Suddenly, the spotlight hit the back of her head and Barbara stood. Applause rang out. She turned around and saw how those around her were cheering, and then from the back two men stood, then a woman rose to her feet, and before long every single person was standing in a spontaneous ovation.

"How spectacular a response! Come on stage, Barbara," Mrs. Kays called to her.

In her crowning moment, Barbara took the few steps to the stage. "All right, students, you, too," Mrs. Kays added.

One by one, the dancers, musicians, actors, and athletes dressed in uniform took the stage to stand beside Barbara. They all took each other's hands and in one long line took a bow.

The crowd remained on their feet, clapping.

Barbara couldn't believe it. They liked her painting! She glanced over at her father, who, to her great disappointment, had eyes fixed on the sports stars, but her mother was staring straight at her, tears flowing down her cheeks.

"Thank you all for coming. Please join us in the cafeteria where several students will receive an award for their talents while we can all dine on the staff's goodies and drinks."

As the lights came back up, the students shuffled off the stage to rejoin their parents. Barbara tapped Mrs. Kays on the shoulder and gave her a huge hug. "This is the best night of my life."

Mrs. Kays embraced her tightly. "You are the very reason I became a teacher. To know I played some part in your career makes me very proud."

"Mrs. Kays," said a large older man in a suit behind her. "That isn't appropriate at this time."

Barbara backed away, recognizing the principal of the school.

"And you must be our star painter, Barbara Larson?" the principal asked.

"Yes, Sir." Barbara gasped.

"Please, call me Gary or Mr. Johnson," he said.

"Yes, Mr. Johnson." Barbara stiffened.

"After the award ceremony, I'd like to talk to you about how much you'd be willing to sell this painting for. I'd like to hang it in my office permanently."

Barbara's eyes widened. "What?"

"How much would you sell it for?"

"I never thought about selling it," Barbara said.

"Thirty dollars." Mrs. Kays gave her a nudge. "Don't take anything less than that. It's worth far more."

"You're right," Mr. Johnson said. "Fifty it is then." Then he patted Barbara's shoulder and moved in the direction of the cafeteria.

Mrs. Kays wrapped an arm around her, walking her off the stage.

"I sold my first painting. It was Dreamy!" Barbara told her mother excitedly as she came to stand beside her. "Our Principal at the high school paid fifty dollars to put it in his own office!"

"Really? Cat's pajamas!" Her father turned his head to look at the principal, who was now speaking with the ballerina's parents. He almost seemed surprised that anyone would buy it. "He's willing to pay that much?"

"Of course, he is," Mrs. Kays snipped. "It's worth ten times that amount. The principal got himself a bargain."

"Yes," her mother said, dryly. "I've heard of paintings going for that in New York or London but not Maple Hill."

"Barbara is very talented," Mrs. Kays reminded.

"So, you keep telling us," Her father said.

That should have hurt Barbara's feelings, but tonight, of all nights, no one could hurt her. The only thing that hurt was that Loren wasn't around to see the finished painting. She couldn't wait to write her next letter telling him all about it.

CHAPTER 14

Holding a letter in her hand, at the bus stop, Barbara waited. Her heart was pounding. She had waited all these weeks to see Loren again. Just to see those eyes in person, to hold his hand, to kiss his lips; the very thought made her weak in the knees.

She reread his last message. "Barbara, I'm coming home. I'll be there on Saturday, Bus 29. Meet me. I can't wait to see you."

How sweet a note!

The Ford bus marked 29 began to head toward the station. Barbara read the number over the driver's head and gasped. She walked to the edge of the street until the bus came to a stop.

One after another, people left the vehicle. She looked for him until she saw him. His lovely blond hair was cut completely off, now mere stubble. Loren looked so handsome; her breath caught in her throat. He looked thinner and more muscular.

His big eyes shifted to hers and a smile crossed his lips. He dropped his duffle bag, leaned in and embraced her with a big kiss. His hands caressed the small of her back as his breath mingled with hers in passion.

"Miss me?" he asked against her lips.

"Every moment of every day since you left."

"Tell it to Sweeney! So I don't need to run off all the other guys who want to marry you?"

"Other guys?" she asked as she gripped him tightly.

"Marry me, Barbara." She couldn't breathe. She backed away.

"Marry me," he repeated. "While I'm overseas you can live with my mother, and when I return I'll buy us the biggest house with a big white fence and we'll be together for the rest of our lives."

"You want that?"

"Wouldn't that be swell?" Loren kissed her again, then he reached in his pocket and pulled out a simple gold band with a small diamond chip in the middle. "I saved up two months' wages, every penny of my boot camp pay for this and I hope it isn't too small. I bought another band that matches it for me as well."

Barbara kissed his lips as tears rolled down her cheeks. Over and over, she tasted his lips. Relishing the very feel of him against her, she gave him her answer without even speaking.

"What about tomorrow?" he asked. "I called the pastor of that Baptist church where my mom goes. I already asked and he said he'd marry us at once if you agree."

Barbara didn't know what to say; she wanted this more than anything. She had so much to tell him, but her mind couldn't come up with the words. She loved him and wanted to marry him now, not even wait for the morrow.

"Do you have the moxie to be my girl forever?"

Barbara grinned. "You're no lug for asking!"

"So, you'll marry me?"

She nodded yes as he picked her up and swirled her around in circles.

* * * *

With strands of pearls around her neck, wearing a simple white dress with ribbons in her hair, Barbara walked down the aisle toward Loren. She didn't dare tell her parents. They wouldn't approve and would try to stop her. Nor would her mother approve of Barbara borrowing her pearls.

No one could stop her.

As witnesses were the minister's wife, who was playing the piano, and Mrs. Kays, who was the only person sitting in the pew. Her face was covered with a giant smile as Barbara walked toward Loren.

He was in his Air Corps government-issued light brown uniform. Dressed all in brown, except for the cap, which had a blue band and the Air Corps winged propeller symbol in the front.

When they came together, he took her hand and the minister spoke. The words were those she'd heard a few times at family weddings. She barely even noticed what was said.

Her only thought was that Loren would be her husband. At the tender age of eighteen, her parents couldn't stop her, either. She only had two more weeks of school, and she would live with Mrs. Kays until Loren came home.

"Do you take this woman to be your bride?" the minister asked him.

"I do." Loren gazed into her eyes.

"Do you, Barbara, take this man as your lawfully wedded husband to have and to hold from this day forward for all of your lives?"

"I do," she said on a quick breath.

"Exchange rings," the minister said.

In his hand, Loren held the same gold band ring he showed her yesterday. "With this ring, I thee wed." ·

Barbara took the matching gold ring he handed her and then put it on his fourth finger. "With this ring, I thee wed."

"What God has brought together, may no man put asunder," the minister said. "Now kiss your bride."

Loren leaned in and kissed Barbara's lips. "I love you."

"I love you, too." She sighed.

The kiss lasted what felt like only a moment. They heard Mrs. Kays thanking the minister and his wife for playing such a beautiful song. Barbara had no idea what it was. She didn't care. All she could think about was that now she was the luckiest woman on earth.

She was Mrs. Loren Kays. He was her husband.

If time ever stood still, it did at this very moment. When his lips left hers, Barbara realized this was it; they were wed.

"Are you happy?" he said.

"Yes." She grinned.

"Now, I have to do something very unpleasant," he said.

"What?"

"I'm going to talk with your father, gather your things and bring them to my mother's house. I mean, our house."

Barbara held him. "I can't believe this is happening."

"It's the right thing to do. I have to tell him, man to man. Let's hope he doesn't call a prowl car. I'm a square John."

"Can I go with you?" Barbara asked.

"I think it's best you don't. Go with my mother. She's going to stay with my aunt for a few days to give us privacy on our honeymoon."

Barbara blushed and looked down. She honestly hadn't even thought about that. Soon she would know what it felt to have a man make love to her. It thrilled her to her very core.

CHAPTER 15

Barbara waited in Mrs. Kays' house alone. Worried about Loren and what her father might do when he learned of their marriage, she paced around the small house until she had memorized every inch of where the furniture was.

Her nerves made it impossible to stay in the bedroom, which she realized was now hers as well. Loren's room was simple enough, a large bed covered in white sheets; solid blue curtains framed the window and tin model planes hung from the ceiling and across a large wooden shelf.

Next to the bed sat a table with a blue lamp. The only paintings in the room were of the sky. Those she adored. How fascinating that his mother had made sure he could see the sky before he shut out the lights before sleep.

When the door shut in the living room, Barbara rushed from the bedroom to the front of the house. There Loren stood, his face ashen. His eyes lowered and he took in a breath before saying, "Your father is not pleased."

"I could have told you he wouldn't be."

"You'd think he would appreciate my love for you." Loren moved past her and into the kitchen. There he pulled out a bottle of wine and poured himself a glass. He raised it up in offer. "Would you like some? It sure beats the panther piss our parents had to drink during prohibition."

"No thank you."

"I will never tell you what he said, so don't bother to ask," Loren grumbled, gulping down the wine.

"If I know my father, it wasn't a kind word."

Loren nodded. "How such an angel like you came from such a crab patch I will never know."

Barbara took a deep breath, watching him pour himself another glass. She wondered if this was how the next few days would be, him angry at the argument with her father.

"He brought up your uncle and said he hoped I had the same fate!" Loren shook with rage. "He has no soul!"

She couldn't believe it. Her father's brother had been killed in WWI. He had been shot; not by the hands of the enemy but by friendly fire, an accident in the front lines every member of the family mourned greatly. Her father hadn't had a close relationship with him, but even he cried at the funeral. It was the only time in her life she saw her father weep.

"My father loved his brother."

Loren finished his second glass. "I'm trying to be a man and tell him how I feel about you, that we are wed, that I plan to take care of you for the rest of my life and what does he say? 'I hope you don't come back!'"

"He's angry." Barbara knew. "Think how he must feel. He just lost his daughter to someone he hardly knows."

"He said I was beneath you," Loren snipped, pouring another glass. "He's probably right, but there was no need to say it. I'm coming home a war hero. I'll show him."

"You knew this wasn't going to be easy. I should have done it for you."

"No, I'm glad I went." Loren smirked. "I needed to see just what I am protecting you from." For a few moments he held the glass up to his lips but didn't swallow, then he lowered it. "He wants you to live there, not here, until I return from duty overseas. Actually, he said if I return from overseas."

"I can't apologize enough for what my father said." Barbara walked over to him and leaned in. "He's not me and you're no chump. I think you'll come home a war hero. I believe when you get back we'll buy that house with that white fence you want so much; we'll have babies and be a family."

Suddenly the grimace on Loren's face weakened. He glanced over to her and the hardness in his eyes loosened with tears. "At least you believe in me."

"I never doubted you."

"You make this all worth that confrontation."

"Then forget it ever happened. My father doesn't know what he's talking about. He only thinks he knows what's best for me. He's wrong. You are what's best for me, a life with you. I can't see myself anywhere else or with anyone else. I love you, Loren."

He smiled then, the anger leaving him as quickly as it had come. "You are a gift from God."

Barbara moved closer, her lips inches from his.

"Our love is like the sky," Loren said. "Endless."

With no warning, he wrapped his arms about her, picked her up, and carried her into the bedroom.

Underneath the planes dangling from strings, he undressed her in one big swoop. Her eyes relished his body as well as the way he was touching her. There she saw a man for the first time. By her amusement, she proved she was indeed an innocent.

For an hour he lay on top of her, kissing her lips and, when they were so caught up in the passion, she felt no pain; he made her wife in every way. After he had claimed her, he held her tightly in his arms.

This closeness made Barbara cry with joy. In her entire life, she hadn't been treated so kindly. For once, she didn't feel rejected or belittled. She felt as if she was high.

"I love you, Barbara," he said.

"I love you, too. I'm so sorry my father ruined this night for you. I wanted it to be the best night."

"It was." He smiled. "How did I get so lucky to have you as my wife? To know I'll have a rare dish to come home to."

She kissed his lips again. "I'm the lucky one." And so, she felt she was. Barbara gazed into those blue gems so fascinating that it took her breath away. They were the same color as the sky above on a crystal clear day when the sun shined brightly on their small town.

Those eyes filled with passion and love, no sight was more incredible. She told herself that on lonely days she'd remember the color and that he claimed their love was as endless as the sky above.

CHAPTER 16

Moving out of her father's house proved harder than she thought it would be. Several days had passed, so Barbara had hoped her father would be at least cordial.

When she walked through the door, her father simply walked out. He didn't speak to her or Loren, who was waiting on the stoop. He slammed the door, stomped past Loren and headed across the street to the newsstand. Barbara watched him pay for a paper, grab a coffee and sit down on a nearby bench. He obviously didn't want to be anywhere near either one of them. She walked toward her bedroom to gather her clothes, and there she discovered her mother sewing near the hallway.

"Good morning," her mother greeted without looking up.

Barbara smiled and said, "How are you, Mother?" "I've missed you."

She peered up through her glasses. "I'm also very disappointed in your actions."

"Loren and I are very happy," Barbara said.

"You adore him," her mother replied. "Of that I have no doubt. It's just I wish you had invited me to the wedding."

"You would have gone?"

Tears entered her mother's eyes. "Of course."

"But I thought because of Father you would not approve."

"Not everything is up to him," her mother said, finishing the hem of a long blue sundress. "Here, this is your wedding present. And…" She handed her a box. "I made Loren some handkerchiefs for when he is away."

"Loren!" Barbara called.

He rushed in and quickly walked down the hall. "Are you all right?" He peered down at his mother-in-law.

"No, it's not that. Here, this is from my mother." She handed him the box.

Loren opened it and lifted a white handkerchief up. On the bottom, inscribed in small letters was: "Barbara and Loren Kays." He immediately bent over and kissed her cheek. "Thank you, Mother."

She wiped her eyes and sniffled. "I may not approve of how fast you did it, but I do think you'll make a fine husband for my daughter." She stood.

Barbara rushed to her and hugged her. Her mother reached out for Loren to join them, too, and all three hugged for quite some time. By the end, Barbara had to wipe her eyes several times.

"Thank you, Mrs. Larson, for such a wonderful gift. I will take these with me."

"Do you have to move out now?" she asked Barbara. "She can still be married and living at home until you return."

Loren turned to her. "What do you want, Barbara?"

"I have a choice?"

"Of course you have," Loren said and chuckled. "I don't want you to be where you don't want. Would you like to remain here or live with my mother?"

Barbara glanced over her shoulder, and through the screen door she could see her father still stewing over a cup of coffee. He saw her looking his way and opened up the newspaper in a huff.

"Well?" Loren asked. "Your mother seems to accept us. I have no doubt she'll let me in when I return."

"What of Father?" Barbara said. "I don't know if I can live under the same roof with him now."

"Let me take care of that crab patch," her mother said. "Please, let me get used to this idea of not having you around much more. I know when Loren gets back, you'll be off, and I want to spend as much time with you as I can."

Barbara felt torn between her two obligations. "I don't know. Father upset my husband so much yesterday."

"I'm over that," Loren said.

"You are?" her mother asked, surprised.

"If you ask me, some of the things he said were quite unforgivable and nothing but horse feathers."

"True, but they were said in haste." Loren knew.

"I'd imagine it would be hard to lose a daughter in this matter."

"We haven't lost her," her mother said proudly. "We gained the most handsome, sweet son."

"Thank you." Loren got choked up. "I appreciate that you see me as more than he does."

"You are a bright young man with a brilliant future. I admit I was upset at first but then I ran into the farmer and he told me how dedicated a pilot you are. You are a hard worker, he told me. You're a good man, he said. I'd be thrilled if he married my own daughter, that's what he boasted."

"You never met his daughter." Loren shook his head.

"He'll be lucky if anyone ever marries her."

"Oh," her mother laughed, "I take it she wasn't pleasing to your eyes."

"Not my cup of tea."

"But my daughter is," she added. "The moment she came into this world, I knew she was special. I know you will take care of her."

"You have my word."

"I do apologize for what my husband said in anger. He didn't mean such horrible things, especially regarding his brother. He loved his brother very much. He was quite upset when word came of the accident. I'm sure he especially didn't mean that."

"I think he did," Loren said.

"Perhaps it would be better to move in with Mrs. Kays, Mother. It's not like I can't visit you when father is at work."

Her mother lowered her chin. "Reconsider, please. It is so hard for a mother to let go like this. My daughter is no charity girl."

Barbara still didn't know what to do.

"I have an idea. Why don't we just take a few of her things and let her ponder over it for a week or two where she wants to live. For my part, I don't mind either way, as long as I will be welcome and she can get my letters."

"I'd make sure she does. I see the mail first, long before her father comes home."

"What if he forbids it," Loren asked.

"It doesn't matter. You are her husband and what God has joined I will not try to separate."

Barbara nodded. "That sounds good. I will stay with the Kays until Loren leaves and then I'll come back and see how things go, Mother. If Father gives me too much grief about getting married, I'll move back out."

"That is reasonable," Loren agreed.

"It is," her mother concurred. "That will give me a few weeks to work on your father and let him know that this will be his last chance to come to grips with the fact his daughter is now a woman."

"I understand," Loren added. "This is hard for a father but remind him he owes me an apology for the things he said. It was all I could do not to raise my fist."

"If it is any consolation, you showed me the man you are by restraining," her mother said. "You are a fine man who loves my daughter. With the military and your piloting skills, even when you return you can provide for her. Your mother told me long ago without you she wouldn't have been able to pay her own bills. It was an honorable thing you did by providing for your mother."

"You've done your research," Loren said.

"I felt the need. But now I see how wrong my husband was about you. There were a few past girlfriends, or should I say Debs I learned of, but all of them missed you when you broke up, which tells me you were quite a catch. They all said this, that when they were with you, they cared so much."

"Who are these girls?" Barbara raised a wary brow.

"No matter." Loren shrugged. "They were all nothing compared to you and how we are."

Mrs. Larson straightened, wiped her eyes and held up the sundress to Barbara's shoulders. "Yes, this will fit just fine. I'll make you a hat as well. I know how much you love those hats."

CHAPTER 17

Waving farewell to the Ford OTC bus this time proved harder than the last. Barbara would rather feel the pain in her leg again than the aching in her heart that hurt so badly tears didn't give any comfort.

Mrs. Kays and she watched the bus leave. There was sadness in Loren's eyes, mixed with a bit of fear. Barbara saw it but chose not to believe anything bad would ever happen to him.

He was far too good a pilot.

On the way home, Mrs. Kays asked, "So will you stay with me?"

"What would you prefer?" Barbara wondered. "My mother calls me three times a day; she misses me so."

"I'd miss you as well."

Barbara felt torn. "I haven't made any decisions yet. Can I stay with you one more week—at least until I've decided. My father isn't speaking to me yet and until then, I don't feel comfortable going home."

"So you'll be leaving," Mrs. Kays said. "I'd hope you'd stay and keep me company."

"How lucky am I that so many people want me?" Barbara grinned.

"True," Mrs. Kays agreed. "How about some lunch? This diner has the best fried chicken and dumplings around."

"Actually, it's their sundaes I love."

"Both will be on me." Mrs. Kays opened the door to the small diner.

They sat down at a red booth. A green oilcloth tablecloth was spread across the table; paper napkins marked each setting. Around the counter came a jolly, thin woman with her hair tied up in fancy pigtails and wearing bright white bobby socks.

"Good afternoon; what can I get you both to drink?"

"Sodas," Mrs. Kays said.

"What a treat." Barbara grinned.

"Well, we both deserve it after today."

After the drinks arrived, they both ordered the chicken and dumplings dinner and talked about Loren. They were interrupted when the door to the diner flung open to reveal a woman crying. Two other women were trying to console her.

Mrs. Kays recognized the woman. "What is wrong with Mrs. Neighbors? She's the music instructor at our school."

"Do you know her? She looks so upset." Barbara stopped eating.

"Not Henry! Why Henry?" Mrs. Neighbors wept.

"Yes, I know her well. Every year I'm invited to her big red house on Cranbrook Avenue for the teachers' Christmas party. I should go and try to see what is wrong." Mrs. Kays walked across the room and placed a hand on her shoulder.

Barbara couldn't hear most of the conversation but then four words rang out across the diner and everyone looked up. "My son is dead!" the woman wailed.

Mrs. Kays grabbed the counter. "Not Henry!"

"Yes, he was shot in Germany. The meat wagon couldn't get to him. He bled to death right in front of his cousin, who was a leather neck in his platoon." Mrs. Neighbors gasped. "Please, some water. May I have some water?"

The waitress quickly poured her some water as the men around her kept telling her it would be all right. Barbara suddenly got a sick feeling in her stomach. This could happen to her and Mrs. Kays. They could lose Loren.

When Mrs. Kays returned to the table, she was as pale as a ghost. She didn't touch her food.

"How horrible," Barbara said.

"We can't think of such things now."

For several more minutes they heard the woman crying. It chilled Barbara to the core. She was openly weeping for her lost son, killed because of a war that everyone knew was worthy of fighting.

"My son came back not long ago and told me what happens in those Nazi camps," Mrs. Neighbor said. "He died soon after. He died to free the Jews."

Barbara glanced down at her dinner and she, too, no longer wanted to eat. She remembered Mrs. Neighbors. Her son Henry had played piano at last year's Talent Show. She saw him in her mind's eye, playing piano. Brown hair with big green eyes and a large, plump nose. Not a handsome fellow by any means, but God had given him so much talent one couldn't help but know how much God loved him.

"He couldn't shoot anyone! He didn't have the heart!" his mother continued.

Mrs. Kays rose. "Come on, Barbara; let's leave her to her misery."

Barbara got to her feet and followed Mrs. Kays back to the house. Neither of them spokes. Barbara guessed she was as worried about Loren as she was.

When they walked in the door, Mrs. Kays went into her room and shut the door. Barbara could hear her crying. She moved past to her bedroom. Instead of crying, she picked up her easel, paint brush and canvas. For hours she painted. She pictured Henry playing piano and drew him that way.

Throughout the night, she heard Mrs. Kays crying. It didn't stop her from creating this piece. She painted onward and didn't stop until even the overly large nose was perfectly created.

At dawn, so tired she could barely open her eyes, Barbara took the painting and walked out the door, still in the clothes she had worn the day before. She walked three blocks to Cranbrook Avenue and looked for the big red house Mrs. Kays had mentioned yesterday.

There were two houses that were of reddish shade. One was small and the other a two story with a giant shed in the back. Two collies were jumping at the white fence as she approached.

After several minutes of the dogs barking, Barbara wondered if this was a mistake. Should she bother this woman in her grief? Then the door opened, and a man leaned down to pick up the newspaper.

He saw her at the gate holding the painting. Barbara turned it around so he could see. The man grabbed his chest and nearly fell over. Tears came to his eyes. He rushed for the gate and opened it.

"For you and your family," Barbara said. "It's still wet so be careful."

"How much do I owe you?" he asked. "You're the Larson girl, right?"

"Nothing," she said, and she turned and walked away.

She didn't tell anyone she did it. She didn't even sign the painting, but Mrs. Kays informed her that it was hung during the funeral and she knew her work by the master technique that could only have been Barbara's.

CHAPTER 18

Barbara took a walk after Mrs. Kays returned from the funeral. This tragedy only made her remember that Loren was in great danger. Although she didn't care much for bloodshed, she agreed with the cause to protect the Jews from Hitler's wrath.

To get to the dirt path behind town, Barbara took a street she normally didn't walk, a side path rightfully named, "Briefy Road." It was a dirt street with only a few houses, but they were divine. As she traveled, she saw one before her with a "For Sale" sign up on the white fence. She gazed over the house. How incredible it was. It had a large front porch, with large Victorian doors that were painted as white as the picket fence that was short enough to see over. Even the windows were slender by design and long. Below every opening was a window box which held dozens of pansies in yellow and purple.

What a place to live!

This had to be one of the most charming homes she had ever seen. Although it was smaller than the other homes on the short street, there was a creek in the far back and a wooden bridge.

How absolutely charming!

She wished she could afford such a house. Passing it, she couldn't keep her eyes off of it. She pictured herself hanging clothes out back with Loren trimming the bushes in front.

Nearly tripping, she pivoted and continued to the dirt path. How close it was to her favorite crab apple tree, so near the burger shop that Loren had taken her to. She sat down underneath the tree and searched for the bunny she had seen the last time she had needed to get away.

To her surprise, the bunny was a short distance away. He must have a hole nearby. The bunny got up on two feet and sniffed the air. He glanced over at her briefly and then returned to eating grass.

How much she wished Loren was here. She missed him so much that her heart ached to just look upon his face. "So this is love," Barbara said to herself. "There is no better or worse feeling."

A couple came out of the burger shop and sat on the bench. Barbara watched them. They were so oblivious to the fact that a war was going on. She almost felt like saying, "How dare they be happy when my love is off risking his life?"

Her head leaned back against the tree and she glanced through the branches and saw a few bees buzzing around the flowers. She watched them for a moment, listening to the buzzing they made. She'd never painted bees before, she realized. Could she capture that movement? An interesting subject such a small creature could make.

"Excuse me," a voice interrupted her thoughts.

Startled, Barbara glanced up and saw that the girl of the couple was a few yards away from her and moving closer. "Yes?"

"Are you that painter I've been hearing so much about?"

"I paint," Barbara said. "But I doubt you've heard of me."

"You're famous," the girl said.

Barbara tried not to laugh. "I'm sorry, but you must be mistaking me for someone else. I've only done a few public paintings. There were some at my father's store, but they were removed."

"Barbara Larson?" she asked.

"That's me. How have you heard of me?" Barbara said, rising to her feet out of curiosity.

"I saw that painting you did at the funeral earlier today. So many people asked who had painted it and I remembered the cow picture in your father's store."

"He took it down." Barbara's eyes glanced downward.

"He did? When? I went there for milk yesterday and it was hanging. You also did the jug over the dairy. There's also a fruit picture somewhere on the left. My boyfriend," she pointed to the guy chowing down his burger, "told him how much he loved that one."

Surprised, Barbara smiled. "I'm glad he hung them again."

"He went on and on about you. That you just got married to a pilot in the Air Corps. My brother is in the war. He's a Commanding Officer, a real Butch."

"My father spoke of my husband in a kindly manner?" Barbara gasped. The girl tilted her head, curiously.

"Is that odd?"

"Yes, it is," Barbara said, matter-of-factly.

"The reason I came to speak to you is my family would love to have you paint a portrait of my brother. We'd be willing to pay you to do it. The only problem is we only have pictures. Could you paint from seeing pictures?"

Barbara shook her head no. "I've never done that before."

"What about Henry? He wasn't even around to pose, was he? You painted that, right?"

"Yes, but I knew Henry."

"I see." The girl sighed. "Poor Henry, he sure was the bee's knees around here."

"So sorry." Barbara headed off toward the path. "You might want to ask my teacher Mrs. Kays; perhaps she could do it."

"I know her. I'll ask her then," the girl said, behind her back. "It's a shame you can't do it. My grandfather said he'd be willing to pay one hundred dollars."

Barbara stopped in her tracks. She thought for a moment, realizing she could use the money. That could buy her so many supplies. She could paint dozens of bees if she wanted with that kind of loot.

"Should I ask Mrs. Kays?" the girl questioned.

Barbara whirled around and extended her hand, "Let me have a go of it first. If I can't do it, I'll ask my teacher myself."

"Swell," she said. "We live at Twenty-One Oak. Please come by tonight and I'll have my grandfather give you the pictures you can use to paint the portrait. I'm not sure how he'll want him to be dressed but probably in his uniform. My grandfather fought in WWI and he is so proud of him."

"As well he should be." Barbara shook her hand and smiled.

"See you tonight around seven."

CHAPTER 19

Twenty-One Oak Street proved to be a mansion. Barbara walked up the long driveway, up the ten steps to the double doors and used the brass knocker to announce her presence.

A maid answered the door and asked, "Are you Barbara Larson?"

"I'm Barbara, but I've recently married, and my last name is now Kays."

"Come in." She lowered her head as Barbara walked in.

The ceiling was so high, Barbara had to squint to see the tapestry so high on the wall. It was of several boats at sea. The sun was shining high above, reflecting off the cool waters. Below was a beach where several shells were scattered around, and a child was placing one in a bucket.

"Hello," came a low elderly voice.

Barbara turned and saw a man standing in the dining room. His hair was slicked back. On his face was a pair of thick glasses and he walked with a cane which had a decorative silver tip. He was a handsome man, who she guessed was near eighty in age. His blue navy suit was in perfect condition.

"I'm Barbara Kays." She moved forward to shake his hand.

He refused to shake it. "No need for formalities in my house. I don't mean to bat my gums, but I know you. I've heard so much about you that I find you family."

Barbara shyly glanced down. "Thank you."

"Henry was my nephew and when I saw your painting of him I was deeply moved by your art. Is it true you refused payment?"

She admitted, "I refused."

"You have a good heart." He headed toward two formal leather chairs in the parlor. He sat down with some difficulty and pointed to the other chair. "Please, have a seat."

Barbara helped herself to the large chair. She hadn't sat in leather before. She liked the feel of it underneath her hands. Immediately, she decided she would paint his grandson in one of these chairs. "I would like to begin as soon as possible."

"Here." He pulled four pictures out from his pants pocket.

She rushed up, took them, and sat back down. Admiring the quality of the photographs, Barbara realized this would not be as hard as she thought. She could use this with the lighting in this room to create a portrait to please him. With confidence she continued to gaze at the man in the photo. Although she had never seen the man in the picture before, he felt familiar. He had dark brown hair with streaks of lighter brown near the tips. His eyes were very deeply set and shined a golden brown.

"Donnie is quite a lady killer," he said, "a real he-man kind of fella."

"He looks like a younger version of you," Barbara complimented.

"I've met a few charity girls in my day," he said and chuckled, proudly. "That would take me many a day to tell so I'll dummy up."

Barbara felt her pride swelling. "I am sure I can capture his essence. I really like this picture of his face. His eyes have a certain appeal."

"I'm willing to pay you five hundred dollars to paint them all."

Barbara couldn't believe what she just heard. "Five hundred dollars?"

"Yes, for those three pictures to be painted on canvas." The grandfather tapped his cane. "And especially the last picture of the woman."

"Mr…" She realized she hadn't gotten his name. While she spoke, she pulled out the last photo of a brunette woman with a bun in her hair.

"Mr. Reaves, that is my name," he replied, pulling out a piece of paper from his other side pocket and holding it out to her. "I hope you are prepared for all the paintings I have recommended you for."

Barbara rose, took the paper and began to read. On it was a list of names, addresses and who they would like to be painted. Next to their names was the amount they were willing to pay. One had written down that they would pay two hundred for one family portrait to be hung in the museum.

Speechless, Barbara stood, her hands shaking.

"I suppose that is a lot to take in. I told them all that the list was long and that in no way had you agreed, but that I would let them know. I put a star by the ones who were willing to pay double if they were moved to the top of the list."

"Mr. Reaves, I don't know what to say."

"We'll keep you out of Hooverville." He smiled. "Are you pleased that I took such liberties as to mention to my friends I knew you?"

"I'm flattered that you would entrust me with painting your grandson. Now I learn you've got me commissioned to your friends for six months or more. Why?"

"Rejecting my offer?"

Barbara grinned. "I can't believe that you would help me. Why?"

"You can bring the dead back to life," he replied.

"What an odd thing to say," she said, briefly. "I accept. Please inform all on the list I will begin right away."

"Indeed," he said. "Can I offer you something to eat or a cup of Joe?"

"I must be going," Barbara said. "I want to get painting on your grandson tonight. I will be by in the next few days."

"Do you need money for supplies?" He pulled out his wallet and opened it. "Take a hundred skins up front to help you get what you need."

Barbara couldn't fathom a man so generous, but seeing his house, she knew he could afford it. A hundred dollars to him was pocket change. She took the cash and said, "Thank you."

"If there is anything that I can do to further assist you, let me know," Mr. Reaves said.

She leaned over him and kissed his cheek. "I don't know how I could ever repay you."

He laughed. "You just did."

Barbara let herself out, down the steps and out onto the driveway. She decided to take the long way home. She would walk past the house on Brief Road and jot down the seller's number. If she could afford it, she would put a down payment on that little house on the corner.

She had finally made her decision as to where she would live until Loren returned. It was near both her mother's house and Mrs. Kays'. Yet, she would have privacy and a yard with a fence.

CHAPTER 20

Removing the For Sale sign gave Barbara a thrill. She tossed it into the sink. Moving around her new home, she felt as if she were floating on air. The house was small but it was near perfection in her eyes.

Three bedrooms and two baths with a small kitchen; any more would be too much. She moved into the back bedroom and saw the bay window. It overlooked the wooden bridge and creek. Ducks were waddling around the water's edge along with a wild swan.

Barbara knew this would become her studio. She would set up office in the living room and have a desk and a few chairs. A few of her older paintings could hang on the walls and she'd add some nice potted plants. That would keep the patrons in the front. No one would ever see her workplace in the back bedroom.

That would remain a mess. How wonderful to have a place she could leave a mess and not have one complaint! Even better, on cool summer nights, she could open the bay window and see the reflection of the moon on the water. This was paradise. A feeling of warmth filled her to the core. This was a feeling she hadn't ever felt before; she was home.

Walking around, Barbara realized she didn't have even a bed to her name. The house needed many things, furniture for one, and a paint job in the inside, but that would only take a few weekends.

She stepped outside and took a look around the grounds. The landscaping included bushes and a few flowering trees. In the center of the front yard was a giant elm that looked older than dirt.

Nearing the creek, she watched as the ducks moved into the water. She peered in and saw several minnows and a blue crab with bright red claws. She could paint a hundred paintings from these surroundings.

"No time for that."

Hurrying back to the house, Barbara grabbed her suitcase and opened it up. Among her few belongings she pulled out a canvas and two bottles of paint. She painted the entire back a shade of ivory and in giant black letters she slowly filled in: Kays' Studio. Artist for Hire.

She set it outside on the porch to dry and sat down. A million things she needed to do, but for the time being, it felt good just to relax. Celebration can come in all ways, and sometimes just being happy in silence is one of them.

The paint dried quickly in the sun and she took it over to the large kitchen window and nailed it up to the sideboards. Hurrying out front, she saw it even from the road. "Artist for Hire" stood out.

"I should put office hours," she concluded. "How often do I want patrons to come by?" Not too often. An artist needs privacy to create masterpieces.

In the back bedroom, she wouldn't hear the door that well either. So, it was decided. She walked back inside, wrote on a sheet of paper *OPEN SATURDAYS FROM 9-12*. She stuck this piece of paper on the side of the sign and thought if that didn't work out, she could always change the time.

When a knock came at the door, Barbara turned around and was surprised to see Mrs. Kays.

"I got your note that the sale went through," she said.

"So, what do you think?" Barbara raised her hands. "This is Loren's and my house. I can move in anytime."

She glanced down at the suitcases and tears stung her eyes. "I see that."

"Please don't be upset," Barbara said. "I need a space to work. I'm going to make a go of painting as a career and use the back as a studio. You should see the view." She took Mrs. Kays' hand and pulled her into the last bedroom. "See what I mean?"

"This is just divine!" Mrs. Kays grinned. "It's all coming together so nicely."

"Mr. Reaves commissioned me and…"

"I heard," Mrs. Kays said. "That's why I've come. I'd like to know some of the names he gave you as clients."

"What is it?" Barbara noticed the panic in her voice. "Don't you like Mr. Reaves?"

"He is a member on the museum board. I know him well." Mrs. Kays raised her hands to her hips. "Tell me the names."

"I don't know offhand." Barbara gasped, hurrying back to her suitcase.

She pulled out the piece of paper and handed Mrs. Kays the sheet. "Your work will be seen by thousands."

"Thousands?" Barbara chuckled. "In our museum?"

"No," Mrs. Kays glanced out to the creek, "I'm afraid you don't understand. Mr. Reaves owns twelve museums across the country. Many of the clients he gave you on this list are the owners of those museums."

Barbara took a step back. "Are you pulling the wool over my eyes?"

"I'm telling you that your work is going to be in almost every major museum in the country." Mrs. Kays pointed to a name. "Look here, this man owns the largest museum in New York City, and this woman lives in California."

"Why would he do this for me?"

"I'm not sure," Mrs. Kays said. "I'm thrilled for you, though. This opportunity doesn't happen to most artists. Now my star pupil will become a star on her own."

Barbara couldn't help but notice the oddness in her voice. It almost sounded like jealousy. "Are you upset with me?"

"I waited my whole life for Mr. Reaves to even say my name, to hang even one of my paintings up in our museum."

"But he did hang the one of you. I saw it."

"I didn't paint it," Mrs. Kays reminded, angrily. "I was the subject. No better than any model and, quite frankly, he made me a real pig's coattail."

Barbara's smile diminished. "I'm sorry you didn't like it. I thought you looked like a peach in it."

"No matter." Mrs. Kays stepped away. "I just want you to see what is happening to you. The fact you say you can paint pictures from a photo may make you one of the most famous artists in the world."

Barbara recalled she hadn't actually accomplished that feat yet. "Is that so unusual?"

"At the quality that you paint, absolutely," Mrs. Kays said. "Let me see the photos he gave you."

Barbara walked slowly back to her suitcase. She didn't know if she should be rejoicing or upset. Mrs. Kays didn't even seem happy with this news. This was the biggest opportunity for her; didn't she like that? Barbara opened the suitcase pocket and pulled out the four photos Mr. Reaves had given her.

Mrs. Kays was standing behind her and took them before Barbara could hold them out. "What's this?" She stared at the first three.

"Just his grandson…oh, yes, he gave you a picture of his beloved Bernadett."

"Bernadett? Did you know her?" Barbara said, curiously.

"She was the woman who drowned by falling off his boat on the way to the island. Some say he murdered her."

"Surely you are mistaken." Barbara's voice caught in her throat.

"No one could be sure. They were engaged. One morning, they left for the island where they were to be married by a friend of his, a captain. You know that island off of the Bay where the big lighthouse is?"

"It no longer has a light."

"But once it was very intriguing to all the men at sea. To marry on such an island was to bring luck to your marriage. Now it's seen as a curse because of what happened to Bernadett."

"So, what happened?"

"On the way, the boat sprang a leak and began to sink. She was in a very large gown and he could not keep Bernadett a float in it," Mrs. Kays informed. "At least, that's what he told the police. No one saw. By the time the wedding guests heard him calling for help, she had drifted away to the bottom of the Bay. She washed ashore two days later, colder than ice."

"How horrible a fate," Barbara said. "Thank you for telling me. I had planned to paint her near the water. I'll remember not to now."

"Yes, Dear, paint her away from the water."

CHAPTER 21

Barbara waited for the mailman out on the porch. Every afternoon she did this, in hopes that another letter from Loren would come. When the mailman walked up, he held out a letter and she knew a new letter had arrived.

"Another letter for you," he said.

"Thank you, this is a wonderful sight!"

Quickly she tore through the envelope and read:

Dear Barbara, How are you?

How is your painting?

I'm doing fine in France, and the bombings are harder than I imagined. It's hard to pull that lever. Every time I do it, knowing a bomb will fall, I pray that there is no one underneath and that it is only the buildings I am hitting. They try to shoot back, but I am far too good a pilot for them to hit.

It's tragic what we are doing to the countryside here. France is lovely even though the war is ugly. I wish you could paint what I see before it is gone. Take away the meanness of it all, and there is beauty in the trees, grass and even the buildings which the war is taking away.

The good news is I'm told that I will be able to come home for a week in the spring. I'll be looking forward to seeing you again. There isn't a day I don't think of you and wish I were with you.

So, we now own a house? When I read your last letter, I couldn't believe it. I know of the place that you are talking about it. I've walked past it a hundred times on the dirt path. That's great; it's near my favorite burger shop. How much I wish for one of those now! You should see what they feed us. Nothing like my mother's cooking, believe me. When I get home, I'm going to request her homemade peanut butter pie.

No matter what house you bought, any place with you will be paradise. I'm looking forward to putting my tools in the garage. My own garage, now that is something to be happy about. I've never had a place of my own before. Thank you for putting my name on the title. I'll sign the papers in the spring to make it legal. As long as it is in your name, it's good enough for me.

I'm writing you as often as I can. Hope you get this soon so you know how much I love you and think about you every day.

Tell Mom hello for me. I wrote her a letter yesterday. You didn't mention her in your last letter. Are you not seeing her as often now that you've moved out?

Love, Loren

She folded the letter, walked in and placed it in a box near the doorway. The only piece in the room. It served as a holder for all of his letters. Each one meant so much to her.

A knock sounded on the door just as she closed the box lid. The door slid open and in came Mr. Reaves, clicking with his cane.

"Good afternoon, Mr. Reaves." Barbara smiled, then she remembered the story Mrs. Kays told her of Bernadett. She wondered if it were true. Could the man before her now be a murderer? Her eyes lowered and chills ran down her spine.

"Sorry to bother you. I was just curious how the painting of my grandson was coming along."

"I finished," Barbara admitted. "Wait here and I'll bring it from my studio." Barbara strolled back to the bedroom, took the canvas covered by a towel off the easel and returned to his side. In one quick movement, she unveiled the painting. It was an exact duplicate of the picture he had given her. The only difference was that his grandson was sitting in the large leather chair.

Mr. Reaves' eyes grew big as a smile crept across his face. "That is perfection."

"Thank you," Barbara said. "I thought it was swell and I will begin the next painting tonight."

"You work nights?"

"I prefer it, actually," Barbara admitted. "I enjoy painting as the sun sets over the creek. A view to inspire me."

"So, the creek and the bridge are your muse." Mr. Reaves nodded. "Water and I don't mix."

"Not a swimmer?" Barbara asked, lowering the painting. "Could you put that in my car?" he asked.

"Certainly." She moved past him and walked toward his luxury automobile, one of the last Pierce Arrows which was much larger than her father's Model T tin Lizzie. She opened the door and placed it in the passenger's side. When she turned around, Mr. Reaves was behind her, startling her. She nearly lost her balance. "Excuse me," she said and stepped to the side.

"Here is two hundred dollars." He handed her two one-hundred-dollar bills. "That is well worth it."

"I appreciate your praise," Barbara said, still wondering if the rumors were true. How could such a nice man be a murderer?

"I hope you don't mind, but I took some liberty as to pay for some furniture from *Tables & Decor* around the corner for you. You have a five hundred dollar deposit there to pick out whatever you need."

"Mr. Reaves!" Barbara gasped. "Surely I can't accept."

"You must," Mr. Reaves said. "It is a gift."

Barbara couldn't believe it. What did he think he was getting by giving her so much money? "Mr. Reaves, I don't know what you think you are buying, but I am a married woman."

Suddenly laughter escaped his full lips. "No, Dear, it isn't like that. Nothing like that, I assure you. I have a lady friend, many in fact."

"Oh." Redness came to her cheeks.

"Don't fret. I'm moved you would even consider it."

"Well, I didn't!" Barbara said. "I thought—"

"You thought wrong," Mr. Reaves said. "You are a kind woman who treats me with respect. That is an odd thing in this town. Many here remember what happened to Bernadett and avoid me like the plague."

Barbara took in a deep breath. She wondered if she should mention anything, but curiosity got the better of her. "Speaking of your once beloved, I was told by my teacher not to paint her by the water. I see now that she was correct in that assumption since you don't like the sea anymore."

"Find that odd for a sailor, do you?" Mr. Reaves stepped closer and leaned in.

"I do find that unusual."

"Think nothing more of it. Paint only her face and her torso; that's all you were required to do. Even with my grandson there was no need to paint the chair. Although, I must agree, it makes it better to see him. Also, makes him appear more dignified."

Barbara felt his breath on her skin and it made her skin crawl. She inched backward and said, "I'm glad you like him seated."

"You seem afraid of me now." Mr. Reaves sighed. "I suppose you didn't know of the rumors and now you do. That's what always happens to me. I befriend someone and then they hear the gossip and then no more friend."

"I am not your friend, Mr. Reaves. I am your business associate."

"You've made that perfectly clear." He tapped his hat and began to head around the car to the driver's seat.

She saw she had offended him and regretted the harshness in her tone. "I am flattered, however, that you would want me as an equal."

He gathered himself and heaped into the car. It gave him some trouble, but he scooted his left leg underneath the wheel and closed the door. For a second, he stared at her, and then he said, "My Dear, you are far more than I." He turned on the engine and drove away.

CHAPTER 22

Barbara walked into the Tables & Décor shop and glanced over all the new furniture. She was admiring a green sofa and dark maple tables when a man approached, lowering his glasses.

"Mrs. Kays," he greeted. "I was told you'd be coming."

"Have I met you before?"

"I saw your painting of Mr. Reaves' grandson when I was at the museum. It's an incredible depiction of the photograph. When you have some time, I'd like to talk with you about painting for my store. I'm always in need of paintings to hang, to match my living and dining room sets. I'd pay seventy-five dollars a painting and sell them for a hundred and fifty; that way we'd both make money."

Barbara was stunned. "I'm quite busy at the moment."

"I've heard." He nodded. "There's no rush. Whenever you get them done, the offer stands."

"Thank you." She smiled. "What exactly are you looking for in subject matter?"

"Fruit and bread always are a big seller with the dining rooms, and any type of landscape would be fine for the living areas." His eyes shifted. "Although, if you feel that is beneath you, I'd be happy to look at any painting you finish."

Barbara was surprised by the offer. "I certainly will paint for you when my portraits are completed. I am honored that you'd even consider making me a painter for your company."

"There's no pressure on time of course," he said. "Just come on in and ask to speak to the manager, Ray Mondel."

"Mr. Mondel, it is a pleasure." She smiled.

"Nate put down a five-hundred-dollar credit with agreement of additional financing if you need more to furnish your home." The phone behind the counter began ringing, and Mr. Mondel moved to grab it.

"Thank you, I'll take a look around," Barbara said.

As soon as he picked up the receiver, she began to scale the store. Up and down the aisle she strolled casually. What amazed her the most was how much that amount would buy. She could have furniture in every room of her home, even the spare bedroom which no one might use. *Better yet, perhaps I'll make that a nursery for when Loren comes home.*

A smile crossed her lips just thinking about having Loren's child. She loved him so much it made her proud.

She stopped when she noticed the living room set in the window. The chairs were leather, similar to what Mr. Reaves had. The sofa was made of the same, but it had tiny gold buttons around the top to hold the fabric in place. *Exquisite.*

Picking up the tag, she read *$150.00.* That was an excellent price for such fine quality. Behind the living room set was a dark redwood table and six matching chairs. Against the wall sat a matching buffet table and china cabinet. The tag read, *$200.00 for the set.*

To the left of that was a desk with a chair. That would look excellent in the parlor when her patrons walked in. The desk had a tag of *$50.00.* Barbara was pleased she could buy all this for four hundred and fifty dollars. Suddenly, she realized what she needed the most, a bed.

In the back of the store there were many mattresses and a few wooden frames. These were simple but would work just fine. One even had a matching stand which had a lamp on it. The price was fifty dollars for the bedroom set.

Within five minutes, Barbara had picked out her entire household worth of furniture. She would be responsible for the tax, but with all this for free, how could she complain? A part of her wondered if she shouldn't walk out. Why was Mr. Reaves being so nice to her? Why was he going out of his way to help her?

"So have we decided?" Mr. Mondel asked.

"Yes." Barbara pointed to all three sets. "I think those are just fine and dandy."

"We can have it all delivered tomorrow," he informed. "What time will be good for you?"

"The morning."

"I'll have it there first thing." Mr. Mondel began jotting down the numbers on a piece of paper.

"How much do I owe you for tax?" she said.

"It's all taken care of." Mr. Mondel began to lead her out of the store. He opened the door for her and raised his glasses. "Mr. Reaves made sure."

"Are you a friend of his?" Barbara wondered.

Mr. Mondel said, shortly, "I take his money for services rendered. That's all."

She understood. "Have a nice day, Mr. Mondel."

"It's been a pleasure." He smiled then shut the door. "Please don't tip the delivery man. Mr. Reaves will take care of that as well."

Barbara watched as he walked away. She couldn't help but get the feeling Mr. Mondel didn't care too much for Mr. Reaves, but he wasn't above taking his money. She was in the same boat. To her, he'd been nothing but kind, though. Even if this town had its rumors about his past, Mr. Reaves seemed to be a changed man and so willing to help her. That's what bothered her the most; why did he? And why did Mrs. Kays get so upset just by the mention of his name?

She moved down the street to return to her home. One more painting of Mr. Reaves' grandson and then she'd begin on Bernadett. That would be hard to try to hide her feelings on the matter from her work. Behind those green eyes, she would struggle not to show sadness or rage in them. In fact, the way Barbara wanted to depict her was with love in her eyes.

How much she wanted to believe Mr. Reaves was innocent! "There she is," Barbara heard a voice whisper behind her.

She turned to discover three women in the alley next to the ice cream shop. One of the ladies looked familiar and she recalled seeing her in church one Sunday. Her name was Patricia and those were her sisters. All considered spinsters in their mid-thirties, not one had a friendly face.

"Good morning." Barbara nodded then pivoted to move on.

"Heard you are being kept by Mr. Reaves," the blond sister said. "Is he your sugar daddy?"

Barbara stopped. "I am his painter."

"A painter," the blonde said and laughed out loud. "That's not what we heard."

"Of all the nerve." Barbara gasped. "I assure you, you heard wrong."

"Not his charity girl? Still, you better watch out." The brunette grabbed her belly. "Mr. Reaves bumped off the last one."

"Threw her in the water to drown," the blonde added.

"Got all the money from the father." The last sister made sure she knew. "It's said he threatened him as well."

"You'll be next." The blonde chuckled. "So, you better amscray."

"If you like old, w r i n k l e d men," the brunette said. "That is, now that your husband is in the war."

"Futz!" Barbara snipped. "You are wrong about me and Mr. Reaves. And don't speak of my husband in such a tone. He is a war hero who is risking his life for an excellent cause."

"All the women take his money at first and then they disappear." The brunette moved closer and gave her a push. "You might seem so high and mighty now, but it's only a matter of time before you'll be swimming with the fishes too."

"If you touch me again, you'll regret it."

"Complain to the sheriff. He won't even cast a kitten for you now, or did you forget the sheriff is Bernadett's cousin."

Barbara decided that's exactly what she would do, speak to the sheriff about these women spreading such gossip. She'd seen the sheriff several times in her father's store before. How hard would it be to go ask him of Mr. Reaves' history? She was going to find out.

CHAPTER 23

Barbara stormed into the police station, slamming the glass door. All eyes flashed up as she hurried over to the desk. A woman wearing a blue dress and a police hat asked, "Is this an emergency?"

"I have a few questions for the Sherriff."

"Please have a seat. He is on prowl." She waved over to the many seated in the chairs. "We'll call you when he is in. Sign, here, thank you."

Barbara placed her name on the list, sat down on the only available seat, next to a man slumped over his chair. She guessed by his smell that he had far too much to drink at the bar around the corner.

Staring at the clock on the wall, she listened to every tick-tock as the hand slowly moved around the wooden face. After an hour had passed and no one had gotten up or had been called, she went to the counter again. "Is the sheriff going to see me soon?"

"When he returns, you will have to wait your turn just like everyone else."

Barbara gasped. "You mean I've waited here over an hour, and he still isn't even here?"

"He does have other duties." The woman gave her a rude look then said sarcastically, "We've had several moll-buzz cases and even a wife beater."

Barbara went and sat back down; by now, her foot was tapping on the ground. The background music was grating on her last nerve, and she felt as if she would explode from rage.

She realized that her anger had been brought on by the three sisters. In her head, she heard them laughing at her and making fun. She'd get to the bottom of this and hell hath no fury until she proved them wrong. After all, if Mr. Reaves had nothing to do with the death of his beloved, then the police had a duty to stop all this gossip from destroying his reputation.

Surely, that must be of importance!

Once she found out the truth behind all this fiction, Barbara would march right back and tell the sisters what they could do with their wrong information. She'd tell them that they had no souls and that spreading such lies was an abomination to justice. They should stop immediately, or she'd tell Mr. Reaves to sue them until everything they owned was his!

The door to the police station opened and the sheriff pushed in a man who was handcuffed and struggling. The man cussed him up and down as he was being led to the jail at the back of the building. The sheriff stuck his key in the door and pushed him in, slamming it shut. He muttered, "You'll get a phone call after you cool down."

"I didn't hit my wife," he said. "She fell down."

"Or your son too, right?"

"He was in her arms when she fell! That's all!"

"You're as innocent as they come." The sheriff walked over to the counter and asked the woman, "Who is the next lucky fellow I can put in the pokey."

Barbara stood. "I would like to speak to you, Sherriff."

He glanced over at her, stared for a second, then picked up the list and said, "Is your name Claud McBornin?"

"That's me." A man in a seat far from Barbara's rose to his feet. "I need to speak to you about the ticket my wife got last week."

"All right, come into my office," the sheriff said.

Barbara waited another hour, but at least this time one by one someone was called in until her name was finally called. She stood, her feet half asleep from sitting in such hard wooden chairs.

"Mrs. Kays," the sheriff said, not even raising his head. His hand scribbled writing on a sheet of paper marked, *Unlawful Investigation*. Then he put that paper on top of a pile on the right side of his desk.

"I would like to know the history behind some of the rumors of my employer, Mr. Reaves. I was hired by him to do some paintings, and quite frankly, the things I am hearing are far from pleasant, especially from the three sisters."

The sheriff pulled out a form titled, *Complaint*. He jotted down her name and asked, "What exactly is your beef? What did these women say and was there any crime mentioned?"

"Several, I assure you and I want to know the truth behind these accusations. If they are true, I will no longer accept his employment."

"I can see your dilemma. What rumors?" he asked matter-of-factly, leaning back in his chair. "I bet I have an idea."

Barbara got a good look at the sheriff then. His brown wavy hair swooped over his dark hazel eyes. He was a dreamboat of a man, not much older than her, but he was thin and very muscular. In fact, his looks made her glance down. She shouldn't find another man handsome now that she was married. And this man was as beguiling as they came. She even forgot the gun strapped around his waist which should have scared her.

"What have you heard about Mr. Reaves?" he repeated.

"There are these women I think you should arrest for slander of my employer. They said that Mr. Reaves murdered the woman he loved. That he drowned her in the Bay, in her wedding dress. There are more crimes they said he committed as well."

"I assure you if the murder were true, he would have been arrested a long time ago." The sheriff began writing on the form. "Would you like me to speak to these chatterboxes and tell them not to speak of your employer that way?"

"Yes, I would. That would be swell." Barbara took in a deep breath, gazing up again.

He glanced up at her and then quickly jotted down more. "I don't like to see a pretty dish so upset."

Barbara blushed. "Thank you, kind sir."

"I take it you married Loren Kays, since your name changed?" he asked.

"I did," she said.

"My brother went to school with you," he said. "I saw you a few times when I was picking him up. You're the grocery store owner's daughter, correct?"

"Yes." She couldn't look at him now.

"Congratulations on your marriage. So if that will be all, I'll stop by sometime next week." He handed her the paper and pen as he pointed to the address lines which were blank under her name.

She filled in her address and handed him back the paper. "I hope you will be able to stop these rumors about Mr. Reaves. It seems many people believe he had something to do with Bernadett's death."

"I've heard the rumors behind her death." The sheriff smiled. "Worse, in fact, that he was involved in a drug trade and that he kept women as his personal possessions."

"So, you know about the rumors!" Barbara gasped.

"It's my business to know the truth behind these things," he said. "Believe me, Mr. Reaves got a raw deal in this town. The rumors are not true or, believe me, we would have loved to arrest him. He's not the most charming of men. He has a tendency to speak ill of people who don't believe him."

"He has that right! He hasn't kept women either then?"

"Mr. Reaves sponsors artists. The only one who had legal problems was Bernadette. I can't get into the specifics, but her death is still under investigation. Many were questioned about it, Mr. Reaves being the prime suspect."

"I was told he pushed her out of the boat on the way to be wed on the island."

"I can't get into specifics of the case," he said.

"Did he or didn't he push her into the water?"

"He was on the island, not even on the boat at the time she drowned. There were dozens of witnesses to that effect. What you are hearing are rumors, nothing more. I'll be sure to clear up the matter. I can see how upset you are." His hand moved over hers and patted. "In a town like this, rumors spread like wildfire and believe me, once they start it's hard to extinguish them. They've practically ruined the man. Good thing he's rich, or no one would deal with him at all."

She was shocked he took the liberty to touch her hand in such a way. She pulled it away and placed it on her lap.

"I'll talk to these women and tell them to stop. If they don't, I'll arrest them for harassing you. How does that sound?" He smiled at her.

His smile melted her, and she rose and walked to the door. "Shame you're married," he said, as she shut the door.

CHAPTER 24

The painting of Bernadett began late in the evening. Fog was coming in the bay window, and that inspired Barbara to sit and begin. With a new love for this long-lost woman, Barbara was confident now that Mr. Reaves didn't have a thing to do with her death.

His love for Bernadett was what drove Barbara to make sure the painting would have every detail the most correct. Her untimely passing was something straight from a romantic novel. Time could not erase the feelings they had, nor could death part them.

Barbara glanced over at the photo Mr. Reaves had given her. For a long time, she studied it, and then she closed her eyes. In her mind's eye, she saw Bernadett coming in from the fog, dressed in fancy designer clothes. When Barbara was fifteen, she saw a red suit that tailor Tom Athens made and that is what she pictured. A finely cut red suit with black trim to represent her death. Over her short blond curly hair, she would wear a red-black hat. Those gray eyes of hers would be misty. Guessing she was about five foot five and weighed not much more than a hundred pounds, Barbara would make her figure thin and beguiling.

This woman would be painted as one of the most beautiful women she had ever seen. It wasn't a far stretch from the truth, but the fog and the misty eyes would capture love and sadness all in one.

Tears stung her eyes as the brush touched the canvas. The entire time she painted Bernadett walking closer, and it gave Barbara such a feeling of compassion mixed with pain. How much Mr. Reaves must have loved her once!

For hours, she worked nonstop. The dawn came and went. Hunger finally droves Barbara to quit and make a sandwich from out of the kitchen. Shaking from exhaustion, she knew she needed to rest, but a part of her didn't even want to.

Barbara washed her hands and lay down on the leather sofa. That's when darkness overwhelmed her, and she finally got some well-deserved rest. When she woke, she shouted, "Darn it, the eyes need work!" and marched back into the room to finish the painting.

The moment she walked in, her breath stopped. The woman seemed almost alive in the painting. She had never painted anyone so lifelike before. She'd accurately captured the mix of both emotions; it shook her to her core. "It's perfect."

The eyes were so mesmerizing. The mist in them could not be altered. How funny that when she walked away, she had thought it needed more work, but now, to look at it she saw how absolutely incredible it was.

Pride made her smile. "Bernadett, you are a lucky woman to be so loved. An entire town misses your lovely face."

She touched the edge of the painting and found it dry enough to move. Quickly she took a shower, dressed and rushed down several streets to Mr. Reaves' mansion. There, she knocked loudly.

Answered by the maid, Barbara simply turned the painting around for her to witness. The maid jumped back at the sight and backed away. "My goodness" were the only words coming out of her mouth.

Barbara moved in and discovered Mr. Reaves sitting at the dining table drinking some scotch and lifting a spoonful of vegetable soup to his lips. She held out the painting and walked closer.

His eyes moved to it and that's what Barbara wanted to see, his first sighting of the portrait of Bernadett. His eyes focused and then it happened, the same thing that had happened to her, but much more emotional. His spoon dropped. Tears came as a hand flew to his mouth in agony.

The pain of a love lost written over his face, he said, "A masterpiece. Never have I seen such a painting."

"Then I have pleased you?" Barbara placed the painting in the chair to his right.

He couldn't take his eyes off of it; the tears by now were streaming down his face. Not another word was able to come out of his lips. Barbara leaned over and wrapped an arm around him as he wept.

The maid came forward, crying herself, bringing him another scotch. He didn't bother to take it. The maid walked around the table for another look and wiped her eyes. "She can almost walk out of the painting she looks so real."

Barbara nodded.

After several minutes, Mr. Reaves sniffled and took a handkerchief from his suit jacket. He wiped his eyes again and again, and then finally drank the drink, nearly choking on it with emotion.

"My Dear, this painting will hang in the middle of the museum, and it will never be taken down."

"You honor me." Barbara smiled.

"No." He grabbed her arm, weeping. "You have honored me, and if you ever need anything, anything at all, you'll have it."

"I didn't paint her for that."

"I know." He wiped his eyes again. "You painted her as I saw her. You captured my love for her and my pain."

Barbara was glad she knew he wasn't involved in Bernadett's death. If she hadn't known he was on the island and not even on the boat, she might have guessed that his pain was linked to a crime. Now she understood. His pain wasn't really from the guilt. No, his emotion was drawn from what drives us all, love.

He missed her.

"We would have been very happy," Mr. Reaves said. "I assure you, if I had been given the chance, I would have made her the happiest woman alive." He leaned his head against her arm.

Barbara felt a tear falling down her elbow. This kind of love, she understood. This missing someone so badly that it hurts you to the very soul. Wanting to touch them, see them, talk to them, she could now relate because of Loren. But for Mr. Reaves, Bernadett never came home.

She patted Mr. Reaves on the head as he cried. She didn't mind how awkward this was. In her heart, she now found him her friend. She didn't care about the rumors or how badly everyone thought of him and now her for working for him. To see this, to know that he had this kind of reaction to seeing the painting of Bernadett, proved how much he had loved her.

Mr. Reaves cared so much for this woman. How painful it must be for him to have the entire town hate him for it as well. Perhaps it was because she was so beautiful that so many had wanted her for themselves.

"I'll have the director of the museum pick it up in the morning." Mr. Reaves sat back in the chair.

"I'm surprised you don't want to keep this for personal viewing."

"You don't understand the whole of the situation, or you would understand why I want the world to see it."

"Perhaps I do see," Barbara said. "You want the world to know how much you loved Bernadett."

"Some may hate me for hanging it," he said. "But word must spread, good or bad, so that the world will know."

"And what if they don't see what we do?" Barbara warned him. "They may just take it as an action out of guilt or even insanity."

"There is no guilt here, only remorse for never speaking to her again. I had so much I wanted to say. If they call it insanity, then so be it. Call me madly in love with the wrong woman. If that is a crime then I surely should have been arrested long ago," he admitted.

"My father told Loren he was beneath me too. Others can never understand what truly lives in a heart. One may look at the same couple, many will say it is madness or perhaps won't survive. It isn't if they do or don't, actually, that's not important. It's the moments that make love divine that is craziness at its best." With that, Barbara left him with the portrait, knowing he needed one more chance to speak to Bernadett, even if she could not hear him speaking back.

The painting may have been a way for Mr. Reaves to find closure, but it certainly proved with real love, there never really is.

Chapter 25

The next afternoon, Barbara was sitting on the stoop of her house waiting for the mailman. He had become a welcome sight every day. They had worked out a system by now. As he walked down the sidewalk, if he smiled and tilted his head, she had a letter from overseas and if he shook his head and kept moving, she would know today was not a lucky day.

The second he turned the corner, the young man smiled at her and pulled out an envelope. Barbara immediately ran to him, grinning. She took the letter, thanked him and hurried back to the stoop to tear it open.

She read:

Dear Barbara,

My mother wrote me about your upcoming showing of "Loving Bernadett," at the museum and the big party Mr. Reaves is planning for the entire town. I must have read her letter a dozen times. I'm so thrilled! To have my wife's painting hanging in the center of the museum! Isn't that the biggest honor bestowed upon an artist?

My infamous wife, how much I love and adore you.

I know my mother is upset about your working for Mr. Reaves and to be quite honest I wasn't sure what to think. Now I am fully aware of how beneficial working for him can be. I'm glad you are his benefactor.

Therefore, seeing how much this day means to you and our family, I wrote a letter to the Air Force letting them know how important this event is to our family. I'm hoping they will give me time enough to fly back home to be there for the painting unveiling next week. I'm not sure if they will be as happy as we are, but clearly, they must know how amazing this is.

I want you to know that I also wrote Mr. Reaves a letter. I've never met him, only seen him in town a few times. He always seemed like an interesting fellow who enjoyed staring back. There was always a smile on his face which I found pleasant. I wanted him to be aware of how proud of you I am and how thankful I was that he was looking out for you in my absence. Hopefully, he will appreciate the letter. I also told him how excited I was that you were working for him and that he had great taste in art. As a thank you, when I return, I promised to take him flying in the crop duster. I'm not sure he will like doing that, seeing how dignified and rich he is, but he might like the fact I offered. If he agrees to go, I'll show him the sky.

If you don't hear from me before the showing, know I am with you. Whether I am physically there or not, my heart is filled with you. I'm very proud to be married to you. God truly blessed you with a gift, and I believe the entire town is about to see it firsthand. I want to be there to see it with my own eyes, to kiss your lips and to let you know how much I am proud of you.

Keep your fingers crossed. Loving you,

Loren

Barbara finished reading the letter and closed it. When she turned around, she discovered the sheriff parking his car in front of her house.

"Mrs. Kays," he called, stepping out of his vehicle.

"Come in, Sherriff." She greeted him with a smile.

The handsome officer of the law closed the distance between them. Barbara had a hard time not noticing the gun on his belt or what appeared to be a very long stick of some kind.

"I spoke to the sisters," he said.

"And?" Barbara opened the door to her house. "Can I get you something to drink or eat perhaps?"

"Actually, I haven't eaten lunch," he admitted.

"Do you like turkey? I have plenty of lunch meat and fresh bread from the bakery."

"Sounds good." He sat down at her dining room table. "Nice furniture."

"Mr. Reaves bought it for me," she proudly admitted.

"He sure has helped you a lot, hasn't he? I got my invitation to the museum showing next week."

"Will you be going?" Barbara began to make two sandwiches and placed them on separate plates. When she was finished putting the turkey between the white bread, she then placed fruit on the side. "It should be quite the evening."

"That's not my sort of thing." He nodded.

"Art isn't just for the elite," Barbara disagreed. "If everyone doesn't enjoy looking at art, I'd find painting not of any value."

He took the plate and began to eat. "You have an interesting view of things."

"I wish you would go. I'd like to hear what you think of my painting," Barbara admitted, then realized that seemed too forward. "I mean, if you had the time to take a glance at it."

"I'll think about it if I'm not on flatfoot duty," he said, chewing. "Delicious."

"It's from my father's store. He still isn't talking to me, but every week I go down there and buy as much as I can. I figure eventually he'll get over the fact I got married."

"At least Loren's a square John, a real flyboy and not any grifter." He chuckled.

"So did you arrest the sisters?" she asked.

"There wasn't enough evidence to arrest them. In fact, many down at the station found it quite Dillinger."

"Funny?" Barbara gasped. "I don't find any of their meanness humorous! That's all it was, meanness."

"They said you were just as cruel."

"They started the conversation," Barbara assured. "It was they who angered me. Everything I said was in justification of what they were doing."

"True," the officer said. "Isn't it divine to forgive?"

"Perhaps," Barbara sighed, "as long as they stop harassing me."

"I spoke to them and mentioned to only speak to you kindly." He finished eating his grapes, and then said, "They did say Mr. Reaves gave them an invitation as well."

"He didn't!" Barbara sat up, her eyes bulging in horror. "Oh, but then he doesn't know."

"You never said anything to him about the rumors they were spreading?"

"Didn't want to crush him," Barbara said. "He loved Bernadett very much, and that alone is enough torture."

"Looks like I should go to the event after all," the sheriff said. "I'll put out any fires if need be."

"Do you really think they'd be so bold as to try and ruin the party?"

"That's exactly what I think they will be up to. Women like that find pleasure in getting away with things. Don't fret; I'll be dressed like a fly dick."

Barbara shivered. "They are so cruel."

"Clearly they weren't to be taken lightly."

Barbara glanced over at him, but quickly changed direction by peering downward. She found him very charming and too beguiling not to notice. Her body had only known one man, Loren. She couldn't believe even now, at this very moment, she was wondering what it must be like to be in the arms of this man in uniform. His smile alone would melt any woman's heart.

For a second, the officer sat across the table not speaking, and then he rose and scooted in his chair. "I should be going. Thank you for the sandwich." With that he left, his belt clicking as he walked.

Barbara didn't look after him; she couldn't, in fear of what her next thoughts of him might be. When he closed the door to the house, she rose to her feet and began washing dishes.

This event was going to be very interesting indeed.

CHAPTER 26

Barbara found a dress on her doorstep and knew who it was from. The long black garment was classy and so expensive there was only one man she knew who could have afforded to buy it. Mr. Reaves' generosity was beyond comparison to her own father who hadn't even mentioned going to the museum, and she had been at the store every day.

In fact, he didn't mention that her mother would be in attendance either, but she hoped her mother would come. When Barbara walked up to the museum, the doorman bowed and opened the door.

Bright lights blinded her and when her eyes adjusted to the light, she saw that the museum was filled to the brim with men in tuxedos and women in designer gowns. Flashes of camera lights blinded her as several men approached with pen and paper.

"Cal from the Maple Newspaper here," a man said, jotting down her name. "How do you feel about being featured today at the museum?" Barbara was flabbergasted. Reporters were interviewing her! What should she say? She wasn't a star.

"Dekota Martin from the Hill Home Magazine." Another man greeted her. "What do you think about everyone saying you are the artist of the year?"

Mr. Reaves closed in and wrapped his arm around her. "Please, please, give Barbara a chance to enjoy her party." He began pulling her away.

"I need a quote!" the Maple Newspaper followed.

"All right," Mr. Reaves said over his shoulder. "You're looking at one of the greatest painters of our time."

"Can I print a picture of the painting too?"

"Absolutely," Mr. Reaves handed Barbara a cup full of punch, "if it appears on the front cover."

Moving around the room toward the buffet table, Barbara saw that her painting, covered by a white cloth, was hanging from ropes, suspended high above in the center of the room. A ribbon hung from it, ready to be pulled to reveal the painting of Bernadett.

She couldn't wait until everyone saw this piece of work. This was her pride and joy. Bernadett had inspired her to paint her greatest portrait and she couldn't believe how many people would catch a glimpse of it.

The flashes of light continued as Barbara strolled beside Mr. Reaves. So many were photographing them! They were being treated like royalty. A hand touched her back and she spun around to see the sheriff.

He didn't appear at all like he did in uniform. Indeed, he looked far more handsome in a black suit jacket and white button-down shirt. His hair was slicked back and from his large lips came a pipe.

"Barbara," he greeted.

"Who is this?" Mr. Reaves gave him a worried expression.

"The sheriff," Barbara announced. "He's a friend."

"Of the family," the sheriff held out his hand for Mr. Reaves to shake. Mr. Reaves quickly shook it and then wrapped an arm around her waist.

"Oh, yes, I recognize you now. I've seen you around town. You are friends with Loren, who is now her husband, right?" The tone of his voice sounded more like a warning than a question.

"I've never met him," the sheriff announced then he asked politely, "May I have a word with you, Barbara."

"Certainly." She stepped away from her benefactor's side and said, "I'll be right back."

"Don't be long. I plan to unveil it as soon as the reporters are ready to take their photos."

The sheriff led her away from the buffet line and pointed to the three sisters in the corner. All three of them looked hideous in their frumpy black suits. Not one had any prettiness to them. In fact, Barbara thought, their ugliness goes clear to the bone.

They gave her dirty looks and then spoke between themselves; every few minutes laughter escaped their lips.

"Shall I ask them to leave?"

"Have they done anything?"

"Actually, one walked right up to the newspaper reporter and told them a bunch of lies about you. They thought it would be funny, but it only showed how shallow and pitiful their attempts are to ruin your reputation. Clearly, they are sick women."

"By all means escort them out," Barbara said.

"With pleasure." He smiled.

She grabbed his jacket. He turned around and their eyes locked for a brief moment. "Thank you for saving me from further embarrassment."

He leaned down and kissed her cheek. "You look amazing tonight." With that he walked away, clearly on a mission.

Suddenly a single drum sounded in the center of the floor. Mr. Reaves stood beside the drummer, his hand on the ribbon to pull the string. He motioned Barbara to stand beside him.

"Ladies and Gentlemen, without further delay, I would like to show you the most incredible portrait. It's called, "Loving Bernadett." It's named after the woman I loved many years ago. Although there are many lies spread about my feelings for her, I assure you only an artist as talented as Barbara Kays could have possibly captured it in such a way."

Barbara saw her mother to the right as the crowd opened and turned around. Thrilled to see her, she gave her mother a wave. Her mother raised her wine glass. Behind her, the sheriff was speaking to the three women who were clearly arguing about having to leave.

No one heard them. Their pleas were so unimportant to the greatness of what was happening.

"Wait," a voice cried out. "This is going to be just peachy, a real humdinger."

Mr. Reaves who was about to pull the ribbon, but stopped as if he knew who had cried out. From out of the crowd came Loren. Barbara screamed with glee when she saw him. As she ran to him, the newspapers took photos as they embraced and kissed each other on the lips.

When they finished, the crowd was applauding. Then Barbara realized how she had ignored what was about to happen to see Loren. She was worried that she'd upset Mr. Reaves. She twirled around to see him with a big smile on his face.

"Excuse them—Newlyweds," Mr. Reaves explained to the crowd. "Now, Loren, the town war hero, get over here and pull this ribbon for your wife."

"You want *me* to do it?" Loren asked, delighted, his eyes widening.

"No one else should," Mr. Reaves said.

Loren reached up and yanked the string. The white cloth fell to the ground. The oohs and the ahhs came in wild form. For several minutes everyone in the room stood mesmerized by the painting.

"That is incredible." Loren gasped, wrapping his arm around his wife. "You painted that? This is no flimflam!"

"I did." Barbara beamed.

"My goodness, it's perfect! My mother couldn't have even done something…"

"That good." Mrs. Kays hugged her son with a grin.

"I thought you weren't coming," Mr. Reaves said shortly to the teacher, Mrs. Kays.

"She's still my student," she snipped back.

Ignoring the two, Loren hugged his mother and said, "It's good to see you."

"Good that you are home."

Barbara stepped back to give them a moment together. Mr. Reaves stood beside her and said, "Dear, please tell your husband I would love to go flying with him."

"So, you got his letter?" Barbara asked.

"I did," Mr. Reaves said as a smile crossed his lips and reporters closed in to ask more of their questions.

CHAPTER 27

When the reporters finished, Loren came back over with his mother.

"I am very impressed with your painting," Mrs. Kays said. "It is your greatest work. No one could have done it better."

"Do you really think so?" Barbara placed a hand over her heart.

"You captured Bernadett as beautiful as ever." Mr. Reaves' eyes lit up as he glanced back up at the painting.

"Actually, she was a bit larger in the legs." Mrs. Kays titled her head. "But I'm sure you gave Barbara her best photo to copy from."

"You have the nerve to insult Bernadett?" Mr. Reaves raised his voice. "How dare you."

A few turned around to see what the new commotion was about. When he didn't reply, they pivoted again and went about their own conversations. Barbara couldn't believe Mrs. Kays' rudeness. Even if she didn't like Bernadett, she was dead, and no one should speak ill of those who have passed on.

"I'm going to ask you nicely to go, Aleavia," Mr. Reaves finally said.

"With bells on my shoes," she replied and then she kissed Barbara on the cheek. "Your painting is lovely despite the subject." She turned on a heel and walked out.

"I will speak to her in private tomorrow," Loren said.

"After our plane ride?" Mr. Reaves questioned.

"So, you read my letter?" Loren smiled. "I wasn't sure you got it. It's hard to know if my mail ever arrives."

"I've been looking forward to being on a plane," Mr. Reaves announced.

"Have you never been?" Loren questioned.

"Never." Mr. Reaves leaned on his cane. "I will enjoy it immensely; I can assure you. A ride of a lifetime."

"You will," Loren promised. "I'll fly you as far as the waterfalls. You'll never believe what they look like in a plane."

"Perfect." His eyes teared up. "I've been looking forward to it longer than you'll ever know." Mr. Reaves grabbed his handkerchief and wiped his eyes.

Loren noticed and glanced over at Barbara.

Barbara quickly explained, "It's the portrait. This is a big day for him."

"Yes, how hard it must be for him." Loren understood. "Can I get you something to drink?"

Barbara's mother rushed forward and hugged her daughter. "I love your painting," she said.

"You do?" Barbara asked.

"Yes," she admitted.

"Did Father come?"

"He's waiting for me outside, but I'm going to tell him all about how absolutely lifelike it seems."

Barbara was disappointed but she smiled. "Tell him then."

The sheriff approached and announced, "The sisters have gone."

Barbara sighed with relief. "You are my hero." She saw that her mother was leaving already.

"Wasn't that your mom?" the sheriff asked.

"Yes, she is when my father lets her be," Barbara said.

"He didn't come?" He seemed to know.

"No, he didn't."

"His loss." The sheriff touched her hair. "Truly it is."

Loren whirled around and stared at the larger man. The sheriff didn't take his eyes off of Barbara. "And you are?"

"This is the sheriff," Barbara announced. "I've had some problems with some local women who don't like me very much." She turned back to the sheriff. "So, what did they say?"

"They said you would never make it and that you should get a real job."

"They didn't!" Barbara gasped.

"Then they laughed at your dress; you know, the usual childish stuff women do when they are jealous."

"How repulsive they are!" Barbara said. "Those lap happy dams who think they know me when they know me not one bit."

"Surely," Mr. Reaves interrupted. "This night is not turning out how I had planned. This was supposed to be a celebration of a fine artist, a real super night, not this whole circus of silliness. Can't we speak about these things later? Tonight, is for Barbara."

The sheriff nodded in agreement. "Forgive me. I just wanted to make sure she knew I forced them to leave her alone."

"I can't thank you enough."

"Sorry," the sheriff apologized to Mr. Reaves. "You're right. Tonight, is for Barbara and Loren, for your family."

Barbara spied him as he walked away. She couldn't help but think the way the sheriff said her husband's name that it was hard for him. She wondered why. There was a tension between them, but clearly, he understood she was married, right? She hadn't led him to think otherwise, had she?

"I do believe that man is smitten with you," Mr. Reaves said in her ear.

"Don't be ridiculous." Barbara shrugged.

"You are quite charming, a dilly in that dress." Mr. Reaves raised a brow. "Not that I am noticing, mind you. You're far too less wrinkly for my taste."

"Wrinkles?" She chuckled. "You like wrinkles?"

"And veins on the legs makes a woman a real woman," he admitted.

"So perhaps I should have painted Bernadett with veins and wrinkles?" Barbara grinned, teasing him.

"I would have adored that."

Then, screams came from the crowd. Roars of shock erupted as the sea of people parted all the way to Loren, Barbara and Mr. Reaves standing in the center of the room. A woman wearing a large black coat and a scarf around her head approached. Her face was shadowed by the headpiece.

Cameras started clicking and flashing; Mr. Reaves backed away. His body was shaking from head to toe; he almost fell to his knees.

"Mr. Reaves." Barbara panicked. "Are you all right? Help me, Loren."

Loren took Mr. Reaves by the arm and held him up. Right then, Barbara had to know who this woman was that moved Mr. Reaves to almost pass out. The scarf was moved down to rest around the woman's shoulders; Barbara would know that face anywhere.

Her face had aged. Around her eyes were small lines that most would hardly notice. Her body was thicker in the legs, but her figure was hourglass and short. As she sashayed closer, Barbara spoke her name.

"Bernadett?" she asked.

The woman removed a cigarette from her purse and lit it. She glanced up at the portrait and then gave a slight nod.

"You're Bernadett?" A reporter came closer. "Aren't you dead?"

"I assure you, my designers from London don't dress dead women." She took a drag off her cigarette, still glancing up at the painting.

"You done good," she said to Barbara.

"Mr. Reaves, is that her?" Barbara had to ask him.

The panicked expression on his face proved she needed no more reaction. This indeed was the woman he'd loved for all these years.

"You said you'd never come back," he shouted. "Not unless you had forgiven me. Have you? Have you forgiven me finally? Have you returned finally to be my wife?"

Bernadett shook her head no. "I just had to see it with my own eyes."

"See what?" Loren asked her.

"That he still loves me, even now, after all these years. My aunt mailed me a copy of the invitation and when I saw the name, *Loving Bernadett*, I couldn't believe he would commission something over me."

"Flattered?" Loren wondered.

"You have no idea."

CHAPTER 28

The sheriff barreled his way toward Bernadett and quickly took her arm. He held it close to his chest and spoke angrily, "Bernadett, I'm going to need you to come with me down to the station."

"The pokey? Am I under arrest?" She blew smoke in his face. "Surely I haven't done any crime."

"You can either come with me willingly or by force and in cuffs; that is your choice in this matter."

"She hasn't done anything wrong." Mr. Reaves closed in, trying to force the officer to remove his grip. When the sheriff's hand didn't raise an inch, he ordered, "Take your hands off of Bernadett."

"Her case is still open, Mr. Reaves. By law, this woman has legally been dead almost twenty years. I have every right to question her of her whereabouts since then." The sheriff motioned her to step in front of him. "Please, Bernadett, I'm offering you a less embarrassing way out of the room."

"When will I see you again," Mr. Reaves asked his beloved. "I must speak to you. I have so much to talk to you about."

"Soon," she promised, moving away with the sheriff. "We will speak again before I get out of town."

"Do you at least like the painting?" Mr. Reaves tried to keep pace. "I had it done for you."

"Yes," she admitted. "Your new artist is far better than your first."

"Mr. Reaves, I can arrest you for obstruction of justice. I implore you to step away from Bernadett and let me handle matters. When I am finished, she will be released, barring any other problems or situations that might arise."

Mr. Reaves angrily threw his cane to the floor. "Horsefeathers; this is injustice. I haven't seen her in twenty years!"

The sheriff led Bernadett out the door. Barbara couldn't believe it. Bernadett was alive! She wasn't dead. She had left Mr. Reaves at the altar. There had been no drowning. The crowd was still in shock, many watching her every movement. Barbara realized that to change the crowd's focus she would have to alter the mood. Loren wrapped his arm around the small of her back.

"We should dance," Barbara said.

"I'll tell the musicians to start." Loren hurried toward the string quartet in the corner. The second he leaned over to the violinist, all four musicians began to play, "A Tenor Waltz," in D minor. The drummer took to the bells and the music soared out through every corner in the room.

By now, a few couples had begun to join at the hip and sway in unison; Loren came closer and took Barbara by the hand. She didn't even know he could dance, and she was surprised when they melded together perfectly, gliding across the dance floor, underneath the portrait of Bernadett.

"This has been quite an evening," Loren boasted. "I would have never believed it if I hadn't seen it with my own eyes."

"It has been a night of surprises." Barbara blushed. "And pleasures."

"This evening has just begun," he whispered.

"Surely the return of Bernadett is far more upsetting for Mr. Reaves," Barbara replied. "Unless he knew she wasn't dead."

"I'm not so sure he didn't." Loren glanced over to Mr. Reaves who was clearly seated near the buffet table. He sat there watching them from a distance. "Although, he did appear quite shocked to see her."

"There's something odd about that man," Loren continued. "She knew Mr. Reaves knew she wasn't dead, yet all these years she said nothing."

"A lover's quarrel?" Barbara wondered.

"No matter," Loren said. "Your canvas showed her how he felt about her. Perhaps it will rekindle a spark."

"I hope so for his sake. I'll never forget when he saw her." Barbara leaned her head on his shoulder. "Clearly his feelings for her have not changed."

"That is quite obvious," Loren agreed, checking on Mr. Reaves with a quick glance. "He still appears to be quite rattled."

For several songs they danced to "Cheek to Cheek," "I'll be Seeing You," and "I'm in the Mood for Love." When Barbara's feet tired, she asked to go sit at a table. They seated themselves next to Mr. Reaves who didn't speak; he was peering up at the painting. In front of him were a plate of cheeses and a bottle of wine which he hadn't even touched.

"Is there anything we can do for him," Barbara asked Loren as they headed toward Mr. Reaves table.

"I'll ask," Loren said. He leaned down and questioned, "Mr. Reaves, do you need to see a doctor? You've had quite a shock."

"I'm afraid my beloved lover may be in far more trouble than she thinks. I'm worried about her and that sheriff. He may be a fine man, but his heart can be like stone. I'm not sure he'll understand things."

"She did fake her death," Loren reminded. "That is illegal in all states."

"You wouldn't understand such matters." Mr. Reaves patted his shoulder. "She looks as lovely as ever, doesn't she?"

Loren nodded, rose and went to the buffet table. He piled his plate full of freshly cut vegetables, dips and salmon pieces wrapped in bacon. When he returned, he showed Barbara his plate, but she knew what he had. Hungry was the last thing on her mind.

Worried about Mr. Reaves, she finally asked, "Shall we call it a night?"

"I do believe we should leave," Mr. Reaves said.

"I'm so sorry this was ruined," she said.

"Ruined?" He shook his head. "You brought Bernadett back to me even if it was for a moment."

"You'll see her again," Barbara promised. "I don't think she'll ever forget you had her painted. She truly liked it."

"That will never be enough," Mr. Reaves admitted. "Our hurt goes too deep."

"Anything can be forgiven," Loren said.

"Ah, the young!" he burst out in response. "How lucky you both are to not know how wrong you can be. Surely, in matters of love, I've got quite a few years on you both."

"Shall we take you home?" Barbara asked.

"I'm going to be fine," he admitted, rising. "I'd much rather you two enjoy the evening."

Loren promised, "We will. This has been a night to remember. I don't think I'll ever forget how proud of Barbara I am."

"I as well." Mr. Reaves kissed Barbara's cheek. "I'm off. Drop by tomorrow and we'll take to the sky."

"I'll see you then," Loren agreed.

Mr. Reaves took his cane and headed out the door. The reporters took several pictures as he left.

Barbara felt sorry for him. "Even with all that money and all those things, he isn't happy."

"What I don't comprehend was how rude my mother was to him and to Bernadett, even to you. I'm starting to think my mother is jealous. She always wanted Mr. Reaves to help her and now he's helping you. That must be a thorn in her side."

"She still came to wish me well," Barbara reminded.

"As did your mother."

"Yes." Barbara smiled. "At least she saw the painting even if it was for a short while. I'm glad she saw how impressed the public is. Maybe now my parents will realize that my painting is more than a hobby."

"Perhaps." Loren leaned over and kissed her forehead. "What do you say we follow Mr. Reaves' advice and leave the public to its own devices? I've never seen my home, and there are many rooms to explore, especially the bedroom."

Barbara kissed his lips and forgot all about her painting or all the drama surrounding it. The only thing on her mind was Loren, and that was the most delightful of distractions.

CHAPTER 29

"Come with me," Loren begged, wearing only a towel.

Barbara couldn't believe how lucky she was. Her husband was home; they had made love for half the night and now he even wanted to take her flying with Mr. Reaves.

Flying hadn't entered her mind before today.

She hadn't even conceived of the notion that her feet wouldn't always be securely on the ground. "I think if God wanted me to fly, he'd have given me wings."

"Didn't he?" Loren leaned over the bed and kissed her again on the lips. "He made you fall in love with me, right?"

"Good thinking." Barbara laughed.

"Hurry up and get dressed. It's almost noon."

"Noon!" She gasped.

"We slept in," Loren announced. "I couldn't believe it myself when I got out of the bath."

Barbara got out of bed. Loren grabbed her and kissed her naked shoulder and then let her pass. While she moved past him, he gave her a quick slap on the butt which made a snap sound.

"Ouch." She giggled.

"You are going to love flying."

"As long as we stay in the sky and don't come plummeting down, I'll enjoy it." Barbara snickered as she went to the closet. From out of the back, she pulled down a pair of knickers, a long sleeve white top and a matching white hat.

"If you think you'll be able to keep that on, you're sadly mistaken."

"Right." She tossed it back in the closet.

After she brushed her hair, Barbara dabbed on some make-up while Loren dressed in a pair of slacks and a shirt. She enjoyed watching him dress. This all was so new, having a male roommate.

The sight of him thrilled her. Having Loren near only reminded her why she fell in love with him and how happy she was to be his wife. Barbara couldn't imagine herself with anyone else or feeling this way about another.

"Do you think we should inquire about Bernadett?" Loren asked her.

"I'm not sure," Barbara said.

"If she's there, we might change the date to when I return next time."

"Leaving?" Barbara said.

"I only have until tomorrow," Loren announced. "That's all the Air Force would give me, because it wasn't a death in the family."

Barbara's smile turned to a frown. "Only today? And I have to share you with Mr. Reaves for half of it?"

"Don't be bitter." Loren wrapped his arms around her, the grin widening on his face. "If it wasn't for Mr. Reaves, we wouldn't have this amazing house, and you wouldn't be the next Picasso on the way to international stardom so quickly."

"I see your point." Barbara raised her eyes to meet his gaze. Staring into those crystal blue gems, she couldn't help but slowly lean in and kiss his lips. This kiss lasted for quite some time until Loren was forced to pull away.

"We shouldn't be late."

She gave him a look of regret, and then together they moved through the house and out the door. Loren wrapped his arm around her on the stoop, and they were both surprised to find Mr. Reaves in his automobile parked on the street.

"Are we ready?" Mr. Reaves asked, excitement written all over his face.

"We are." Loren opened the car door for Barbara. She scooted into the middle and Loren hopped in to sit beside her.

As the car started down the street, Barbara watched ahead at the people going in and out of shops. Just last week she was lonely in her studio, following her same old routine, but today everything was fresh and new because she had Loren. The excitement of having Loren home made her realize how wonderful things would be when he got done with his wartime duties. She wouldn't get as much work done, but her paintings would be far more vivid and joyful.

"I stopped by the police station," Mr. Reaves said suddenly. Loren didn't skip a beat.

"And Bernadett?"

"She was released last night by your tin-wearing friend," he said. "I waited for her all morning, but she never came back to see me. Then I went to the hotel, and Mr. Parker's Inn; she checked out from the Inn last night."

"So, she left without speaking to you," Barbara said, shocked.

"With another man," Mr. Reaves announced. "The clerk told me there was a man with her."

"Perhaps it was the sheriff?" Barbara wondered.

"She didn't leave in his pie wagon from the hoosegow," Mr. Reaves said. "Beauty like that rarely remains alone for very long. It's probably her new acquaintance. In her eyes, I've been long forgotten, not even a faint memory." He patted her hand. "At least I saw her again. Your painting did that for me, and it was well worth it."

"We should remove it from the museum," Barbara mentioned, angrily. "I don't want my finest piece to be of a woman who broke my benefactor's heart."

"She did that long ago," Mr. Reaves said. "That painting must hang. At least I can see tears in her eyes that way. Believe that somehow, she felt once that way about me."

"You have a romantic heart, Mr. Reaves," Barbara admitted. "I think you deserve a woman who realizes how special you are."

"There's more to our story."

"Did you know she was still alive?" Loren asked.

Silence entered the cabin for quite some time. Barbara realized that he wasn't going to answer that question, meaning that he had known.

"You let everyone in town think that you pushed her off the boat?" Barbara said. "Why didn't you clear your name?"

"I tried." Mr. Reaves sighed. "The day before she got on that boat, we had quite a spell. I knew there was a good chance she wouldn't arrive to marry me. When word came, they found her shoe, I feared the worst for a while. Then a note came in her handwriting. She didn't sign it, but she used a word, my nickname for her, "Doll," in the first line. I showed the last sheriff the note and told her she wasn't dead, but that wasn't proof enough for him. The town preferred me a murderer, a drug pusher and a man who keeps loose women. None of that was true, but it supplied them with rumors for years. As the years passed, the rumors only got worse."

"All because she left you." Loren shook his head, disappointed.

Barbara said, "You don't deserve that kind of treatment."

"After Bernadett left me, the things people said about me would curl your toes," Mr. Reaves admitted. "I was called the most hideous of things. But I couldn't blame them either, because they just believed what others were saying. So many believed I hurt her and did those things that it seemed impossible to change anyone's mind, and even those I trusted eventually stayed away, because they didn't want to be seen socializing with a murderer, or junk peddler who went to hook shops. After a while, I got used to their lies and I got angry too. I said things back on occasion; I shouldn't have in certain situations. It was hard to always keep my cool about being treated so horribly."

"Why didn't you find her and bring her back to clear your name?" Barbara wondered.

"My Dear, I loved her. Sometimes you let loves get away with things, even when it hurts you. You give them space to grow and hopefully someday they'll realize what they did. They'll know then that they did once love you after all because of all the sacrifices you made."

"She made you her pawn in a game of chess." Loren leaned back and said, "Mr. Reaves, I do believe you loved that woman far more than she deserved."

"I want her to be happy, even without me, even if it hurt so bad that I needed her to be painted just so I would be close to her again." Mr. Reaves parked the car next to the lake. Loren's crop duster plane was parked beside a red barn with doors wide open.

"Mr. Reaves," Barbara let Loren jump down from the car before she added, "if you ever change your mind about removing her painting from the museum, don't think twice about it. I don't think I ever want to see her face again."

"All great art has incredible pain behind it," Mr. Reaves said. "If you remember that, you'll know our love was a masterpiece."

CHAPTER 30

The sensation of butterflies fluttering in her stomach was making Barbara feel very sick. She didn't like this feeling of uneasiness. Fear was gaining control of her as Loren was buckled her into the plane seated in front of Mr. Reaves.

He kissed her cheek. "Don't be frightened." Barbara gulped.

"Can you tell?"

"Not at all," he lied. "Your shaking body gives you away."

She looked down and saw her knees practically knocking together. A part of her was terrified. Her heart started to pound. "I think it's best I wait here."

"Don't be silly." Mr. Reaves reached over her seat and patted her shoulder. "You have nothing but fear. People fly every day."

"But I don't." Barbara pulled at her seatbelt, trying hard to remember to breathe. "I don't want to die today."

"I'm the best pilot ever." Loren laid his hand on her head. "Do you really think I would put you in danger?"

"I didn't think you'd do it intentionally." Barbara exhaled.

"If you let what frightens you stop you from doing great things, then you will never be great," Mr. Reaves said.

"Finely said," Loren agreed.

Barbara realized she was out-voted. She took another deep breath and tried to calm her nerves. Her hands dropped from the belt, and she nodded. "All right, if I am married to a pilot, then I best become like a bird."

"Good girl." Loren winked then jumped into the seat in front of hers.

The plane's propeller began to twirl as the engine started. Slowly the plane rolled out of the barn and into the pasture, onto a dirt path. It began to speed up. Barbara closed her eyes as tightly as she could as the plane left the ground.

When she didn't feel the wheels pounding the dirt, she opened one eye and peered out between her fingers. Half afraid of looking up, down or even to the side, she kept her gaze on the floor.

Mr. Reaves was screaming sounds of immaculate joy. He was tapping his cane on the floor and shouting, "What fun!"

Gathering courage, Barbara told herself that she wasn't going to die. That the only thing she feared was fear itself. She calmed herself with thoughts of her paintings, how she would someday paint that one of the bees and the fence outside her house. What a simple work it would be… she opened her eyes… then she saw the most amazing thing, a cloud.

It wasn't far from the plane itself and it appeared as if it were a big piece of cotton to reach out for. It was shaped like a fish with an open mouth and four fins that were in all the wrong places.

"Hold on," Loren shouted back.

He took the plane lower above the town and there Barbara could see all the people shopping and looking up at them. It was quite interesting to see how small everything seemed from above. After he passed the town, he headed above the forest.

So many trees of all shapes: birch, maples, oaks and mixes of pine by the hundreds that remained unchanged by man. It was such a sight. On one high oak was the giant nest of a large osprey. Barbara could even see its eggs.

"That would make a fine breakfast," Mr. Reaves leaned over and said in her ear.

"I think not." Barbara smiled.

"So do you like the sky?" Loren asked her over his shoulder.

Her gaze moved to his blue eyes. They matched the color all about him. What a sight to see; how happy he was. *This is where his home truly is.*Now he had both his loves together for the first time; she could read his enjoyment in the way he smiled. How much he wanted her to love it too. Gladly, she didn't disappoint him.

"I am having fun," she said.

"Attagirl! Now watch this." He turned the wheel fast and all of a sudden, the plane rolled midair. It did a turn and then righted itself.

Barbara couldn't believe he did that. It would have frightened her half to death if she had known it was coming. But now that it was over, she didn't mind one bit. In fact, what a thrill this was!

"Do that again!" Mr. Reaves begged, now no longer with a hat.

"Don't you dare," Barbara said.

It was too late; this time Loren rolled the plane twice before righting it again. "That's a very serious move. Only the best pilots can do it."

This time Barbara spoke up. "Please, Loren, this is my first time."

He winked again at her. "Don't worry; we're about at the falls. Look down."

The plane began to lower and down to the right was a very rocky river. The current was strong and then all of a sudden, the expanse of land dropped down into a waterfall. Loren dove the plane downward with the water.

Barbara let out a scream. Mr. Reaves shouted, but by the time Barbara gripped the seat, Loren had leveled the plane and turned it around again for the most amazing sight. The waterfall was enormous, with so much water falling that a mist appeared at the bottom. A single tree with purple leaves sat on the edge in the middle of it all, clinging to a rock.

"That's my lucky tree," Loren said.

"Lucky?" Barbara argued. "To be in all this mess of water? It's a miracle it doesn't get ripped apart."

"Exactly the point." Mr. Reaves understood. "It remains no matter how turbulent the water is."

Barbara smiled. "That's quite poignant."

Loren turned the plane around, flew over the falls again, this time against the flow of the water. The powerful wind from this angle whipped her short hair and made her squint. Once high enough, the wind died down a bit with the clouds. Barbara spied out the Osprey nest once more to count the eggs this time. She found there were three, but one was black, and she guessed it would not hatch. When the town came again, Barbara started to worry again.

She forgot about looking at how nice the townsfolk looked so small and focused on the fact the plane would be landing shortly. Her teeth began to clench as the plane began to lower over the field again.

When the wheels hit the dirt, Barbara let out another quick yell, and then when it came to a stop, she breathed a sigh of relief and happiness all at the same time. She was pleased to be on the ground, but another part of her wanted to try it all over again.

"What an afternoon," Mr. Reaves said, unbuckling his belt.

Barbara followed his leave. Loren jumped out from his seat and began to assist her. "Do you need a hand down?" he asked.

"I'm swell." But when she rose, she noticed she was a bit unsteady.

"Here." Loren jumped down onto a wing, grabbed her by the waist and slowly lowered her to the ground. "All right?"

With her feet on the dirt, she said, "Yes, I am."

Mr. Reaves stepped onto the plane's wing, sat down and rolled off of it with one big hop to the dirt. Landing on his feet, he quickly used his cane to steady himself. "That was the most fun I've had in years."

"Glad you enjoyed yourself, Sir," Loren said, and then he noticed. "Where is your hat?"

"Lost it somewhere over the forest, I'm afraid." He patted Loren on the shoulder. "Never mind my headpiece. That was an experience of a lifetime. I've had so much fun it will take me weeks for it to sink in."

"We'll have to do it again the next time I'm in town then."

"I would relish it." Mr. Reaves nodded. "What about you, Barbara, will you come again too?"

She looked up into Loren's face and saw how much he wanted her there too. "I wouldn't miss it."

Loren leaned down and kissed her lips. He didn't seem to be bothered that Mr. Reaves was watching. When Loren stepped away, Mr. Reaves was blushing and was wiping his forehead with a handkerchief. "Hot one today," he said. "I best be getting home."

"We'll walk down the path so no need to wait for us," Loren said, kissing Barbara on the cheek.

Mr. Reaves didn't seem to mind. He seemed to skip almost to the car. And with a wave of a hand, he drove off with a smile on his face.

CHAPTER 31

Saying goodbye to Loren proved harder this time. Barbara cried all the way home from the bus station. Walking up her steps, she sat down on the stoop and noticed a piece of paper tucked under the door.

She guessed it was another note asking her to call for a painting. Next to it was a newspaper wrapped in a rope. She rolled down the string and uncurled the pages. Headlines read, "Bernadett alive!" The headline spoke of how Mr. Reaves was once accused of killing her; it mentioned some of the rumors as well, which made Barbara cringe. Why repeats such gossip?

There was mention of her painting being excellently done, but it was only a brief line. Clearly, Bernadett had taken the spotlight. She folded up the paper and left it beside her on the stoop. Barbara grimaced. How horrible for Mr. Reaves to read all this about the woman he once loved. Now the entire town knew she'd left him and even worse, destroyed his life. For a while she ignored the newspaper and turned toward the note of paper under the door, and then curiosity got the best of her. She reached out and took it.

Your painting was incredible. I'd like to commission you to paint the town for $100.00. I'll hang it in my office.

Mayor Jake Newton.

Barbara rose. This was an honor. The Mayor wanted her to paint something for him. Could any award be higher! Deciding that she would spend the day painting the town from the view of the plane, she didn't want to sulk about missing her husband any longer today.

Grateful to have an exciting distraction, she hurried back into her studio.

She flung on a canvas, sat in her chair and closed her eyes. Without even looking, Barbara took her brush and pictured what she would paint. Her mind went to that very second when, in the plane, they swooped down right in the middle of town. All those people strolling on the street, their heads turned up and smiling at the plane.

That is what she would create. It would capture one of the most frightening and exciting times of her life. Barbara wanted every stroke of color to show how thrilling it was to be in this town.

By mid-afternoon, the painting was halfway completed. Instead of focusing on how sad she was, Barbara was encased in the desire to relive a moment in time. Successfully, she had pulled herself from loneliness.

The phone rang, but Barbara didn't answer it. She kept her attention clearly on her mission. She wanted every detail of the foliage correctly portrayed, especially the giant oak tree that was near the marketplace.

Thirst finally made her quit. When Barbara went into the kitchen, she discovered she had a guest drinking in the parlor. Mrs. Kays sat quietly; a smile crossed her lips when Barbara began to fill her glass.

"I didn't get much of a chance to see Loren this visit," she complained.

"Oh." Barbara realized that Loren should have stopped by his mother's before getting on the bus. "We woke up late," she lied, not wanting to tell her that they got up early to go to breakfast and make love.

"A friend of mine saw you both eating pancakes," Mrs. Kays said. "That's a problem when you get famous. Word spreads quickly."

"We got up and then went back to sleep. It was such a busy night last night." Barbara sighed, knowing she had just been caught in a lie, trying not to hurt Mrs. Kays' feelings.

"I see." Mrs. Kays rose and went to the counter.

Barbara raised her pitcher full of lemonade and offered Mrs. Kays a refill. She nodded and Barbara filled her glass.

"I came to apologize for how I acted at the showing." Mrs. Kays lowered her glass back to the counter instead of taking another sip. "It was wrong of me to cause such a scene."

"How long have you been waiting for me?" Barbara questioned.

"I've been here since noon," Mrs. Kays said. "I saw the light on in the back bedroom and didn't want to disturb you. A new work?"

"For the Mayor," she said and then regretted mentioning that. Barbara didn't want to seem as if she was bragging.

"Wonderful." Mrs. Kays smiled, but there was a weird sound in her voice.

"Are you upset with me?" Barbara asked.

"I'm all wet by a very odd set of circumstances which I have fallen into," Mrs. Kays announced.

"Can I help you with anything?" Barbara questioned. "I feel that there is this tension between us."

"Not you," Mrs. Kays said. "It's Mr. Reaves who I do not care for. I'm quite troubled that he is your benefactor. In fact, I have a hard time sleeping in fear of what your allegiance is doing to your reputation. Since you are married to my son, I have a duty to make sure you are kept far away from scandal. Out of respect for my son, of course."

"I understand." Barbara grinned. "You haven't a thing to worry about. I've spoken with the sheriff about Mr. Reaves' past and learned it was rumors, that's all. Bernadett is alive and therefore that's proof."

"He's into illegal matters." Mrs. Kays spit the words out. "That isn't good for you or Loren. What scandal will this bring to my family name?"

"Mrs. Kays," Barbara sipped on her drink, "the illegal matters of women and substances was checked out and he was found innocent of those as well. Mr. Reaves is simply the product of everyone's cruelty. He is a fine man. His only flaw is loving a woman who doesn't want him. And even she has left town now."

"She's gone?" Mrs. Kays' eyes lit up.

"Are you pleased?"

"Glad." The teacher nodded. "Good riddance to the bimbo broad."

"Mrs. Kays, your finding gladness in Mr. Reaves' heartbreak isn't kind. I assure you, Mr. Reaves is a good-hearted soul."

"He is a scoundrel, and you are being fooled!" Mrs. Kays raised her voice. "I'm looking forward to your gaining so much favor that you'll no longer need him."

"I'll always want him near." Barbara gasped. "He's my friend."

"Friends like that are enemies in disguise."

"Mrs. Kays, if you continue to speak of my associate with so much hatred I will ask you to kindly refrain from talking about him around me. His money bought us this house and the people he knows buys my paintings. At first, even I was startled by how good a man he was. I feared the worst. He hasn't done a thing wrong. I feel sorry for him; he's lonely like me, and surrounded by so many who want harm to come to him."

"You think you know everything." Mrs. Kays walked toward the door. "You haven't a clue why he's helping you. Revenge isn't sweet."

"Vengeance for what?" Barbara almost laughed. She covered her mouth, pretending to wipe it and then took another sip.

"Out of love for my son, I do not tell you."

"Let's say I want to give this some thought. I want to. You've been kind to me and taught me everything I know. I owe you more than I do Mr. Reaves, but you seem determined to hold onto this grudge and not see how much he is helping us."

"It's a family matter concerning Bernadett."

"A family matter? Am I not family?" Barbara took that as an insult.

"Bernadett's family," Mrs. Kays explained.

"I do want to spend time with you," Barbara said, walking around the counter, giving Mrs. Kays a hug. "Perhaps you can come for dinner next week. Right now, I must finish what I started."

"Please listen to my warnings," Mrs. Kays begged. "Mr. Reaves isn't quite what he seems. I worry about you and your reputation."

"We'll speak further on it at dinner." With that, Barbara left Mrs. Kays. She was curious about why her teacher thought this was about revenge. In truth, it didn't matter. Mr. Reaves was her friend and Mrs. Kays her mother- in-law. Clearly, they would have to find a way to coexist.

Chapter 32

Mr. Reaves insisted on escorting Barbara to the mayor's office to reveal her latest masterpiece. When she ventured into the majestic office, Barbara noticed the fine furniture and mahogany desk. Behind it sat the square-shouldered Mayor, Jake Newton. His thick jaw rose, and his double chin appeared as he greeted them with an interested smile.

"I finished your painting," Barbara said, dutifully. "I hope you will enjoy looking at it."

The mayor waggled a finger for her to bring the painting closer. She put the canvas on his desk and flipped over the protective cloth cover. Without glancing at her work, she stared into the mayor's big brown eyes.

Staring blankly, the mayor responded guardedly, "That is fine. I'll have my secretary pay you twenty before you leave."

"Twenty!" Mr. Reaves voice thundered. "That is an insult. This painting is worth far more."

Then Mr. Reaves hurried around the desk for the same view as the mayor. His eyes brightened, then he grinned awkwardly, almost knowingly.

"I'll pay twenty," the mayor repeated. "Take it or leave it."

"We'll leave it." Mr. Reaves wrapped his arm around Barbara's shoulders.

"It would be an honor to have this hung here," Barbara whispered to her benefactor. Then she straightened. "Is there something wrong with the painting that you don't like?"

"It lacks nagging details."

Mr. Reaves stood rooted, then he prodded Barbara to recover the art piece. "Well, that will be all, then."

Together they headed back for the door. Barbara's worst fear had just materialized. A client didn't like her finished product. Perhaps it was the angle he didn't like. He probably didn't want one from the sky? It was an unusual direction to go, but it was still good. Wasn't it? Doubting herself, she waited as Mr. Reaves put his hand on the doorknob.

"Wait." The mayor stopped them. "Twenty-five."

"Don't say a word," Mr. Reaves told her.

"Well, take it or leave it?" the mayor added.

"Sorry," Mr. Reaves said, dismissingly.

"Thirty," the mayor said on a snarl.

Looking mildly astonished, Barbara concluded that he indeed liked her work but wasn't happy with the price. By the looks of his suit and his office, surely the mayor could afford the hundred dollars he'd offered on the note.

"You promised the girl one hundred," Mr. Reaves said ruefully.

Unimpressed, the mayor challenged, "Thirty is a good price for a painting these days."

"That will only cover her cost in paints and canvas," Mr. Reaves charged matter-of-factly.

The mayor opened the drawer on his desk, pulled out a pen and checkbook and with a vice-like grip signed his name on the bottom. "Fifty dollars it will be then."

Before the mayor's pen touched the amount line, Mr. Reaves hurdled across the floor with his cane and slammed it down on the checkbook. The loud sound caused sweeps of murmurs from the office across the hall. A few faces poked in the door of the mayor's office, curious as to what the loud noise was.

The mayor raised a hand to ignore the interruption and responded guardedly to Barbara, "You come on like gangbusters."

"You said one hundred dollars on your note." Barbara came forward and maneuvered between the desk and two chairs. She took a seat in front of him, her face enthusiastically grinning. "I believe you should keep your word."

"Seventy-five!" He shot back.

"One hundred." Mr. Reaves grabbed the pen from the mayor's hand and took it as if he would stab her work.

"Please," Barbara said, feigning shock.

"You'd destroy it?" the Mayor asked distinctively.

"I can't have others thinking they can cheat her." Mr. Reaves raised the pen higher, ready to drop.

"And you'd let him?" the mayor turned to her.

"I thought you didn't like it anyway. One hundred dollars," Barbara reminded casually, not taking her eyes off of him.

"Give me the pen back." He took it and scribbled the amount they sought as quickly as possible. "One hundred I'll pay now, but with the promise to paint my neighbor's son Dayton in his uniform for his mother. Mr. Jackson will pay you one hundred as well, but he doesn't want to wait in that long line of other soldiers' families you have on your list. His son has been gone one year already in the war and he's missed dearly by them." He signed the document and handed it over. "I promised them that I would put in a good word."

"I'll paint your neighbor's son, but he'll wait his turn." Barbara rose. "I'm no dumb Dora."

Mr. Reaves pushed her out the door with a hand on the small of her back. Her heart soared; although she could take what just happened as an insult, it was quite exciting.

"Do you think he'll hang it now?" Barbara questioned.

"By paying that much, he will and brag about it as well." Mr. Reaves opened the door for her of his vehicle, Barbara took the step and climbed up into the passenger's seat, smiling awkwardly. "Now where to?" She felt the growling of her belly. "I hardly ate yesterday."

"I'll remedy that. I'll have my maid stir up something good for you," Mr. Reaves said.

"What about the diner?"

"I no longer dine in public," he admitted. "Too many servers that like spitting in my food."

Barbara was horrified. "All because of Bernadett?"

"Don't blame her." Mr. Reaves got behind the wheel and started the engine. "She can't control every person's reaction. So, what will you have?"

"Mr. Reaves, I do believe you need to fall out of love with that woman. Please forgive me for saying it, but it's true. All she's given you is heartache and she's so selfish she doesn't even care what happenings have destroyed your life."

Mr. Reaves maneuvered his leg further under the wheel, then turned the car around the bend heading back north, toward his estate. "Asking me to stop loving her is like telling me not to breathe. It can't be done. It would be like telling you to cease painting. It's who you are."

"It isn't my place to say." Barbara nodded. "But I am curious as to why my mother-in-law is so set on hating you as well."

"That's another tale altogether." Mr. Reaves chuckled. "She has spirit, Aleavia. I used to find that an appealing thing. It's what attracted me to Bernadett, that fire in one's spirit. It came out in her paintings. Aleavia, before you, was the greatest artist I've ever seen."

"Yet, you've never helped her?"

"That depends on your opinion. Many would say I did." He cocked his head in her direction.

"I wish you two would get along for the sake of Loren and me. In fact, maybe we should swing by her house and invite her to lunch with us. We should open the door to let her know that if she accepts our friendship, we can all be friends."

"You ask the impossible," Mr. Reaves said, glumly.

"It would make me happier to know my favorite people in this world could at least be civil. Could you at least try?"

Mr. Reaves turned the car around with a huff. He rolled his eyes and glanced over at her. "For Loren and you, anything, even if it means… her."

CHAPTER 33

Mr. Reaves drove Barbara to Mrs. Kays' property. In the living room, a light shown softly through the lace curtains softly blowing in the breeze. Barbara opened the door to the vehicle, climbed out and walked up the path to the door.

She knocked vigorously.

Mrs. Kays opened it. When she saw Barbara, she immediately straightened with a happy greeting. "How nice of you to stop..." She noticed Mr. Reaves waiting in the car on the street.

Barbara broke the uncomfortable silence. "We were wondering if you'd like to join us for lunch at Mr. Reaves' estate."

Mrs. Kays said dismissively, "I haven't the time. Perhaps you could stop by tonight? You and I could go out for dinner, just the two of us."

Barbara realized she would have to be more forward. "Mrs. Kays... Mother... I would like all three of us to dine together. Perhaps we can work through the past and get through all this animosity."

"That's impossible," Mrs. Kays corrected her. "To be in such a drip's house would make me quite sick to my stomach."

"For me?" Barbara begged. "You two are some of the most important people in my life. I just wish we could relate as a family."

"How dare..." Mrs. Kays lowered her tone. "You have a sweet heart. As you get older you will learn that sometimes it isn't the niceties that are important but the little things."

"It's just lunch," Barbara reminded. "I'm not asking you to marry the fella."

Mrs. Kays blinked frantically. "So now he has the nerve to tell you that I turned down his proposal? Of all the blasted things a tyrant can do! He probably said that I asked him. Well, I didn't. You can tell him to keep any ideas away from me that have to do with wearing that ring again!"

Barbara went speechless. Did Mrs. Kays just believe that Mr. Reaves liked her? Not only that, but did she just claim that he once proposed to her and that she won't wear his ring… again? She actually said the word, again. That would imply that there was more than once that she had been betrothed to him.

Barbara spun on her heel, but before she could climb back into the car, Mr. Reaves was headed toward the stoop. Mrs. Kays had her hands on her hips and her face was turning crimson with anger.

"Get off my property before I call a flatfoot!"

"Hiding behind Johnny Law, are you?" Mr. Reaves stomped down his cane, almost hitting her in the toe. "I never told her our past, Aleavia! Now you've done it! You done told that girl that we were once engaged and who do you think she's going to tell that information to? Can't you ever keep your trap closed?"

"Don't you speak to me that way. I have half a mind to tell her the whole thing."

"Go ahead now," Mr. Reaves said. "You might as well."

Barbara, worried how upset Mr. Reaves was getting, returned to his side and said, "Let's do this another day. I was wrong in my assumption that we could all be friends. I didn't know that you were once sweethearts."

"There was not one thing sweet about us," Mr. Reaves said in a dark tone. "You're looking at the woman who drove Bernadett away from me and this whole town."

"I did nothing of the sort," Mrs. Kays shot back.

"Please," Barbara begged. "I didn't know that there was a history here more than what lies beneath the gossip. I'm sorry. It's my fault for not trusting both your judgments. I had hoped that we could all relate well and be like the family I've never had. Now I see that is impossible.

I certainly won't put either of you in such an awkward state. Clearly, this bond will never grow. History makes it impossible between you both."

"Oh, but Bernadett," Mrs. Kays added, "anything that woman does is the cat's pajamas in his eyes, and I treated him twice as good."

"I didn't care for you," Mr. Reaves blurted.

Her hand rose and Mrs. Kays slapped Mr. Reaves across the cheek. Stunned, he tumbled backward. Luckily his cane swung behind and steadied him so he would not fall to the ground.

"Was that necessary?"

"Yes." Mrs. Kays took in a deep breath and calmed herself.

Barbara took Mr. Reaves by the arm and said, "Forgive me. I didn't know. I'll never ask the two of you to be friends again. We'll just work things out where I do things with each of you."

"That suits me just fine." Mr. Reaves tapped the tip of his hat to Mrs. Kays. "You are not a lady."

"That's because you are no gentleman," Mrs. Kays snapped.

Then a car pulled in behind Mr. Reaves. A military man dressed in an Air Force uniform, not more than eighteen, climbed out. He took several steps toward the house and stopped on the path, blocking Mr. Reaves and Barbara's path.

Suddenly, Mrs. Kays let out a bloodcurdling scream. "No!" Barbara whirled around.

"Oh no!" Mr. Reaves gasped, the blood rushing from his face. "This can't be happening."

The young soldier walked over to Mrs. Kays and said, "Mrs. Kays, I'm looking for Loren Kays' wife, Barbara. She wasn't at the address listed on my envelope. I'm told you're Loren's mother; is that true?"

"No!" Mrs. Kays cried out, her knees failing.

"What's wrong?" Barbara asked.

Mr. Reaves rushed to Mrs. Kays' side. He dropped onto his good knee, holding her up, starting to weep. Mrs. Kays couldn't speak; she pointed to Barbara, tears streaming down her face.

The soldier turned. "Barbara Kays, wife of Loren Kays?"

"Yes, that's me." Barbara started to shake. "What's wrong?"

"I regret to inform you that Loren Kays' plane went down over in Italy. There are no survivors." With that, the soldier handed her a letter and walked away. His eyes never met hers.

Barbara's hands clutched the letter as tears rolled into her eyes. She faced Mr. Reaves and Mrs. Kays, only to find them grieving in each other's arms.

"Come here," Mr. Reaves said to her. "I haven't the strength to get up to make sure you're all right."

Barbara walked to him. With her worst fear materializing, she tried to open the letter, but her fingers fumbled over the crease. Too horrific for the mind to assimilate, she too let out a whispered, "No."

Mr. Reaves struggled, but he managed to rise to his feet. He came to her and held her in his arms. That was well and good, for that was the last thing she remembered as she collapsed.

 Chapter 34

In the dark of the night, a crowd gathered, dressed in black and surrounding a white coffin. Loren was buried in the town cemetery. A big hole had been dug next to the seats; his remains were not inside.

A picture of him lay in the center of the open casket.

There were murmurs behind Barbara; she could hear many ask why there wasn't a painting done of him. Truth be known, since the moment she had been told the news of Loren's death, she hadn't picked up the brush.

Art was the last thing on her mind.

Pain and grief had caused such depression; Barbara could barely fathom love could hurt this badly. How cold she felt. Even though the sun was setting in the distance, she felt not one bit of warmth as it crawled lower in the sky.

She could no longer look at the clouds.

For some time, Barbara tried to listen to what the pastor said.

"We gather this evening to say farewell to a soldier. A brave young man who gave his life at the age of twenty for a cause. It is said he died flying a plane which was his favorite of all things. That should give us some help in knowing that he died where he loved to be. Those who knew and loved him will forever remember how kind a man he was. I remember him sitting on the front pew, sitting next to his mother. He wasn't always the most quiet of boys, but as he grew, he learned to be a man who kept his word. Men like that grow here in this town. Men who live and go to fight a war."

The pastor went on about how tragic this was and how so many had died in the war. "I've held too many funerals these days in our town as many more Jews die at the hands of Hitler. We lose our boys, so that many others will be able to live. We are battling hatred at its core. Loren hadn't a bad bone in his body; he was good-hearted and even shy. We will not forget him, and he will be deeply missed by his wife Barbara and his mother, Aleavia. We must cherish our memories, and they will pull us through. This will take time."

The agony that Barbara felt grew in her belly like a fire wind. No comfort came from his message.

She seemed empty now. Life felt hopeless.

Loren's mother had her arm around her. Mr. Reaves sat two chairs down. His tears met between his nostrils and dropped to the dirt. For once, these two ex-lovers didn't argue. Mr. Reaves even had the kindness to sit next to Mrs. Kays. Not one harsh word had come between them since the tragic news arrived.

Barbara knew she should be pleased that at least something came out of Loren's death—two who hated each other putting aside their differences for him.

How life can change in the blink of an eye. Just a week ago she was in his arms, loving him, hoping to start a family when he returned. That dream was gone and with it, the light in her soul.

Barbara's eyes rose to the people surrounding her. So many had come and now they slowly passed her, saying, "sorry," or "he went too quickly." Those words seemed to tear at her, coldly ripping her apart.

"I'll be having guests today for food and drink," Mrs. Kays said in her ear. "Join us."

Barbara nodded that she would but turned in the opposite direction to walk home. Mr. Reaves rose as she passed him and he said, "I'll drive you."

"I'm just ginger," Barbara muttered.

"Pastor, won't you join us?" Mrs. Kays asked him.

"Thank you for your kind words," Mr. Reaves added.

"Would you like me to take you to our house?" Barbara's mother asked Barbara from behind.

"I'm fine," Barbara said again, surprised to see her.

"Are you sure?" her mother questioned.

Barbara noticed she was wearing black. Her father was standing behind her. How ironic, he finally accepted she was married at her husband's funeral. How sad that was and how it made her angry. The things her father said to him, Loren never forgot. How coldly he treated her. He never gave Loren a chance.

"Come with us," her father said, removing his hat. "You can for a while until you are well."

"I'm fine," she said, again.

What lies came from her lips that day. She was not fine. Would she ever be again? Sorry didn't cut it and it didn't matter that he went too quickly. Loren, her love, was dead! How foolish all this seemed at this very moment. She'd been to a dozen funerals before, but it hadn't seemed to register until this one.

She traveled further to the dirt path where she came upon the crab apple tree. Today, she didn't look for the bunny or the crows flying about. She ignored the wasps in her path and walked among them as if unafraid of being stung.

Moving on, she came to the creek behind her house and walked up the path until she came onto her porch. There she sat on a chair and stared at the floor. Hours must have passed. She heard knocks, her phone ringing.

She didn't answer, nor felt any need to move.

Night came. In the blackness, she didn't move an inch. The moon was casting a light reflection onto the creek. And that's where her eyes stayed, on the line over the water. She heard the faint distant washing of the shore then the sounds of a clicking coming her way.

By now, she'd know that sound anywhere, the cane of Mr. Reaves. He came to sit beside her in a chair. He too sat and didn't breathe a word. His hand rose to her shoulder once, but only for a second.

This way, they mourned the loss of a good man; no words were needed. Eventually, Barbara fell asleep. When she woke, Barbara found a blanket over her and his cane in the chair beside her.

She went inside and found him cooking breakfast.

"I'm not good in the kitchen," he announced, forcing a 40's smile. "But I know an overcooked egg isn't bad for you."

Barbara moved to the table where a place was set. He tossed a few eggs on her plate with a piece of ham. She didn't want to eat, but she lifted the fork and forced herself to.

"There were quite a lot of messages on the phone this morning. I wrote them all down. Mostly grievances, but a few for paintings that were for payment," he informed.

She took in a deep breath.

"Don't worry," he said, confidently. "You'll find your brush."

She ignored the comment, ate, and then trotted off to the bedroom. When she saw the bed, she wept openly, falling into the sheets. She held them in the palms of her hands, smelling them, gripping at the pillows to find any scent of Loren.

CHAPTER 35

"It's been several weeks, and she hasn't painted one bit," Mr. Reaves said to Mrs. Kays.

Barbara could hear their conversation from her bedroom. The room she hadn't left other than to barely eat in twenty-two days. Her sheets smelled now of sweat and tears. The room was covered in half empty water glasses and used tissues.

"She needs to find her bearings."

"There are many paying customers that could go to another painter," Mr. Reaves reminded.

"Then let them."

"I know this isn't easy on you. It isn't on me either…"

"You haven't the right to say that." Mrs. Kays' voice was snippy. "My son hardly even knew you. I'm the one who raised him."

Mr. Reaves said, "Someone has got to help her back on her feet. The Ranglers' son just died yesterday, and his parents are willing to pay her five hundred dollars if she can paint his burial portrait by Friday. That's a lot of money, enough to last her now that Loren's money isn't coming in anymore."

"If she has a problem with financing, I'm sure you'll pitch in. You didn't seem to have a problem before."

"That isn't the point."

Barbara sat up. She knew Mr. Reaves was right; she needed the money and didn't want to take his money any more. She rose and went to the doorway. Mr. Reaves and Mrs. Kays didn't notice her standing there, listening. Their backs were turned to her and they were deep in conversation.

"Of course I'll always help her," Mr. Reaves insisted. "That dame doesn't know, though, and it looks odd to the community. I've been trying to help her get self-sustaining."

"No different than the others." Mrs. Kay's reply was curt.

"There were no others," Mr. Reaves reminded. "That was speculation. They were rumors which you started, might I add, all because of jealousy."

"Jealous?" Mrs. Kays laughed. "Of the others, even on my worst day, I was more beautiful a doll than they."

"On the exterior," Mr. Reaves said, coldly.

"I have a right mind to slap your face." Mrs. Kays' face reddened. "I'm too much of a lady."

"A lady bent on destroying people when they don't do exactly what she wants. You were a bully then and you're still a bully."

"You are so dramatic. Really, you should have been a drama teacher at my school. Maybe then some would respect you."

"So you could get the kids to hate me next, was that your plan?" Mr. Reaves asked. "When will you take responsibility for what you did?"

Barbara finally interrupted. "I'm not painting any more soldiers who are dead so stop arguing about it."

Mr. Reaves and Mrs. Kays faced her. The look of shock quickly diminished with Mr. Reaves coming forward and placing a hand on her shoulder. Intensely he bent over and stared in her eyes.

"Painting is your bread and butter."

"I can't live on bread alone," Barbara said. "Nor will I ever pick up a brush again."

"Don't be ridiculous." Mrs. Kays traversed the floor. "You have a gift, that I helped mold. You've established a following that only very few artists ever establish. You can't quit now."

"I can't paint what I can't feel."

Mrs. Kays sighed. "I know. Sometimes you just have to force it and hope for the best."

"Force it?" Barbara shook her head no. "That isn't how I do things. If it doesn't feel right then it doesn't comes out."

The door opened and in walked a familiar face. The waitress at the Seafood restaurant where Loren had taken her on their first date. She was in a black dress and wearing a large brim hat.

"She isn't seeing anyone today." Mr. Reaves quickly walked over to the grieving woman.

"You must paint him for the funeral," she begged. "I only have one picture and it is ripped. That isn't good enough."

Barbara turned so she wouldn't see her.

"Leave," Mrs. Kays told her. "This girl is going through her own crisis at the moment."

"I know." The woman came forward and handed Barbara a letter. "Read this. Please."

"Go." Mr. Reaves grabbed her by her shoulders and began leading her out. "Your husband went to boot camp with…"

The door shut and Barbara left the letter on the table.

"Oh, dear." Mr. Reaves sighed. "I hope it doesn't get out that now she's refusing paying customers."

"She's in no condition," Mrs. Kays said.

Mr. Reaves sighed. "Barbara, I have always tried to let you live your own life."

"Really?" Mrs. Kays gasped sarcastically. "I would have never guessed that, not with all that money, parties, and showing her about."

"Perhaps, I have overstepped at times. Truly, I only wanted what's best for Loren and you. I've been here day after day now for weeks and you know what I see? I see a woman who was in love. Loren wouldn't want this for you. He wouldn't want you crying day after day for what could have been. He surely wouldn't want you to stop what he admired in you. Loren is gone and that is difficult for any of us to accept, but you can't stop living because he did."

Barbara didn't care. She raised a hand for him to stop. Instead of ceasing, he took her hand and forced her around by grabbing her chin to look at him.

"I know what you are going through. I miss my grandson every day. He was the only person in my entire life that knew about my reputation and didn't care what people said about me. He used to stand up for me. He loved me, honestly, because I was his Grampy, because I taught him how to fish and hunt. That's what he called me, 'Grampy.' Boy, do I miss hearing him say that. I'm the one who talked him into signing up for the army, and each day I wake remembering that.

"For a long time I felt guilty, but then I saw how proud he was to wear that uniform in your painting. That he was doing what he wanted to do. He died a hero, just like your husband. And, yes, you have every right to feel what you are feeling for Loren, but you can't let this destroy who you are. If I am anything, I am a role model for those who survive even the worst of circumstances when no one likes them. No one does. No one even wants to admit knowing me half the time, even when I support their businesses, but I keep on keeping on. I may not find pleasure in the company of my fellow man, but I do in your paintings, and in the sunrise, and in the..." he started to cry, "birds that fly outside my window in the morning."

"Find me a violin." Mrs. Kays rolled her eyes.

"I love you, Barbara. I love you like a daughter. In my eyes, you will always be family, just like my grandson. You're all I've got, and I'll always be here for you even if you don't want me to be."

"Because I paint." Barbara tried to force her chin out of his hand. "If I wasn't a painter than I wouldn't even know you and you wouldn't even care."

"That's not true. You don't even know the real reason."

"It is," Barbara said then turned to Mrs. Kays. "That's the only way you think about me too. Those days are over. I'm no longer a painter, so leave me alone. Both of you. Leave me alone!"

"No," Mr. Reaves said.

"Leave me be!" She pushed him; he stumbled back on his cane and fell on the floor.

Mrs. Kays left him there for a second then she bent over to help him rise again to his feet. Mr. Reaves hobbled to her. For several moments, he gazed deeply into her tear-filled eyes which mirrored his own.

Finally, he said, "I'll be back tomorrow."

With that, he hobbled toward the door and let himself out.

Chapter 36

Barbara knew Mr. Reaves was right. Loren wouldn't want her to give up one of the things he admired most in her. He loved that she was a painter, even commented once that she was one of the greatest painters of their time. She just wasn't known yet, but on her way.

She loved that about him.

How he always believed in her. When no one else did, not even her parents, Loren and his mother lifted her spirits and gave her the wings to soar like the crow sitting outside her bay window.

She sat in her studio, gazing at the bird on the sill. It seemed as if it was watching her as much as she was staring at it. Its eyes were coal black and lifeless but behind them was life.

Tonight, she felt like that crow.

Mrs. Kays checked in on her from time to time and Barbara could sense her peering in the door, waiting for her to pick up that brush and stroke something on the blank canvas before her.

Minutes passed like hours. The crow finally got up and flew off, bored of watching her, the dead shell of the woman she had become. Barbara remembered dancing in Loren's arms, holding him in their bed, his laughter, his eyes. The woman who had given her that picture never mentioned that her son had a wife.

Her hand reached over and touched the brush. It felt the softness of the bristles, lay there, flipped through the horsehair, and then grabbed the handle. She lifted it to the bottle of black paint, looked one time at the photo, and touched the canvas.

In front of her, she saw what she would paint, the young man standing in front of the Seafood Restaurant, his mother waitressing in the background. It would remind the woman of how many times her son had visited there. He was in uniform, a young boy to the right saluting him. "That's how I shall paint you."

And then, like magic, it began.

Barbara forgot her pain and focused on the woman's. She cornered every detail with perfection, not missing one color or stroke. Even the "S" in the sign would be tarnished just like it was. On the tables, Barbara painted even the dish that made her ill. How she enjoyed painting that; she put Loren's hand reaching for hers in the corner table. The faces were hidden but Barbara would forever remember.

The young man she portrayed as handsome and fit. The mother would love it, she perceived.

Mrs. Kays came in and set down the letter the woman left in the living room. "You should read it," she said.

"No time for that," Barbara said, finishing the last few strokes. "What do you think?"

"One of your best pieces, I especially like the couple in the corner, the sign hiding their faces. That," she pointed down to the lobster, "is Loren's favorite dish."

"So, you know."

"Only a teacher can see the story behind the lines."

"Do you like it?" Barbara knew she would, that she would be happy that she was painting again.

"There hasn't been one I haven't liked." Barbara glanced over to her, disbelievingly.

"Perhaps I wouldn't always paint the same subjects in a particular order as you, but I can see the talent in every work of art you create," Mrs. Kays admitted. "My son would be proud that his dish is in this painting, and his hand with yours."

"No one will know." Barbara smiled.

"We will." Mrs. Kays nodded. "Isn't that all that matters?"

Barbara dropped the brush and pulled Mrs. Kays into her arms. The initial shock of the embrace startled Mrs. Kays, but then her limbs rose and wrapped around Barbara. "I will miss him so much."

"Me too." Mrs Kays' eyes watered. "When you are ready, I want you to paint him like you've done for so many others. Until then, paint his eyes, his arm, whatever makes you happy."

Barbara released her. "You don't understand."

"There could be a million ways you could. I could show you pictures of him flying his plane, or perhaps from your wedding."

"No," Barbara said.

"What?" Mrs. Kays gasped. "You won't paint Loren?"

"Never."

Mrs. Kays backed up. "How could you not paint my son? It's what you do! How many other soldiers have you portrayed? Now my son dies, and you won't paint him! I thought that you would need some time, but now that you are creating again, soon you should."

"I can never paint him."

"It's the only way to see him again!" Mrs. Kays said. "The way you do it, it will be almost like looking at him."

"I can't!"

"I won't take that for an answer." Mrs. Kays' voice rose to a roar. "You must paint him. You must for me!"

"Loren wouldn't want to be just another man in one of my paintings. He would want to be seen as more."

Mrs. Kays shook her head, her face in total horror. "How can you say that? He loved your work."

"Paint him yourself!"

"I can't paint as good as you, not even on my best day."

Barbara knew she should have been flattered, but instead, rage overtook her. "I cannot paint Loren! It would be too hard. I don't want him stuffed on some mantel somewhere."

Mrs. Kays sighed. "It will just take time."

"There will be no time long enough. If you think I will ever paint him then forget it. I can't. It would be too hard. If it wasn't my best painting, then I will have failed and I could never live with painting him less than what he meant to me. That feat is impossible. I can't capture the sky in two feet. I couldn't possibly get all that he meant to me, or you, in one painting. It would take one thousand paintings, two million brushes and even then, it would not be enough."

Mrs. Kays started to cry. "I can't paint him, not like you. Please."

"And you expect *me* to? If you can't paint your own son, then how can I paint my husband?"

"You only knew him a short time. I knew him his whole life!"

"That doesn't mean I didn't love him." Barbara tossed down her brush and it stuck to the side table.

"I know you did; that's not what I meant. I just want to have something of him."

"We have our memories."

"I don't even know what he last saw. What about a landscape, his last view, what of that?"

"What do you want from me?" Barbara cried. "I've given you all I have, and I can't give any more. Get out! Get out!"

"It will just take time, that's all. You're back to painting and soon you will have the strength to paint my son. I just know you will. I have faith in you. You can do this." Mrs. Kays turned on a heel and left, her face covered in tears, her body trembling.

"I can't capture what I feel for him; it's too deep to ever convey."

"Even if you get a part of your feelings, it would be enough."

"I will only say this once. I will never paint Loren. Do not ask me again, ever. Because I love him so much, I cannot do it. If you want him on a canvas, then you do it. Paint him, his last view, paint until your heart's content, but don't ever expect me to look at it. I see him…" she touched her heart, "… here."

CHAPTER 37

In the morning, Barbara woke and went into the studio. She looked at the painting she had done and decided it wasn't as good as her other portraits. She knew the woman would love it and even pay, but in good conscience Barbara couldn't take the money.

This painting was nowhere near the quality that she could perform.

It wasn't for lack of trying; she had painted what she saw in her mind's eye in perfect detail. The portrait was fine by most standards, but when Barbara looked at it, it didn't make her feel that sense of pride.

She picked it up and walked down the block to the Seafood Restaurant. For some reason, she didn't want to go in. The place reminded her of Loren. Although it had been a devastating evening, their worst perhaps, it was still time with him, and she recalled the worry on his face when she'd gotten ill.

In the window, she held up the painting. The waitress wasn't working, but another came out and said, "She'll love it. She'll think it's real swell."

"How much? I'll pay you and she can pay the restaurant back."

Barbara simply said, "It's free."

She moved away with a wave and a smile. It wasn't long before Mr. Reaves drove past and stopped on the street. "I was on my way over," he said.

"I did the painting."

"I see that." He glanced over it.

"Not your best."

"No kidding." Barbara sighed.

"Still damn good," he said, "for a lamb pie."

"Thanks." She glanced down and stared at an ant climbing up his very large black tire.

"Aleavia came to see me last night."

"I'm surprised you're not black and blue," Barbara said and chuckled.

"True enough." His eyes lit up. "It wasn't always that way between us, you know. We were once…friends."

"I'm guessing she told you I got upset with her and told her I would never paint Loren."

"I agreed with you," Mr. Reaves said. "It isn't right for you to paint him."

Barbara was surprised by his support. "Why do you even care?"

Mr. Reaves face dropped. "Don't say that to me. I've done nothing but support you and… Loren."

"I am well aware of why you and Mrs. Kays keep coming around," Barbara said. "You like my work to hang in your museums and make money off of people coming to see your protégé. My teacher finds me someone she can boast about. She wants me to paint Loren. I mean nothing to either of you, except because of my hands." She held them up.

"That isn't true." Mr. Reaves gasped. "It isn't. I wish I could tell you otherwise."

"Don't bother. I know when I am being used. I've meant nothing to both of you but what you can get out of me."

Mr. Reaves turned away.

"I don't want you coming around my house anymore," Barbara said. "Please be kind and stay away. If I am going to paint again, I'll do so on my own terms. I'll paint what I want, when I want. If I'm going to make it, I'll do so on my own."

"It isn't that easy," Mr. Reaves said. "What I've given you is a way into the highest places."

"I have no need for fame and glory."

"That is what you need!" Mr. Reaves stopped the engine and got out of the car. His hands reached for her. "I didn't do all this to let your grief ruin everything that I've done."

"I don't ever want to see you again."

"You don't mean that," Mr. Reaves said. "You couldn't."

"I do." Barbara began to walk away. "Your reputation is one I want nothing to do with. I believe that you are innocent, that your only crime was being too nice to the wrong woman, but that is your problem and no longer mine. I might do better without you. Did you ever think of that?"

"You're being foolish."

"I'm standing on my own two feet."

"That don't know where solid ground is." Mr. Reaves kept pace with her. "I'm not letting you shove Mrs. Kays and me out of your life. We love you."

"We… now you two are a we?"

"Not for a long time," Mr. Reaves shook his head. "But that doesn't mean I don't love her either."

Barbara stopped. "What?"

"I love Aleavia."

"First Bernadett, now Aleavia? Commission that one, next? I'm not going to fall for that again?"

"You don't understand," Mr. Reaves said.

"I don't care anymore," Barbara said confidently. "I'm on my own now."

"You've been on your own your whole life." Mr. Reaves spat the words out. "Don't you think that it's been too long?"

"What do you mean? I was married."

"Yes! And you loved Loren, but you've never truly had a family, because you push us out of your life. You're too afraid that everyone is going to hurt you like your own family did."

"My parents love me," Barbara said. "My mother calls all the time."

"But she doesn't really know you, does she? She doesn't really support what you need. She does whatever your father wants and when you need her, she backs away just because he snaps his fingers."

"What is your point to all this babble? If you don't mind, I'm going to go for a walk near the creek and then I'm off to paint a portrait of another soldier." Barbara stiffened her lip. "I have plenty to keep me busy."

"Busy from life," Mr. Reaves said.

"Really?" Barbara fought back tears. "I think I've done enough living in my life to know enough."

"My Dear, I love you like a daughter. How many times do I have to tell you that until you believe me? I want to help you. I want to be here for you even when you want me away," Mr. Reaves said. "Aleavia cares for you, too. She's at her wit's end. You're all she has. We're all we've all got."

"Aren't we in a sad state," Barbara said, walking away from him.

"She left," Mr. Reaves announced. "Aleavia left today to go to Italy. She's going to paint the landscape where Loren's plane went down. She said she could never paint his face, but she would paint that. I'm worried about her traveling so far alone. With all this fighting, this is a dangerous situation. She isn't thinking clearly, losing Loren, and now she thinks she lost you, too."

Barbara's heart skipped a beat.

"What shall we do?"

"Even if she gets to Italy, she won't be able to paint it. It would be too hard."

"I know. It would be so painful for her." Mr. Reaves cast an accusatory glance at Barbara. "This is all your doing. You could have lied and told her you would paint him someday, but since you said you never would, she went to do it on her own. It just isn't safe! She was so upset last night I couldn't even console her."

Barbara stood motionless.

Mr. Reaves turned her to him. "It isn't safe for her."

"I'm sorry, Mr. Reaves. I do regret that Mrs. Kays took off on her own, but like I said, that is none of my concern." With that, Barbara stepped away from him, hurrying quickly so he couldn't catch up.

Chapter 38

Weeks passed.

Time moved like molasses for Barbara. Over these weeks, she hadn't seen anyone at all, not her parents, not Mr. Reaves or Mrs. Kays. She didn't even know if Mrs. Kays had returned and Barbara thought of her often.

Barbara was worried about her. Mrs. Kays was Loren's mother and Barbara really shouldn't have been so abrupt with her or with Mr. Reaves, for that matter.

At night, she painted. None of her paintings were like before Loren had died. They lacked a certain spark that had made her previous canvasses masterpieces. Barbara knew it and felt it in every stroke.

She missed Mrs. Kays and Mr. Reaves. Alone was lonely.

Paint could not give her the warmth of another's smile, or the feel of a hug, or the sound of a voice. Isolation was wearing on her, and when the sound of a knock came at her door, Barbara rushed from the studio to the front of the house to answer it. She was hoping it was Mrs. Kays returned or Mr. Reaves.

"Hi," the sheriff said.

Barbara was surprised to see him. She smiled, though, shyly glancing over his handsome face. What interesting features he had; she had forgotten. "Please, come in. Can I get you something to drink?"

"Beer?" he asked. "Just one, I can't get bent."

"Sorry." She sighed. "You'll have to go to the tavern for that. I don't drink a lick, only water and juice.

"I heard Mrs. Kays went to Italy. School is starting next week; do you know if she'll be coming back?"

"She isn't back?" Barbara asked, worriedly.

"No, and people have been wondering about her. I mean, some of the kids' parents and all."

"I see." Barbara guessed he was a bit concerned himself. "Have you seen Mr. Reaves?" he questioned her next.

"No, I haven't seen him either."

"I called his house every day for a week, and when one of his brokers called me, I broke into his house."

"You did that?" Barbara said, curtly. "That was intrusive."

"We have the right when we think someone might be ill. He left a note on the table for you saying he was going to Italy after Aleavia. He said that he would see you when he got back; that's why I'm here."

"I see." Barbara raised a hand to her chest.

"You didn't know?"

"No," she admitted. "Now they're both gone."

"No word then to when they were supposed to return?" The sheriff removed his hat and moved to the sofa. "May I?"

"Of course, have a seat. Make yourself comfortable."

"It's been a long day. A Mary Magdalene on the lam and I had to break up two fights, and then a drunk out in the meadows refused to go when his wife was having a baby at the doctor's."

"You do see a lot of goons in your line of work," Barbara said, understandingly. "That must wear on you after a while."

"Doesn't painting dead soldiers wear on you?" he questioned with a smirk.

She found that smirk quite charming. In fact, she couldn't help but to return the gesture, tilting her chin.

"I'm sorry; that was cold of me seeing about Loren and all. I didn't mean it that way."

"It's been hard."

"There's another reason I came by," he said, glancing down.

"Why's that? I hope not business purposes on your account. I haven't broken any laws, have I?"

"No need to arrest you today. Actually, I was wondering if you'd accompany me to a dinner party."

"A dinner party?" Barbara raised an eyebrow.

"My brother throws one every year. A bit fancy for my taste, but I figured if you were free that night, we could go... as friends. It would get you out and it would really help me out. I'm always teased about going alone every year."

"My husband just died," Barbara reminded, suddenly feeling queasy. "I'm not sure how that would look."

"I should have figured you'd say that." He sighed. "I meant no disrespect. I just thought even widows have friends. It wouldn't even be a date, really; it would be just a dinner."

"Is that what you want us to be, friends?"

"I'd like that," he admitted. "I find you a bombshell of a broad and I think we have a lot in common."

"And what do we have in common?"

"We both like art," he said.

"I thought you browned off."

"How could I not like what you do?"

"I'm not good at friendships," Barbara said, getting up and heading toward the door.

The sheriff rose, putting on his hat. "Have I offended you?"

"No, not at all."

"This is about Mr. Reaves then," he guessed.

Barbara sighed. "I think that what happened to Mr. Reaves was horrible; to be investigated for a crime like murder when you are innocent must have been very hard on him. You pegged him as a wise guy."

"We didn't send him up the river. My department just did its job."

"Yet, you knew that there was no body found in that bay and that he wasn't into drugs or whores. The whole town treated Mr. Reaves so wrongly because of those rumors. You let them believe the worst in him and did nothing to redeem his character."

"Mr. Reaves did that to himself," he said.

"How did he do that? He didn't take drugs. He didn't hire whores, only painters! He didn't kill Bernadett! How did he do that to himself? I tell you how it happened; your department allowed these rumors to continue."

"I'm not supposed to tell you this, but I did go to my sergeant and tell him what was happening to Mr. Reaves five years ago. I suggested that we make a public statement so that some of these rumors would end."

"And what did he say?"

"That it was not fair to Bernadette's family in case he was involved."

"But he wasn't," Barbara said. "He was in love with her."

"She left him at the altar," the sheriff said. "For that, he paid a heavy price. I admit it wasn't fair. That's life."

"That's life?" Barbara barely could believe her ears. "Let me get this straight, the police allowed all this to happen to him and then summed it up as 'that's life.' What justice is that for an innocent man?"

"It wasn't right. I'll be the first to admit it, but what else could I do?"

"More!"

"What? It's not a crime to gossip."

"You saw what was happening in this town. How could you not, living here, knowing how bad it got for Mr. Reaves?" Barbara asked. "I'm afraid I don't find rumors destroying a man's life funny."

"I spoke to those broads on your and his behalf to get them to back off of you."

"What about him? All these years, your department did nothing but allow all these lies to grow and it ruined him." Barbara opened the door. "What else did you do to make sure the town knew the truth?

My teacher even believed them, and it destroyed what friendship they had. You could have corrected the situation by letting the town know that he was innocent instead of letting everyone else make up more."

"He could have moved," the sheriff reminded.

"But then who else would the town have to laugh at?" Barbara showed him the door.

"I made a mistake by coming here," the sheriff decided.

"Believe me, I wish I could be honest with you about how I find you, but in my opinion, we are at odds." Barbara shut the door behind him.

He simply said, "Sorry." He stomped down the steps in a hurry. Then Barbara heard his footsteps coming back to the door. "What do you mean be honest about how you find me?" She didn't reply through the door. "Please, tell me."

"I don't know what you mean," Barbara said.

"I think you like me." By the tone in his voice, Barbara knew he was smiling. "Don't you, Barbara. You're pushing me away just like everyone else."

Quickly, she returned to her studio. She was upset about Mr. Reaves, but mostly because she was angered that a part of her would have admitted to liking the sheriff. She loved Loren and she wouldn't go out with any other man, not even one as attractive as the sheriff. Mr. Reaves would serve as the excuse, for now.

CHAPTER 39

Another week passed and Barbara was so worried she could no longer sleep. She walked past Mrs. Kays' house and knocked, no answer. She then took the dirt path to Mr. Reaves' house. She didn't even stop at the crab apple tree.

When she got to his front door, she noticed it a jar. "I let myself in," she remembered the sheriff said.

She pushed the door open. "Hello, Mr. Reaves?" Inching her way in, she could see that there was no sign of him. From the door, she spied the note on the table and went to see what he had written for her.

Dearest Barbara,

I write this in hopes that you will read it. I've left money for you in a canister in your kitchen, take the money and see a woman named Lucy. She will make sure you get on that plane to Italy. Don't be frightened by her appearance. She's a good-natured girl that will help you. Please come to Italy. I may need your help to bring Aleavia home.

Mr. Reaves.

Barbara put down the letter and hurried for the door. When she opened it, she caught a reflection in the window. Hanging above his mantel was the painting of his grandson. It really was a great piece.

She turned and walked to it. To paint someone so well seemed foreign to her now. How easy it had been to do that piece. She wasn't attached, she realized.

Behind every amazing piece of art comes a great story. Barbara heard Mr. Reaves' voice in her head. Looking down, she noticed a photo album. She guessed that there were more pictures of his grandson. She touched it and then decided that it was too personal for her to thumb through.

What would Mr. Reaves think of her meddling in his things? She pivoted, but her fingers knocked a loose photo from the pages. Barbara quickly bent down to pick it up and flipped it over to stick it back inside. Her eyes hardly focused on it, until she saw Mr. Reaves so young.

She then really looked. He was a young man in this picture. His arm around Bernadett. How incredible a couple they made! The look in their eyes, there was no lying in that. They were in love, young love, that foolish kind of love that she had with Loren. The kind where nothing matters but each other.

How sad, Bernadett fell out of love with him. Then, because of her disappearance, any chance Mr. Reaves had of being with Aleavia had vanished. It hit her then. Aleavia must have dated him before Bernadett! Of course. Barbara sighed. That would make sense. Aleavia hates Bernadett. *She wasn't jealous of my painting her.* She hated that Barbara was painting the woman who he left her for.

With time, everything is answered, even the darkest secrets in the deepest parts of the human heart.

"Breaking and entering now?" A voice came from behind her.

She knew the voice and gasped. "Sherriff, I was invited in." She put down the picture, rushed to the table and held up the note. "See, he left it for me, even you saw that."

"I know." He sneered. "Don't worry; I'm not going to arrest such a *sweet* girl."

"Horsefeathers, you're angry."

"You never answered my question last night."

"Are you following me?" Barbara asked. "It seems you know far too much about me, and everywhere I go, you show up."

"Maybe you're under investigation." The sheriff laughed.

"I don't find that funny," Barbara said.

"Neither do I," he said. "In fact, I don't like being forced to watch you when I know that you don't like me very much."

"I never said I didn't like you," Barbara reminded.

"That I lack compassion for Mr. Reaves, that's all you said." He moved over to her and leaned down. "I'm sorry if it upset you. The more I thought about it, the more I realized you were right. I should have pushed harder to protect Mr. Reaves' reputation. He got a bad rap and it wasn't fair."

"Are you following me?" Barbara backed away.

"Actually, since this morning, I have been. I'm afraid I have some troubling news. You're a victim of a very serious crime," he said.

"Victim?" Barbara gasped. "What are you talking about?"

"Something's gone," he said simply, "missing."

"Missing?" Barbara's heart started to pound. "What's missing— Mrs. Kays or Mr. Reaves? Did they go to Italy and get hurt?"

"Your painting of Bernadett. It was stolen last night from the museum. The director is saying the painting is worth five thousand dollars, which makes this a felony that I have to check out. Both Mr. Reaves and Mrs. Kays are gone and now so is the painting, which is considered your best work."

"I assure you they don't have it." Barbara's knees felt weak. She grabbed the mantel and took a few deep breaths.

"Calm down," he said. "Don't get the vapors."

"You tell me my painting is gone and expect me not to get upset. I'm very upset." Barbara dropped to the ground, fighting desperately to breathe.

"Breathe in, breathe out," he said. "Concentrate on something else for a moment." He took out his wallet and flipped out a picture. "This is a photo of my cat. His name is Frighto. I call him that, because when I got him out of the dump, he was fighting off three other bigger cats for this head of cheese. It was rotten cheese even, but he didn't even care; he just wanted that cheese for his…" Then he stopped and placed a hand on the small of her back. "You look better, just keep breathing."

Barbara started to feel better, and the room stopped spinning. She took the picture and glanced at it. "It's a cat."

"Let me guess? You don't like cats?"

She smiled. "You're wrong. I appreciate the beauty in every animal. I especially like the sounds cats make."

He leaned over and kissed her cheek. He did it so suddenly she didn't have time to react.

She gasped. "What was that for?"

"For being you." He stood and, offering a hand, helped her up. "I promise you, I'll do whatever I can to find your painting."

"Thanks," she said.

"I want to go with you to Italy, but I think I better stick around here and see where the trail leads me. Someone here wants your painting bad enough to take it out of a building with four locks and an armed guard."

"Please find it," she begged. "I know that Bernadett doesn't love him anymore, but that painting shows how much she did, once. It means a lot to me, especially the way I had mist in her eyes."

"I'm not going to stop until I find it. Go be with your family in Italy."

When he went toward the door, Barbara grabbed his hand and said, "We'll have dinner when I get back then."

A smile crossed his lips. "Don't do that just because I'll find your painting."

"Even if you don't," she said. "I want to have dinner with you. I've changed my mind about that."

"You do change your mind a lot, don't you?"

"I shouldn't have been so rude the other day. It's just hard for me... right now, to deal with anyone."

His eyes flashed a hint of surprise, and then he leaned down and kissed her cheek again. "Things are going to get better," he said. "I want to hear all about Italy at dinner when you get back."

Chapter 40

Barbara disembarked and stepped into a new world. The green hills and valleys amazed her, and there was a serenity she hadn't felt since before Loren died.

Men in zoot suits rushed forward to take her luggage, and Barbara thanked them with a smile. The men stuffed her bags into the trunk of a waiting car; Barbara climbed in as the passenger side door was held open for her.

The driver nodded to her, and then started the car down a long dirt path through incredible hills with villas sitting on top. Barbara was in awe of Italy.

She hoped that the reason Mrs. Kays and Mr. Reaves hadn't returned to America was because the scenery was divine and not because something had happened to them. Then she recalled something had. Back home, Mr. Reaves' prized possession—Bernadett's painting was gone.

In a weird way, it was almost a compliment to have a painting stolen. That some person would want her painting so badly that he or she would defy the law and common decency to get it.

Barbara had mixed feelings about this.

On one hand, she felt proud that someone would do whatever it took to get that painting, even glad that Mr. Reaves would not hold so much passion over such a woman who obviously cared so little for him. Perhaps it was good that it was gone.

It somehow gave a light to the dark badness of what had happened to them and their love. Barbara wondered if Bernadett ever loved him. Why hadn't she returned before?

The loss of the painting would devastate Mr. Reaves, though. That was the odd thing about all this, how much Mr. Reaves never got over Bernadett even after he knew she faked her death.

"Good morning," a voice came from the passenger side door.

Barbara had been so entranced with the landscape and her thoughts, she hadn't noticed the car had parked outside a small home. It was a square, two-story house, and on the front door was a painted shield.

"My name is Antonio Bantanria; welcome to my home, Ms. Kays."

"You know me?"

"Yes, I am friends with Lucy. She called yesterday to tell me you'd be arriving, and you'd be heaven sent."

"It's been a long trip," Barbara admitted.

"There is a bed made upstairs, cups of Joe and food in the kitchen."

"I don't want to rest until I find Mr. Reaves or my mother-in-law. Do you know where they are?"

"Of course." He tapped his hat. "They are staying here."

"Hot dog!" Barbara jumped down from the car. A thrill ran through her at the thought of seeing them again. She had missed them so much. How could she have ever sent them away?

"They aren't here now," he announced.

"Oh." Barbara's heart fell.

"Every afternoon they take a car to where Loren's plane went down. I believe Mrs. Kays is painting."

"I see." Barbara felt a twinge of guilt. "Can this driver take me there?" she asked.

"Don't you want to come inside and rest?" he questioned, worriedly. "Such a long trip for a young woman traveling alone."

"Please." Barbara jumped back up into the car.

"Are you sure?"

"It would be just swell," she said and nodded.

The man leaned into the car and spoke to the driver. "Take her."

The car started and Barbara sat back with her heart pounding. She hadn't realized how hard this would be. To see the place Loren died. She pictured the plane crashing into bits and she turned her head so the driver would not see the tears welling in her eyes. This was going to be the most difficult thing she'd ever done.

For a mile or two, the car drove up a hill, and then, when it came to the top, Barbara gazed down on villas overlooking the sea. The water matched Loren's eyes it was so blue. It was a blue she thought she would never see again.

"It's beautiful," the driver said with a broken accent.

"Yes." Barbara wiped her eyes.

"They don't have this in America," the man boasted.

"No," she admitted. "Your country is something an American would never forget."

"War has ruined much," he said, sadly, "but not everything." Barbara smiled. "We are almost there." He drove along the hilltop, around the small town by the sea and stopped in a field.

Among the grasses sat two people on wooden chairs. In front of them was a scorched ground, but no piece of the plane remained. There was a canvas covered by a cloth sitting on an easel in front of the woman.

"The plane was carried off," the man announced.

"What about my husband's body?" Barbara asked.

"Nothing much left of the flyboy." He choked a bit. "It upset the town to see the plane, so we removed the shells and the pieces."

"Shells?" Barbara then knew what he meant; he meant bomb shells.

"I'll park here," the man said. "It's a walk. Watch out for snakes and live eggs that haven't exploded."

Barbara climbed out of the car. At first, she took a few steps in the grass, and glanced down. The warning about snakes made her shiver, but then Barbara glanced up and saw Mr. Reaves turning around.

Seeing his face brought tears to her eyes. It had been far too long since she had seen his friendly, caring smile. She ran to him. He rose from the chair and opened his arms.

By the time she reached him, Barbara was nearly out of breath. Mrs. Kays was standing, and they all embraced in one big swoop of tears mixed with a love that only a family could understand.

"I missed you." Mr. Reaves kissed her forehead.

"I'm sorry," she said. "I was a real bitch kitty to say those things. I love you like a father, too, and I'm so angry at myself for what I said. Can you ever forgive me?" Then she faced her teacher. "Can you forgive me for saying such horrible things? I don't even know why I said them. I missed you both so much."

"Forgotten." Mrs. Kays wiped her eyes.

"You couldn't say anything that could make me go away." Mr. Reaves chuckled then he sat down and continued to stare at the grass.

"That's where he landed," he said, his voice dropping.

"I know." Barbara could barely look.

"I tried to paint it," Mrs. Kays said.

"Well, let me take a look." Barbara went to the canvas and raised the fabric.

What she found below made her step back. Her eyes turned downward as Mrs. Kays took the second seat beside Mr. Reaves. Barbara took in a few breaths and understood completely.

"I've been here weeks and…" Mrs. Kays stopped when Barbara raised her hand.

"I know why." Barbara nodded and glanced back up at the canvas. The blank canvas.

Chapter 41

"I have the picture in my head," Mrs. Kays said. "It's right before me as clear as day. I wanted to paint this scene with Loren in a plane."

"Crashing?" Barbara gasped.

She shook her head. "On the ground safe."

"You wanted to create a different ending." Barbara understood. "Just like I did with Bernadett."

"It doesn't happen that way, does it?" Mrs. Kays picked up the brush. "It just doesn't work out the way we want."

"That's life," Mr. Reaves abruptly said. "The key to it is to let go of the pain and try to find another starting point."

"I want to paint him. I need to have this part of the land forever sealed in my memory." Mrs. Kays trembled. "I want to know what he last saw and that I was a part of it."

"You wanted to be here," Barbara said, understandingly.

"How could this happen?" Mrs. Kays wept. "How could one man's rage kill so many people?"

"I don't know." Barbara wept. "Loren wanted to fight. He wanted to do the right thing."

"He never expected to die." Mrs. Kays sniffled.

"Whoever does?" Mr. Reaves placed his arm on the arm of Mrs. Kays' chair. His fingers caressed the middle of her back.

She glanced over to him with a smile and said, "You have been so kind to be here with me. After all I did to you. I can't imagine why. Both of you, I've been so horrible sometimes I don't know how either one of you puts up with me."

"I could say the same thing," Barbara said.

"I should have told him," Mrs. Kays whispered to Mr. Reaves. "He had the right to know you as his father."

"Your husband was protecting your reputation," Mr. Reaves said. "And his. He was an honorable man who married you when I wouldn't."

"I said yes." Mrs. Kays laid her head on his shoulder.

Barbara could barely fathom what she had just overheard. Mr. Reaves was Loren's father!

"What are you saying?" Barbara kneeled down in front of them.

"Loren was my son," Mr. Reaves announced. "We kept the secret all these years because Aleavia married another man. After he died, I wanted the truth told, but with my reputation, I didn't think Loren would like having me as a father."

Barbara's hands flew in front of her mouth to stifle the cry. "You're his father."

"Which makes you my daughter-in-law. You see, I am your father." Mr. Reaves laid a hand on her shoulder. "That's why I helped you, why I fell in love with all that you are. You are family, my only family."

"So it wasn't that I could paint?" Barbara gasped.

"I only gave you a hand. If you didn't have the talent, none of what happened to you would have."

Barbara hugged him. "You are my father."

"Yes." He held her tightly. "Loren was my only son, and you know what you did for me?"

"What?"

"You gave me the day flying with him on that plane. It was the greatest day of my life and I'll never forget it. Never!"

Mrs. Kays inched over to them, leaning closer. "Thank you. I know Loren never knew the truth, but he met Mr. Reaves because of you and even liked him."

Barbara didn't know what to say. This was almost too much to take in all at once. Sitting on the same field where Loren had died brought such enormous grief, and now to learn that Mr. Reaves was indeed more than just a friend… But then again, he always had been. He had been more of a father to Barbara than her own. She finally had a father who appreciated her talent and her gift of art.

She rose then and walked to the canvas. "I'm no flub-a-dub. Give me the brush."

"But you said you'd never paint him."

"I'll paint the scenery and you paint the plane in front if you like." Barbara tabbed her brush in the color of blue and wiped it across. The color lit up the empty space, and before long, it molded into several trees, the Italian kind that climbed to the sky in a brilliant shade of green.

She colored until her heart ached from crying and from capturing the very space where her husband died. When she got to the clay color of the sand, Mr. Reaves stood and put his hands on her shoulders. Mrs. Kays did the same and it was as if they all were painting the final strokes.

All were crying.

All needed rest but didn't care.

This was far too important for each of them, grieving in their own way. When the background was finished Barbara handed her the brush. "It will dry soon and then you can do the plane."

"No," Mrs. Kays said.

"No?"

Mrs. Kays grabbed her shoulders and spun her around. "Look. Look what you did. Look what magic your fingers created." Tears rolled down her face. "It's the most incredible painting I have ever seen."

Mr. Reaves was beside himself. "It can get no better," he agreed.

Together they took the chairs, the paint and the canvas back through the fields, carrying all to the car parked near the street.

"I got my gift back," Barbara said. "Loren gave it back to me."

"He never left you," Mr. Reaves reminded. "He died loving you."

"I didn't think I could paint this way again," Barbara said. "It felt as if I were alive again."

"I knew you would paint again the way you wanted." Mr. Reaves opened the door for the two women. "This is as good as *Loving Bernadett*. In fact, I believe many would say it is better."

"Oh, that work." Barbara shuddered, remembering.

"Now I think it's time we get back to America," Mrs. Kays said. "I think we did what we came for."

"I agree, Aleavia." Mr. Reaves kissed her hand.

How could she tell Mr. Reaves? Barbara decided to tell him later, perhaps in the morning or on the plane ride back. She would have to find a way to let him know his painting of Bernadett was missing. Someone had stolen it right out of his private collection at the museum.

CHAPTER 42

When Barbara entered the plane, she was not looking forward to the long trip home. The trip to Italy had seemed endless and to travel again so soon after arriving she knew would be difficult.

Mr. Reaves had problems getting up the steps and Mrs. Kays held his arm to steady him. This startled Barbara; the two people she thought would never get along were now almost bosom buddies.

Death can bring even the worst of enemies together.

When they sat down in the small seats, Barbara noticed that Mr. Reaves and Mrs. Kays sat together. Then what she considered a miracle happened, they held hands. Mrs. Kays even smiled when his fingers interlocked with hers.

Barbara closed her eyes and leaned her head back against the seat of the plane. How long it had been since she'd held Loren's hand. Love was a gift. No matter how hard it comes by, it can withstand the test of time, space and even anger for one another. Deep down, Barbara knew Mrs. Kays had always cared about Mr. Reaves. Perhaps that was why it hurt her so much what the town was saying. Yet, she believed the rumors or perhaps she wanted to believe to save herself and her child from public ridicule.

"Will you marry me?" Mr. Reaves said.

Mrs. Kays looked up at him and asked, "Are you sure? What about Bernadett?"

"She never loved me," he said.

Barbara gasped just as the plane started up the runway. She watched as Mr. Reaves pulled out a small box from his jacket and placed the big gold band on her finger. In the center was a large diamond with small red rubies shaped like a heart on each side. Barbara watched as Mrs. Kays kissed him.

Was she dreaming? Barbara wondered. It was so surreal that it seemed impossible.

"I always loved you," Mrs. Kays said. "I never stopped."

"I know," he claimed. "Why else would you have gotten so mad about Bernadett? You were jealous."

"Jealous! I would never be jealous of that hideous beast. She was just… in the way."

Mr. Reaves burst out in laughter. "Okay, then, you weren't jealous."

"I was angry that you still dated Bernadett even after I told you I was pregnant."

"Let's not bring up the past," he said. "From this moment on, let's concentrate on the future, our future with our daughter." He glanced over to Barbara. "I guess I should have asked you for permission to ask her to marry me."

"Don't be ridiculous." Barbara grinned.

"This must surprise you." Mrs. Kays showed her the ring.

Barbara stared at it sparkling from the sun coming in from the windows. "You're right. I'd have to say this is a shock. I thought you two would always hate each other for the rest of your lives. I would have never guessed this."

"I never want to talk about Bernadett again," Mr. Reaves said. "Can we all agree on that?"

Barbara sighed. She wanted to tell him that the painting was gone. Even if he didn't love Bernadett anymore, that painting was valuable, and it had been stolen right out of his museum.

"Promise me?" Mr. Reaves asked of her.

"I… have to…" Barbara tried to find it inside her to tell him but couldn't find the strength nor did she want to ruin the moment.

Mrs. Kays had her head on his shoulder now, staring down at her ring. Even Barbara could tell how in love with him she was. She should have known that all that hatred came from somewhere—a hurt that only someone so in love could ever face.

"Well?" Mr. Reaves questioned. "Do you promise us never to bring her up ever again?"

Barbara knew she had to. It was his property. One of her greatest works and although he may never look upon it again, he had the right to know. He had commissioned it himself.

"All right, but..."

"But nothing," Mr. Reaves interrupted. "I don't want to hear of that woman again. I had this fantasy about her since high school that she was the perfect woman, and I was so wrong, I should have been locked up in the bughouse for crazy people."

"Don't apologize to me for loving her," Barbara said. "I completely understand what happened."

"You do?"

"Yes," Barbara admitted.

"And how could you know when you weren't there?" Mrs. Kays chuckled.

"I can guess," she said, "that you two were in love and dating. Bernadett who always enjoyed Mr. Reaves' attention got jealous and decided to ruin your relationship by finally dating him. By then you were pregnant, but Mr. Reaves who had always had a crush on Bernadett left you for her. Pregnant and scared, you meant another man who agreed to marry you. Mr. Reaves asked Bernadett to marry him, to which she agreed. She waited until you were wed and showing to make the date. On the day she was to marry you, Mr. Reaves, Bernadett took off. The entire town assumed you had her killed, by her disappearance. and then the rumors started."

Mr. Reaves turned to Mrs. Kays. "I do believe she figured it out."

"Attagirl! She did." Mrs. Kays' eyes widened.

"This was all a rouse to get you two not to marry. Now, although, I believe Bernadett did care for you, Mr. Reaves..."

"Call me Father," Mr. Reaves said.

Barbara swallowed. "Father, I believe that she really put it upon herself to decide that if she couldn't have you, no one else would. She didn't want you to be successful. Once she had you, she moved on and didn't even help after your life was destroyed. Bernadett was ego-filled but vindictive. Your attention is what drove her to do it. She had to have it and when you commissioned the painting, she had to see it with her own eyes that she had won."

"You know then," Mr. Reaves concluded. "Now let's never speak of her again, ever. I do believe my wife and I have lost enough time because of her."

"There's just one problem," Barbara alerted. "*Loving Bernadett* has been stolen and the sheriff is now looking for who stole it."

Their gazes locked, her father's filled with rage, then the feelings diminished, and he sat back. "I shouldn't care about that now."

"The painting is gone?" Mrs. Kays shook her head.

"You sound more disappointed than I," Mr. Reaves said, aghast.

"It's just a fine piece of art," Mrs. Kays admitted. "Barbara's greatest piece, and I would hate to think it is in a hand that might do it harm. Don't get me wrong, I never want to hang it up in our house, but I can see why it holds such fascination."

"How important you are to have some painting stolen." Mr. Reaves smiled openly. "That is the first time the museum has ever been robbed."

"It is?" Barbara said.

"As long as I have been on the board," Mr. Reaves announced. Of course, the person who stole it might have reason."

Barbara suddenly knew what he meant! "Bernadett stole the painting. Of course! Your love for her drove her to commit the harshest of crimes. What is stealing a painting! Bernadett stole it so she would keep it as a trophy of your love for her that she had broken up your relationship."

"She may have taken years out of our lives," Mr. Reaves said. "But she hasn't won anything. We are still together, bonded, closer in fact. If anything, we know who to trust and who not to more now than ever."

"Perhaps we should move," Mrs. Kays said. "I could teach in the city and then we wouldn't have to deal with the people who think so low of you."

"No one runs me out of my hometown, not even the President of the United States. This is my home." Mr. Reaves tapped his cane. "I'm not running from anybody, especially from her."

"Good for you both," Barbara said. "I do believe this is a start of an incredible marriage and family."

"Yes," Mr. Reaves leaned over and grabbed her hand, "Daughter."

"When we get home, I will tell the sheriff my theory on Bernadett, and then we will never speak her name again."

"Promise," Mr. Reaves repeated.

"With all my heart, I promise. And you know what? I admired you more every day that you loved her, even despite what she did to you. That only shows how great a person you are, that you can love unconditionally like that. Those who can't see it are fools. You are a good man, Father. A good fella who I am proud will marry Mother. Loren would be so happy for the both of you."

Mrs. Kays wiped her eyes and said, "I think you are right. When he took Mr. Reaves out for that plane ride, he wrote to me several times on how much fun he had taking you both. That he liked Mr. Reaves and that it was a great time for all three of you that day."

"I will keep those letters until the end of time," Mr. Reaves said.

"Then it is agreed," Barbara announced.

"It is." Mrs. Kays sighed. "Bernadett will not stop us from having a future. She has stopped us for far too long." She brightened for a moment. "Maybe she'll rot in the hoosegow, now that she's on the lam."

"No," Mr. Reaves said. "I wouldn't want that for her."

Barbara knew no matter what, he would always care for Bernadett. Putting her in the past was what was best, though, and Barbara admired his strength for doing so.

"Me either. She's miserable enough. She just lost the one man who is capable of more love than she will ever know, and she'll have to live with it."

CHAPTER 43

Barbara slept most of the trip home, and when the plane arrived in America, she was very happy to set foot on solid ground. Mr. Reaves had parked his car at his friend Lucy's house, which he collected and drove them back into town.

Barbara wanted to speak to the sheriff but didn't dare want to bother Mr. Reaves and Mrs. Kays anymore. They were cuddling and holding hands, discussing what kind of small wedding they wanted.

When the car turned the corner on her street, Mr. Reaves said, "The sheriff is out front."

Barbara was pleased. "Good."

"Should we see him, too," Mrs. Kays asked.

"Why worry?" Mr. Reaves grinned. "I think we have more important things to discuss, like how long it will take you to move into my home."

When the car parked, the sheriff got out of his and went around to the driver's side. "I need to speak to all of you, inside."

"That decided that," Mr. Reaves complained.

They exited the vehicle and walked up the steps. Barbara pulled out her house key and noticed that the door was open. She moved in and saw that Bernadett was sitting on the sofa in handcuffs; the painting lay on the coffee table.

"I found her inside," the sheriff announced. "I was driving down the street last night and noticed your studio light on in the back. I thought you were home, so I walked up and noticed the lock broken. It didn't take me long to catch her."

"Why was she here?" Barbara asked, then she decided, "To get more paintings."

"I didn't take any more!" Bernadett said.

"Then why did you break into my house?" Barbara asked her.

"I merely wanted to know if you were painting another portrait of me, that's all."

"This painting," the sheriff pointed to *Loving Bernadett*, "I found in her car trunk along with a train ticket to Boston."

"I was returning it," Bernadett said. "I borrowed it for photographs and then I was going to bring it back. I didn't think I'd be caught."

Barbara wondered how much of that was true. She knew Bernadett loved the painting. She would because she was the subject, but how much did she want it, bad enough to steal it forever, or just photograph it for mementoes?

Bernadett struggled to stand in handcuffs, and then she rushed over to Mr. Reaves. "Thomas, talk to the sheriff."

"That ship sailed long ago," he said.

Bernadett turned to Mrs. Kays in desperation. "Aleavia, please!"

"You should be in prison for breaking and entering, faking a death, stealing a painting… what's next?" Mrs. Kays glared at her.

"I'm not a criminal." Bernadett's voice was a roar. "This is insane."

"I would like you to come down to the station and press charges, Mr. Reaves," the sheriff said. "For stealing from your museum collection."

"A ride into town would be lovely this afternoon."

"Thomas, you couldn't!" Bernadett gasped.

"I would love to accompany you." Mrs. Kays stuck on a pair of sunglasses. "It is an incredible day for a long journey."

"Barbara," the sheriff added, "I need you, too, to sign a paper that she broke into your home."

"What will happen to her?" Barbara asked.

"I'd imagine for both crimes at least a year in prison," he replied.

Barbara glanced up at him. The pride of catching the criminal showed across his handsome face. He was proud he had figured out the crime and that he had done exactly what he had promised. She was impressed, but still didn't hate Bernadett enough to send her to prison. In fact, Barbara even felt sorry for her.

"What's that?" Bernadett noticed Mrs. Kays' hand and the ring. "Finally got a chump to wed you?"

"Actually, we're engaged again." Mrs. Kays wrapped her arm around Mr. Reaves' arms.

"Are you?" The sheriff slapped him on the back. "Congratulations! Isn't that the best news?"

Mr. Reaves grinned from ear to ear, but then he turned and saw Bernadett. The pain was evident. The fear had turned to pain; her body lost its life and her eyes deadened from every word.

Barbara wouldn't wish that kind of pain on anyone. Bernadett, despite her horrible ego that landed her in so much trouble, did love him back… once. Mr. Reaves must have seen her expression change, too, because the smile lowered just a bit.

"What's wrong, don't you think someone would find me attractive even if you don't anymore?" he asked Bernadett.

"No, it isn't that," she said. "Sherriff, please uncuff me, please."

The sheriff looked over at Mr. Reaves, took a step forward and unlocked the cuffs. Bernadett wrapped her arms around Mr. Reaves and started to cry. Mrs. Kays, her hatred for Bernadett dimmed, stepped out the door to give them some privacy.

"Don't marry her," Bernadett begged.

"You only want me when there's another woman involved," he said.

"That's not true. I love you. It's just I hate this town and you would never leave."

"Then you go where you want." He backed away and went to the painting. "I love another woman now."

"No, you don't. When things got bad you couldn't depend on Aleavia. She didn't believe you," Bernadett reminded.

"And you never saved me either from shame. Did you? You were too busy with those flyboys in the big city to ever think twice about me," he said.

"That isn't true. I thought about you every year, especially around the holidays. I wanted you to be happy. I wanted that more for you than this town and these dreadful people."

"This is my town. These are my people whether they like me or not. I have a daughter now, and I am going to live my life the way I want," he said.

Barbara felt as if she was eavesdropping. The sheriff must have, too, because he took her hand and began to lead her out the door to wait near Mrs. Kay on the stoop.

"Wait, Barbara," Mr. Reaves said. "I hate to ask this of you, Honey, but will you drop the charges against her?"

"I never would have pressed them anyway," Barbara admitted.

"I'm not pressing any either," Mr. Reaves informed the sheriff.

A wave of disappointment washed across his face then the sheriff nodded. "I understand. This is more of a family matter."

"You're not sending me to jail?" Bernadett's eyes widened in surprise.

"Of course not. I love you, you foolish girl," Mr. Reaves admitted. "A part of me always will. You want the painting, right?"

"I like seeing myself the way you saw me," Bernadett cried out.

"Then," he reached down and took the painting, "if Barbara will allow it, I'll let you have it."

"It's worth a fortune!" the sheriff reminded. "It's Barbara's finest work. You couldn't possibly give it to this thief!"

"She's not just a thief to me," Mr. Reaves said.

"Only if you come with the painting," Bernadett begged. "Just forget about Aleavia and come with me to Boston. We could be so happy. I have this big house near the lighthouses, and you can watch the sailboats all day. I bought it even thinking about you."

Mr. Reaves leaned down and kissed her cheek. "Take the painting. I can't look at it anymore."

"You hate me that much?"

"No, I love you that much," he said, tears in his eyes. "I finally realized you aren't the one I'm supposed to be with. However, I would really, really, really, like to be friends even if we never see each other again."

"I want to see you."

"Perhaps when you get over this," Mr. Reaves said.

"Then I never will see you again." Bernadett held him, embracing him in her arms. "I admit I hated you, I loved you, I cared for you, I cried for you, and I would die for you if need be. Don't let this be it."

"Take the painting." Mr. Reaves backed away and handed it to her. "Remember how much you meant to me. Forget the bad. Bad always happens when two people love each other."

"Love doesn't end."

"It hasn't ended." Mr. Reaves started to cry. "It's just changed places, that's all, to another section of my heart where it will remain for the rest of my life."

Bernadett sat down on the sofa. Her hands rushed to her face as tears streamed down her cheeks.

"Excuse me, Honey," Mr. Reaves moved past Barbara. "It's time I finally took Aleavia home."

He walked out without saying goodbye to Bernadett. Barbara guessed it wasn't a goodbye and there would never be one. It was better to leave things like that, open. Things not said, things not known. That was the right thing to do for all concerned.

Mr. Reaves took Mrs. Kays by the arm and escorted her to the car. There he helped her up and drove off down the street. Bernadett couldn't watch. The sheriff stayed put. Barbara couldn't watch Bernadett cry over the portrait.

Art had mimicked life.

With true love, it had always done.

Behind every great piece of art is great pain. Mr. Reaves' words echoed in her head.

For half an hour the woman cried, until finally, she thanked them both, took the painting and walked out of the room. Barbara didn't need to ask if she would take care of it; she knew Bernadett would treasure it always. At times, Barbara guessed the painting would be just left somewhere where Bernadett couldn't even see it, but that was all right. It was hers now.

"What a day." The sheriff sighed. "You okay?"

"It's been a long week," Barbara said.

"I'll let myself out." He headed toward the door.

"I'll see you on Friday."

"Friday?" he questioned.

"The wedding, I'd like you to escort me."

He nodded with a smile. "Good thing I bought that jacket."

"I know. You've already had two uses for it already." Barbara walked over to him and gave him a hug. "Thanks for finding my painting. At least I know that it will be fine where it is, and someone appreciates it."

"All that work to give it to the thief." The sheriff chuckled.

"Then she's not a thief after all." Barbara laughed. "Besides, everything always comes out in the wash."

"I hope so, because I got this wine stain on my shirt collar." The sheriff walked down the steps with a smile. "See you Friday."

Chapter 44

The wedding took place in Barbara's backyard. The sun was setting, and lines of crows sat on her roof as the music of the band played out. The moment after the kiss, Mr. Reaves grabbed a bottle of wine from a nearby table, rushed back to his bride and said this toast:

"For my friends that are few, Thanks for coming.

For those who didn't show, Thanks for not.

And for those who love us, Let them know,

We married today so that our love will forever grow."

The few that came rose and cheered; glasses were tossed into the creek symbolizing that nothing could break their love. And then, the band began to play, and they danced: Barbara with the sheriff, the newly wed Mr. and Mrs. Reaves.

Barbara with the sheriff, Mr. Reaves and Mrs. Kays. What a celebration it was!

* * * *

"What a celebration it was." Aunt Barbara's voice cracked from talking so long. "That sunset was so amazing. It was as if God knew this was an artist's wedding, so He made the sky twice as colorful. It almost seemed like Loren was watching from up above, making the sky so beautiful for them."

"Did Bernadette show up?" Mia asked her Great Aunt Barbara, raising the glass for her aunt to drink. "Did she ruin it?"

Her aunt took a sip and Mia sat back to listen.

"No, Thomas didn't see Bernadett again for many years, but they did run into each other at a gallery. They hugged and it was a good meeting, I was told. They were still friends."

"And what of the painting of Bernadett," Nathan asked.

Great Aunt Barbara turned her head and announced, "It landed up in a museum in New York City where it still hangs today. Bernadett had connections, too."

Mia clapped. "That was such a great story!"

"And it's true, Dear." Great Aunt Barbara laughed. "That's the funny thing about life. Real life is always better than fiction."

"And what of the sheriff; did you ever date him?" Mia's husband wondered.

"Yes, for many years we were together, but Loren was my first love. That's why I want you to have the painting Aleavia and I did of Italy. It hangs in the hallway."

"You want me to have it?" Mia's hands flew up in glee.

"Yes," Great Aunt Barbara said. "It's what I leave you."

Mia got up and walked into the hallway. She found the picture with the landscape. It was unsigned, but it was the most incredible painting Barbara had ever seen. It had the tall trees that reached the sky and tall grass. They didn't put in the burn spot. Nor did this perfect picture need the plane either; Loren was in every detail.

Knowing how much this was a treasure to her Aunt, Mia removed the painting from the wall, clasped it close to her chest, and walked back into the room where her Aunt lay waiting.

"I will hang this in my house," Mia said.

Her husband rose and thanked Great Aunt Barbara with a kiss to the cheek.

Her aunt shut her eyes and started to snore. The four of them rose from around the bed, walked out into the garden and watched the sun set. In Mia's thoughts was the wedding of Thomas and Aleavia.

She pictured them dancing underneath the orange and red colors that lit up the sky. "Loren's beautiful sky," Mia said to her husband.

"Looks like he wanted to make it come back again tonight."

CHAPTER 45

The next morning Mia woke up early, crept out of the guest room and checked in on her aunt. Her nurse had already given her coffee with a straw. Mia could smell it the moment she walked into the living room.

Mia gazed out through the giant picture window and noticed the woodpecker clutching a tree not far in the distance.

"Isn't that a bird?" her aunt commented. "What a big one."

"Thank you, again, for telling me about Loren, Aleavia, and Thomas."

"Do you like the painting?" her aunt asked, insecurely.

"More than words can ever say," Mia admitted.

"That's quite a compliment coming from a writer." Her aunt smiled, having a difficult time moving her head to see her.

Mia inched forward so her aunt wouldn't have to struggle. "It's wonderful to learn about your life."

"You should write about it," her aunt said.

"I can't."

"Why, because of what your ex-husband, the Literary Agent said!" Aunt Barbara raised her voice. "Do what I said and show them you're the shit!"

That stunned Mia and she sat down. "Please don't get upset over this. What's done is done. I was spit out before I was ever given the chance to prove myself."

"Do you know why I picked that story to tell you? Believe me, I got hundreds of paintings and many tales to tell." Aunt Barbara gazed deeply into her eyes. "I told you that one and gave you that painting, not because I wanted you to write it, but because I wanted you to learn about Mr. Reaves particularly."

Mia wondered. "Why your father-in-law?"

"Because he had so many against him, too; for years he was right where you are now. I know how you feel, defeated. You're depressed. You think your whole life is coming to a stop because they are kicking you when you are down."

"You can only kick a dog so much before it doesn't come back, or it doesn't get back up. I'm not getting back up this time." Mia fought back her emotions.

"Nonsense, you're letting the bullies win."

"I have no choice. I could write forever and that ex-husband of mine will destroy every chance I ever had of having my work known. He hates me that much! He told the whole world I couldn't write and that I was a joke!"

"No one owns the literary world, but the fans," her aunt reminded. "You've been through a lot; there's going to be a break someday. It will come."

"He's got a lot of friends that hate me in all the right places."

"Bernadett did, too, in that town. Mr. Reaves' life turned around. I almost quit painting myself after Loren died, but we were put on this earth with gifts that we've got to use. That's what needs to be done."

"I'm finished, Auntie. That book has been written."

"You're not done with the craft until you can't lift a hand like me." Aunt Barbara started to cry. "When you get like me, when you can't lift a pen, that's the only time I'll allow you to quit; do you hear me? Don't you dare take the gift you were given for granted. Not everyone can write like you."

Mia fought back every tear to stand strong. "I can't take it anymore. I can't take those reporters making fun of my work; it's hard. Fame isn't what I thought it was going to be. Being married to him showed me exactly what it was like; if you're not on top, you're not anywhere but a joke."

"You got me, don't you? I believe in you," Aunt Barbara said. "In that top drawer is a gold sailboat pendant on a chain. I want you to wear it, to know, someday your ship is going to come in."

"You don't have to keep giving me things, Auntie." Mia took the necklace, placed it around her neck and sighed. "I love you, regardless. You remind me so much of my grandmother."

"I'm not going to be here much longer."

"Don't say things like that." Mia touched her hand even though she knew her aunt couldn't feel it.

"I tell all my friends about your writings and show them those articles you've had published in all those fancy magazines. I'm so proud of you. You are an artist like me, and I know what it's like to be down. Your ex- husband is just like Bernadett. That's what the problem is. It isn't fame or money that's hurting you so much. It's the fact you never got over him. Let him go and write. Write for me. Write for yourself and someday the whole world will read you."

"Thanks, Aunt Barbara, for believing in me."

"Behind every great piece of art is great pain. Remember that. My second father told me that."

"My life is more than a sad story. I can't write them anymore."

Aunt Barbara said. "You've got a great new husband now. You've got lots of people who do love you and think you're great; concentrate on them. Follow your dreams."

Suddenly, the side door opened, and Nathan appeared. "Well, you both are up early," he said.

Aunt Barbara gasped. "Promise me, that you'll not quit."

"Not in front of my cousin," Mia whispered. "He doesn't know."

"He should. The whole world should know what almost happened because of that guy who only thinks of himself."

"Quit what?" Nathan grabbed the container of coffee and poured himself a cup.

"Promise me," Aunt Barbara said. "I can't get up to shake you, but if I had the strength, I would."

"I'll try." Mia did, wiping her eyes.

"Now what's going on here?" Nathan asked.

Aunt Barbara grinned from ear to ear. "I have a painting for Toby and you."

"You do?" He raised a brow.

"See that painting of a woman in the hallway?" Aunt Barbara asked. "It's yours if you want it."

"Thank you." Nathan leaned down and kissed her cheek. "We'll love it."

"I painted that a long time ago. That's one of my best friend."

"Really?" Nathan sat down. "And who was she?"

"Oh, my." Aunt Barbara grinned. "Now that's a whole other story. Go get the others, pull up some chairs. This is going to be another great day for us all."

ABOUT THE AUTHOR

*M*ichele Wallace Campanelli has had nine stories which have appeared on the best-sellers list, including two that reached #1 on the New York Times. She lives in Florida and is a graduate of Writers Digest School, Keiser College and Brevard Community College.

Her short stories have been included in over 30 anthologies. She has also penned numerous novels, screenplays, magazine and newspaper articles in both fiction and non-fiction. She's been published by Simon & Schuster, Chronicle Books, Adamsmedia, HCI and America House Publishing. An estimated over fifty million have read her work internationally.

When she isn't writing, Michele is CEO of Regal PA & Entertainment Services LLC which performs concerts in Central Florida. She enjoys singing, writing and acting.

Prologue

Jyres exited his hut in the morning and went into the village to see what all the commotion was about. He was not surprised at all to see two knights on horseback in the middle of the village. Jyres decided to go closer so he could hear what they were talking about with Hans, the village leader, who had gone out to talk to them. Jyres wondered what the knights wanted this time. He joined the small crowd of people who had gathered and heard the knights were again making demands of the villagers. Hans was doing his best to satisfy the knights without giving in to them. Then one of the knights brought his hand back as if he was going to strike Hans, and Hans stepped back.

"Provide me with your monthly quota of supplies, or I will tell Meslar you are not cooperating," said one of the knights. The knight laughed to himself, knowing that Hans would have to give in. Hans knew it too, and he ordered the set quota to be brought out. It was two baskets full of food from the recent fall harvest and a small bowl of healing salve. The salve was made from a mixture of sand, water, and the roots of a cactus that grew in the desert that had been discovered to have healing properties. Satisfied, the knights took the baskets and trotted the horses out of the village.

Hans turned to face the crowd of people. "Today we did not have a choice but to listen to their demands. But I tell you, somehow our luck will change, and our hard work will pay off." Hans looked over the crowd and knew they were unsure about his words but hopeful that he was right.

After the crowd cleared, Jyres approached Hans. Hans was an older man, maybe just past sixty years, and had led the village for almost twenty. He smiled at Jyres, but Jyres could see the worry in his eyes. "I don't know, Jyres, I just don't know," the gray-haired man said. "Something has got to be done." He patted Jyres on the shoulder and walked away toward his hut.

1

The Week of Peace

The sun was starting to go down. He knew it was time to go. Alhazar was a long way to travel, but he was determined to get there. Jyres collected his things and set out at a fast pace toward the Catastrophic Cliffs. He knew he had to hurry, because if the Knights of Enchantment found out what he was up to, he would be in a heap of trouble. If he could just get to the cliffs, he would be safe.

Even though nightfall had come over the land, it was still hot. The human village where Jyres lived is right outside the Desert of Despair. Although it had quite the desperate name, it was not an inhospitable place. While it was dry and hot, only in summertime could it live up to its name. By heading to the cliffs, Jyres could avoid going right through the desert that was wide open with only sand dunes to hide or take shelter by if needed. He took a swig from his canteen and continued his march toward the cliffs.

The dwarven folk had made their home in the cliffs in recent years. They used to live in the Alhazar Mountains, but they were overrun by orcs and goblins. Jyres had never seen an orc or goblin before, only heard the stories. Stories his uncle used to tell him of those horrible creatures who killed and destroyed anything in their path.

Jyres was of average height for a human and had a medium build. He wore a plain white shirt and dark pants and had an old sword hanging at his hip. His muscles were not busting out of his shirt, but he was not skinny either. His hair was fairly dark, but not quite black, and his face was handsome looking, but because of hard work over the years, he looked older than what he was, which was twenty. His eyes were a rich-colored blue, and living in the desert underneath the hot sun had darkened his skin.

It was very dark now as Jyres continued his walk. He was very tired and could no longer see the cliffs because it was so dark. He had to hope he was still going straight toward them. He knew he had to press on and that he had to get to Alhazar. Hans had said something had to be done, and Jyres knew it too. The Knights of Enchantment had oppressed them for long enough. He would represent his people at the meeting.

The region of Alhazar always held a meeting around the same time every year. The creatures of both Tomackus and Alhazar were invited. The humans had never been truly represented however, because the knights and their leader, Meslar, saw to it that they were the ones to represent the human village at the meeting.

Suddenly, Jyres could hear something in the distance. He listened closely. *Thump, thump.* It was the sound of hoofbeats. There were after him. Jyres mustered up all his strength and ran straight into the darkness. Up ahead, he could now make out the cliffs; he had managed to stay on course; if he could only make it to the cliffs before the chasers were upon him.

*****

Lalatco peered into the forest. It was a pretty quiet night tonight; it was the day before the week of peace. No one ever came through the forest at this time. If you participated in anything that can be considered nonpeaceful during the week of peace, the dragons hunted you down. Lalatco often wondered why the dragons were seen as the rulers of the world. There were only two of them. Sure, the dragons were powerful, but they were greatly outnumbered. Lalatco often wondered if he could stand up to a dragon. He had heard many legends of dragon slayers, who existed when the humans ruled the world. Lalatco laughed at the thought of this. Humans were so weak compared to the elves, and even more so when compared to the dragons. If legends were true, however, the humans once had an empire beyond the Alhazar Mountains and rivaled the power of the dragons.

Lalatco was fair looking, as all elves are, and had long hair that was almost white in color but often appeared to take on a soft version of the strongest color near him. He was very slender, but fine-tuned muscles hid under his thin shape. His eyes were a dark green as if they were meant to match the color of the trees. He wore a long-sleeved light-green shirt and dark green pants as many of the elves did.

Lalatco left the tower and headed down to the main complex. The elves had made a nice home among the trees; their wooden structures kept getting bigger and bigger. As he walked, he exchanged greetings with those he passed. Lalatco was a respected warrior, and others often sought him out, including the young elves who wanted to learn from him. Lalatco proceeded to the throne room to find both the king and the queen there and gave a bow as a sign of respect. As usual, both the king and the queen were wearing long cloaks that went all the way to their feet. The king's cloak was a dark green, and the queen's was white. The queen also wore a small golden crown in her hair, and the king's sword lay at his feet.

"How can I help you, Lalatco?" asked King Malick.

"I was just wondering who all will be making the trip to the Valley of the Dragons." Lalatco really wanted to go this year and was hoping the king would tell him he was.

Malick responded in a rather serious tone, "Rumor is that the dragons have some important news to share, so I must attend. I have not decided who I will bring with me. I will let you know if I need your services."

Lalatco then asked, "Who from the other races will be in attendance this year?"

Malick replied rather quickly, "The dragons are expecting Vurth, Demorous, and I, and even a representative from the orcs and the goblins, so pretty much everybody."

"If I am needed, I am eager to serve my king." With that, Lalatco bowed again and left with a disappointed feeling but tried not to let it show.

*****

The sounds of horses kept getting closer and closer as Jyres kept running. Then from out of nowhere, a massive creature grabbed Jyres from behind. A shout of surprise was stuck in Jyres's dry throat. Jyres's fear of the creature was displayed on his face as the creature roughly forced Jyres onto his back. The creature ran much faster than the speed at which Jyres had been running and soon was at the cliffs and started to climb. The beast had claws that drove into the side of the cliffs as the creature climbed with Jyres on his back. A little ways up the cliffs, the creature stopped and sat on a ledge. Jyres got down from the creature's back and sat down a few feet away from the mighty beast, still unsure of its intentions. Both of them looked down at the horses and their riders who were now at the bottom of the cliffs.

One of those riders shouted, loud enough for them to be able to hear, "Vurth, come out here! There is someone hiding in your cliffs, and we want him!" Jyres recognized the voice; it was Demorous, the leader of the Knights of Enchantment, who was also known as Demorous the Fierce. He was calling for Vurth, the head of the dwarves who are residents of these cliffs.

The creature, while still gazing down at the horses, asked in a deep voice, "Why are they after you?"

Jyres, who was almost as afraid of the creature as he was of the knights, was slow to answer. Eventually, he said, "They think of me as their slave. They try to enforce a curfew on us."

He then quickly asked, "What are you, and why did you help me, or I hope that is what you did?" The fear was still evident in his voice.

The creature responded in that same deep voice, "I am a gargoyle, and you seemed to be in trouble. You have no reason to fear me."

The gargoyle was very large, larger than anyone or anything Jyres had ever seen. His pale-green skin seemed to enhance his mammoth size, and his wings that stuck out behind him were a deeper green color than his skin. The creature folded his wings in around him, covering his back and touching each other over his shoulders and under his neck. Around his neck, he donned a small medallion of silver color and square in shape.

Inside the caves of the cliffs, Vurth could hear the shouts of Demorous. He did not care very much though, because the coming morning would start the week of peace. Vurth did not want to subject his dwarves to any punishment from the dragons. He was, however, unsure of whom Demorous was talking about. Vurth called a few of his soldiers and sent them looking for whoever else had taken home in their cliffs.

After some time had passed, Vurth lost his patience, and eventually he went out to send Demorous away. Vurth exited the dwarves' caves and walked toward the knights along with a couple of other dwarves. "What do you want, Demorous? Whatever it is, come back in a week, and then maybe I will help you. It is the week of peace. Now get out of here." Vurth turned away and started to walk back to the caves in the cliffs.

Demorous replied in an angry voice, "Vurth, come back here! Don't walk away from me. Vurth! Vurth! You will pay for this, Vurth, you will pay." With that, the knights turned and headed back across the desert as Vurth made his way back to his room.

*****

"Listen, do you hear that? It sounds like someone is coming. Get on." The gargoyle looked over at Jyres and got down on all fours.

Jyres heard the noise too; dwarves usually were not very quiet. With a slight hesitation, Jyres climbed onto the gargoyle's back, who then extended his wings and leaped into the wind and rose above the cliffs.

"You can fly! Wow!" Jyres yelled in astonishment.

Gargan responded, "I cannot fly, not like a bird anyway. I glide. I need the wind to fly. What is your name, human?"

"My name is Jyres. What is yours?"

The gargoyle said something Jyres could not understand and then went on, "Gargoyles have their own language, but humans once called me Gargan." After a while, Gargan then asked Jyres where he wanted to be taken.

Jyres had to think about this, because he really did not have much of a plan beyond getting to the cliffs. "I need to go to Alhazar," he finally answered.

"What is Alhazar?" Gargan asked.

Jyres did not know what to say in response to this, so he told him just to land somewhere safe where they could talk.

Although he didn't know the names of the lands, Gargan continued to glide over the hills of Tomackus and into Alhazar. Jyres looked down to see the rolling hills. From his perch, they looked nothing more than bumps on a brownish-green backdrop. Gargan continued through Alhazar to the Alhazar Mountains where he swooped down and landed. They landed on the mountains at the edge of Alhazar. The mountains went on for quite a while; no one Jyres knew, besides the dragons, had ever been on the other side.

Jyres found himself happy to have his feet back on solid ground and said as much. "Well, that was an adventure. Not sure if I was born to be in the air."

Gargan simply said in a matter-of-fact way, "Of course you were not—you have no wings."

Jyres smiled and shrugged and took in their surroundings. They had landed in the mountains, on a natural overlook. Not interested in being anywhere close to the edge at the moment, Jyres walked away a few paces and sat down with his back against the rock face. Gargan came and joined him.

"So," started Jyres, "what is a gargoyle?"

Gargan thought about that for a second, perhaps unsure of how to answer the question before he said, "A gargoyle is a race that has been in the shadows. Long have we been content in our home. We are strong, determined, patient, and have a storied past. Each one of us is unique. No two gargoyles are the same. Some of us have true wings like dragons. Others glide as I do. Still others cannot fly or glide at all. But there is one thing that each gargoyle has in common."

Jyres, listening intently to his every word, said, "What is that one thing?"

"I tell you this in necessity. Every gargoyle's energy is sapped by the sun. We cannot live under the sun as you do. During the day, we must protect ourselves, and our bodies do that for us. You will see this soon, and that is why I share it with you."

"I don't understand. How can that be?"

"You will see."

Just then, the sun had started to rise, and the first rays of sunlight started to shine over the land. Gargan got down on one knee, looking toward the sun. Jyres was just about to ask what he was doing when Gargan instantaneously turned to what looked like stone as the sunlight hit him. Jyres did not know what was going on. Gargan's green skin had turned to a dark gray. He called to Gargan, trying to talk to him, but it was no use. Gargan was as motionless as the rock cliff they stood on.

Jyres examined the huge creature, now statue, which had just been gliding him to safety. Gargan had an almost square face, its features very distinguishable on the statue. Jyres was impressed by the creature's very defined muscles and large legs, an indication of how powerful he must be. Jyres walked a circle around Gargan, and while at the back of the creature, he marveled at its massive wings. He had seen them in use and now was able to see them close-up in their what looked like stone form. The wings were connected to his back, folded in, and they partially went around the gargoyle when they were not in use. Jyres completed his circle and remained astonished. The creature was nothing like Jyres had ever seen.

2

Travelers

Vurth was awake with the sun; he knew he had much to do today. The dwarves made a horse and a donkey ready to go and packed everything that the travelers would need. Vurth and two other dwarves were getting ready to set out for the Valley of the Dragons. Depending on which way the dwarves went, the trip could be long or really long. Vurth had decided they were going to take the shorter way. During the day, the goblins and orcs kept to the mountains so the three dwarves were going to go right over the hills of Tomackus. Even if they did not clear the hills by evening, the goblins and orcs should not attack because it was the week of peace. Even they should know that is one thing creatures do not do. The punishment was too much to bear. With Vurth on the donkey and the two others on the horse, they set out toward the Valley.

Soon morning turned into day as the travelers stopped by a stream to fill up their canteens and rest the animals.

"Vurth, look, two knights riding this way," said one of the dwarves.

Vurth responded in a confident voice, "It is probably Demorous on his way to the meeting, and he is trying to catch up to us because of last night. Do not worry about him; he is not as tough as he looks."

The two dwarves' confidence grew by just looking at their leader. Vurth's hard-set face and piercing stare showed the dwarves he was ready for anything Demorous the Fierce would throw at him. Vurth had always been a good leader. He was a stubborn dwarf, even by dwarven standards, but he knew how to lead his people. Vurth had a long orange beard, which was peculiar, seeing that the rest of his hair was the color gray. He often tucked his long beard under his brown belt, which matched the color of his long coat he often wore over his chest plate. He was on the taller end of the average height of a dwarf but was still only about four feet tall.

The dwarves were soon ready and began crossing the hills. The two knights were not too far behind and would catch up shortly.

"Vurth, are you not scared of me? Why aren't you running? I told you, you will pay, and you will right now." Demorous kept yelling words of intimidation to Vurth.

Before long, Vurth had had enough; he stopped and waited for the two knights. The knights, as always, were fully armored from head to two in fine silver armor. Demorous trotted his horse up next to Vurth and his donkey. Demorous drew his sword from its sheath and stared down at the dwarf though his helmet. Vurth had not thought Demorous was really truly upset, but he must have been wrong. Demorous the Fierce was not just playing one of his games; he was irate and showing how he had earned his name. Demorous continued his stare when out of the caves of the not far-off mountains, many goblins rushed on to the hills toward the five warriors.

Vurth knew they were all in trouble and barked out directions, "Everyone to the top of the next hill. We will be able to fend them off from there." The dwarves and knights forced their animals to run to the top of the hill. "Now hold your ground. Do not let them see fear. Show them you are not afraid. Intimidate them." After saying this, Vurth grabbed hold of his ax and sat ready on his donkey.

All five of them ready, they stared down at the approaching mob of goblins. The multitude of goblins filled the warriors' vision and flooded their ears with shrieks. Vurth's companions were frightened at first, but one look at Vurth and they forgot that in a hurry. Just before the goblins were about to strike, an almighty dragon descended from the sky and opened his maw. The goblins saw him coming and retreated faster than they had charged. The dragon unleashed a steady stream of fire from its mouth as the goblins tried to run from him. Not all the goblins got away from the fire; about a dozen goblins could be seen torched on the ground, and a few goblins running away still had flames licking at them. The dragon landed and let out a roar loud enough the whole area could hear.

Vurth started to laugh out loud as the magnificent beast approached him and the rest of the group. "Hello, dragon," he said with a smile, "what a pleasant surprise."

In a low, deep, and powerful voice, the dragon replied, "Not a moment too soon." The dragon then leaped into the air and beat his wings. As the goblins continued their retreat, the dragon bore down on them and unleashed more flames from his gigantic mouth. Screams, shrieks, and yells of agony filled the sky as the fire consumed its victims. Only a few goblins reached the safety of their caves.

*****

The sun was about to go down as Lalatco finished his meal. He wondered what time King Malick would leave tomorrow. If it wasn't for having to cross the river, the trip would not be long at all. Lalatco got up, left the mess hall, and started to walk toward the front gate. As he was walking, he saw Malick approaching him.

"There you are, my good friend." Malick looked to be in a very good mood, as he continued to talk. "I would love it if you would accompany me to the meeting."

Lalatco was ecstatic. "Well, of course I will. When do we leave, sire?"

"We will leave at the start of the second arc, and it will just be the two of us traveling after we have crossed the river."

"Very good, sire."

Arcs were established as the way to track time by the elves long ago and has been used ever since. The second arc Malik referred to would be early in the morning. Arcs refer to the two moons that can be seen in the sky throughout the day and night. During the day, one moon is more visible than the other, with the second moon barely seen during the day. Thus, the two moons received the names day moon and night moon. As the day moon follows its arcing path across the sky, its location and brightness mark the time of day or the numbered arc. The day moon then starts to become harder to see as the night moon pops up and gets brighter and higher in the sky. A full cycle of arcs by both moons contains somewhere between twenty-one and twenty-five arcs in a day depending on the time of the year.

The next day came quickly, and Malick knew he could follow the forest all the way to the Mitelow River, but he still sent some elves ahead of them to be on the lookout.

It is a cool morning today, Lalatco thought as he mounted his horse. Cool, but good, and Malick and he started to trot through the forest. There were not too many people who liked traveling through the forest of Malkin, but the elves did. It was their home, even though there are many stories about scary creatures that are in the woods. Lalatco and Malick arrived at the river Mitelow in almost no time at all. Now they had to cross it. The scouts Malick had sent out were there waiting for them.

"The river is fairly deep, my lord," said one of the scouts.

Malick responded in a frustrated voice, "We will have to leave the cover of the woods then and follow the river north until there is a place to cross."

The elves did as Malick said and followed the river north. The elven scouts continued to test the river's depth and the speed of the current. A little while later, they found a spot that was deemed crossable. Malick was happy to hear this. "Scouts, thank you. It looks like you may then head for home."

*****

Jyres was starting to wonder if he had made an error, waiting for the mighty creature. But he had nowhere else to be, so waiting was just fine with him. Jyres spent the time resting and thinking, pondering his next moves, and second-guessing himself. He stood up and took in the view.

Never before had he glimpsed on the world as he did now. Alhazar spread out in front of him the grasslands nearest to him. The river Mitelow flowed just past that, and the forest of Malkin went on for what seemed to be forever. Somewhere in those trees was the home of the elves. A place Jyres had never seen, but a place he had hoped to visit one day. Jyres focused his gaze to the north, where he had come from, Tomackus. Not as pleasant of a sight. Whether it was the actual scenery or the life it represented that caused this feeling, Jyres wasn't sure. Tomackus was by nature bleaker, dryer, and dull when compared to Alhazar. But so was his and his village's current state. Just north of his lookout, Jyres's eyes fell on the Valley of the Dragons where all his hope rested. Would they come to the aid of his village if Jyres continued his current course?

The last rays of sunlight seemed to vanish to the west, and finally Gargan started to move. He roared as the gray color seemed to melt away from him, first by his face and then down his arms, to his legs and into the ground he stood on. Jyres had never seen anything like it. When the sun goes down, Gargan is alive; and when the sun comes up, he seems nothing more than a statue. He stood there, speechless, staring at the very much alive and well Gargan.

"I am glad to see you are still here," commented Gargan.

Jyres looked up at the tremendous creature with a look of amazement and asked, "How many of you are there?"

Gargan said with a sigh, "We are strong in numbers, but not all are as of the same manner as me. Only some. For there are other gargoyles who only seek out that which will grant them personal gain." Gargan lifted up his medallion around his neck and said, "This signifies me as the leader of my clan. I take great pride in that honor and in leading those who have bestowed this upon me." Gargan appeared to be lost in thought for a moment before he asked, "Do you know where you need to go?"

Jyres sighed and said with conviction, "Yes, I have sat here unsure of my decision, but I know I must continue. If you could take me down to the foot of the mountains, that would be all I need."

Gargan picked him up and jumped into the wind. As the gargoyle drifted down to the ground, Jyres asked him "Will I see you again, Gargan?"

"Yes, you will, but I must continue moving." With that, Gargan set Jyres on the ground and started to climb back up the mountains. He only climbed a little ways, however, before leaping into the air and rising into the clouds. Jyres watched him head to the west, over the mountains.

3

The Meeting

Early in the evening of that same day, everyone had gathered in the Valley of the Dragons. The Valley of the Dragons is nestled in between mountain ranges. The opening to the valley was at the southern end, and a small waterfall started at the northern end of the valley and flowed into the Mitelow River, which rushed out the southern end of the valley. The Valley of the Dragons was always a wonderful sight but was even better when the weather allowed it to be green and full of life. The end of fall, which it was, did not allow for that. The grass was brown and ugly, and the valley seemed to be devoid of life.

One dragon was in the middle of the valley and another one kept watch from afar, sitting on a high mountain ledge. Malick, Demorous, and Vurth went to sit next to the dragon in the valley, while the others, including Lalatco, stayed at the southern end of the valley. Soon an orc named Ogla came and joined the group in the valley.

The dragon, in a deep yet womanly voice, started to talk. "I believe this is everybody, so we should start the meeting." The lady dragon's name in the basic language was Esmeralda, simply because of her scales that showed to be the color of emeralds in the sunlight.

Not long after Esmeralda had started speaking, there was some loud yelling heard from the south side of the valley. Jyres had come, and Lalatco and the others would not let him enter the valley. The dragon who was watching from afar flew down to where they were and roared as it landed. The arguing quickly came to an end as the group beheld the red dragon, a magnificent and powerful-looking creature. Crimson, the name that the dragon went by, said that Jyres could be allowed into the meeting.

Jyres started to walk toward the middle of the valley, and he tried to stay calm. He was very shaken up by seeing the dragon so close up. It was very intimidating. He had only seen them in the sky from afar. What a sight they were, so beautiful and powerful. Gargan was no longer the biggest creature that he had ever seen. It seemed like a very long walk to where everyone was seated because all eyes were on him as he drew closer to the group. He noticed someone who must be an orc or goblin sitting in the group. Jyres was experiencing a lot of firsts, and it was not even midday. Focusing back on the task at hand, he told himself he had a right to be there and that no one would do him any harm.

"Welcome," said the dragon, as Jyres walked up to the circle of people.

Demorous stood up and yelled at the human, "What are you doing here? You do not belong here! You must be the one who broke Meslar's curfew."

"Sit down!" roared Esmeralda. "We have some important matters to discuss." Demorous was quick to sit down, though he still protested to Jyres being there. "First of all," Esmeralda went on, "there was an attack made on the first day of the week of peace. The goblins attacked the five travelers from Tomackus. Now, Ogla, can you tell me why?"

Ogla was the most intelligent orc you could find; he is also the calmest one, and probably the only one who could sit through a meeting of this sort. He responded slowly and tried to speak clearly, "I can only control the orcs, not the goblins. The goblins are too stupid to realize it is peace week. After the dragon's attack, they will be afraid to come out for a while."

The dragon knew the goblins would not come out after the death of so many of their kin. She did not see any reason to discuss it further, so she started the next topic. "It seems that lately everyone has been doing well, and there have been no fights. Is that true?" Everybody said yes it was. "Before we move on to other topics, are there any other matters that need to be discussed?" The dragon knew that there must be, since there was a human at the meeting. Demorous had always just represented both the knights and the humans. Meslar and his knights were human, but they were of the kind often called the delga, which meant "the gifted" in the old elvish tongue. They were a race miring the human in every way, except each delga was embodied with a certain level of power or magic and longevity. This is the race of wizards, clerics, charmers, and often dragon killers.

Jyres, finding courage somehow in front of this mightiest of beasts, stood up and started to talk. "For many years the humans have been pushed around and treated like slaves, and we will no longer stand for it. We will no longer be controlled by Meslar and Demorous. If there is nothing done about it, we will attack Castle Mystic."

Demorous just started laughing hysterically. "You and what army?"

Jyres fired back a response, "I have made some new friends, Demorous, friends who are more powerful than that magical Meslar." Jyres really wasn't sure what to say and was saying the first thing that came into his mind.

"All the creatures in the world are represented here at this meeting, Jyres. Do not try and fool us, you puny human." Demorous was starting to become uneasy but would not let it show.

"Be quiet, both of you." Esmeralda had had enough of this bickering. "Demorous, you are wrong. There are some new creatures that have been seen in the area. This is one of the topics I wanted to discuss. I am interested in how this human knows about them."

Jyres knew he had to tell the dragon what he knew. "I told you they are my friends. They saved me from the hands of Demorous."

Vurth spoke up as he stroked his beard. "Where did these creatures come from?"

The dragon was quick to respond. "They come from beyond the mountains, and they can fly. I think that they may be gargoyles. Gargoyles are creatures that thrive in the night. Only they are much smarter and stronger than orcs or goblins." The dragon bowed his large head in the direction of Ogla as if acknowledging the orc despite the words she spoke before continuing. "Demorous should know of the creatures of whom I speak."

Jyres wondered how the dragon knew all this about his new friend and what Demorous would know but did not want to share more information than needed and did not confirm that the creatures were gargoyles.

Malick asked a question, "So what is to be done about these creatures?"

The dragon looked straight into Jyres's eyes. He wondered if Jyres really did have the protection of the gargoyles. Jyres tried to match the dragon's stare even though he knew it would be impossible to do so.

"Okay," Esmeralda stated, "this is what shall be done. Demorous, you will tell your leader Meslar that the humans shall be left alone. From this point forward, they are released from his care. If they are not left alone, you and he will pay dearly. Jyres, you tell your gargoyle friends to leave everyone alone. That is the deal. Demorous leaves you alone, and the gargoyles leave everyone alone. Are there any questions?"

Vurth had one. "What if these creatures do attack, and then what?"

"Then the dragons will have to respond," roared the dragon.

By the time the meeting was over, it was fairly dark, and the night moon was already high in the sky, so no one would return home until the next day. Many other topics were discussed, the coming winter, the river that seemed to be running rather high and could cause flooding, and many minor issues. The news that came out of the meeting that everyone was talking about was the gargoyles. Many seemed a little nervous about these newly discovered gargoyles. No one was quick to go asleep either. Lalatco was tending to both his and Malick's horses when Jyres walked by.

"Who are you?" asked Lalatco, genuinely curious.

"I am Jyres. You are Lalatco, right?" Jyres said, having to look up just a touch to the taller elf.

"How do you know my name?" Lalatco asked as he studied Jyres closely.

"I heard you are great with knives and have quite the collection."

Lalatco gave him a nod in return and continued to question Jyres. "How do you know these gargoyles?"

"One of them saved me" was all Jyres said.

Jyres knew Lalatco did not trust him and his story about the gargoyles. Jyres also had heard how talented of a warrior Lalatco was and did not want to be on his bad side. Just then, when Jyres was looking up in the sky, he could make out the form of a gargoyle flying over the valley toward the mountains. Jyres pointed it out to Lalatco. Lalatco grew curious now of the creature and of Jyres's story. It was not too hard for the two of them to leave the valley unnoticed and walk toward the nearby mountains.

Jyres and Lalatco walked to the base of the mountains and started to climb. After climbing a short ways, the two rested on a small outcropping. Jyres and Lalatco were talking on the small ledge getting ready to climb a little higher, in hopes of seeing the gargoyle again. Jyres really wanted Lalatco to see one up close so he would believe him.

After climbing a little more to another outcropping, they looked into the sky again. After a few moments had gone by without any gargoyle sightings, Lalatco mentioned that it was getting pretty late in the night, and perhaps they should head back. Jyres was about to agree when a green gargoyle swooped in and landed next to them. Jyres smiled at the huge creature; it was Gargan. Lalatco quickly drew two knives and retreated a few steps, ready to fight.

"Gargan, this is Lalatco." Jyres gestured toward Lalatco as he said it. "What have you been doing?" Jyres asked.

Gargan replied quickly, "Just overlooking the land, searching this side of the mountains." After a slight pause, he continued, "It is a long way from my home to yours."

"Where is your home?" It was the first time Lalatco had said anything to the gargoyle. Lalatco was noticeably less on edge as he sheathed his knives.

"I live on the other side of the mountains, with other gargoyles."

Intrigued, Lalatco asked, "Does anyone else live on that side of the mountains? I have heard the whole land has been destroyed."

"Well." Gargan paused. "It is not what it once was. But my clan still lives there, as does another gargoyle clan. There are others also, but only two castles are left standing: my clan's castle and the other clan's castle. Gargoyles have no real threats over there, besides themselves. In your land, it seems there are many who could threaten us."

Lalatco wanted to ask more questions but knew they should get back to the valley. Jyres and Lalatco said goodbye to Gargan and headed back to their camps. In the morning, everyone would start to pack and soon would be on their way to their respective homes.

The sun was bright and sunny as Jyres awoke. He made it a point to talk to Lalatco before he and Malick left. "Well, what did you think of your first meeting with a gargoyle?"

"A very impressive creature. I am glad they don't seem to intend us any harm as of yet. It was a pleasure to have met both him and you. Best of luck to you." They exchanged goodbyes and shook hands.

Jyres knew it would take him a long time to get back to the village by walking, so he headed toward the mountains, hoping to see Gargan again. Jyres made camp on the same ledge where he and Lalatco had talked the night before and waited to see if Gargan would arrive. The whole day and night went by without any sign of Gargan. The same happened with the second day and night, and now Jyres was worried he would run out of supplies. He decided he would wait one more night, and then he would start the long trip home. On the third night, Gargan did show up, and Jyres was relieved.

4

Home

Demorous and his fellow knight reached Castle Mystic on the second night after the meeting. Castle Mystic was the home of the wizard Meslar and his Knights of Enchantment. The Knights of Enchantment included twelve delga warriors, all of whom wore a full suit of armor that was enchanted with spells from Meslar and had inherent power of their own. All of the knights were very skilled and had been with Meslar for many years. Demorous the Fierce was the leader of the group and Meslar's right-hand man. The rest of the knights were Felix, Bartholomew the Bold, Brigand, brothers Oliver and Oscar, the Silver Shadow, Lemont the Lost, Karth, Lord Kapel, and brothers Sigmon and Digmon.

The castle itself stood like a fortress in a land bleak and colorless. The castle often appeared to be a stark black color against the landscape. At night, the torches made gray shadows dance upon its walls. Lemont and the Silver Shadow currently stood upon the main lookout that was located high above the main gate. The rear corners of the castle had tall towers as well, giving it the appearance of a throne when looked at from a distance. Lemont gave the word for the gate to be opened for his fellow knights returning from their journey.

Meslar waited for Demorous to come report to him in his chambers. Meslar wore a long hooded robe of dark purple, with gold trim, and was hardly ever seen without his staff. The staff was made from a dark wood, smoothed and oiled to give it a sheen look. It was curved at the top three times, giving it a look of a maze with a gem in the middle of it. The gem was a purple color as well.

As he waited, his mind lay restless. He absently dragged a hand across his smooth face before running it through his spiky hair. Thoughts of his plans and his frustrations fought each other for full attention from the wizard. But Meslar fought them both off by focusing on his path so far. During the early summer, out of what seemed to be pure coincidence, Meslar's path was crossed with a creature's who was not from this land. The two of them seemed to be of the same ilk, and by the second meeting, both their minds were fixed on the same goal. Their secret meetings had continued since then; not even his own knights knew of these meetings.

Demorous walked in and removed his helm, revealing his full dark beard, shaved head, and crooked nose. Meslar's attention now turned toward his trusted warrior. "Well, out with it," the always impatient Meslar almost yelled. Demorous reported what the dragons and the human Jyres had said, to Meslar. Meslar was enraged by the news and decided to act on it. He was afraid this Jyres character would interrupt his goal. He also did not take orders from anyone else, including the dragons.

"Demorous," he said, almost calm, "you will take the knights and raid the human village on the very next night."

Demorous questioned the order, "What if the human is telling the truth, and he has the protection of the gargoyles?"

Not pleased by the question, Meslar yelled in return, "I am Meslar! I am not afraid of some winged monsters. Let them try and attack us. Nor do I believe that this Jyres speaks for all gargoyles. The gargoyles were never rulers of their land in the past, and they do not scare me. Let anyone try to best me. I am more powerful than those creatures." *Soon to be even more powerful*, he thought to himself. When Demorous left to carry out his orders, Meslar was again left to be alone in his thoughts, wondering what his fellow schemer would think of this news.

*****

Jyres explained to Gargan what had happened at the meeting and almost sheepishly said, "The dragons ask that you leave others in this area alone. I may have given them the indication that I know you better than I actually do."

"I do not intend any harm to those that live on this side of the mountain. There is no need for worry."

"Good, because that has saved me from the knights. They have been told to leave my people alone. I must return home and tell everyone that we have our freedom."

Jyres hung on to Gargan's thick neck as he glided over the land. Jyres and Gargan talked as they continued to draw closer to the human village. "Why are you helping me, Gargan? You did not know me. You are not from this place."

"You were in need. I lead my clan with that in mind at all times. To help those who are in danger. It only seemed natural to help you."

"I can't thank you enough, but that doesn't explain why you continue to help."

"This has also given me the opportunity to learn about this world and its inhabitants. For too long have we lived in isolation. It is good to have met you, and I am happy to help your people."

They were getting along quite well, and often something Jyres said would cause laughter to escape from Gargan's mouth. Jyres had to hang on tight, because if Gargan really laughed hard, his body would shake, making it a bumpy ride. Finally, Gargan entered the desert air, but in the distance, they could see fire and smoke. It was coming from the direction of the village. As they got closer, they could tell that the village was indeed on fire.

Jyres was astonished. *How dare the knights do such a thing? So much for the week of peace,* he thought. Gargan landed in the village and stayed out of sight for the time being as Jyres ran up to the first person he saw, asking them what happened. The gentleman who was carrying an empty bucket stopped running and talked to Jyres.

"Where have you been? The knights attacked us an arc ago. They put everything to fire. We could not do anything. We have tried to put the fires out, but everything is too dry, and we do not have enough water. We are going to lose everything. Almost all of our shelters have already burnt to the ground."

Jyres knew there would not be enough water to tame the fire. The one water source was a deep well, which made it hard to retrieve water fast; and even with the well, it was still a limited supply.

Jyres could not believe it. He thought a deal had been made. The Knights of Enchantment would pay for this; somehow they would pay. No one in the village was trained for battle, nor could they have hoped to defend against the knights' attack. The arc after the attack had been chaos. Everyone looked to Hans to lead the people, and Hans had just stood there in shock and sorrow.

Jyres found Hans, still overcome with melancholy, watching the blaze. "Hans, what happened? What now?"

Hans replied, "There is nothing left, nothing left to do."

"We have to do something. Come on, Hans, the people need you." Hans just turned and watched the smoke rise from the ashes.

Jyres decided it was useless to stay here any longer and that he would have to be the one to take charge. It took a little while, but Jyres slowly got all the people together along with anything they had managed to save from the fire. They all started heading south. Going south was the fastest way out of the desert area, and without the village, the humans had no source of water.

Gargan had stayed out of sight, not wanting to frighten an already terrified group. Now that the humans were on the move, Gargan wanted to talk with Jyres. He landed with a thud at the head of the group. As expected, some of the villagers screamed, and some fell to the ground in fear. Gargan kept the conversation with Jyres quick. Then he took to the air and went out ahead of the group, scouting for a good place to camp for the night. Jyres quickly tried to ease the villagers' concerns and assured them that Gargan was a friend and everything was going to be okay.

A little while later, Gargan landed on a very large plateau and looked over the land. To the southwest, he saw cliffs, a waterfall, and a river, but nothing else worth noting. As Gargan overlooked the land, he decided that his plateau would perhaps be the best option. Although it was very steep and the humans would have trouble reaching the top, it would also offer them natural defense against their enemies. Gargan watched as the group, Jyres at the lead, continued their slow but steady trek in his direction. There were probably only thirty-five of them, but Gargan had noticed they needed a true leader. After a while, Jyres was in clearer view. Gargan motioned to Jyres with his hand and made sure Jyres knew where he was. Gargan nodded his head and pointed at the ground. Jyres nodded back, understanding the gesture. The gargoyle then turned to face the rising sun. Gargan's body again went into its solid form.

5

The Humans Rebuild

It did not take long for news to travel, and within a couple of days, everyone knew that Meslar had attacked the human village. No one was very happy with what he had done, and the dragons decided they should pay Meslar a visit. Demorous was standing in one of the lookout towers of the castle, when in the not-so-very-far distance he saw two enormous creatures flying toward the castle.

"Sound the alarm!" he yelled. "Dragons are coming!"

Meslar figured the dragons would be coming, and he was not worried. Even the dragons could not harm him in his castle. Castle Mystic was too full of power and magic. He and his knights had built this castle. Each block of stone being embedded with magic as those blocks were used to build the castle. Although it was a long process, it was well worth it. The castle was a home filled with consistent energy. He and his knights fed off it, making them strong.

Meslar went outside to the main terrace. As the dragons drew closer to the castle, Meslar just stood there waiting for them. He guessed the dragons were here to try to talk to him, not fight. The dragons flew straight over the castle, their wings spread and scales glowing from the reflection of the sun. Meslar had to admit they were magnificent creatures. The dragons flew around the castle once, and then one of them yelled in a deep voice, "Meslar, what was the meaning of your attack!"

Meslar responded without hesitation, "I do not need to answer to you. I have my reasons, dragon. Now go, and leave us alone."

"I asked you to leave them alone," came the dragon's reply.

"My actions are none of your business, dragon."

"The attack was uncalled for, and cowardly."

"What are you going to do, dragon? You can't harm me!" Meslar yelled angrily.

At hearing this, both dragons swooped down and spewed fire upon the castle. The castle repelled the fire as if the fire were trying to set water aflame. The dragons attacked again, this time sending fire toward Meslar. Meslar reached up his staff and yelled words of power. The fire was absorbed by the staff, and the cloaked figure remained unscathed.

"Shoot them down, Knights!" commanded Demorous.

His words were followed by arrows as seven of the knights let arrows go into the air. They continued to rain more arrows into the sky. The dragons quickly retreated to a safe distance, the arrows missing or bouncing off their tough scales. The dragons circled about the castle, watching the movements of Meslar and the knights. The short skirmish was over, with neither side doing any damage to the other.

Meslar returned to his chambers and leaned his staff against the wall. The staff had been given to him long ago, and its gem was a powerful item in its own right. Gems of its kind were often referred to as Delga Stones. It allowed its user access to the stored power it held. Although anyone could access the stone's power, a Delga Stone was used to its fullest when used by a delga to help focus or enhance their inherent power. There were many different possibilities of inherent abilities that a delga might possess. Some delga may be gifted with specific powers, such as incredible speed or strength or the ability to heal injuries. Meslar, a delga, had learned early on that he had the power and abilities to be a wizard and cast spells. A power he believed was almost unmatched. Meslar had started to learn different spells at a young age and had continued to add to the number at his disposal throughout his life.

To cast a spell, three things were needed. First, you needed a power source. For Meslar, that was being a delga, and he also had a Delga Stone to augment that power. Second, you needed to know the ancient words that formed the spell. Finally, you needed to be able to have control and concentration. The ancient words could be learned and memorized, but the control and concentration only came with practice. Meslar sat down and closed his eyes and brought his mind through an array of different spells, concentrating on the words, and eliminating distractions. He practiced. And then practiced again.

*****

When the news of the attack on the village had first reached Malick and the elves, they did not respond. Although they feared what Meslar might do, they thought it would be in their best interest to stay out of the situation. When they heard about the dragons being virtually ineffective, however, they knew they had to at least try to do something. Malick decided to send three elves to find the humans and help in any way they could. Lalatco would lead the small team, and they would be able to travel through the woods for a better part of the journey. With Lalatco leading, and the group traveling through the trees where the elves were most comfortable, Malick was confident that they would succeed. One of the elves who went along was a woman warrior named Elonda. The elf to complete the trio was named Hex. Hex was known for his craftsmanship.

The three elves started their journey toward Tomackus, each riding on a horse. Although they did not know for sure where the humans would be, they had heard they had left their village. Lalatco had a good idea where to look. By the route Lalatco would take, they would be in the cover of the forest the whole trip. They would travel through the forest of Malkin until it reached a river, which starts at the Catastrophic Cliffs. The river starts inside the cliffs and flows out of them in the form of a waterfall. No one has ever found where the river truly begins, and so the river received the name of Eternal. The forest was massive and covered much of the area, so the elves' journey would be about a two-day journey.

On the first day of the trip, the elves made good time. Nothing unexpected interrupted the trio. They knew the woods very well and the best paths to take. Hex had what he considered to be an amusing trip. For Lalatco and Elonda used to be inseparable; where one was, the other would be. Hex and all the other elves were certain the two would be bonded together. But then something happened between them, and no one really knows what. Although they still talk, it is not like it once was. Hex found the conversation quite humorous, the other two elves trying to not offend the other by anything they said.

During the first night of the trip, the elves made camp in a small clearing among the trees. The elves would rotate keeping watch as the others slept. Lalatco watched more than he slept, but he did not mind it. The others needed rest more than he; he was used to journeys of this sort. He played with his knives to stay awake during the last shift of the night. He was juggling three knives at a time and only dropped a knife once. His skills with knives were just amazing. He had many knives of all shapes and sizes. He brought about ten or twelve with him on this trip. They were all hidden among his clothing, including one in his boot. Sometimes he wore a bandolier across his chest that held all of his knives.

In the morning, they had a quick breakfast, repackaged their horses, and were on their way. If all went well, they would reach the river by early evening.

*****

Jyres guessed that as soon as Gargan would awake, he would leave to go back to his home. Jyres was left to fend for himself and for the thirty-five or so people who relied on him now. Jyres knew Gargan had determined that the safest place for them to be was on the plateau, and Jyres agreed. He also knew that most of the people would not be able to make the difficult climb.

After the trip in the middle of the night, not much was done in their new location on the first day. Many people were shaken up by the attack or too exhausted, and all were perfectly fine sitting or sleeping at the base of the plateau. Jyres was not sure the reason for the attack, but he figured if it had anything to do with him and that meeting, the knights would be back soon. So Jyres knew he had to come up with a plan to get the people on top of the plateau. He sat down to rest his legs, suddenly realizing he too was exhausted. The thought of getting these people to the top of their new location was still in his head as he drifted off to sleep.

Jyres woke up near midday. Others were starting to move around as well. He got up and stretched his legs and looked around the area. To the southwest were the cliffs, and to the south was a waterfall flowing out of the cliffs, creating a river that moved out steadily from it. Jyres contemplated taking the people to the cliffs and asking the dwarves for safety. But Jyres didn't know the dwarves, nor did he want a temporary solution. Jyres also noticed what looked like a pretty big forest starting just past the river.

Jyres walked around taking note of the condition of the people and their belongings. As he did so, he took into account what they had saved from the attack and what the area around them offered, and started formulating a plan in his mind. The group of humans was able to save a few tools, an ax, and a rope from the fire; and someone was smart enough to bring them along. Jyres was also thankful that a couple of buckets, as well as some of the healing salve, were brought along.

As Jyres expected, when the sun went down and Gargan awoke, he had to be quickly on his way. The two exchanged goodbyes, and Jyres thanked him over and over again for his assistance.

On the second day in their new location, Jyres recruited a couple of people to help him, and they walked over to the nearby river. It took a little while, but they found a place they could cross the river and started to chop down a couple of small trees, including two that were long and slim. Jyres had come up with a plan to build a ladder that would reach the top of the plateau. Everyone would then be able to use the ladder to climb up to safety. It would have to be a big ladder to reach the top of the plateau, but Jyres was confident they could do it.

Work on the ladder continued on the third day and was completed on the fourth day after the knights had attacked the village. Meanwhile, while Jyres was working on the ladder, he had recruited people to find food and water. They had collected a lot of berries and also found some edible vegetation called waterweed and found that the river would do just fine for drinking water. After the completion of the ladder, it was time to put it to the test. A couple of people were sent up the ladder with no problems. The rest of the group was then sent up the ladder, as were all of the supplies.

Early in the evening, Jyres and two others were returning from the river with buckets of water. All the members of the group had done a lot that day and were now safe on top of the plateau. Jyres had said this would be the last trip of the day. It was starting to get dark as the three neared the plateau with the buckets of water. The three of them were almost to the ladder, when the sounds of hoofbeats could be heard very near. Jyres turned to see five horses coming fast toward the plateau.

Jyres yelled to his companions, "Leave the water and run for the ladder!"

As the three of them reached the ladder, they saw that the knights were almost on top of them. Jyres's two companions had already started to climb, and Jyres yelled up to them, "Pull up the ladder as soon as you get to the top!"

The ladder was pulled up just in time, but Jyres was left on the ground to fend for himself against five knights. Demorous trotted his horse right up to Jyres and drew his sword. "It is time for you to die," he said. "You should have never gone to that meeting. You are an insignificant human, and that is all you ever will be." With that, Demorous raised his sword and prepared to strike.

*****

The three elves made it to the Eternal River by early evening, and they also found a place to cross it. Not long after they crossed the river, they could see horses in the distance and small figures huddled at the top of the plateau. Lalatco knew that it must be the humans, and they might be in trouble. He urged his horse to sprint toward the plateau. The other elves could not keep up with Lalatco, as he had his horse sprinting extremely fast. Lalatco had gotten just inside fifty yards or so of the plateau and could see Demorous on his horse looking down on Jyres. Lalatco drew a small slender knife from his boot, aimed, and threw; all the while the horse was running on. It was a very long throw, even for Lalatco; he could only hope it would make it to its target. Lalatco watched as Demorous raised his sword to swing, and then Demorous's horse suddenly reared back hard and sent Demorous to the ground. The knife had struck the horse in its underbelly, causing the horse to buck. Lalatco smiled, surprising even himself on that throw, and charged on.

Jyres immediately ran away from the knights; if they followed, he knew he would not get far. They were on horseback, and he was outnumbered. Jyres had seen a knife hit the horse Demorous was riding, but he had no idea how or where it came from. As he started to run, he saw three horses coming his direction, and Jyres could tell there were elves riding them. Immediately Jyres knew Lalatco had saved his life. Who else could make a throw like that?

Jyres looked behind him and saw three horses right on his tail. The three knights chasing Jyres were Oscar, Oliver, and Bartholomew the Bold. They were gaining ground when a knife went whizzing by Jyres and hit Oscar's horse right in the neck, causing both horse and rider to fall to the ground in a heap. Then Oliver and Bartholomew were right on top of Jyres, who dove to the right as a blade swished over his head, just missing him. Lalatco was there in time to block a second swing of Oliver's sword with his scimitar. Hex and Elonda were there moments later and clashed swords with Bartholomew. They exchanged a few blows before Bartholomew knocked Hex off his horse, who fell to the ground. Elonda more than made up for it, blocking a swing of the knight's sword and countering with an aimed strike of her own that sent Bartholomew's sword out of his hand and to the ground.

The fourth knight, Brigand, had regrouped with Oscar; and the two of them saddled the good horse and joined Bartholomew and Oliver in combat. The warriors fought to a standoff. The knights knew Demorous would not be able to come to their aid without his horse.

Elonda blocked two quick slashes from Brigand and slipped her sword through the knight's defenses only to have it clang off the enchanted armor. Bartholomew, having lost his sword, pulled out a knife and threw it at Elonda who ducked just in time, the knife stuck in the back of her cloak. Jyres and Hex charged at Bartholomew who now had no way to defend himself and quickly retreated.

The rest of the knights slowly worked together to create an escape route. The elves showed no signs of being interested in a chase as the knights rode off and picked up Demorous, still standing by his downed horse. Demorous could be heard shouting curse words as they trotted away.

After the battle, the group gathered together at the top of the plateau, and the elves immediately began the conversation. The elves spoke in the basic language but caught themselves a time or two speaking out of frustration in elvish. Elonda wanted to report what happened to Malick immediately, but Jyres had more pressing concerns including getting shelters built for his people. Jyres and the elves talked long into the night, most about what they would do next, but also some things to lighten the mood. Ultimately it was decided that the elves would stay and help build shelters. Hex was excited for the opportunity to show his skill to the humans.

The next day the plateau was extremely busy. Everyone was recruited to help. Much of the work involved cutting down trees and cutting them into logs. Thankfully, Hex always had tools with him. Lalatco saddled a horse to scout out the area and keep watch for any intruders in the distance. Lalatco was chosen for this task as the others had confidence in his ability to give everyone ample warning if they were attacked.

As Hex supervised the construction, Elonda and Jyres went out to do some hunting. They crossed the river and entered the woods. Jyres had not had a lot of experience with a blade, but he did carry an old sword with him.

Jyres took the time to observe the first female elf he had met. Elonda was about his height, maybe a bit taller even. She had long dark hair that she had tied back in a ponytail. While both Hex and Lalatco wore shades of green, Elonda stood out with colors of gray and blue. Her tight-fitting shirt was a very dark blue, a touch darker than the blue of her eyes, and her short cloak was gray. She sported a sword at her hip, and she had her bow ready with her quiver full of arrows and strapped to her back.

After just a short time, Elonda had already shot three good-sized birds. Jyres, itching to catch something, got excited when he saw a rabbit and chased after it. It was of course gone in a flash, and Jyres scolded himself for reacting so. Jyres saw Elonda smiling at him as he walked back toward her. Her smile turned into laughter, and to Jyres's own surprise, he joined her with his own laughter. After two arcs had gone by, the two had exchanged conversation and returned with four birds, a rabbit, and a deer, in which Jyres had a small part in catching. By the time the evening was growing old, the humans now had one shelter atop the plateau that would be used to house all their supplies, including the food Jyres and Elonda had just provided.

Hex did a marvelous job in the coming days. The village now had four structures. Two of them were completely enclosed buildings, the one to be used for supplies, and the second building with wooden tables for meetings, learning, and eating. The two other structures had wooden posts supporting a roof made out of sticks and leaves that Hex assured Jyres would do just fine. These shelters would be used for sleeping and protection from the sun and the rain.

Jyres could not believe what was accomplished in just over a week's worth of time. He was so thankful for his new friends. Not only had they saved his life, but they were making his people's lives a whole lot better. Jyres had grown to be friends with the elves, especially Lalatco, and was sad that they would be departing. He had learned a lot from him about elves and about Lalatco himself. He always talked with such confidence and honor. Not an overconfidence, but an understanding that he had the skills necessary to protect his people. He saw that role as an honor and as a responsibility. Jyres shared some of those same feelings but didn't possess all those same skills. Nor did he feel the same connection with his village that Lalatco felt so deeply with his kin. Already in this short time, Jyres felt more connected to Lalatco than to those he had spent most of his young life.

"You look deep in thought. Everything all right?"

Jyres looked up from his seat, which was a wooden stump, to see Lalatco looking down on him. Lalatco had surprised Jyres, and it caused him to pause for a second before saying, "Yes, I was just thinking about your people. How that bond has formed, the way you speak, it has left me envious."

"You don't feel the same connection with your people?" asked Lalatco, taking a seat on another stump by Jyres. They were sitting in one of the newly made buildings.

A few humans milled about, and Jyres's eyes seemed to look from one to the other before responding. "No, not really, I guess."

"Meslar has taken that from you. It is hard for them to put in the work to create friendships when many may not see why they should. Your people have been trodden on, the energy and zeal stomped out. But you have begun to reverse that process. You have stood up to it, and now the healing may begin. For your people here, and for you with us."

That caught him off guard. Jyres looked up, a confused expression clear on his face.

"You should come back with us," Lalatco provided.

"What?" was all Jyres could think of to respond.

"Come see our home! Also, there has got to be more to why Meslar attacked you and the village. It just does not make sense to me that he would attack just because you went to the meeting."

"Lalatco is right," added Elonda, coming to join them at the table. "You should come back with us and talk to Malick. He may have learned more of what Meslar is up to."

"What if we get attacked again?" responded Jyres in a concerned voice. "These people need my leadership to defend themselves."

"Look back at the actions of the knights, Jyres. It's you that they are after. If you stay around here, you will only endanger the lives of your fellow humans." Elonda frowned after saying it; she did not like how it sounded.

Standing up, Lalatco reached out his hand to Jyres. "Come, see our home and see the bond of which we spoke."

"I think that you are right," Jyres conceded and grasped the offered hand and rose to his feet. "If I go back with you, perhaps they will be safe. First, I need to talk to them and find someone who will lead them."

This turned out to be a difficult task, and most of the humans didn't understand why he would leave. Eventually he had talked to two brothers to share the role of leader. They both were tall and dark skinned and were older than he was. He hoped they would prove a good choice to lead them in his absence and, again, hoped he was making the right decision for the people. He put faith in Lalatco's and Elonda's words. If he stayed away, they would be safe.

6

Dangerous Decisions

The return trip for the elves and Jyres went almost as fast as the trip to the plateau. At first, Jyres was low in spirits because of leaving his fellow humans, but deep down he knew that the elves were right. Somehow he knew that Meslar was after him. On the trip, Jyres rode along with Elonda on her horse. It was an interesting ride to be sure, riding with the female elf. Jyres was not quite sure what to think about it all.

Elonda interrupted his thoughts, "So, Jyres, tell me more about you. Other than the fact a delga is trying to kill you." Elonda, who was in front, turned her head slightly to the side as she spoke. "What else is there to tell?"

Jyres, holding on to Elonda's waist, and feeling uncomfortable about the whole thing, took a moment or two to respond. "There is really not much to say. I grew up in the village. My uncle is the only family that I can remember. My parents died young, as many in the village have. It was hard work and has only gotten harder as the years have passed."

Elonda, unsure that she understood, asked, "Why did your people stay there?"

"It is what we had. Meslar wasn't going to help us, and where else could we go? Only with help like the help you, Hex, and Lalatco provided could we change our fortunes." Jyres let out a sigh. "Perhaps I should have done something earlier, or perhaps

I shouldn't have done anything at all." Wanting to change the subject, Jyres asked, "What about you? All I know is that you can hunt and fight."

Elonda laughed and responded, "Well, that is about right! Those are certainly two things I am good at. I am a trained warrior, and I serve my King and kin, which too often involves fighting. Though if I am truthful, I perhaps seek it out more than I should." This comment caused Lalatco to give them a sideways glance. Changing the subject again, Elonda in an excited tone said, "Just wait until you see our home, Jyres, you are going to love it."

On the second night of their trip, they had made it to the safety of the elven abode. Jyres was enamored by the elves' homes. The whole village was constructed in the trees. Jyres laughed at the thought that his former village now used elevation as a defense as well. All of the structures were beautifully constructed. Jyres thought of how fast Hex was able to build the human structures but wondered how long it took him and the elves to create such elaborate designs and beautiful buildings. Not too long ago, Jyres had been hoping to see this place, and here he was. It was a breathtaking sight with the colorful leaves in the trees surrounding the beautiful structures. Jyres wished he could have seen it just a few weeks earlier with less leaves having fallen to the ground. It would have been a magnificent sight.

Lalatco, his hair showing a shade of pale green now, took Jyres with him into the throne room where Malick and a couple of other elves were waiting. The elves greeted each other with ceremony, bowing to their king. Then the king said to Jyres, "Welcome, my friend, to our home."

Jyres and Lalatco took turns telling the story of what happened, and when they were finished, Malick motioned for them to sit down. They both sat in the elaborate chairs, Jyres laughing to himself for going from a tree stump to this work of art.

"Like what Lalatco was alluding to, the most important question is, what is the real reason for Meslar's activities?" The others were silent as Malick continued. To Jyres, it seemed he spoke in a noble and almost unworldly tone. "Let us reflect on all he has done recently. He attacked the human village, discovered Jyres was not there, and destroyed the village yet caused no harm to anyone. He then sent his knights out again, this time getting very close to killing Jyres. Jyres, did they say anything to you?"

"Yes, he did. Demorous said, 'It is time for you to die. You should have never gone to that meeting.'"

Malick continued, "And we can't forget about the dragons' failed attempt to scare them into submission. Although Demorous said what he did, I agree with Lalatco that there has got to be more to it than getting back at Jyres for going to a meeting in which Meslar has unrightly spoken for all of the humans in the past. Something about Jyres has him scared."

"I believe we are all in agreement that there is more to it," said one elf, "but how do we find out what it really is about? We can't just go knock on the door and ask him what it is all about. The dragons tried that."

Lalatco smiled. "Why not do a little eavesdropping?"

Another elf replied, "Are you thinking straight? You can't sneak into Castle Mystic unnoticed."

Malick questioned Lalatco as well, "How do you propose we would do this?" The nobleness of his manner and voice was always present.

Lalatco nodded and said, "I was hoping we would not have to sneak into the castle to do it. Perhaps we could catch someone off guard while outside the castle."

After Malick spoke his next words, he had caught on to what Lalatco was thinking. "With the exception of sitting outside the castle for a week, how would you know when a knight was leaving the castle?" Malick's eyes opened a little wider. "You want to draw them out somehow."

Lalatco smiled. "Exactly!" was all he said as all eyes turned toward Jyres.

"Hold on!" Jyres shouted and stood up. "You want to use me as bait. Are you sure that is such a good idea? I didn't exactly enjoy my last meeting with Demorous."

"Don't worry," replied Lalatco, "we will be sure nothing happens to you." Lalatco stood up, put his hand on Jyres's shoulder, and gave him a nod.

With the plan all settled, Lalatco, Jyres, Elonda, and two other elves had all set out the next morning by the second arc of the day on horseback for the Valley of the Dragons. Their plan involved a little bit of help from the dragons; the group just hoped the dragons would agree to help.

It only took a day to arrive at the Valley of the Dragons. The dragons were not happy to be disturbed as they tended to think that their time was more important than anybody else's. After finally convincing the dragons to hear them out, Lalatco and Jyres laid out their plan for the dragons. The dragons thought it quite clever, which is a huge compliment coming from a dragon, and they agreed with the plan and said that they would help.

The next morning, Jyres and the four elves were traveling again, this time headed toward Castle Mystic. The dragons promised to keep watch over them so they did not have to worry about the orcs or goblins as they traveled over the hills. As the horses traveled along, the group talked to each other, Lalatco and Jyres growing closer all the while. Lalatco and Elonda seemed to grow more distant, neither speaking to the other. At his next opportunity, Jyres asked Lalatco about Elonda. Lalatco decided to tell Jyres a little about her and what had happened.

"Elonda and I used to be very close. Not too long before I met you, I was all set to be bonded with her. But when we started talking about that possibility, we did not see eye to eye. We wanted different things. In the end, we hurt each other with offensive words, and now I fear our friendship may be lost as well."

Jyres offered his sympathies but was thinking to himself that he wanted to know more of the story. Why didn't they see eye to eye? They were both elves, lived in the same woods, both warriors. Maybe he could learn more at a different time. For now, he would have to be content.

When the group started to get closer to Castle Mystic, they traveled carefully, to avoid being seen as they traveled the desert. The desert was full of sand, dunes, rough dirt, and patches of dry growth. They soon found a place close to the castle where they could hide. When the time had come for them to finally execute their plan, Jyres had grown quite nervous. Lalatco and Elonda both talked to him, trying to instill confidence. They were all hiding behind a sand dune out in the Desert of Despair and not too far away, behind one of the biggest sand dunes you're ever going to see, lay a bigger surprise. Jyres climbed into the saddle of his horse, and began to trot out toward the castle. Once he was a little bit closer he started to walk the horse aimlessly around the desert.

A knight keeping watch spotted him from a tower in the castle. He called to Demorous who was just as eager now as he was before to please his master and end the life of Jyres. Demorous called Digmon to his side, and the two of them were on horses and galloping across the sand to catch the wandering Jyres.

Jyres played his role beautifully, bopping in the saddle as though he was exhausted; he lifted up his canteen only to find it empty. He slumped in his saddle and almost fell off in his supposed exhaustion. Jyres heard the thundering hoofbeats coming, but still he waited, keeping up the ruse. He waited until the very last moment, and then he kicked his horse into gear just as the two knights arrived. Jyres urged his horse on as the two knights drew their swords and were so close they could almost slash him. Jyres maneuvered his horse around a small dune and headed straight for the huge dune, where lay his safety.

Demorous swung his sword, just missing Jyres as he turned his horse. Jyres led the horse to the middle of the dune, and the horse turned amazingly sharp to the right. Demorous matched the move, and the other knight fell just a little behind. Jyres's horse gave it everything it had as it came around the dune;

Demorous was right behind. Both horses tossed their riders as the horses beheld what was waiting for them. There lay a dragon, waiting for them to come around the corner. Jyres hit the sand hard and blanked out for a moment; Demorous never hit the ground, for he was caught by the dragon's tail. Demorous pushed and pulled, but there was no way he was getting away. His helmet and sword went flying away. The other horse came around the corner and tossed Digmon as well, who landed on the sand. The knight didn't move, knocked unconscious by the hard fall.

"Now," said Crimson, holding Demorous in front of his massive maw, "what is your master up to?"

"I don't know," Demorous stammered in response to the dragon's question.

The dragon roared, "Yes, you do! Now tell me before I set you on fire!" A few flames left the dragon's mouth to emphasize the point.

"Really, I... I don't."

The dragon reached his massive head forward and chomped his teeth, a hair's length from the knight's exposed head.

"Okay, okay." Demorous was obviously scared as the dragon licked his lips. "All I know is that Meslar was reading some prophecies, and somehow Jyres could have interrupted his plan."

"Is that really all you can tell us?" asked the dragon.

"I don't know the full plan, really I don't." Demorous's fear remained present in his voice.

A warning call from Esmeralda circling above put everyone in motion. With a flick of his tail, Crimson threw Demorous to the top of the dune and then sent the other knight to follow him. Crimson leaped into the air and beat his wings to join his fellow dragon in the sky, as Jyres and the elves got on the horses and started galloping back the way they had come.

Meslar and the other knights had quickly come riding out on horses in hopes to find out what had happened, and that is why the dragon had called the warning. Jyres and the elves had left in a hurry, and Meslar had no hopes of chasing them down. He sent some of his knights to fetch his injured warriors; he was going to have a word with them.

*****

Once again, Jyres found himself in the throne room talking with Malick and the others.

"Did the plan work?" asked Malick.

"The plan worked very well, though Demorous did not talk as much as we hoped. He did say Meslar was reading prophecies and saw Jyres as a threat." Lalatco had been the one who responded.

"All right, so we have confirmed what we suspected. There is another reason Meslar is after Jyres. Unfortunately, I only know a few of the old prophecies, as most are from before my time. We will have to search my old books or parchments to see if they contain any." Malick looked as though he was in deep thought as he spoke those words. "Althea"—who was an older female elf—"take a few elves to our small library. Look for any prophecy you can find and bring them to me."

After Althea had left, Jyres joined in the conversation for the first time. "Who would know these old tales?"

"Not many" was Malick's response. "They would be from a time long ago and a place far away."

"Well, obviously Meslar got them from somewhere."

"Yes, that is another question to consider. The only name that comes to my mind that would have knowledge of such matters would be Zar."

"Who is Zar?" questioned Jyres.

"He was a great wizard, a delga, like Meslar and the knights. But he lived a long time ago. His power was beyond that of any other, but he never used his power to harm anyone who did not deserve it. He was revered by everyone. He lived in the time when the humans ruled the land and when all of civilization lived beyond the mountains."

Interested, Jyres asked, "What happened to him?"

"No one knows for sure," Lalatco had chimed in on the conversation. "Zar is mentioned in many of our old tales and songs."

"Many say he died in the old wars." Malick was talking again. "Some say he died of old age. Still fewer say he still lives on the other side of the mountains."

"What do you think happened to him?" Lalatco and Jyres had asked the question almost in unison.

"I am not sure, and if he is still alive, I do not know if he will be able to help us. There may be others on the other side of the mountains that could know more as well. We know so little of what has transpired there over the last hundred years. Long ago, the dragons set forth the rule that no one shall cross the mountains. There are elders among us who lived in the old world. We will also seek their council, but great effort has been made to put the past, the old, behind us." Malick paused, considering their options. "What I do know is that right now we are in the dark, while Meslar continues his plans. There is a small possibility that Zar is alive. The question is, is such a long and dangerous journey worth it, when so many doubts surround it? I would like to hear what everyone's thoughts were on the subject."

Some of the elves voiced their opinions, but none of them were strong one way or another. Though they did point out they could not spare many men if Meslar was to continue to fight. Jyres knew what he had to do. "I will go look for Zar." Jyres's voice was too quiet at first, and so he repeated himself in a more confident, louder voice. "I will go look for Zar!" All eyes turned toward him in surprise.

"I will go with you, Jyres." Lalatco was not about to let his new friend go alone.

The other elves did not like that idea at all. "He cannot go. We need Lalatco here," said one of the elves.

Although Malick somewhat agreed with the elves' last statement, he also knew that if anyone could find the old wizard, it was Lalatco. "If Althea cannot find anything in our own parchments of old, and our elders cannot shine any more light on the situation, Lalatco and Jyres will go and look for Zar." Malick's voice was stern, and his mind was set. "Jyres leaving to begin the search will actually serve many purposes. Jyres will be safer in the short term until Meslar realizes he has crossed over the mountains. In the long term, Jyres, I am sorry to say, perhaps your feeling of safety will decrease. For more than likely you will draw Meslar's attention, and those you leave behind will be safer because of it. You and Lalatco will rest until Althea has finished her search and the queen and I converse with our elders. You will leave there after if nothing of use is found. Let's hope that is not the case."

7

The Journey Begins

A day or two of rest was good for both Jyres and Lalatco. They spent the time relaxing and trying not to think about what may lie ahead of them. They walked among the trees and rested on the grass, feeling closed off from the world. That was fine with Jyres, anything to keep his mind from focusing on the task ahead. The elven home and the forest it resided in did seem to exude a calming feeling to those in its midst. Jyres observed the elves walking peacefully and talking with each other with their quiet words and smooth tones. Simple gestures of greeting, pleasant smiles, and soft music enhanced the experience for Jyres. Lalatco's descriptions and feelings of his home were more than accurate; but being here, in this place, was something Jyres had only dreamed of.

Despite the serenity, he was still afraid of their possible journey. He had no idea where they were going or what would be in their path, but he was happy he would have Lalatco with him. He knew Lalatco gave them a fighting chance.

After two days of research and reading by multiple elves, any writing that could be seen as a prophecy was brought to Malick. Malick looked them all over, but as he feared, there was nothing of use. Most of his collection of writings were of a more recent nature, and nothing that he or his queen read seemed to connect to recent events in any way. Nor did the oldest elves have any more information on either Zar or prophecies from the old world. He called Jyres and Lalatco to him to tell them the news. They tried not to let disappointment show on their faces as Malick reported the bad tidings. The three of them talked for a long while, and by the end, both Jyres and Lalatco were two determined travelers. Malick wished them well and told them that they would leave with the morning.

Jyres and Lalatco got a good night's sleep. A big breakfast was served to them, and three horses were prepared for them. The third horse would carry their supplies for the long journey. After breakfast, they met quickly with Malick and his queen for some final advice, including different ways to try to cross the mountains and the reminder that the dragons did not like the idea of anyone trying it. Malick also handed Jyres a sword. Jyres took the magnificent-looking weapon as Malick said in his serene voice, "May it help you on your journey." He and his queen each in turn blessed them in the elvish tongue. It sounded beautiful as most elvish does, but Lalatco needed to translate it for Jyres, which he did. "May your feet be light, your path clear, and your heart brightened."

It was into the third arc of the day when the two travelers were on their way. Lalatco and Jyres traveled west until they reached the Mitelow River. The river was still very deep, but Lalatco did not want to follow it north because the dragons would easily see them heading toward the mountains if they went that way. Their only choice was to follow the river south until they found a place to cross. Lalatco did not know the area to the south as well but was confident they would find where they needed to go. As the two traveled south, they lost the cover of the forest.

As they rode along, Jyres inspected the sword given to him by Malick for the trip. His own sword had been old and damaged. The one given to him by Malick was an amazing sword in comparison. The elves were very good at the crafting of swords, and this weapon was no exception. Jyres also noticed that the handle had an inscription, but it was written in a language that Jyres could not read.

"What does the sword say?" Jyres asked Lalatco.

Lalatco did not have to look to know what it said. "That sword has been in Malick's family for many years. An elven cleric once blessed the sword and inscribed those words." Lalatco turned in his saddle to look at Jyres as he said, "It says, 'May this sword keep you safe, and may you return home victorious.' It is a great honor Malick has given you by allowing you to use that sword. Never before has a human carried that sword, and never before has the carrier not returned home. Let's hope the sword works for humans as it does for the elves."

Once they left the forest, they hurried their horses along the riverbank. The sun was out, and it was warmer than it was underneath the trees. The travelers were happy to go without the heavy coats they had been given for a little while.

The river appeared to be shallower, but it was also moving faster here than it had been to the north. By the time Lalatco found a spot he saw as crossable, the water was moving very fast. Both Jyres and Lalatco dismounted their horses to help them cross the river through the rushing water and to the other side. They both made it across. The horses were happy to be out of the water, but Lalatco had to go back to get the third horse. Lalatco made it back over to the other side without any problems. He urged the third horse into the river, helping and pulling it across the river. Jyres could tell the horse was struggling, must have been all the weight from the supplies. Finally, it looked like Lalatco and the horse would make it to the shore. The horse had just a few more steps to take. As Lalatco pulled the reins, he tried to put his back foot on the riverbank, and he slipped. Lalatco went flowing along with the river as the horse managed to get on to dry land.

Jyres was running then, along the river just a little ahead of where Lalatco was in the river. Up ahead he could see a low-hanging branch over the river. He climbed the tree and crawled out on the thick branch, calling out to Lalatco as he did so. He reached down, expecting to see a distressed Lalatco reaching up for him, but Lalatco was nowhere to be seen. Jyres desperately looked all around the river, looking for any sign of the elf. Every moment of his frantic searching seemed to take too long, and Jyres feared the worst. He could not believe it as he climbed down from the tree. Jyres scanned the river and the shore looking for Lalatco. He stood, for what felt like eternity, scanning the area for any sign of the elf. How could their journey be over so quickly? Decimated and in disbelief, he turned and walked back toward the horses. There, to his overjoyed astonishment, he saw Lalatco, standing very alive next to the horses. Lalatco was untying the rope from his knife, when Jyres walked over to him. Lalatco smiled, as did Jyres.

"I thought you were gone! I looked everywhere. How did you manage it?" asked Jyres.

Sheathing his knife in his bandolier, Lalatco said in his confident, quiet tone, "I quickly stabbed my knife through the rope and slung the knife into a tree trunk on the shore and was lucky enough to be able to pull myself to safety."

After Lalatco changed his wet clothes for some dry ones and donned his coat, the two started out again. They had gone far enough south already, and Lalatco led the horses west away from the Mitelow River and toward the mountains. With the dragon's rule in mind, the travelers hoped to be able to avoid being seen. Lalatco thought they would be far enough south of the Valley of the Dragons. Although when it came down to it, the dragons could fly anywhere, so it may not matter how far south they had traveled.

The land they had to travel between the Mitelow River and the mountains was all grasslands. It was late fall, and the area was not nearly as green as it often is. In some places, the grass and weeds were out of control; and they hid the travelers, the tall grasses being taller than the travelers themselves. While in other places, they traveled on wide-open terrain. The two had not gone all that far before the light of day began to vanish into the darkness of night. They traveled a little farther and made camp amidst a few rocks and boulders. Jyres started a small fire, and the two of them had a small dinner. As they ate, they talked about all sorts of things other than their mission and Meslar. After the small dinner, conversation turned more serious; and Lalatco started to tell Jyres details about the time before, and of Zar, and of their enemies.

"There are many stories of the past," said Lalatco, "some of which are true, and some of which have been retold and rewritten so much that they no longer hold any truth to them. I feel there are many things I need to tell you before we continue this quest of ours." Lalatco paused as he ate his last chunk of bread and had a sip of water. Lalatco started again, "One hundred years ago now, all of civilization lived beyond those mountains. No one had ever been on this side of the mountains. It was an age of war. A countless number of dragons roamed the skies. Humans were strong in numbers as well, and some say they were the rulers of the time. Humans and delga had always been united, and together they were powerful. The humans and dragons, however, were in a constant battle with each other. Dragon slayers were rich if they were skilled. The elves, dwarves, and all other creatures were trapped in between the two sides. Some of those races played both sides of the war, depending on whichever side got them more gold."

Lalatco looked over to Jyres and said, "Are you with me so far?" Jyres merely nodded, and Lalatco continued on. "Gold was highly sought after back then, and the war continued to escalate until creatures could no longer stand it, so the stories say. The dwarves decided to pick up and leave. Almost every dwarf in the land moved. They began to mine and live in the mountains. The closest anyone had ever got to crossing them. Another few years went by, and war was leading up to what would be the final battle. Everyone knew what was about to happen, everyone except for the leaders of the power-hungry humans and arrogant dragons, and it was obvious that no one would survive."

Lalatco paused a little while letting Jyres process all of the information before he started talking again. "Two dragons decided they did not want to fight in the war. Those two dragons spoke with Zar and with Malick's grandfather. It was decided that the two dragons; sixteen renowned delga warriors, Meslar included; seven human families; and a whole lineage of elves would cross the mountains and create a place where one could live in peace. The family of elves was led by Malick's father, and the delga and the humans were led by Demorous the Fierce. The two dragons are of course the ones we know and who live in the valley. They all crossed the mountains and left a path behind them, so those who wanted could come and join their new world of peace."

Lalatco again gave Jyres a few moments. "Now, pay close attention to this part. Then the Battle of Ages took place. It was the biggest and deadliest battle anyone has and ever will see. All of the creatures in the land found themselves on either the dragon's or human's side. The battle lasted for weeks and weeks. Fighting was nonstop. When it was all over, thousands upon thousands of creatures, humans, and dragons had died. The battle ended when all the dragons had been destroyed. By the time this happened, the damage was done. The humans and the delga were almost wiped out. Few were left to cherish their victory. The land was destroyed, ravaged by war."

Jyres stopped Lalatco there. "What about the dwarves? I thought you said they had left."

"Oh, you have been paying attention," said Lalatco. "The dwarves luckily had not been involved in the battle. The dwarves' population probably now outnumbered the whole world's. But some creatures that did survive the battle, including orcs and goblins, moved into the mountains. Living so far and deep into the mountains, even the dwarves did not know they were there. Slowly their number began to grow, and soon the dwarves no longer had the mountains to themselves. Vurth's father soon found himself in a war, just after avoiding one. The dwarves battled for a while but learned quickly that the goblins and orcs were too relentless. Vurth's father led his dwarves out of the mountains and followed parts of the path that was left by the dragons. He led them to the cliffs, where the dwarves still reside today. He is also the one that brought the news of the final battle and the terrible result."

Once Lalatco had finished the tale, Jyres asked him many questions, most of which Lalatco was able to answer. Jyres was confused about how Meslar was already alive one hundred years ago. Lalatco explained that not only were the delga blessed with power, but they often lived for many years, and that Meslar was just twenty-five at the time. He also mentioned that if Zar is still alive, he would be at least one hundred and fifty years old, maybe even one hundred and sixty. The two friends talked long into the night. Lalatco finished by singing a song about Zar and Malick's grandfather.

The song was actually a story that told of an adventure Malick's grandfather had had. The song started out by introducing Malick's grandfather as a great warrior and saying no one matched his abilities. It went on to tell a tale how Zar had actually saved him once. Zar had protected him from a dragon's fiery breath.

The morning came fast for Jyres and Lalatco. They got a later start then was desired, but thought they could make it to the mountains by nightfall. They traveled across the grassland quickly; the terrain was very smooth and open.

8

Another Attack

Meslar was awaiting the return of Demorous and a few of his knights. He had sent them to attack the humans again and this time capture Jyres. From the moment Meslar heard about Jyres walking into that meeting, he knew Jyres would be dangerous. He needed to get rid of him as soon as possible. Meslar looked out over the desert and saw the knights returning, with no prisoner. Meslar stormed down to the front gate.

"Where is the prisoner?" he yelled.

Demorous responded in the most confident voice he could muster up, "Jyres was not there."

"The dragons will know where he is. Come along, Demorous, and fetch four other knights as well."

Soon Meslar, Demorous, Felix, Lord Kapel, and the brothers Sigmon and Digmon were mounted on horses and riding out of the gates of Castle Mystic in the direction of the Valley of the Dragons. After a long, loud command from Meslar, the horses lifted into the air, as if they were flying.

Meslar's frustration boiled over as they were flying toward their destination. He often wondered if he had made the right decision with the delga warriors. Since they had first arrived on this side of the mountains, he had slowly used his magic to inch by inch gain complete control over the knights' desires. He had sealed their fate when he promised them a mighty spell that would protect them, and although that was not a complete lie, hidden in that spell was the final spell to dominate their mind. There were, however, a few unforeseen ramifications to what Meslar had done. One, they started to either lose or forget their own delga abilities that they each possessed. And second, they were somewhat less effective at times then when they had been in complete control of their own thoughts.

Recently, for example, they had been unable to capture or kill the human Jyres. An action that should have been within their capabilities, despite the help the human had received. Had he made a mistake? Meslar pushed that thought away as he remembered the reason he had done it in the first place. Meslar doubted considerably the possibility that they would still be in his service without it. Meslar shook off the last of his thoughts and concentrated on the task at hand.

*****

After traveling over much ground, Jyres and Lalatco reached the bottom of the mountains. Lalatco knew from the instructions of Malick that they had to go further north to find the mountain pass. Malick was born on this side of the mountains, but his father had told him many times the story and showed him the pass when he was a young boy. Malick's father died much earlier than expected for an elf, as elves were immune to the passing of time, and old age didn't affect them. But injuries, wounds, and diseases still affected them just as they did other races; and Malick's father had developed a deadly infection that the elven clerics could not remedy.

As day turned into night and the day moon grew dim as the night moon brightened, the two explorers followed the mountains north. A gasp and an "oh no" escaped Jyres's lips, for he had seen something in the distance. Lalatco looked up and now saw what Jyres saw. In the distance, six flying horses could be seen over the Valley of the Dragons. Just after they saw the horses, two dragons emerged out of the valley and into the dark sky. Both Jyres and Lalatco watched as they circled around each other, most likely engaging in some sort of conversation. After a few moments, fire filled the sky as the dragons fought with Meslar and his knights.

"What now?" asked Jyres. "Must we help them if we can?"

Lalatco thought they should, though he did not know how they were going to do it, with the battle being raged in the sky. "If we go out there, we lose our ability to cross the mountains unseen by both the dragons and Meslar." Another second of indecision took place before they made up their minds. Leaving the third horse, Jyres and Lalatco charged out from the base of the mountains toward the valley.

Meslar was aware of two horses approaching and, unsure of who they were, sent four knights to deal with them, keeping Demorous to help against the dragons.

A dragon sent a ball of fire at Meslar, who maneuvered his horse around it and sent one of his own balls of flame from his staff back at the dragon. Crimson simply swallowed the incoming fire. Demorous and his flying horse charged at Crimson, taking him by surprise and slashing his side. Meslar continued to cast all kinds of spells on the dragons as the fight wore on. A lightning bolt from Meslar's staff hit Crimson, who was already injured by Demorous; and he began a slow fall from the sky, too injured to stay in flight. Just then, Esmeralda whipped her tail around and knocked Demorous off his horse, and he also fell toward the ground. His decent was not so slow.

Jyres caught up to the motionless horse of Lalatco's. Both of them could see the four horses that were descending from the sky toward them. Lalatco pulled out a knife from his bandolier, thinking to take a throw, but thought otherwise. The wind was blowing strong and would knock the knife down from its upward course. With no better ideas, Lalatco and Jyres turned their horses around, thinking to at least continue to draw the knights away from the dragons. And that they did. The knights, however, had the angle on them and were almost to the ground after getting closer and closer to their targets. Jyres blocked Felix's swinging sword as the horses touched the ground.

Lalatco knew they were in trouble against the four battle-tested knights. Not only were they skilled, but Meslar's spells protected them. Lalatco shouted to Jyres as they urged their horses to go faster, "Don't try to beat them! Just defend yourself!" After saying that, he broke off to the left, and Sigmon and Digmon followed.

Jyres was riding as fast as he could but could not pull away from the knights. Jyres reached back and blocked another strike from Felix, but Lord Kapel swung and clashed with Jyres's sword. Jyres could not hold on to it, and it fell from his grip. He leaped from his horse as Lord Kapel barely missed him with what would have been a fatal blow. Jyres hit the ground hard and rolled to a stop. The two knights trotted their horses up next to him, looked down at him, and started to laugh in delight. They had done what Demorous could not. They would please their master.

Lalatco saw Jyres on the ground and quickly changed his horse's direction. Lalatco reached his arm back to throw a knife; but Sigmon, one of the pursuing knights, swung and whacked the knife out of his hand and onto the grass. Lalatco tried to get away from the knight but had lost track of his second pursuer. Lalatco saw an incoming arrow and jumped off his horse to try to avoid it. Digmon had taken advantage of his brother's distraction of Lalatco and slowed his horse enough to take a good shot at Lalatco from his bow. The two brothers trotted up to Lalatco and found him lying facedown with an arrow sticking in his side.

As Jyres lay on the ground, Lord Kapel got down from his horse and pulled some rope out from one of the saddlebags. The knight bent down to tie Jyres's hands, when from out of nowhere something swooped down and knocked Felix off his horse. Lord Kapel stood up, only to find a massive creature standing behind him. A loud growl came from the creature, which then sent the knight flying with a mighty punch. The knight flew back about ten yards and lay motionless on the ground.

"Gargan!" Jyres cried as he stood up.

Gargan and another gargoyle, the one who had knocked the knight off his horse, had come to his rescue. That gargoyle was skinnier than Gargan and had blue-colored skin. Jyres jumped onto one of the horses and yelled, "Come on!" He could see Lalatco lying in the grass and feared the worst. The two gargoyles ran on all fours behind Jyres who was on the horse.

Meslar had swooped down to catch the unconscious Demorous and landed his horse on one side of the valley; the dragons landed on the other. With another command, the horse leaped back into the air with both Meslar and Demorous in tow. Meslar was feeling very drained. He had used a lot of magic and was not any closer to defeating the second dragon, though one injured dragon was still good work. But he looked to his knights on the ground and saw the gargoyles and knew that his knights had not succeeded either, and he called a retreat. Those gargoyles had interrupted his plans again. He had someone he was going to talk to about that inconvenience.

Sigmon and Digmon who were near Lalatco heard the call and also had seen what these creatures coming toward them had done to their brethren. They quickly retreated and tried to circle around to help the injured knights, Lord Kapel and Felix, get back on their horses.

Jyres and the gargoyles let the knights retreat and hastened toward Lalatco and found him still lying on the ground. Jyres knelt down next to him. "Lalatco, can you hear me? Wake up." He saw the arrow, and Jyres's heart sank. But wait, there was no blood. Jyres carefully rolled his companion over to find the arrow sticking through his coat. The arrow had not hit Lalatco's body at all. After a few moments, Lalatco came to and was happy to see Jyres looking at him, and not a knight. As Jyres corralled Lalatco's horse, Esmeralda landed close to them. It eyed the gargoyles and then spoke.

"Thank you for your help. Your distraction allowed us to fight off Meslar. Four more knights would have added to the challenge. I am curious though, what are you doing out here?"

Jyres hesitated before answering. Should he tell the dragons their plans? What would their reaction be? Jyres didn't know those answers but decided telling the truth to the dragons was the better option. Jyres answered, "We have come to cross over the mountains in hopes of finding information or someone who can help us with Meslar. But we saw the battle and felt obligated to help."

The dragon nodded in return. "A little help would be nice, though I don't know what or who you expect to find. It has been made a law that no one was allowed to cross the mountains, but times are desperate. I do warn you, the other side has been decimated, and I find it hard to believe there will be anything there that can help us. But go if you must. I must tend to Crimson." The mighty creature beat its wings and left in a flourish.

"Gargan, I owe you my thanks again. We were really in trouble there. Where did you come from?" said Jyres in an excited tone.

"Luck is with you, my friend, for as we had just glided over the mountains, we saw riders in the sky. We came with all speed not even knowing you were in danger at first. Only when we got close did I realize it was you." Gargan patted Jyres on the back, and Jyres smiled back, even though the pat was perhaps a touch too hard.

"Well, thanks to you we can continue our journey."

"Where is it you are going?"

"We are going to visit your side of the world," replied Lalatco, still a little dizzy he realized as he took a step toward the green gargoyle.

"I see," said a confused Gargan.

"We hope to find an old wizard named Zar. Do you know him?" Jyres's blue eyes were filled with hope as he asked the gargoyle the question.

"I am sorry, I don't not know that name, but we will help where we can."

Lalatco and Jyres gathered their lost weapons, and the group of four followed Malick's directions and Lalatco's lead and found what must have been the mountain pass. It had taken a little longer than hoped, and Lalatco and Jyres were both exhausted as the night grew very old. There was a small statue of a creature near the start of the path. It was a combination of many creatures, including a dragon, a human, and an elf. On the bottom inscribed in the statue were the words "A pathway has been forged to this new world, and in this new world we will live together in peace."

Gargan then spoke to the others. "It is almost light, and we must regain our strength. We will stop here. You may continue you on if you like."

"We will stay here. We are too tired as it is," exclaimed Jyres.

With that, the two gargoyles knelt down and took on the appearance of the statue next to them.

Lalatco just stared at the gargoyles, unsure of what was going on.

Jyres chuckled at his companion's expression. "I know what you mean."

9

The Pass

Jyres and Lalatco were very tired and took turns standing watch as the other one slept. It was late afternoon, or the thirteenth arc before Lalatco's headache had dissipated and both of them felt as though they had recovered their strength. They made a small supper as the sun started to go down.

"Lalatco, watch this."

Lalatco looked at Jyres with a confused look who pointed at the gargoyles. Darkness came over the land, and the two travelers watched as the stony appearance of the gargoyles just melted away. Jyres enjoyed watching Lalatco's expression as the gargoyles roared back to life.

Jyres looked at the second gargoyle more closely now, realizing he was very different from Gargan. His wings were attached to the bottom of his arms, and not his back, and hung down at his side when not in use. His face was quite long and not of human features; he looked more like a bird than anything else.

Jyres asked the gargoyle his name, and the gargoyle responded, but just like Jyres could not understand or pronounce Gargan's real name, so it was with this gargoyle.

"Well," Jyres said, "how about Hawkins?"

"Hawkins it is," the gargoyle replied.

The four of them started out on the path that would bring them to the other side of the mountain range. As they walked, Jyres realized it would take them days to cross the mountains, and perhaps that is why he only saw Gargan every so often. It was a long trip. The gargoyles could have glided in the air and traveled faster, but they decided to stay with the weary travelers. The small group traveled well into the night and finally stopped to make camp a little off the pass in a secluded opening in the trees to the south of the path. Lalatco made a fire to warm themselves, more concerned over warmth than about anyone seeing the fire.

As the group sat around the fire, Gargan talked about his world and what they would be entering into, and Lalatco and Jyres thought many things that he said may be helpful for them to know in the future. "I warn you of many creatures, including some that are fierce. There will be many things that neither of you have ever seen before. I further warn you that all gargoyles are not like us but that the evil Bram and his clan would not be as kind." Gargan talked for a long time, and before he was done, both Jyres and Lalatco had fallen asleep. The two gargoyles were content to keep to themselves as they kept a keen eye aware of anything around them.

When Jyres and Lalatco woke up, both gargoyles were there in their statue form. Jyres and Lalatco picked up camp and packed the horses. Knowing the gargoyles would catch up quickly and should not be in danger, they decided to start out, following the pass forged long ago. The path, wide enough for multiple horses at times, and sometimes narrower, was rocky but clearly marked. As they moved along at an easy pace, Jyres wondered aloud to no one in particular, "How would they have made this path?"

"What was that?"

"Oh, sorry, Lalatco, I was just wondering how they would have forged this path so long ago."

"My guess, dragon's might and delga's power."

As they trotted along on their horses, Jyres and Lalatco tried to take in the wonderful view. At times on the path, the two travelers would be near the top of a small mountain, and they could see far and wide. It was a breathtaking view. Jyres was awed by how far the mountains went and that they could see the land they just left behind as well. Jyres looked back toward the cliffs that hid his view of the plateau. He wondered how his fellow humans were doing, but in his heart, he knew he was doing the best thing for them. If he was the reason for the attacks, they would be safer without him around, and only after Meslar was dealt with would they truly be free.

As they continued, Jyres looked over at Lalatco. He noticed his hair had a grayer look to it now, the small tint changes of his hair color often now detectable to Jyres after spending a lot of time with him. Jyres decided now was his chance to ask again about Elonda. "So we have some time, and I was wondering if you wanted to fill me in on the rest of your story with Elonda."

"Well, there is not much more to say, I guess. Elonda is a free spirit. She is independent and an adventurer. She didn't want to be tied down to me. She feared that I would try to change who she was." Lalatco looked distant as though he was thinking of these times in the past.

"Why would she have thought that? Why would you try to change her?"

"I didn't want to change her, but in the end, I think she was right. I would have been too afraid for her to let her be herself." A smile came across his face. "I would have held her back, tried to keep her safe." A comfortable silence fell between them, each of them lost in thought.

During the night, Gargan and Hawkins rejoined them on the path, and they traveled together for a while again before stopping for the night. This pattern continued for a while, and on the sixth night of their journey, the four of them had reached the end of the mountain pass.

Jyres looked out over the old world; it went on and on. Jyres wondered how they would find the wizard named Zar in such a big world. Lalatco looked over the land in a kind of reverence. He knew his ancestors once lived in this land; Malick's grandfather made his name known in this land of chaos. Although Gargan's words may be of some help, Jyres and Lalatco were entering a land new to them and really had no idea what lay ahead.

A small creature could be seen in the air flying toward them. As it got closer, Jyres realized it was a small gargoyle. Once the small gargoyle landed, all three of the gargoyles were talking in their own language. Gargan then explained to Jyres and Lalatco that the other gargoyle clan was up to something, and they would have to leave. Jyres thanked them for their help, and then all three creatures were in the air and gliding away over this odd-looking land.

10

The Old World

In the early morning, Jyres and Lalatco looked over the land nearest to them. The land they would have to travel through immediately after leaving the mountains looked like a barren wasteland. Sharp rocks were everywhere, and it did not look like an easy terrain to try to navigate. They eased all three horses slowly down the slopes, and once down, they mounted two of the horses and brought along the third still carrying the food and supplies. They trod very carefully over the dangerous terrain.

Before long, they came to a point of complexity. Ahead of them was a chasm more than eight feet across. Even if they could make all three horses try to jump, the horses would not be able to clear it. As Lalatco looked for another route, however, no clear path could be seen among the rocks and canyons. Both travelers continued to look around them, and neither one had a solution. They looked at each other, both wondering what they would do now.

As they pondered the best course of action, Lalatco caught something out of the corner of his eye. It was something that was moving extremely fast. Before they knew it, the little creature was standing alongside them. Neither Jyres nor Lalatco had been able to follow it with their eyes because its movements were so quick. The creature was no more than two feet tall and had pointed ears and black fur. Its face looked almost like a dwarf's face. It looked up at them and muttered something almost inaudible. Jyres did not hear it at all, but Lalatco thought it sounded something like "Who are you?" Lalatco introduced himself and Jyres and said they were trying to cross this barren land. The creature made a motion to follow him, and the two travelers turned their horses to follow. It was no easy task to follow this creature; every move he made was lightning fast. Night started to fall, and Jyres and Lalatco started to wonder where the little guy was leading them. An arc or two later, however, they finally emerged from the treacherous area and could see a forested region to the west. The little creature was then gone, as fast as he had come.

Lalatco and Jyres headed into the wooded area and made their camp just inside the tree line. They did not risk lighting a fire because they did not want any unwelcome visitors. They ate some bread and talked quietly before they lay down for some needed sleep. Among other things, they talked about the new creature they had met and how glad they were for his help. At one point, Lalatco asked Jyres how much he knew about Meslar and his knights. Jyres admitted that he didn't know too much, so Lalatco shared with him a story.

"Well, you will remember when last we talked about the old days that there were sixteen renowned warriors that were chosen to cross the mountains. Out of those sixteen, only thirteen remain. Those thirteen are, of course, Meslar and the Knights of Enchantment. What happened after the group crossed the mountains is not entirely clear. Perhaps you would know more from human stories passed down. But it is said that after a while, Meslar was made the leader of these warriors and promised them long life, power, and riches in exchange for their service."

Jyres thought about it for a second, and then his eyes popped open a little wider. "Now that you mention it, I do remember a few things. It has always been told in our village that Meslar and the knights abandoned the human people and that Castle Mystic was built thereafter. Now that I have seen

Meslar, I suppose that he used his magic and built the castle. I guess I never really thought about that before. Also, the knights, I always remember the same knights, and they never seem to change. In all the years of my young life, they have always looked the same. I guess that makes sense if Meslar has granted them long life, and as you say, delga live longer than humans. I wonder what else he has granted the knights."

Lalatco gave a half smile and quickly continued the conversation. "Well, both you and I have discovered that their armor and weapons are magically protected as most people guessed. You also wonder what effect Meslar has had on their minds. The old stories give conflicting answers, but each knight was selected to cross the mountains for a reason. Now they all seem to answer the master's call without question. Whether that is because of some power Meslar has over them or the knights have extreme loyalty, it is hard to say." Both Jyres and Lalatco thought on that as they drifted off to sleep.

The next morning, Lalatco inspected the area as Jyres packed their bags. This forest was like no other forest the elf had seen before. The trees were much taller than his homeland, and the forest was full of sounds, some of which were totally new to Lalatco. Lalatco could feel a lot of life in the forest. He continued to be awed by it as they started out that day. Very often vines would be hanging down in their way, needing to be cut down or maneuvered around. Sometimes the plant life would be so thick that the two travelers would have to change their course considerably.

As Jyres and Lalatco continued to travel through this weird forest, they learned that the deeper they went into the forest, the darker it became, and the noisier it got. The noises and sounds of all the creatures were almost unbearable. As the two settled down for some rest, neither could fall asleep that night with all of the weird sounds around them. Both stared into the forest wondering what or who could be staring back. Lalatco kept his acute senses alert, hearing and seeing even more than he could register into his thoughts.

Both got up the next morning very tired as they started to pack up their things. As they were finishing packing, a beast sprang out from the underbrush and charged at Jyres. The creature was large, had long sharp fangs, and ran on all fours. Jyres stumbled and fell on his back. Jyres watched in horror as the beast charged him, then an arrow pierced his side, but the beast kept charging. Moments later, another arrow struck the beast, this one in its neck. Five yards away from Jyres and the beast still charged. Jyres could not get a hold of his sword hilt, the beast almost on him. Its fangs and claws lashed out at Jyres, as another arrow and a knife hit the beast at the same time. The beast slumped to the ground, but the beast claws had slashed Jyres's leg. The beast was still breathing, and Jyres rolled away from it and looked down to check his wounded leg as a woman holding a bow appeared from behind the trees.

Jyres looked up at the woman. He was immediately surprised by the sight of her. She looked nothing like that of the women Jyres knew from his village. She had blond hair that fell to her shoulders, a young-looking face, and a slender figure. She was a little shorter than Jyres, and her lighter skin was a contrast to his dark complexion. Jyres and Lalatco both were amazed by the look of the young woman who walked toward them.

Eventually, Jyres got over that and thanked her for her help. She nodded her head, drew her sword, and plunged it into the beast. The beast growled one last time, and that was it. She then retrieved Lalatco's knife, her sword, and one arrow that she deemed as reusable. She did all of this without saying a word.

Lalatco thanked her as she returned his knife. Lalatco noticed mud streaked on her face and leaves in her hair, but her ruggedness just seemed to add to her mystery and his interest in her. Only his elven friend Elonda could compare to this woman, Jyres's savior. Then after sheathing her sword, she finally talked.

"My name is Leah. Lucky for you I have been tracking this sabertooth for over a day now. I was able to catch up to him when he stopped for some lunch. So thanks."

Lalatco stepped toward her and reached out his hand; she placed her hand in his, and he raised her hand and kissed it. "I am Lalatco, from the House of Malick. I am very pleased to meet you. This here is Jyres." Lalatco pointed to him as he spoke his name. Jyres was still sitting on the ground examining his upper leg where the sabertooth had clawed him. Leah knelt down by Jyres to look at the wound. It was not very deep.

"You will be fine," she said. She pulled out a small cloth, and she was about to tie it around the wound.

"Hold on," Jyres said. "Lalatco, can you retrieve the small jar from my horse's pack?" Jyres and she talked while they waited for Lalatco.

"So what brings you two out here? I have not seen you before."

Jyres answered carefully, not wanting to share too much yet, "We are on a search. Thanks to you, I can continue." Jyres gazed into her blue eyes as he waited for her response but realized he was staring and looked away.

Leah knew there was a lot more to it than that but decided not to press. Lalatco returned with the requested item and handed it down to Leah. She accepted with a quizzical look at Jyres.

"Trust me," he said, "it is a healing salve."

Leah used her fingers to scoop a small amount of the tan paste and smoothed it unto the cut on Jyres's leg. Jyres looked her over again as she worked on tying the cloth around his leg. She wore a bright-green shirt that was tucked into her brown pants. What Jyres found as interesting were the leather coverings she also wore. Each elbow had a leather patch covering it. From the patch, strips of leather connected it to her shoulder patches and then again to a thicker leather pad that went around her waist. Strips of leather also curled around her arms and then around her fingers and connected to a patch on her palm. After she had finished helping him, Jyres thanked her; and with a little difficulty, he stood up.

"Well, excuse me while I prepare my catch." She did just that as she drew out her sword and a knife, each sheathed on one hip, and started to skin and cut the animal. While she did this, Jyres and Lalatco picked up their camp and prepared their horses for another day of travel. After Leah had completed her work on the animal, she retrieved her horse from its hiding spot in the woods.

"So," said Leah, "I must get back to my home and prepare the meat before it spoils and it is of no use to me." She said this as she wrapped the meat in some sort of wrapping made of leaves and put them in the saddlebags. She then mounted her horse and made ready to leave.

Not sure of what else to say, Lalatco quickly said, "How far away is that?"

"Not far, but far enough. Where are you headed?"

"We are without a direction at the moment."

"Come, let's talk, and we will see if I can get you headed in the right direction."

11

The Cave

Leah led the way, and the three of them traveled to her shelter, which was a small but cozy place, a little deeper in the woods. It was made of wood and had two rooms, one obviously used for sleeping. She said little as she went about her duties of unpacking the horse, checking over the home, and preparing a fire. So Lalatco and Jyres kept out of her way and saw to the care of their horses. After a while, she invited them into her home where she had a ring of stones and a fire started. She had also pulled a small rope that opened a hole in the roof for the smoke from the fire to escape. And roasting over the fire was sabertooth meat.

Both Jyres and Lalatco sat down around the fire on the dirt floor and gave each other an unsure look. Leah was being rather quiet, and the two were unsure of their approach. As they considered what to say, she let out a satisfied grunt and finally sat down. After a moment, she broke the silence. "Sorry, I am not used to company."

Both Jyres and Lalatco started to talk at the same time, and then both stopped, waiting for the other to say something. The conversation remained awkward until Leah deemed the meat ready. With the food ready, that gave them something to talk about, and both the men thanked her for the very tasty food. Both of them tried to top the other with a better compliment of the food, or shelter, or anything else they could think of. After the meal, she cleaned up and said good night and that they would talk in the morning. She went into the other room, and Lalatco and Jyres stayed the night in a shelter, which was appreciated.

Lalatco again had trouble getting to sleep. This time it was not because of the animals of the forest, but of images in his head. His mind was full of images of Leah and memories of the good times between him and Elonda. He had fallen for Leah in an instant but could not forget what he and Elonda once had. He did not know what it was about Leah, because Elonda was certainly very beautiful, but something about Leah got his mind thinking. She certainly had not talked much, and Lalatco was left wanting to get to know her. He finally fell asleep, his emotions still in an uproar.

In the morning, Leah made breakfast, and then Lalatco finally broke the tension. "We are from the other side of the mountain range. This is the first time we have ever seen your world. So as you can imagine, we are at a loss as to where exactly we are."

"I had no idea there were people past those mountains. What is it like?" The tone of her voice showed that she was genuinely shocked to hear they were from the other side of the mountain.

"Not like here," Jyres answered in almost a questioning tone.

"It is very nice. There is a valley there that is absolutely beautiful in the spring. The land seems less dangerous than here, and the rivers and waterfalls sparkle in the sunlight." Lalatco smiled, his eyes almost sparkling as well as he looked to Leah for a response.

The more they talked, the more comfortable Leah got, and she took a liking to both of them. It had been a long time since Leah had even seen an elf or a human her age, and she enjoyed the attention.

"Do you know of someone named Zar?" Lalatco asked politely.

"I can't recall ever meeting someone by that name, but I know someone who could probably help you find him. It will be a three-day journey from here to the person that can help you. I will show you the way. I am starting to enjoy your company anyway." Leah smiled and started to clean up.

"How is your leg doing, Jyres?" Leah asked.

Jyres smiled immediately. "Much better, thank you. I anticipate it will be good as new in no time."

"Great, then we can leave a little later on today," Leah remarked.

The small group ate another good meal around the tenth arc of the day and readied themselves for the trip. Well nourished and well rested, Lalatco and Jyres followed Leah and started out. The horses also had a good rest, and the group was able to start at a good pace. All three of them rode on a horse, with a fourth still carrying the supplies.

Leah led the way through the trees and hanging plants, and Lalatco said, "Leah, you had asked us about our homeland, and one thing that is for sure different is our forests. This seems so different to me."

Though Leah thought the question a little odd, she responded, "We call this a jungle. There are other wooded areas we call forests. Perhaps those would be more closely related to your home."

They traveled well into the night without stopping and did not stop until the night moon was all but invisible. They made camp in a small clearing. There was a chill in the air, perhaps a sign that winter was on its way, but the travelers did not want to alert anyone to where they were and did not start a fire. They all rolled out their blankets and settled down to sleep.

Almost a whole arc later, Lalatco was up; again, he could not sleep. Leah was now always in his mind. He looked over at her and saw her yawn and roll over, her face now pointing at him. Jyres was breathing deeply and sound asleep. Lalatco walked over and knelt down by Leah. He had no idea what he was doing, acting on impulse for some reason and throwing caution to the wind. Her eyes were closed, her hair falling over her face. He reached down and gently brushed her hair aside, then leaning even closer to her, he kissed her. Lalatco returned to his blankets, wondering why he just did what he did. Leah opened her eyes as a slight smile came to her face. Lalatco did not see her; he was looking the other way.

The three travelers were ready to go again in the afternoon. Lalatco and Leah were talking quite a bit to each other as they packed up their blankets. Jyres was quickly becoming jealous as the group started out again. He tried to think of other things. He wondered how Gargan was doing and wished there was a way to know when he would return. It sounded like there was some trouble when he left, and Jyres hoped everything was all right.

The second part of their trip went by fairly quick, and again, they traveled until late in the night. Leah was very confident she knew where she was going and said it was best to travel in the dark to avoid unwanted eyes. The group slept until late afternoon, this time one person keeping watch for a few arcs at a time and then switching with someone else.

On the third day of their trip, the little furry creature that had helped guide Lalatco and Jyres through the wasteland appeared again. The group would see him from time to time; he seemed to be following the travelers. Jyres was not worried about him; he had helped them before, and there was no reason to think he would do otherwise. He was also fun to watch as he would zip between the trees.

Very late that night, Jyres, Lalatco, and Leah had reached their destination. The three of them beheld a spooky-looking cave. The cave was very dark, and vines had grown hanging down in front of the entrance.

"This is it," said Leah.

"This is it? Who lives in there that is going to want to help us?" asked Jyres.

"Don't worry, I have been here before. There is nothing to worry about."

The group made a camp and tied up the horses a little ways from the cave under the cover of the trees. There they rested a little while, figuring it better to enter the cave in the morning. The little creature came and joined them. Lalatco was the only one who could hear what it said, but they soon learned its name was Flick.

Lalatco and Leah continued to talk and get along well, while Jyres struggled to maintain composure with the situation. He felt as though he was on the outside looking in, and he also wanted to get to know Leah. Jyres had started to feel more connected to Lalatco and the world than he ever had before. But now they had met someone new, and Jyres was afraid that connection was slipping away.

In the morning, the group again found themselves looking at the cave. Flick made no movement to follow as the other three entered the cave. Leah, having been a visitor on a few occasions, led the way; and the cave became very dark, very fast. She tried to recall the direction needed, but for some reason, her mind was a fog, and the cave seemed extra dark. Jyres became very tense; his steps became slower and smaller, as did Lalatco's and Leah's in front of him. Jyres's hand rested on his sword hilt as they continued to walk deeper into the cave. The light had all but disappeared now as the warriors continued on. All of a sudden Jyres let out a scream as the ground beneath him gave way. Lalatco reached for him in the dark but to no avail.

Jyres fell for a while before hitting the ground hard on his shoulder. Jyres just lay there for a second before sitting himself up. His shoulder hurt a lot, and he wondered if he damaged it in any way.

"Jyres," Lalatco could be heard yelling, "are you okay?"

"Yes, I am fine," said Jyres in a voice that showed he was dealing with some pain.

Jyres could see a little better in this part of the cave and looked up to see where he had fallen. It was probably a ten-foot drop or so. He also looked all around him and saw the light coming from his right.

"Now what?" It was Lalatco's voice again.

"Leah, what can you tell us?" asked a hopeful Jyres.

"I don't know. For some reason, it doesn't feel the same. Something is different since I was here last. I am left unsure."

"I see some light down here in this tunnel. I am going to take a look," Jyres said as he looked back up toward where he had fallen and his companions.

"Okay, meet back here within an arc's time if you don't find anything. Leah and I will search up here."

Jyres stood up, and his right hand grasped his left shoulder; the whole left side of his body hurt. He pitied that side as he started to walk. He followed the tunnel to his right, and it continued to get lighter as it turned more to the right. The tunnel came into a larger more open area just a fraction of an arc later. Jyres looked up, and a long ways above him, Jyres could see an opening in which light was pouring in. There was a small lake at the center of this circle-like area. There were no other exits, only the tunnel from which he had entered. He looked into the water and could see his reflection. Not something he had experienced very often. He gave himself a half smile and chuckled.

An old man sat very still. He could see the images of the intruders in his mind. One of them was on his own now, by the pond, and the other two were wondering aimlessly in the caves. He let that image go and focused on the man by the pond.

"Why do you seek me?" he said out loud.

Jyres heard the voice, which startled him, and he drew his sword and looked around frantically.

"Where are you? Show yourself!" Jyres yelled.

"Why do you seek me?" said the voice.

"I am looking for someone and was told you might be able to help."

"I don't like trespassers in my cave, and it appears you are stuck."

Jyres heard the sound of iron boots coming down the tunnel. It sounded like at least a dozen men.

"Now what?" asked the voice.

The footsteps came closer now, and Jyres started to sweat. He tried to climb the wall, but there was no way he would be able to. The footsteps were very close now.

"You must decide!"

Jyres had no other choice; he sheathed his sword and jumped into the pond.

He fell deeper and deeper into the water. Then he saw an opening in the side wall of the pond. He swam through the opening and swam hard, hoping to get out of the water before it would be too late. He gasped for air as his head finally cleared the water into air. He looked around as he moved his arms and legs to keep himself from sinking and saw an almost identical room to the one he had just left. There was a tunnel as before, this time going in a different direction. Jyres climbed out of the water, and he heard the voice again.

"A brave choice you made."

Jyres proceeded down the tunnel and could see it open into a room not too far from where he was. He walked in and could not believe what he saw. A table was set up in the middle of the room, with four chairs around it. Food was set out on the table, and an old man was seated on a wooden chair at the far side of the room.

"Welcome," said the old man. "Please, have a seat."

The old man pointed at the table as he said this, so Jyres sat down at the table with a grimace; he was going to be sore in the morning. The man was tall and thin with a long dark-brown robe. He had a short white beard and bald head, and many wrinkles graced his face. The old man got up from his chair, grabbed his walking stick, and walked over to the table. Just as he did so, Lalatco and Leah entered the cave from the other side. The old man smiled at his guests and said, "Please, everyone come sit, and we will eat."

Lalatco gave Jyres, who was dripping water, an odd look; and Jyres just shrugged.

A very good meal had been prepared; and it included a honey-glazed ham, fruit, and vegetables. It was the most complete meal the three guests had had in a long time. The old man let them eat before diving into conversation.

"So what brings the three of you here?" the old man asked in a voice that showed both his age and his wisdom as Jyres finished dessert.

Jyres quickly swallowed and replied, "How did you know we were coming?"

"He is a powerful man," explained Leah. "And I think, the reason I could not find my way." It was said more as a question than a statement.

"It is good to see you, Leah. It has been a long time since your adventures took you here." The old man continued with a smile on his face, "Always into some crazy adventure, this one. And yes, I did want to make it interesting for you since you had company along with you. Who are your friends?"

"This is Jyres and Lalatco," replied Leah.

Then Lalatco asked, "Your name, sir?"

"I go by a great many names. Don't bother yourself with them. Again, why are you here?"

"We are seeking a man named Zar, and Leah thought you would be able to help." Lalatco had let a little impatience slip into his voice.

"Oh, did she now? Yes, I have heard that name, Zar, but not for a long time. More recently, I have heard the name Zarth, even more recently, the name Aramith, and most recently, the name Ranith. The names are all one and the same. Whether Zar, Zarth, Aramith, or Ranith, they all refer to me."

"What?" questioned Leah in a surprised tone. "You said your name was Ranith!"

"That is one of my names, yes," replied Zar.

Jyres and Lalatco could not believe it. Their search did not take long at all. It was him, Zar, the wizard, the one who could help them and the one from all of the songs and stories. Lalatco burst out into a song simply titled "The Wonderful Zar." Zar sat back and listened to the song that he had not heard in many a year.

Jyres and Lalatco then went on to explain why they were searching for him. They told in detail about Meslar and that he was after Jyres because of a prophecy or something, and they hoped Zar could help explain it. The old man did not say anything, and his mood did not change throughout any of the explanation. Only once did Jyres see the man blink, and that was when the name Meslar was mentioned. After Jyres and Lalatco were done talking, Zar stood up.

"I will think on this matter tonight, and we will talk more tomorrow."

Satisfied for now, Jyres, Leah, and Lalatco went back to the front of the cave. Leah had no problems this time leading them out of the cave. They brought in the horses, and Flick came in as well, making camp in the mouth of the cave.

When all three guests had left his room, Zar grabbed a torch from the wall and walked to the back of the room and proceeded down a nondescript tunnel. He walked along with the help of his walking stick, and finally he came to a huge cave room. The ceiling in this room was very high, and the room was in the shape of a circle. The only entrance to the room was the way he had come. Zar walked forward into the dark room, holding the torch high. The light that touched the walls revealed pictures and old writings. Many stories, tales, and prophecies were inscribed in these walls. Zar had found them long ago.

There was one prophecy Zar was looking for, so he walked around the room looking for the prophecy. The language used in the inscription was very old, and very few could still read it. Zar was one of those few. Zar gazed up at the beginning of the inscription and read it out loud.

"In the years to come there will be war, famine, and many other disasters. This world will sometimes struggle to survive. In the far-off years, this world will be doomed, unless one man changes the fate of the world. Evil will rise and threaten all life. The evil will unlock the gate. One man will come along who can close the gate. This man will surprise many but must close the gate or it will all be for naught. One man can save this world. Only he has the chance."

In all of Zar's years of study and research, only a couple other times had he read something about the gate, and it was long ago, and he did not remember where. It was not in any of his old scrolls. The location of the gate was not a secret. How could it be? But any history of it seemed to be lost or out of his reach. What was it truly?

Zar knew Meslar once, and with Meslar stirring up trouble, he was worried about the prophecy he just read. At one time, Zar had thought Meslar would be the one who would save the world, the one from the prophecy. Zar had not thought Meslar would be the evil from the prophecy. There were other prophecies as well, but this one had jumped straight to his mind while he listened to the travelers talk.

Zar read some more before retiring. There was one funny story inscribed on these walls that he read every time he was in this part of the cave. It was a very funny story to the old man, and he laughed every time he read it. No different this time around.

12

Back at Home

Elonda had been on her trip for about three days now. Malick had ordered her to find out what had been going on of late in the other parts of the land. She had already been to the Valley of the Dragons and learned of the battle that took place there. She also learned that one dragon had been injured, but they had forced the retreat of Meslar, with a little help from Jyres, Lalatco, and the gargoyles. She was now on her way to meet with the dwarves. It was the night of her third day, and since night had fallen, she headed to the east and camped among the trees. She decided not to attempt to go over the hills of Tomackus. Not when goblins and orcs would be about in the dark.

Elonda awoke with the sun and got an early start. She mounted her horse and left the trees for the hills. The wind was strong and blew her long black hair across her face. As she rode at a moderate pace, she wondered how Lalatco was doing. She did miss him, though she was not sure how much. Nothing had been right between them lately, and to be honest, she was not sure how she really felt. She told herself she would know when she saw him next. She focused on the task at hand and rode a little faster toward the cliffs.

*****

Meslar stood silently on a rock far to the north of Castle Mystic. This was a predetermined location, and Meslar would be meeting his fellow schemer at a predetermined time. It was the middle of night, and complete darkness enveloped him as he waited. Meslar mulled over in his mind the questions he wanted to ask and how to ask them, as every interaction with this creature had to be planned and calculated. This was the sixth such meeting between these two, and Meslar enjoyed the challenge the interactions with the creature presented to Meslar's analytic mind. Their meetings had made a lot of progress when the creature had brought him a copy of a prophecy that they had discussed the meeting before. The creature giving him the actual old parchment put much more stock into their discussions and Meslar's trust of the creature. That was on their third meeting, and since then, this game of intellect had ensued.

Meslar continued to wait but did not have to wait long before he saw the creature emerge from the rocks across from his location. The creature, barely visible in the darkness, stood across from Meslar just as it had on their other meetings. Each waited for the other to speak. Meslar finally broke the silence.

"It is good to see you, my friend. I am glad you honored the time we set."

"I hold to my words," came the response from the creature whose hold on the basic language was solid even though it was not its native language.

"I hope that we both do, for that is the only way that this agreement can succeed." Meslar wondered how being able to see the other's facial expressions would affect their conversations, for each meeting had happened in the deepest of nights, and neither had that luxury. Meslar waited for a response, but after hearing none, he asked his first question.

"Gargoyles from your part of the world have been stirring up trouble in mine. I am assuming that you know this and hoped you would be able to share some insights." Meslar had phrased his question like this on purpose, giving credit to the creature for knowing events taking place.

"I do know this but is not time yet to reveal our plans or partnership."

This was the typical short answer the creature always gave Meslar, and he was ready for it. "You are correct." Again, Meslar was trying to give credit to the creature. "But I believe there must be something you can tell me, some piece of knowledge that just by me knowing it would not reveal our partnership." Meslar waited patiently, knowing the creature would think before responding.

"For reasons unknown, the gargoyles you speak of have been exploring more of the world. The happenings thereafter are of mere coincidence."

Unsure whether to believe the creature or not, he moved on and asked his next question. "How will I find you when I deem that the time is right?" Meslar this time asked in a way that gave himself the upper hand.

The creature, however, turned it around on him right away when he said, "I will find you."

The next day, Meslar stood in his chamber looking out the window. His battle with the dragons did not go as well as he had hoped, although the very brief conversation with the dragons before the battle was encouraging. None of them knew why he was really after Jyres. Meslar chuckled to himself. The dragons were supposed to be the overseers of the land, and they had no idea what was going on. The knights were now fully healed from any of their injuries they suffered in the battle, and he himself was feeling as powerful as ever.

He also was not overly fond about how his conversation last night went either. He still didn't know how much he could trust the creature but knew he would need it to complete his plan. Overall, that was not the immediate problem; Jyres was. He must find Jyres and put an end to him. He called for Demorous, who was quick to respond and came to his chambers.

"Yes, my lord, what is it?"

"Do you remember the battle with the dragons? Was Jyres one of the men who charged in on his horse?"

Confused, Demorous answered even though he knew Meslar already knew the answers, "Your knights have reported that, yes, he was, an elf was the other one, and of course the gargoyles."

"Oh yes, the gargoyles," Meslar said. "Jyres and the elf were obviously going somewhere. We must find out where. If only I could have bested the dragons, then I could have aided the knights, and Jyres would have already been dealt with."

"Maybe the elves will know where they were going. He does appear to be in league with them," Demorous commented.

"Yes, he does." Meslar smiled. "Ready the men."

*****

Elonda's horse thundered up to the cliffs. The cliffs were a mix of the colors brown and green, some grass patches often present on the brown rock formations. As she observed the cliffs, two dwarves came out to meet her. She asked to see Vurth, and the two dwarves started to lead her to him. Elonda had met Vurth on more than a few occasions, but he still made her nervous. He was always so demonstrative and had a voice so deep and loud that it sounded as though he could wake the dead. The dwarves stopped at the door to Vurth's throne room and motioned for her to go in. Preparing for a typical Vurth welcome, she took a breath and entered the room.

"Elonda, nice to see you. How can I help thee today?" Surprised by his very cordial reply, she didn't know what to say. "Dragon got your tongue, girl?"

That was more like it, she thought. "No, just waiting for my usual greeting." The two shook hands and talked a short while, Elonda filling him in on some things that had happened before walking outside to stand on a naturally made lookout. The cliffs gave the dwarves a nice view of much of the area.

"Malick has you out and about, I assume," said the orange-bearded dwarf.

"Yes, I have already learned that another battle took place at the valley. The dragons were attacked by Meslar. They were able to defend themselves, but Crimson was injured. Lalatco, Jyres, and the gargoyles were also there."

"I figured as much," replied the dwarf in his often gruff-sounding voice. "We could see fire in the sky above the valley." He paused before saying, "It has been a while since we have talked. We can see the humans' new home from our cliffs. You mentioned that Malick thinks Meslar is specifically after Jyres, and now you tell me that Jyres is not there. So Jyres and the elf, what were they doing by the valley?" Vurth eyed Elonda, waiting for an answer, and realized he would not be given one. "They have crossed over the mountains then?" Elonda just nodded in return. "Makes sense. Send him far from everyone else, aye?

"What is that?" shouted Vurth in that voice that could make the ground shake.

Elonda followed his gaze and looked across the desert and saw a cloud of dust moving in their relative direction. "It must be the knights. They are the only ones who live out in that direction. Meslar must be casting some spell, causing us not to be able to see them clearly. Where do you think they are going, Vurth?"

"By the direction they are traveling, it does not look like they are coming here. My bet would be your home."

"Mine too," said Elonda.

Elonda was quick to react and was off in a hurry to her horse. She could hear Vurth shouting after her, something like "Hold on, girl" or some such thing. She had to warn the elves before it was too late. Elonda jumped on her horse and was on her way. She stayed to the east side of the river, and her horse was sprinting toward the lake. Before long, Elonda was in the forest and nearing the lake. She could tell her horse was getting tired, but she pushed on. Suddenly the horse reared, and Elonda flew from the saddle. She hit the ground hard but rolled to her feet in one smooth motion. Many creatures had formed a circle around her and the horse. The creatures were the size of wolves but had a rubbery skin and were some kind of water creature. They also had fins for tails. Elonda saw a few more creatures appear out of the lake. All of the creatures started to howl, and she drew her sword.

The first creature jumped at Elonda, but her blade was faster and found its way into the animal's belly. Quickly, she removed the blade and batted away a second creature. Three of them attacked at once, they charged her, and she could see their deadly fangs. Elonda swung out her sword, desperately trying to block the attacks. Her blade crashed into the side of the first creature as more leaped at her. Just then, an ax blade sent both creatures right back to the ground. Vurth had followed on a horse of his own and came galloping in with ax swinging. Elonda whistled for her horse as she and Vurth fended off a few more of the water creatures. She sprang onto the horse with ease, and the two warriors kicked their horses into gear. As they escaped from the ferocious creatures, Vurth bellowed over the huff beats, "Well, I guess the woods do have some dangerous creatures after all."

The horses were exhausted when Vurth and Elonda made it to the elven home. Elonda and Vurth were very tired themselves as they made their way through the trees to see King Malick. Their rapid pace had made a trip that usually took a day and a half into a day. They reported the news that Meslar was on his way, and the elves made ready for whatever was to come.

Early in the morning, before the second arc, scouts reported that Meslar and six knights were very close. Vurth decided to stay out of sight, as he was unsure if his presence would be a hindrance. In the distance, talking could be heard. The knights had been stopped and questioned by some elven scouts. The scouts led Meslar and the others into an opening among the trees. There they waited, and King Malick appeared above them at the other end of the clearing, on a wooden walkway.

"What do you want, Meslar?"

Meslar smiled a crooked smile and responded, "That is not much of a welcome, King. That is what they call you, is it not? Here amongst the trees." Meslar held his arms out wide, gesturing to the forest around him. Meslar paused before continuing. "I am wondering where is Jyres and your elf, oh, what is his name, Lalatco, I believe it is. I was wondering where they are."

King Malick gave a short chuckle. "Get out of here, Meslar. There is nothing I can help you with." His voice showed no fear or change from its usual tone. After the king had said that, he turned to walk away, but Meslar wanted an answer. He pointed his staff at Malick and barked out a spell. The purple gem in the staff started to glow, and Malick was lifted from his feet. King Malick hovered in midair, as a battle cry was shouted. Elonda, yelling at the top of her lungs, emerged from the trees on Meslar's left with ten elves, arrows notched on their bows. Ten more elves appeared to Meslar's right, the elves also with bows and arrows ready.

"Set the king down, Meslar, or suffer the consequences!" yelled Elonda.

Meslar turned and looked at Elonda standing tall with sword held high, ready to give the command to let the arrows loose. Meslar wondered to himself how he did not see it coming.

"Do it now, Meslar," came Elonda's voice again.

Meslar gently set the king back down on his perch and lowered his staff. A little tension was eased among the elves as Malick found his feet firmly planted on his spot in the trees. King Malick took a deep breath and climbed down the wooden steps built around the tree. Meslar dismounted from his horse and waited as Malick approached Meslar until he was inches from his face.

"Look here, Meslar," he said, "you cannot just come in to my forest and demand your questions be answered. This madness had gone on long enough. Jyres has done nothing wrong, and you have no reason to hunt him down."

"Oh, don't I?" Meslar smiled as he questioned the king. "Have you not figured it all out yet, Malick? Are you not up on your ancient history? If you think this is about Jyres doing some great injustice toward me, then you are wrong."

"Well then, please enlighten me, oh, masterful Meslar," Malick answered sarcastically, his voice finally revealing his frustration.

"All in due time, King. I am merely fulfilling my prophecy. Now if you would please tell me the whereabouts of Jyres."

"No" was Malick's simple reply.

"It was a simple request. Why not give a simple answer?" asked Meslar. Again, Malick's response was the same, but Meslar knew he was hiding something.

Meslar lunged out his staff at Malick who had turned enough to take most of the blow on his shoulder, and he then rolled to his left. By the time Malick had completed his roll, Elonda's sword had dropped, and twenty arrows were leashed into the air. The arrows were upon them before the knights could react; many of the arrows bounced off shields and armor. About five arrows hit horses, with one or two finding a spot in between a knight's armor. Miraculously, it seemed that neither Meslar nor his horse was struck, and none of the horses fell or threw their riders.

Still determined to get an answer, Meslar went after Malick again, swinging his staff. Another elf stepped in front of the king and blocked the staff with his sword. At the same time, the knights charged the elves who had fired the arrows. The elves dodged the charging horses nimbly. Meslar realized that he was severely outnumbered as more and more elves came running to defend their king. Meslar turned and took two big steps and let his power run through him and then used his staff to vault him onto his horse. Meslar yelled a retreat, and the seven intruders rode out of the clearing, and no order came from Malick to follow.

Meslar and the six knights continued the retreat and urged the horses on fast until they had completely left the trees behind. Meslar slowed his horse to a walk and called Demorous to him. "Demorous, I have a feeling that Jyres and the elf are up to something. There was a reason they were close to the valley, and Malick was hiding something from me. Perhaps they have even crossed over the mountains. We will have to accelerate our plans. Everyone come in close. I will heal you and your horses."

The knights did as instructed, and Meslar got down from his horse and planted his feet and staff firmly on the ground. After a few moments, Meslar began a slow, quiet chant. After a few more moments, small waves of energy came up from the ground and found their way to the horses and knights who were hit with arrows. Just like that, the wounds were healed. Meslar took a few moments to rest before talking to the knights.

"I will take four of these knights with me and proceed over the mountains. We will search for signs of Jyres, but continue with the main mission. The four that I choose are the Silver Shadow, Lemont the Lost, Sigmon, and Digmon. You, Demorous, shall report back to the castle and gather supplies. Set out again from the castle once you have supplies, and bring three more knights with you. That will leave four knights to guard the castle. I will let you choose those that stay back. Once you cross the mountains, I will find you or send instructions. Any questions?"

"No, sir, good luck."

Demorous and Bartholomew watched as the five riders rode toward the mountains. The two of them then headed back to Castle Mystic to gather supplies.

*****

Back in the woods of the elves, King Malick, his queen, Vurth, and Elonda sat together discussing the events of the day. Much had been said, but little had been decided. Soon silence fell over the group. It was not long before Elonda had enough of that.

"Listen, we sent Jyres and Lalatco out on their own hoping they would find some lost wizard. Now they will need our help.

Meslar has proven he will look everywhere for Jyres. I will not just sit here and do nothing."

Angry, she got up from the table and left the room. As soon as she had exited the room, she began to cry.

"She is right," Vurth said to Malick. "We have to do something." Vurth's voice sounded very deep and strong. "At least ask the dragons for help, Malick."

Elonda stood alone now, on a lookout constructed very high in one of the trees. There were still a few tears that could be found running down her face. Her thoughts were not really on Lalatco though, which surprised her. She was dwelling more on what had happened to this land that was supposed to be a land with no war. *Human corruption again,* she thought. Meslar was ruining everything the travelers who came to this new land had built. Meslar and the knights were even some of those travelers. The humans caused the War of Ages; and now another human, Meslar, was about to start another one.

Why did Jyres seem so different then? she asked herself. Her tears subsided as she thought of Jyres. He was one human who had been trying to do good things for others. Everything he had done was for the good of his village, not for power or pride. She wondered if most humans were like Meslar or like Jyres. A voice interrupted her thoughts. "Elonda." She turned around to see Malick, who had come up the wooden stairs.

"Yes, Your Majesty?" she replied, wiping away the last of her tears.

"You are right," started Malick who sighed. "Go and talk to the dragons and see what they think about all this. Please report back what they have to say. Vurth is going home to prepare his men just in case, as will I." After saying that, Malick descended down from the giant tree.

Elonda took a deep breath and closed her eyes, as a wind gust blew her beautiful hair and gray cloak all around her.

Elonda awoke the next morning with renewed vigor. She and two other elves left the protection of the forest on horseback and rode out toward the Valley of the Dragons. A full day's journey saw them reach the valley after dark. They rode into the valley and saw both dragons lying down in the middle of the valley. The three riders approached the dragons and dismounted.

The nearest dragon, Esmeralda, yawned and said in her deep womanly voice, "To what do we owe the pleasure of your visit?"

"What do you think about Meslar and his actions?" asked Elonda.

"Not much, they have been in constant motion, never content to stay in their castle. We have fought with him twice now, the second time leaving my companion injured, though he is starting to heal."

"He came to our home with his knights, demanding to know where Jyres was," replied Elonda. "He is up to something and will continue to hunt Jyres."

The dragon yawned again and said, "We have done what we can for now."

Elonda started to get frustrated. No one seemed to listen to her lately, and she made another plea to the dragons, the frustration clearly evident in her voice.

"What about the dream you made when you first made the path to this side of the mountains? You wanted all creatures to live in peace. How is this goal going to be accomplished with you, the most powerful creatures, sitting around and doing nothing?"

She realized that this was not a wise thing to say to a dragon. Dragons thought themselves as wise creatures and did not like to be insulted in such a way. She hoped that her calling them the most powerful creatures would save her from getting toasted.

The dragons roared, and Esmeralda got up on her legs. "You dare insult us?" roared her powerful voice. The two elves with Elonda backed away fast, but Elonda did not move an inch. This just made the dragons more upset. Crimson, mostly healed from his injuries, stood up; and both dragons spread their wings, showing their full size, and sent fireballs at the retreating elves. They missed, on purpose of course, and the two elves ran out of the valley. The dragons now walked in a circle around Elonda. They laughed to themselves, realizing how easy a kill this would be. Surprising Elonda, the same dragon spoke again.

"Now is not yet the time to act. Meslar is very powerful as well. Now I suggest you leave before I change what I want to eat for supper."

Elonda bowed saying, "Thank you for your time." She then turned around and walked toward her companions and the horses. She let out a deep breath, thankful that the dragons let her walk away unhurt.

It was a long way back home for the elves and the horses. The horses were already tired from the day before, and all three panicked when they had seen the dragon's fire. Elonda was in despair, and her two fellow elves were not happy with her after almost getting killed by a dragon. To her, it seemed she was alone in her thoughts. She had half a mind to go galloping over those mountains right now and try to help Jyres and Lalatco, but she knew that neither she nor her horse could make it right now. So she reported back what had happened to Malick and went to bed and slept for a long while.

13

A Hard Time for Jyres

Zar slept well but had many dreams and visions. He awoke in the morning with a confused mind. He spent the morning in his study trying to sort everything out. He served lunch to his visitors and after lunch asked to speak to Jyres alone. Jyres and Zar sat together at the table. Zar finally said something after what had felt like forever to Jyres. Jyres had no idea what Zar wanted to talk to him about and was getting anxious.

"Good afternoon," Zar said. "Follow me."

Jyres followed Zar into a tunnel and deep into the cave until they came to a circular room. It was dark, but Zar had brought a torch. Zar let out a deep breath over the torch, and amazingly it sprang to life with fire. Almost as surprising, Zar brought Jyres close to the walls; and on the walls, Jyres could see inscriptions. Zar brought him to a particular spot, but Jyres could not read the weird language. Apparently Zar could, and he translated it for Jyres. It was the same prophecy Zar had read out loud to himself the night before.

"In the years to come there will be war, famine, and many other disasters. This world will sometimes struggle to survive. In the far-off years, this world will be doomed, unless one man changes the fate of the world. Evil will rise and threaten all life. The evil will unlock the gate. One man will come along who can close the gate. This man will surprise many but must close the gate or it will all be for naught. One man can save this world. Only he has the chance."

When Zar was done reading the inscription, he turned to face Jyres. "What do you think?"

"It is some sort of prophecy" was all Jyres could think of to respond.

"Who do you think it is about?" Zar asked.

"I don't know. My guess would be Meslar. Why else would you read it to me?"

"Yes, you are right. I think the evil referred to here is Meslar. Who is the hero?"

Jyres scratched his head in thought. "I don't know. You, I suppose."

"Wrong," exclaimed Zar. "The other person referred to in this prophecy is you." Zar smiled at the shocked expression that passed Jyres's face.

Jyres had no idea why Zar thought he was in this prophecy. "How can that be? How do you know?"

Zar scratched at his white beard and said, "Think about it for a second. First of all, I know that because of the time period this was written in and what was going on, that by using the word *man* in the prophecy, they really mean a human male. Back then, humans were the only ones referred to as men or women. You are a human male. Think of all the humans you know. Humans are not exactly in abundance right now, so there are not a lot to pick from, and even less who have had interactions with Meslar. Name one of them that could stand up to Meslar. Obviously, no one comes to mind, besides you of course."

Zar smiled and started talking again. "Next, think of what you have already done. You have already stood up to him twice. You went to the meeting in open defiance of him ruling over your village, and you attacked him to help the dragons. My final point is this. You came out here looking for me in a land you have never been to before. Why? Because you think I can stop him? No, that is not why you came out here. You came out here for answers. You have been opposing Meslar since the beginning, and you must finish it. It is your destiny to destroy Meslar, and he knows it. That is why he tried to destroy you. He knew what you were destined to do. I can help and guide you, but as the prophecy says, the fate of the world is in your hands."

Jyres nodded his head, turned, and started to walk back up the tunnel. Before long, he was running. Jyres didn't know why he was running; it kind of just started happening. He just felt this need to get away and be alone. He needed some time to go through what Zar had all said. It made sense. He had been opposing Meslar; he went to the meeting knowing he would be in trouble if Meslar knew he was going there. He had been bait for the trap they set on the knights. He and Lalatco had drawn away the attention of the knights to help the dragons before really thinking about what could happen. It was still too much. How was he supposed to save the world? And what was this gate he was supposed to close? He hoped Zar would be able to answer some of his questions later on. Jyres's thoughts continued, and he continued to run, and ran right out of the cave, surprising Flick as he ran by.

That night, Jyres still hadn't wrapped his head around what Zar had told him. Lalatco found Jyres pacing back and forth at the mouth of the cave. "Hey," he said quietly to Jyres. Jyres just nodded and continued his pacing. "Zar told us what he told you," Lalatco said, watching Jyres as he talked. "It does make sense. But you are not in this alone."

Jyres finally stopped pacing. "I need to talk with Zar," he said.

"Agreed, but get some sleep first," Lalatco said firmly.

*****

Lalatco and Leah started spending a lot of time together over the next couple of days. Jyres sought answers and knowledge from Zar, and they always seemed to be talking, which left Lalatco and Leah time to talk as well. The two became close quickly. They both always thought back to that night not so long ago when Lalatco kissed her while she "slept." Today was no different. Zar and Jyres were talking, and Lalatco and Leah decided to take a walk. The two of them were laughing at each other's comments when the conversation took a sudden change in direction.

"What will you do, Leah, if Jyres and I must leave on another journey?" Leah did not have an answer and did not reply. Lalatco spoke again. "Meslar is not from your world. Do not feel like you have to come with us when we leave."

This time Leah answered him, "I know, but I have been living out here for so many years without a purpose. I was just trying to survive. I was always alone. For a while, it was exciting, living in the wild, but the excitement has lessened to a dull roar. Now I have something in my life, you, Lalatco, and I don't want to lose it."

A tear fell down her cheek, and Lalatco pulled her close to him and hugged her. They forgot about everything else in that moment. Meslar and the scary world were distant memories as the two of them embraced each other.

Back in the cave, Jyres and Zar continued to talk about Meslar, the prophecy, and what had to be done next. They also talked about the world, the gargoyles, and Gargan whom Jyres had not seen in a long time. Jyres enjoyed the conversation with the old man and often wondered why he chose to remain in this cave.

The conversation then turned very serious about what must be done. Jyres listened as Zar explained he had only read about the gate once or twice. They both knew that somehow they had to find where Zar had read it before. Unfortunately, neither had come up with any great options. Then Zar came up with an idea.

"There used to be a giant library back before the War of Ages. Although a lot of it has been destroyed, part of the library was built underground. It is possible that part of the library was left untouched by the war. We may get lucky and find more writings about the gate."

"Well, that is the best idea we have had thus far," Jyres replied, running his hands through his hair and then putting his arms straight up to stretch. "Let's see what the others think about it."

Jyres walked out of the cave looking for Lalatco and Leah but found only Flick. Flick waved his hand, and Jyres followed him. They went a ways through the trees and stopped before a clearing. Jyres looked out into the clearing and saw something he did not want to see. Lalatco and Leah were sitting next to each other on the ground giving each other a hug. Then he watched as they gave each other a kiss. Jyres looked away and walked toward the cave. His mind was filled with anger and greed. While he was planning how to save the world, Lalatco had time to take Leah for his own. *I am the hero. Why does Lalatco get Leah?* he thought.

Zar was standing at the mouth of the cave when Jyres came back.

"We go alone" was all he said to Zar.

Zar stood there awhile and saw Lalatco and Leah walking back hand in hand. Zar returned to the inside of the cave and found Jyres. "Listen to me," he said in a tone that made Jyres do exactly that. "I have seen the way you look at Leah. But Leah does not matter right now. You cannot be worried about her as you go about your adventure. It is good that she is close to Lalatco. They will watch over each other. The trials you will face are great enough. You cannot be distracted in any way, and we may need their help. I will also talk to Flick. He likes to travel with me when I travel." Jyres simply nodded, and Zar left the cave again.

A little later during the day, Zar, Jyres, Lalatco, Leah, and Flick were all seated around the table in the cave. They had just finished eating, and Zar started the needed conversation. "Jyres and I have decided to make a trip to an old library that is many days' worth of travel away from here. We are in search of some scrolls that would shed some light on this situation." The old man chuckled. "We don't even know if there will be anything there to grant worth to the journey. It is completely up to you, whether or not you choose to come along." It was silent until Flick made a noise, and Zar said, "Flick will come along."

Lalatco then spoke up. "I started out with Jyres, and I intend to finish beside him."

Zar spoke again. "The road will be dangerous. It is a barren wasteland between here and the scrolls. We don't wish ill will on any of you."

Confidently Lalatco replied, "I understand, and I will go."

"As will I," followed Leah's voice.

*****

Meslar and his four knights had found the mountain pass easily enough. They had come across these mountains years before. They camped for the night at the entrance to the pass and would start the long trek the next morning. Meslar thought about when he was younger coming across these mountains and his young years before that. Meslar had always been interested in prophecies and stories, but there were two prophecies that he knew well, and they both involved the gate. An old wizard named Zar in the past had always told him that one of the prophecies was about him. The prophecy was about one man changing the fate of the world by having a chance to close the gate. The other prophecy Meslar had learned of more recently and is the one he was really interested in. He had the original scroll on which it is written; it was given to him by his fellow schemer. Meslar of course had it memorized though, so he no longer had to read from the scroll. The Prophecy of the Gate read as follows:

> In the deserted lands in the west stands
> the gate. A gate not of metal or rock, but of
> fire and power. To open the gate, two things
> are needed. First a key, a key that has been
> well hidden. The second thing that is needed

is a heart that has no fears. Only the fearless can open the gate. Each person who tries to pass through the fire will face a different challenge. I say again, a person must have no fear. Once the gate is opened an unspeakable power will be realized. Only the person who has the key and passes through the fire can unlock the power.

That is what Meslar wanted, power, ultimate power. To be the most powerful creature now and forever was his goal. The scroll Meslar had was ripped off after the prophecy, which Meslar found interesting. However, this was the least of his worries. Two other things were on his mind. One was Jyres. The second was the key. Meslar assumed that Jyres was the one who had a chance to prevent someone from unlocking the power of the gate. That is why Meslar had been trying to get rid of him. It was still his number one priority. Jyres started to oppose Meslar just as Meslar started to begin his planning. Meslar knew of no other human that would oppose him. The timing was too convenient.

Getting the key was Meslar's next priority; the same creature who gave Meslar the scroll claimed to know where the key was. Visiting this creature who resided on the other side of the mountains would be one of the first tasks. Meslar still didn't like how much he had to rely on this creature. He was the one who had given him the scroll and was the one who knew where the key was. Meslar had tried to gain some ground by trying to control the timeline and did so by coming over the mountains early. But he was still on the mercy of this creature telling when and where to meet up with him.

It was pretty cold up in the mountains, and Meslar could see patches of snow as they began their first day of travel. Meslar thought it may become a little difficult to travel in the highest parts of this path. Their first day of travel went well enough, and they covered a lot of ground before making camp.

*****

Zar, Jyres, Lalatco, Leah, and Flick were ready for the first stage of their journey. Flick rode on the back of Zar's horse as the four horses trotted away from the cave. The weather had definitely gotten colder since Jyres and Lalatco had started their journey to find Zar. Soon, snow would start falling on the now-leafless trees. Zar had warned about the desolate land they would be crossing, and so in preparation for that, the horses would have to carry a lot of food and water.

The travelers started out west from the cave, and by the late afternoon of the first day of their journey, the trees were thinning, and the jungle would soon be left behind. They camped at the edge of the jungle, and after a small meal, they went to sleep early, and they kept watch in shifts. Lalatco had the second watch. Most of his time was spent watching Leah, but Lalatco could still hear the faint sounds of the area around him. He pulled out one of his knives and flipped it in the air and caught it by the handle. Leah rolled over on to a rock, and she woke up with a groan. She saw Lalatco watching her and walked over to where Lalatco was sitting, a little ways away, and sat by him.

"Can't sleep?" Lalatco asked.

"Not very well. Ground is too rough." There was a long pause before Leah spoke again. "What are you thinking?"

Lalatco did not really know how to answer the question. His mind was wandering quite a bit. Eventually he turned and looked into her dark-blue eyes and said, "To be honest, there are few times when I am not thinking about you. But I also know that Jyres has taken a liking to you as well. I don't want this to bother him. The old man has put some crazy ideas in his head, and he needs to be 100 percent focused on what he is trying to do."

Leah looked back at him, and she could not even remember the last time she had seen an elf. Was it for that reason she had gravitated to him and not Jyres? Right away she had noticed they both were interested.

"I understand, but you and I have grown close, and he is your friend. He will understand, and as you said, he will be focused on other things." Lalatco nodded, and they enjoyed the silence together.

Zar roused everybody early, and they were back on their horses as the first light of day crept through the darkness of night. The horses had a nice rest, and thus, the group made good time. The group had left the cover of the trees now and traveled on open ground. With a strong wind and a brisk morning, the travelers grew cold in a hurry.

Jyres said very little as they rode. His thoughts were not ones that made him smile or conversational. It was tough for him to look at Leah, such a beautiful woman, and not be jealous of Lalatco. Then he would get mad and ask himself what he was even doing out here. What had started out as a statement for his people had somehow turned into a fight for the world. It was depressing to think of the great distance Lalatco and Jyres had traveled. And in all of those travels, Leah, Zar, and Flick were the only people or intelligent creatures they had even seen. Jyres then realized how big and devastating a war it must have been. It appears to have wiped out many, or most, of all the living creatures in the region.

As Lalatco and Leah rode next to each other, Lalatco found himself thinking back to before he had met Jyres. He remembered laughing at the fact that humans once ruled the world. Now after meeting both Jyres and Leah, he realized that it was not that far-fetched an idea. It was the humans like Meslar, the power-hungry ones, that gave the humans a bad image. Lalatco was certainly happy to have met both Jyres and Leah.

Later during the day, the terrain started to get rocky as the travels headed a little more north. Zar was their guide, and no one questioned him or the direction he took. The group camped among some boulders that night and lit a small fire. Poor little Flick had gotten awfully cold, and he sat very close to the fire.

As the five of them sat around the fire, no one was talking at all. Jyres did not feel like talking to either Lalatco or Leah, and they did not want to talk to each other and upset Jyres. The old and wise wizard spoke up.

"We need to be a more cheery and talkative group if we are to get through the days ahead. Don't you think?" Then he started singing very softly. The song he sang was an old song even for Zar. Leah had heard him sing it before and recognized it. Zar started by singing the refrain, and it went like this.

> A journey we here have begun
> A long one it will be
> It will seem not so long you see
> If you have some fun with me.
>
> The road may be boring or even hard at times
> But this group a cheery one will be
> If you hear or see us coming down the road
> Join with us and sing a song or three
>
> (Refrain)
>
> We will sing during the day or long dark night
> Or even if we are in a fight.
> Let us hope for many a friend, less foe
> But either way we will sing all the way
>
> (Refrain)
> Look how quickly the dark night has now
> gone by
> It is time now for some needed sleep
> If the journey goes by about half as fast
> Such a shortened journey it would be
>
> (Refrain)

Everyone was in a better mood the next morning, and after a breakfast, the group continued on before the second arc of the new day. The terrain grew very rocky and started to gradually slope upward. It was very slow going, and soon the riders were walking next to the horses to make it easier for the animals. It looked like, to Jyres, they were going up a rocky hill. It appeared there was another one, but bigger, to go up after this one. When they got to the top of the first hill, Jyres thought he could see some sort of structure on the next hill, but he was more guessing than anything. Once at the bottom of the hill, the group stopped to rest and nibble on some wafers. It had grown dark and cold as they started the next climb.

Jyres was proven right. Zar was leading them to the structure he had seen. As they grew closer, the group was shocked at what they could now see clearly in the side of the cliff. A stone castle was built right into the side of the hill. The stone castle blended in so well to the rocky hillside, they could not identify it from far away.

The castle was quite an impressive sight. The castle matched the hill in color and texture perfectly, and it was amazing to see the castle close up. Jyres was amazed that he could not see this before. Even Lalatco could not believe his eyes. There was a small trail leading up to the castle sides; the third side of the castle was the hill itself. It had one high watchtower, and the walls were very high as well. The castle looked like a triangle, with the back side being the hill, and the tower was at the intersection of the two castle walls.

Jyres let his eyes scan the rest of the area. Only now did he see the occupants of this mighty castle. Gliding above the castle and around the hill were gargoyles. Jyres had only seen three at one time before, and he could easily pick out a dozen gliding around the castle. It was quite the sight to see for sure.

Zar led the group down the trail and to the castle. The castle seemed to grow taller as the group got closer. By the time the group was at the front of the castle, the walls seemed to touch the sky.

Gargan and a few other gargoyles were there waiting for them. Jyres was very happy to see Gargan and jumped off his horse, ran up to the giant gargoyle, and offered him a hand to shake. "Welcome to our home, my friends," said Gargan who grasped the offered hand. "Come and join us for some food and drink," Gargan said in a loud and inviting voice with his other arm outstretched.

The travelers looked around for a gate or a door, but none could be seen. Figuring all would be explained to them, they secured their horses to nearby boulders and unpacked a few supplies. Then Gargan and the other gargoyles hoisted each of the travelers on their backs. The gargoyles dug their claws into the now-deep sloping rocky hill and climbed up and up. Soon each gargoyle leaped into the wind and floated up and above the castle walls and into the castle. Another gargoyle still at the foot of the castle gave the horses some food and drink.

14

The Library

Meslar was right: the higher the group got, the worse the weather became. Meslar did use his magic every so often to get them past a blockade of snow. On the fifth night of their journey, they were very close to the end of the mountain pass. All that would be left was the descent down the mountain to the other side.

During that night while most of the knights were sleeping, many goblins and a few orcs crept up on them from the shadows. Meslar was very much aware of their approach. The filthy creatures crept in very close almost close enough to start slashing throats (as goblins and orcs were known for doing). Then out of nowhere came a bright flash of light that filled the sky. The goblins practically ran away terrified with their squeaky growls, and the orcs tried to maintain their ground. The flash came from Meslar of course, who was well aware of the creatures' hate of light. The four knights now were awake and scrambling for their swords.

Meslar approached the nearest orc. The orc growled as Meslar came near. Meslar again worked his magic. This time he took advantage of the orcs' love for metals. With a wave of his staff and some fine chosen words, the orcs agreed to help Meslar in return for some precious metals. Meslar did not have any precious metals, but he was not worried in the least.

By the time Meslar and the four knights were nearing the bottom of the mountains on the next day, they had quite a following of orcs and goblins. About thirty creatures were following the horses. Orcs and goblins have weak minds and were easily persuaded by Meslar. If all they have to do is kill, the promise of precious metals will work every time. They were not quite like the dwarves who mined for their riches; these creatures did not want to work for it. The only question for Meslar was how long he would be able to keep his control over them when no precious metals were given.

*****

Jyres lay back in his chair made of stone. It was suppertime, and he had just finished eating an excellent meal the gargoyles had prepared. It was their second day at the castle, and Jyres knew they would be leaving soon. Suppertime for the gargoyles was of course very late in the night, since they were only active during the night. Gargan had also said it was more out of enjoyment that the gargoyles ate, and it was rare that they had a meal of this kind. He had then further explained that while in their solid state, their body both protected them from the sun and rejuvenated their body, reducing the need for sustenance.

"Can anything awake you from your stone form?" Jyres asked.

"If disturbed enough, a gargoyle can force his stone form to melt away. Some of the oldest among us can even sense this need without any physical contact. Though as I said, the sun is no friend to us."

It was relaxing to be here in the castle, and it also allowed them to have that needed rest and to restock their provisions, but Jyres knew the road ahead would not be so relaxing.

Later that evening, Jyres and Gargan were walking around the castle and talking. Jyres was telling Gargan everything that had happened since the last time he had seen him and how Zar thought he was supposed to be the one who could stop Meslar.

Gargan asked if he could be of any help numerous times, even when Jyres mentioned something about Leah. It did Jyres a lot of good to be talking to Gargan. Talking to Gargan reminded Jyres what friends are for, and every time Gargan offered his help, it made Jyres feel not quite so alone. No, better than that, connected. Even with how complicated his life had become since he left the human village the first time, and his recent struggles with Lalatco, there was more to him now than ever before.

Just before the sun rose in the morning, Gargan and a few other gargoyles helped bring the group back to the foot of the castle by their horses. Gargan said goodbye to Jyres and told him he would try to keep watch over them from the skies. Jyres watched as the gargoyles climbed back into the air and onto the castle walls. He continued to watch as Gargan stood on the watchtower and faced the trail. The sun came up, and the light spread across the land and the gargoyles' castle. Jyres and the others watched as the gargoyles that were standing or sitting on the castle walls, including Gargan, all took on the color of those walls.

Jyres, Zar, Lalatco, and Leah all saddled up on horses to renew their journey. Flick rode with Zar, as always, and they trotted away from the castle. Zar assured the group that they had not gone out of their way at all and would soon be on a direct route to the old library. First, Zar led them back down the path and down one of the hills. After backtracking just over one hill, the group turned northwest. They soon left the hilly region behind; the rocks however increased, making it a bumpy ride.

The first night since leaving the castle, the group camped, and they saw a gargoyle fly overhead; Gargan kept his promise that they would watch over them. It got very cold that night, and the group huddled around a small fire. Jyres had the first watch that night, and it went by without any need for alarm. He walked over to wake up Leah who had the second watch. Every time he looked at her though, he was reminded of his jealousy. He gently tapped her on the shoulder. "Leah, it is your turn to watch."

Leah woke up and smiled at Jyres, gave a yawn, and sat up. "Come talk with me," she said.

The two of them went a little ways away from camp and sat on a huge rock. As they started to talk, the conversation was very general, but Leah had something she wanted to say. Finally, she simply said, "I am sorry, Jyres. I know this is tough for you."

Jyres smiled back at her, not knowing what to say.

"Listen, I know you like me, and I know it hurts you to see me with Lalatco. But you need to get past that. I don't know what it is you like about me, but you just met me. You need to forget about whatever it is and go back to being friends with Lalatco and I. Trust me, I have spent a lot of time on my own. Don't block us out." Leah paused then, trying to think if there was anything else to say. "The three of us need to be comfortable with each other so we can complete our mission. It is our mission, Jyres. You are not in this alone. As soon as you accept that and let me be a friend, your days will go by a lot easier and happier."

"Friends it is," Jyres said, letting out a sigh. "Everything you said is right. I have been foolish. Please forgive me."

"You don't need to apologize. Just be my friend. I have so few of them."

"I think I can say the same thing." Jyres laughed. Leah laughed with him and gave him a smile. Jyres nodded his head and said, "This is good."

"It is."

"One more thing. Do you think you could teach me a thing or two about using a sword?"

Leah smiled. "I sure can try." She then kissed him on the cheek, and Jyres stood up to go back to the campfire and try to get some sleep.

Just then, Lalatco came up behind them and said, "What is going on here?"

"Nothing to worry about, my friend. She was merely talking some sense into me." Jyres patted Lalatco on the shoulder as he said this and walked over to curl up next to the fire. Lalatco and

Leah then talked for a short time before Lalatco also returned to the fire.

Flick had gone out early the next morning to search the area. Leah and Jyres practiced sword fighting, as the group waited for Flick to return. Leah took time to demonstrate different parries and attacks and tried hard to teach Jyres how to handle a sword. Jyres was an average swordsman at best but had never had the chance to learn from someone who really knew what they were doing. Leah certainly did, and their first training session went well.

Flick reported back to Zar that the terrain would soon soften, and no potential enemies had been spotted. Just a short time later, the horses were traveling across dead grass; and after traveling a while, they came across a small town. The group rode into town to find it to be very small with just a few wooden buildings and many a hut. The small town seemed to be made up of all humans, and many looked surprised to see such a company ride into town. Some did recognize Zar, however, and he did receive a few cheers and a few waves. Long had it been since any of these people had seen an elf, and the young ones looked with wonder upon Lalatco.

The travelers decided to stay the night in the town, and they were able to get some rest. It was not long, however, before it was interrupted. Three gargoyles had landed in town, and the people were terrified of the big creatures. When Jyres saw them, he greeted them with open arms. Gargan, Hawkins, the skinny blue-skinned gargoyle, and a third gargoyle that was almost as big as Gargan had come.

Zar had gone to walk about the town and try to acquire a few supplies and was surprised to see gargoyles when he returned to the group with a bag full of supplies. Everyone ate well, and the gargoyles explained they would be willing to travel with them for a little while. They were welcomed with enthusiasm, and Zar warned everybody that the worst part of the trip was about to come and to be prepared.

Zar had been right. A river running through the fields, most likely used for farming by the small town, would be the last river they saw for a long while. The land they now looked upon to the north was a desolate place. What Jyres and Lalatco had experienced before when they first came across the mountains and needed Flick to help them was nothing compared to this.

With the three gargoyles traveling with the group, the time and way the group traveled was different with each passing day. Sometimes they would only travel at night, eating and sleeping in the day while the Gargoyles were in their static form. At other times, Jyres and Lalatco would scout ahead, and the rest of the group would catch up once night had fallen and the gargoyles were free from their protective skin. No matter what shape or form, the group went on, getting closer to their destination and to each other.

Jyres and Leah would often practice fighting, and at times, Lalatco would join in as well. Jyres improved every day with the sword. Whenever the group started to get down and wonder why they were out on this terrorized land, someone would crack a joke or start a song. One night while the group was moving along, Zar explained one of the reasons for some of the scorched land.

"This land here is where the majority of the last battle of the War of Ages was fought. Many, many creatures fought and died on this battlefield. Not too far from where we are now is where the last dragon fell. Tomorrow we will see the statue in the very spot from which the arrow was fired that felled the last dragon. Although the race of men called the battle a victory, so few numbers from any race were left alive. The humans still have one fortified city far to the south. I have seen very few elves. I believe quite a few of them left this forsaken land."

Lalatco smiled. "You are right, Zar, and the elves are great in number on the other side of the mountain."

Zar's promise held true, and on the next day of their journey, they did see a magnificently detailed statue. The polished stone was in the shape of a human male, with long hair. He had one knee on the ground, his other leg bent. In his hands he held a bow, with arrow notched and ready to fly, pointed up to the sky. The group stood impressed and stared into the sky, wondering where the dragon would have been that this human brought down. After a few moments of silence with each member of the team mulling over different thoughts, the group silently agreed to continue on.

On the sixth night since they set out from the small town, the group came across the ruins of a city. "Behold the once great and powerful city of Secord," announced Zar.

Jyres was in awe; the ruins went on for many a mile. Jyres could not believe how powerful the humans once were. This city of men sure would have been a sight.

Zar rode his horse up next to Jyres.

"You will see your race become great in number once again. This is not the end. You will give your people a new beginning." After saying that, Zar led the group into the once-great city of Secord.

The horses trotted through the ruins of the city. Zar explained that the library was very close to the middle of the city, and it would still take some time to get there. The group found a partially standing building to camp in for the night. The first snowflakes of winter started to fall to the ground as Jyres looked around the destroyed city of Secord. Soon they would be at the library, Jyres thought to himself. They had achieved what they had set out to do. Now the question was if they would find any answers. Would they learn more about the gate? What would now be in store for them?

The gargoyles hid themselves among the partially destroyed building as the sun came up. Zar led Lalatco, Leah, Jyres, and Flick to what was left of the library. Even though they knew Zar had told them it was partially underground, they were disappointed to see nothing left of it but rubble.

"We just need to find a way down to the dwarves' masterful underground building," proclaimed Zar.

They searched through the rubble all morning before Lalatco finally found a possible way underground and called out to the others. Lalatco had indeed found a way in, and as the group entered the underground library, they were amazed by the many halls and levels of books. With just a few words from Zar, Jyres's sword began to glow with a bright light, and Jyres held it out, so now the group could see what a truly magnificent place the dwarves had built. When it had been built, the humans had paid a large sum for the dwarves' skills, but if you asked Jyres what he thought, it was well worth it.

No one even dared voice their opinion that they could be in here for a year and still not find what they were looking for. It would be hard enough to look at the books without being distracted by the beautiful pillars and bookcases. No one could rival the craftsmanship of the dwarves. Not even Lalatco's friend Hex.

The group looked to Zar now for guidance of what to look for and where to start. Zar guessed that the scrolls they were looking for would be at the deepest parts of the library. The group walked down the many flights of stairs to the bottom level of the library. The great hall was huge with shelves and shelves of books and scrolls. The group spread out and started to look at all the shelves. Flick was the best at this particular task. He would zoom around even the highest shelves, his small feet fitting easily on a shelf. Apparently he could read as fast as he could move, and he had ruled out a couple of shelves in a matter of moments. Zar had given everyone careful instructions on what to look for, and an arc or so went by without any luck, then another and still another. More than once someone brought something to Zar only to have him dismiss it and wave them away. After searching for a time that spanned many arcs, the group was still empty handed.

Then the group saw Flick jumping up and down with a scroll in his hand. Zar walked over toward Flick as he raced back down the tall bookshelf. Zar then handed his walking stick to Leah to hold, and Flick handed Zar the scroll. The scroll was rolled up around a wooden rod, and the end of the rod had elven markings on it. Zar very carefully unrolled the old parchment. Most scrolls had two rods, but this scroll was ripped at the top, and only the bottom was attached to the rod. Zar thought of that as odd and knew that this scroll was clearly missing part of the original parchment. But he read the words that were there.

"That being said, it is not a power that should be unlocked. Powerful would a man be if he could harness it, but none can. They are uncontrollable. That is why the key has been hidden. Well hidden. May it never be found and the gate never opened."

After reading it, Zar explained a few things. "This is just part of the prophecy; that much I know for sure as this scroll has been ripped in two. A couple of things it confirms for us. There is a key for the gate, and we cannot let the gate be opened." Zar paused and said quietly to himself, "No matter who tries to open it."

"Now what?" asked Lalatco.

"Well," said Zar, "we have been lucky to find at least part of a prophecy that speaks of the gate. I am very doubtful that the other part is here somewhere. My guess is that someone has it, and that someone is Meslar. I dare say that there must be more writings that would be of interest to us, but I worry about the amount of time it would take to find said writings. So first things first, we meet up with the gargoyles."

As Zar looked around the old library, he started to put a few pieces of the puzzle together. Stories and prophecies came flooding back into his memory as he looked at all the knowledge around him. He saw in his mind the fully built library when the city was a thriving place. He wished he had the time to soak in more of the knowledge around him but knew that was not the case. Maybe yet, sometime, before his existence came to an end, he could spend more time in this place. His mind, returning to the present, still hoped and wished he was wrong about every-thing and that Meslar was not the evil one who would try to open the gate.

As the group started to go back up the stairs to open ground, they heard a couple of deep growls. Two very large creatures showed themselves on the stairs leading up to the next level. These creatures were bigger than any orc and had large fangs reaching past their chins and were covered with fur. The creatures were known as thars. They walked on two legs and had enormous feet. They growled their deep raspy growls, swung their clubs, and descended the stairs toward the group.

Leah already had bow and arrow ready and unleashed an arrow at the closest thar. The arrow grazed the leather on her palm as it left the bow. The arrow hit the thar's left shoulder as she loosed a second arrow. Lalatco charged the thars with scimitar drawn. Lalatco ducked under the swing of a club, jumped, and slashed the beast across its belly. Jyres, unsure of his skills, hesitated, but he heard Leah encouraging him, and Jyres also charged. He scored a hit on the same thar Lalatco had hurt by slicing the beast's leg. The second thar got ready to swing at the unsuspecting Jyres, but Leah was way ahead of the beast. Two arrows hit it in the chest, giving Jyres time to avoid the thar.

The fight continued on, and after what seemed like a whole arc had gone by to Jyres, the first beast started to back away. The second thar then attacked even harder. Zar finally stepped in, just as Lalatco was about to be smashed by a club. A bolt of lightning came from Zar and sent the thar to the floor. After hitting the floor, the thar started rolling down the steps, and everyone jumped out of the way as to not be rolled over. The other thar quickly retreated back up the stairs. Lalatco and Jyres sped after it. It did not get very far before Lalatco and Jyres both sliced it behind the knees. The thar crumbled to the stairs, and Lalatco ended its life.

After Lalatco and Jyres tended to a couple of small injuries, scrapes, and the like, the group ascended the rest of the stairs and were once again aboveground. Darkness had fallen, and the gargoyles were waiting for them when the group exited the library. Jyres, like an excited person who had found treasure, shared with Gargan what they had found.

"Well, we have met up with the gargoyles. Now what?" asked Leah.

Zar looked like he was deep in thought as he replied, "I am not sure. We know there is a key somewhere for the gate. I might have a few guesses where it could be, but I am not sure what Meslar knows. Well, let us get out of this city first, and we can talk about what to do on the road." Everyone agreed, and the group followed Zar as they made their way out of the ancient city.

15

A Skirmish

Lalatco, with his incredible vision, could see figures in the distance.

"What do you see?" asked Zar.

"A group is traveling at a fast rate toward this city. I can't tell who or what it is," Lalatco said.

In another few moments, the others could see torches in the distance.

"I am guessing it is not anyone we want to talk to. Hurry this way," urged Zar. He had his horse off at a fast trot, leaving the city the way they had come. The gargoyles ran on all fours next to the horses, as Zar led the way and Lalatco held up the rear.

"They are gaining on us!" Lalatco yelled to Zar and the rest. It wasn't long before he followed it up with "We must do something or they will soon be right on top of us."

Zar was going to do just that. He remembered the perfect spot to spring a trap. They had passed it on the way to the old city. Another quarter of an arc went by, and the torches of their followers were getting closer, but the group had reached the spot Zar had remembered. The rough land sloped up to form a ledge, and the horses jumped down, and Zar stopped the company. The ledge created quite the overhang, and a perfect hiding place that kept them out of view from their pursuers for the time being. Zar, Lalatco, Leah, and Flick brought all the horses underneath the rocky overhang. Jyres and the gargoyles went across a little way and hid behind some large boulders. They were going to spring quite a trap on their attackers.

They did not have to wait very long before many footsteps could be heard. The first of the pursuers dropped down over the ledge. They were orcs and goblins. Zar waited just a few more moments before giving the order. The unsuspecting creatures continued dropping over the ledge and walking toward the big boulders, looking for signs of their hunt. Twelve to fifteen were now over the ledge, and Zar let out a deep yell. Leah unleashed arrows as fast as she could, the leather wrapped around her fingers and palms proving its use and saving her hands from irritation from the arrows. Lalatco threw knife after knife, and Zar let loose a couple of bursts of energy. Before the creatures even knew what was happening, nine of them were dead.

But more came over the ledge; and now Zar, Leah, Lalatco, and flick were trapped under the overhang. The creatures did not realize that they now had their backs turned to Jyres and the gargoyles. Jyres, confident after fighting the thars, led the charge on the creatures. He sliced a goblin in half and plunged his sword into the belly of an orc. Although the gargoyles did not carry weapons, they did just as much damage. Gargan grabbed one orc and threw him into a rock, rendering the orc unconscious with his awesome strength. Hawkins gashed a goblin across the face with his claws and batted him aside.

Leah, Lalatco, and Zar now were engaged in hand-to-hand combat with the orcs and goblins, as were Jyres and the gargoyles who continued to punch forward, getting closer to their friends under the ledge.

Half of Meslar's force was already dead when he led his knights over the ledge and into the battle. Meslar's knights charged in on horses toward Jyres and the gargoyles, slowing them down and pushing them back. Even after killing over half of Meslar's force, Jyres and his friends were still outnumbered. Flick started to run circles around the nearby enemies, distracting them and allowing Zar, Lalatco, or Leah to knock them to the ground.

Meslar now approached that side of the battle. Zar saw him coming. Meslar released a ball of flame toward Zar, but he was ready and redirected it into two nearby goblins. Heart-wrenching screams came from the goblins as the flames enveloped them.

Each of Leah and Lalatco slayed an orc and raced toward Jyres and the gargoyles who were in desperate need of help. Flick ran and hid, leaving Meslar and Zar alone in a wizards' duel. Only bodies of orcs and goblins were left to witness it.

"So the one who I sent with creatures of all kinds over the mountains to start and uphold a world of peace has come back with chaos. Good to see you, my son." Zar sighed.

"I am somewhat surprised you are still alive, Father, but if you stand in the way of my goal, you won't be." A smile spread across Meslar's face.

"And what is your goal, son?"

"I am sure you have figured it out."

"I know you want to open the gate, but I do not see what you will accomplish by doing that."

"I want power, and I will get it. I will be more powerful than you, or anyone else who has ever lived. Ha ha ha!"

"Son..." Zar's voice was drowned out by the sound of Meslar's laughing and the sound of grinding rock. Meslar was using his power and his staff to throw a good-sized rock at Zar. He just barely sidestepped it. The wizard's duel had begun.

As Lalatco and Leah joined the fight on the other side of the battle, Jyres was knocked to the ground by Sigmon. The knight, poised to deliver the final blow, was taken by surprise and knocked off his horse by Gargan's punch before he could strike again at Jyres.

At the same time, the big blue gargoyle ducked under Lemont's slash and rammed his full body weight into the knight's horse. The horse and rider went down in a heap, but the blue gargoyle did not see another knight approach him from behind.

Lalatco yelled a word of warning and tried to react but could not get himself there in time. The Silver Shadow plunged his sword into the back of the huge beast. The point of the sword came out of the gargoyle's chest.

Lalatco, Jyres, and Leah battled with the last of the goblins and orcs. The knights who all had by now been unhorsed were in battle with Gargan and Hawkins. The battle raged on, and Jyres saw the knights pressing hard against the gargoyles. Jyres ran to their aid and caught a knight by surprise and slid his sword past the knight's only to have it clang on his strong mystified armor.

The two wizards cast spell after spell against each other, but neither could breach the other's defenses. Zar could see that his friends were hard pressed now and knew he had to create a diversion. He brought up a dense fog in front of him and moved to his left, as the fog hid his movements. Meslar worked quickly to dissipate the fog with his own powers, but he was too slow. Zar had moved to the other side of the battlefield. The old wizard closed his eyes and mouthed the ancient words; and Jyres's sword, along with Lalatco's scimitar, were bright with blinding light.

The knights fell back and shielded their eyes.

Gargan and Hawkins didn't waste any time and ran to their injured gargoyle friend. They both put his arms around their shoulders and got moving, the sword still protruding from the big gargoyle. Leah also moved quickly; as Jyres and Lalatco continued to point their weapons of light at the knights, she whistled and ran to collect the horses.

The light started to fade as the warriors mounted their horses and galloped at full speed. The gargoyles had moved immediately and were out in front. Zar and Flick were nowhere to be seen.

Meslar ran to his knights, ordering them to pursue their enemy, but the knights still could not see, their eyes not able to adjust so quickly.

16

Events at Home

Castle Mystic was a flurry of activity. The knights were packing supplies and knew they would need to pack as much as the horses could carry. Demorous had decided that he would leave Bartholomew, Karth, and Oliver and Oscar behind at the castle, meaning Felix, Brigand, and Lord Kapel would join him on his journey across the mountains. Meslar had decided to cross the mountains before all was prepared, and Demorous was organizing everything as quickly and as carefully as possible. Once everything was prepared, the knights clasped hands with each other and said their farewells. The four horses thundered across the desert; they had a long way to go to meet up with Meslar.

*****

Vurth smoked his pipe as he listened to the reports from one of his scouts. Vurth had been keeping a few of his dwarves busy by having them continually scout out the land, keeping an eye out for any movement around Castle Mystic. On this particular night, some knights had been spotted moving across the desert. Vurth thanked the scout and turned to the two dwarves sitting across from him.

One of the dwarves sitting there was his son, Tagro. He was just a little bit smaller than Vurth but possessed many of the same qualities. His hair, like his father's beard, was the color orange. Tagro kept his beard short, and small beads were tied into the end of his beard, which was only an inch or two from the bottom of his chin. The beads were colored dark green to match his eyes.

The second dwarf sitting with Vurth was his highest-ranking general and most trusted advisor. General Huff had been a general for longer than Tagro had been alive. He was older than Vurth by ten years, and the age was starting to show on the old dwarf. His hair and beard were both a grayish white, and his body was starting to ache. The general had always been intelligent by dwarven standards and seemed even more so now than he did a few years ago.

"I want twenty-five dwarves ready by tomorrow morning," Vurth said. "I want the most stubborn soldiers we've got." Vurth was not at all surprised to see his son immediately withdraw from the room to go select and prepare the dwarves. He was even less surprised to see his good friend still sitting at the table and looking back at him with a smile. "Something on your mind, General?"

"I was just wondering what you planned on doing with these stubborn soldiers."

"Well, I want to know what Meslar is up to," Vurth said.

"As do all of us. Just be careful of Meslar. Your reign as dwarven leader has been a prosperous one. I would hate for you to be remembered as the one who was torched by a wizard's ball of flame." With a smile, Huff wished Vurth a good night.

When Vurth woke up the next morning, the soldiers were ready, lined up at the foot of the cliffs. Vurth put on his helmet, grabbed his trusty battle-ax, and went down to greet the dwarven soldiers. On his way, he saw General Huff; he nodded to him and said, "You are in charge until I return."

"Companions, I have decided it is time for the dwarves to act. We will track down the knights who left the castle last night, we will capture them, and we will make them talk. Form up, pattern for marching."

The dwarves formed into five groups of five and got ready to march. One group, with Vurth, led the way; then three groups spread out in a line across behind them, and the fifth group led by Tagro brought up the rear. Each dwarf had a pack on his back and a weapon in his or her hand. Most of the dwarves were carrying axes, but there were a few swords in the group as well. Each pack had food and water. Enough, when rationed well, that would last for two weeks.

They marched at a good pace; they headed southwest, keeping eyes out for any signs of the knights. If the knights got a late start at all today, the dwarves could catch up; they had left very early. And catch up they did, later that day when the dwarves started to cross the hills of Tomackus.

When the dwarves reached the top of a hill, they could see four knights on horses a ways ahead of them. They quickly ran down to the bottom of the next hill, where they could not be seen. Vurth, hoping they had not been seen, quickly gave out orders. He kept his group of five dwarves with him and split the other groups in half. He instructed one half to circle around to the east and the other half to circle around to the west. He also knew that the knights were on horses, so if there was any kind of a chase, the knights would escape. He had instructed the dwarves to move fast, but stay out of sight. Even if they managed that, they would still need some luck to be able to catch up. Or would a distraction be enough? Vurth thought.

Vurth and his five dwarves ran up the next hill, and then right before the top of the hill, they crawled up and cautiously looked. On the first hill, they did not see the knights; they must have been at the bottom of a hill. The dwarves hurried on to the next hill. At each hill, they repeated their same actions, only moving when they would not be seen. After a while had gone by, Vurth knew they would not catch up to the knights in this way. To the other dwarves' surprise, instead of crawling, he ran to the top of the next hill and yelled as loud as he could.

"Knights, I want to talk to you!" Vurth did not even know if the knights were in earshot, but his question was answered when the knights came up the hill a few hills away and turned their horses to face his direction. Vurth raised his arm and waved, and the knights descended their hill, starting to come back in the direction of Vurth. Vurth and his dwarves quickly ran down and then up the next hill. They got to the top of the hill and saw the knights already at the top of their hill. Just one hill away now, Vurth did not have to yell quite so loud. Vurth could recognize Demorous as one of the knights, in his splendid armor.

"What do you want, Vurth?" came his voice. "If it is just to talk, why do you have five companions with you?"

Vurth was quick to think of a lie. "I have a proposition for you, well, more for Meslar."

"Well, what is it?" asked Demorous.

"We are having problems with a creature in our cliffs that we have never seen before. We were hoping Meslar and his powers could help us out." Vurth was actually quite happy with himself for coming up with that one. He thought it was rather good.

"Why would Meslar care?" asked Demorous.

"He would be rewarded," claimed Vurth.

"Meslar does not have time for such things."

"Rewarded richly," came back Vurth's deep voice. Knowing Demorous was about to turn away then, he used a different approach.

"Or maybe Meslar does not need to be involved, say, a chestful of silver for whoever kills the creature."

Demorous's voice changed its tone a little. "Maybe when I return I will take you up on your offer. But we must be going." With that, the knights turned and went back down the hill.

Vurth's group ran now toward the knights' direction. He hoped he had bought the other two groups enough time.

*****

Elonda had waited for some time for something to happen, for others to stand up to Meslar. She realized now that Jyres was the first one that had. She knew he and Lalatco would need help. Who knew what Meslar was all planning? And if he found where Jyres and Lalatco were, she knew they would be in trouble. She had decided that if no one else was going to help them, she would, even if it meant doing it alone.

That night she packed some supplies, her sword, and her bow and snuck out of the elven home on her horse. One lookout did see her, but she told him she was merely out for a quiet ride. They would realize that was not true in a short while, but she would be well on her way by then.

Early that next morning, she thought for sure she had spotted some horses to the northwest on the hills of Tomackus. Instantly intrigued, she turned her horse and trotted in that direction. As she started to near the hills, she saw something she did not expect. There at the bottom of the last good-sized hill were dwarves. Not just one or two, but eight or ten. She quickly tied her hair back in a quick ponytail and urged her horse a little faster at seeing that. Then out of nowhere came four galloping horses ridden by knights, with dwarves chasing after them over the hill.

Elonda forced her horse faster and faster until it was going as fast as it could. The knights came down the hill only to be ambushed by the dwarves Elonda had seen at the bottom. One knight fell from his horse as two dwarves jumped at him swinging their axes. The knight fell into the pathway of a second knight, who had to almost stop his horse just to avoid running him over. Those two knights were quickly surrounded by dwarves, as Demorous and the fourth knight broke through.

Elonda could not have timed it better if she had known the dwarves' plan; she charged in sword drawn. She was only fifteen yards away when Demorous first saw her. Elonda slowed her charge just a little as the two knights veered toward her. Her sword felt light, her mind clear, as she directed her horse right between the knights. She parried a strike from Demorous and ducked under a high swing from the other knight, Lord Kapel. Turning her horse around to face the knights, she was able to get a quick glance of the dwarves; some were already trying to run and help her. The two knights turned to face her as well, and she knew she had to try to keep the knights here until the dwarves arrived.

The knights were shocked when Elonda charged at them again, and they maneuvered their horses around Elonda, avoiding confrontation. Looking for an escape route, Demorous realized then what Elonda just did. She had put them in between her and the dwarves. Demorous motioned to his fellow knight and kicked his horse, and it thundered west as Lord Kapel went east. Elonda was to their south, the dwarves to the north.

Elonda thundered east after Lord Kapel. In all likelihood, Demorous would get away, but he would also be the last one who would talk. The knight tried the best he could to stay ahead of her, but she caught up little by little. She held out her sword as she came close, but Lord Kapel tried to make a drastic turn. It was too much for the horse, and both horse and rider tumbled to the ground. As the knight fell, he lost his sword, and his helmet went tumbling away. Elonda leaped off her horse and had her sword pointed at the knight's neck before he could react.

Demorous was fast enough to charge away before the dwarves could cut him off. He looked back and saw all three of his fellow knights being tied up by their enemies. *Meslar is going to love this*, he thought and let out a frustrated sigh.

Quite some time later, the three captured knights and the twenty-five dwarves were at the elves' home. Malick, Vurth, Elonda, and a few others were discussing who should and how they would question the knights. It was soon decided that Vurth would do the actual questioning. One by one, Vurth questioned the three knights; and after the first round of questioning, not much was learned. The knights had been of course stripped of their armor and weapons and locked in different rooms. Guards were posted as well who kept watch during the night.

The sleep, food, and drink gave Vurth much more energy for the second round of questioning. Before long, Vurth was making villainous threats, and soon he found the one knight that might begin to talk. Vurth gave up on questioning Lord Kapel and Brigand and focused his energy on Felix.

"I don't know much, but here is what I can tell you," Felix was saying. "Meslar is looking for Jyres on the other side of the mountains."

"That's it," yelled Vurth, "that is all you know! You are one of Meslar's precious knights. I can pick this ax up and smash the table in front of you," which of course Vurth did, to emphasize his point. "I could also," he continued, "just as easily smash your skull. Now what else do you know?" Vurth demanded.

"Okay, I know he promised us awesome power because of some sort of gate. But that is all I know, I promise." Felix's voice was actually starting to tremble. Vurth gave him a smile, asked the guard to feed the prisoners, and went to see Malick.

Malick thought awhile about what Vurth had told him Felix had said. The comment the knight had told Vurth did not instill any confidence in him. Was there a way for Meslar to become more powerful? After talking with the others, the group agreed that they could not afford any possibility of Meslar gaining even more power. Vurth and Elonda would lead twenty-five dwarves and thirty elves over the mountains and try to help Lalatco and Jyres. Word was sent to the rest of the dwarves what was happening; and with Vurth and Elonda leading the group of warriors, Malick would watch after things at home, including the captured knights.

With winter season starting, the group knew the mountain pass Vurth's father and Malick's father had once walked would not be an easy trip. They started out the next morning with each dwarf and elf carrying supplies. Only a few horses were brought along. All of the dwarves and elves were dressed for the cold harsh weather that was sure to be ahead of them.

Elonda rode on a horse at the head of the warriors. She could hardly contain her excitement. Not only was she going to help like she wanted, she was bringing over fifty others with her. She checked her sword at her hip one more time, even though she knew it was there, and gave her horse an encouraging pat.

The force was quite impressive. Vurth had with him some of the dwarves' finest warriors, and Vurth himself was unmatched with the ax. All of the elves along were also very skilled. Many were fine bowmen, and all of them had melee combat skills as well. It was the first time an army was put together in the new world, but it was bred for the old.

17

A Divided Group

After the escape, the group was reunited a while later when Zar and Flick caught up. The group was huddled around the injured gargoyle. "It is best to leave the sword where it is. Once we change forms, our injuries often heal. I wonder though if this one is too severe," Gargan said with pain in his voice.

From what Jyres could tell, the gargoyle was already dead, but he held on to hope for Gargan's sake.

Gargan, Jyres, and Zar talked at length about what was to be done as Leah and Lalatco tended to the horses. Their primary concern was their water situation. They needed to make the trip out of the barren land and get more water before they became too dehydrated. Gargoyles replenished themselves somewhat while in their resting form, but the rest of the group did not have that luxury. The other issue was Gargan's companion. Gargan said that even though signs pointed to him being dead, when a gargoyle was in its dormant state, it could heal wondrous things; and the gargoyle may wake up again. It could be in the next evening or maybe in five years. It was very important that the gargoyle be moved back to the castle.

The group decided to separate, partly due to Jyres insisting that he would help Gargan in this matter. What water the group could spare would be left with Jyres and the gargoyles. Zar, Flick, Leah, and Lalatco would make for the river they had passed a long time ago on the way to the library. This way, the group could replenish their canteens, which was foremost in Zar's mind. Once the gargoyle was returned home, Jyres would meet them at Zar's cave.

Gargan and Hawkins moved their injured friend to a small group of trees, and Lalatco started a fire to keep the group warm on the cold night. As the group settled down for the night, it started to snow, and it snowed all night until early morning. When the sun came up, all three gargoyles changed forms, and the sword in the injured gargoyle shattered.

The group ate a good meal, something they all needed, though the food was getting low as well. Once back at Zar's cave, they would be able to restock their supplies. Lalatco and Jyres clasped hands before a quick hug. "I don't like this idea," said Leah, coming up and squeezing Jyres's arm in a sign of caring.

"It is the only way. You guys must get water, and I have to help Gargan in this. I owe him so much. Don't worry about me. If the enemy tries to track us after the fight, they will see your tracks, not ours, and they will follow you," Jyres said with a smile.

"That is not exactly comforting," Leah responded with a smile.

Jyres said goodbye to the others and retrieved a few items from his horse's saddlebags. Then he watched as Zar and Flick, on one horse, led the way with Lalatco and Leah, on a horse, leading the other two horses.

*****

When the sun went down, Gargan and Hawkins awoke; their friend did not. "It is as I assumed. He is still in his dormant form, Hawkins," the big green gargoyle said to his friend. "You will take this news to our castle and then bring back with you as many gargoyles as you think we will need to carry our friend to safety." The birdlike gargoyle nodded in return before flapping his wings and taking flight.

Jyres and Gargan each scouted some feet away from their current location, always making sure they could still see each other. After a little while, they were confident in their current safety, and they settled in to wait.

As they were sitting around the small fire, Jyres asked his friend, "Are their girl gargoyles, Gargan?"

"Well, of course, where do you think little gargoyles come from?" Gargan chuckled after responding.

"Are you courting one of them?" Jyres wondered.

"What do you mean?" asked Gargan.

"You know, spending all your time with one girl gargoyle."

"Oh, you mean marding," Gargan responded.

"What?" Jyres was confused.

It was Gargan's turn to explain. "That is what we call it when two gargoyles decide to live their lives together, and no, I am not marding. As the head of the clan, I am too important to be doing such things. I could get distracted from my duties."

"That is not fair," commented Jyres.

"It makes sense to me," replied Gargan.

There was a pause in the conversation before Gargan continued to speak. "What about you, are you marding?"

Jyres laughed really hard and said, "No, you already know that although Leah was interesting to me at first, she took to Lalatco."

The two friends smiled at each other and fell into a comfortable silence.

*****

As Zar's horse rode on ahead with Flick riding along, Lalatco and Leah took their time. It was nice to kind of be alone. Lalatco could not help but smile. Leah had her arms around his waist as they rode to make sure she did not fall off. The two of them talked constantly, and Lalatco realized he had fallen in love with her. She was everything he had dreamed of, only human. It was weird when Lalatco thought about it. He never thought he would be with a human, but after meeting Leah and Jyres, his perceptions of humans had completely changed. They were two amazing people, one a friend, one a girlfriend.

The four of them made it to the river in four days, for they could travel much faster by traveling during the day and the night, as opposed to how they traveled when accompanied by the gargoyles. Lalatco wondered how Jyres was doing. He knew it would take Jyres a long time to finally make it back to Zar's cave, but it could not be avoided. Lalatco also wondered where they would go next and where the key would be. He asked Zar, but Zar would not say much. He would merely reply, "You will learn in time." In another four days, the four riders were at Zar's cave, and a welcomed sight it was. It gave them some much-needed rest.

*****

Jyres stood vigil during the day when Gargan lay dormant. Jyres was on high alert, wanting to make sure the area remained safe. Thankfully, that was the case, although Jyres did jump a little when a rabbit hopped out of the underbrush and ran away from Jyres.

Two nights had gone by before Hawkins arrived with three other gargoyles. It took four of the strong gargoyles to lift their injured friend into the sky. The fifth gargoyle carried Jyres. The gargoyles also took turns carrying Jyres, getting a break from lifting their heavy friend.

When the group arrived at the castle, the big gargoyle was still in its dormant state; and the gargoyles placed him on a spot along the castle wall, hoping at some point he would wake. Jyres decided to get some rest and stayed at the castle for a whole day and then started out for Zar's cave the following morning. Just before the sun came up that morning, Gargan helped Jyres get to the bottom of the castle. Jyres was surprised to see a horse waiting for him.

"You use horses?" Jyres asked in an astonished voice.

"Very rarely. We simply call this one Brown. Used for various tasks, but he would not be used to having someone ride him."

"Well, Brown," Jyres said to the appropriately named horse because of the color of its coat, "let's see how we do." Jyres had to ride bareback on the horse, and Jyres shifted uneasily once he mounted the horse. Gargan shook his friends' hand before patting Brown on the rump. Gargan reached the top of the castle again just before the sun came up.

As Jyres and the horse started the trip toward Zar's cave, it started to snow again. Jyres did not like the idea about traveling by himself, and he had a three-day journey to the cave. He tried to stay optimistic as the snow started to lie heavy on the ground. His mood was helped when he camped for the first night, and his first day of travel proved to be uneventful, and a few friendly gargoyles had passed by overhead.

* * * * *

Meslar and his knights found it very hard to track their query, the snow often creating more of a challenge than a help. Even with his magic, they soon lost the trail.

After a few days of searching for more signs, they were greeted one night by Meslar's fellow schemer, of whom Meslar had yet to speak of to his knights. At first sight, the knights were ready to attack, thinking that they were in danger, but Meslar eased their fears and began conversation with this creature.

"So we meet again."

"You have come earlier than expected," said the creature.

Meslar couldn't help but smile. "Well yes, but it was needed. The time has come."

After a moment of silence, the response was "Very well. You will follow me."

* * * * *

Lalatco and Leah enjoyed the free time they had together as they waited for Jyres. Zar and Flick would often go off exploring, never saying where they were going. It was just as well. Lalatco and Leah would cuddle next to the fire or go for a walk if the snow was light. They grew closer and closer together, each one in love with the other.

Leah always talked about the future. Before Lalatco came along, she had no purpose, and now she could not help but wonder what was next, including what would happen between her and Lalatco when this Meslar business was over. She asked Lalatco that very question.

"Well," he said in response, "I was kind of hoping you would come back with me to my home."

Leah smiled and gave him a big hug and kissed him on the cheek. "I was hoping you would say that."

After the third day of being back at the cave, they started to worry where Jyres was. Their question would be answered later that night.

*****

Jyres's second day and night of travel went by much like the first. He was happy to be among trees again, just one day's travel away from Zar's cave. He finished the last of his bread and once again mounted on Brown. It had taken a few arcs for Jyres to get used to riding without a saddle, and for Brown to get used to having a rider. Since then, however, both horse and rider were doing fine. After slowly weaving between the trees, Jyres stopped after just a short distance. He could spot a couple of wolves a little way away. He slowly directed the horse away, but the wolves had spotted them.

Not two, but four wolves gave a howl and bounded after Jyres. Jyres dug his heels into the horse, and Brown took off running. It was hard to make tight turns with the inexperienced horse, and that worried him as the wolves closed in on him. Jyres drew his sword, now trusting his horse to find its own way through the trees. He swung his sword as a wolf came near, and as he did so, his horse made a sharp turn to avoid some trees, and Jyres almost fell from his uneasy position. The wolves were all around them now as Jyres glanced one of the wolves with his sword, but it hardly wounded the animal. Brown was then bit by a wolf just as arrows sprang from the trees. All four wolves fell to the ground with arrows in their necks and bellies.

Jyres breathed a sigh of relief and then held his breath, waiting for the archers to be revealed. Out of the trees walked Elonda and six elves. Jyres could not believe it. His face showed his relief as he got down off his horse.

Elonda smiled. "It has been a while since I saw you last, Jyres."

"You picked a great time to show your face," Jyres replied.

Jyres thanked the other elves as well who collected their arrows and their catch. He then saw to Brown, trying to calm him and look over his bite. Jyres was confident the horse's injury was only minor and continued to calm down Brown. Once ready, Jyres walked beside Brown, and Elonda led the group to the south as she tried to explain to Jyres why they were here. Before all was told, they came out of the dense trees, and Jyres saw something he was shocked to see. An army of elves and dwarves were gathered and resting among the trees. Vurth gave a shout of excitement as he saw the fresh meat being carried by the elves.

Before long, many were gathered around Jyres as he told his tale. He told them how he and Lalatco had found Zar and gone to the library, and he explained in great detail the battle with Meslar. He ended his tale with how he had traveled by himself and Elonda had saved him from the wolves. It was quite a long tale, and when he was done, he asked Vurth and Elonda for more details of their journey.

The meat was cooked and distributed as they told Jyres about capturing the knights and of Demorous's escape. They also told Jyres what Felix had said, and they finished their tale with their ten-day journey to where they are now. "The mountain pass was a treacherous one," said Vurth. "The snow was piled high, and we had to clear paths for ourselves. It was awfully cold, and we are glad to be down from those mountains."

"We also got attacked by goblins one night," added Elonda. "They did not realize our numbers, and we defeated them easily. We had only a few injuries, no deaths."

"Then we had to try and navigate through that maze of rocks and chiasms with a whole army. We ended up traveling around it. And what do you know, we find you." Vurth laughed out loud and then said, "It is a pleasure to meet you by the way. Though I have heard a lot about you, I believe this is our first official meeting. I do not count the meeting during the week of peace, seeing how we never got a chance to talk."

"Well, I have never been more pleased to see a dwarf in my whole life," responded Jyres.

They talked into the night, and when scouts walked into camp with Zar and Flick, Jyres jumped up and ran to greet them. Zar was extremely happy to see Jyres and was introduced to both Vurth and Elonda immediately. Flick was sent to get Lalatco and Leah. The army had happened to make camp very close to Zar's cave. When Lalatco and Leah arrived, many of the stories were told again.

Lalatco was overjoyed to see his elven friends again. On seeing Elonda, Lalatco quickly approached her, and the two shared a brief hug. In that brief hug with each other, it was as if they communicated their feelings of respect and moving on without having to speak. They smiled at each other, and Lalatco gave her a slight bow. He then introduced Leah, whose story was then told. Jyres had not gone into detail about her story.

Elonda could tell right away that Lalatco and Leah were fond of each other, but it did not bother her, and she was glad for him.

The night was a very lively one. There were singing and dancing; if anyone was near, they would have heard the group. If enemies were near, they would have known where to strike. But there were none, and the party lasted until morning. Jyres and

Elonda spent part of the night talking to each other and even danced when an energetic elven song was sung. They sang it in the basic language, and it went like this.

It has been a while since I saw you last
Let's have some fun while we got the chance
We will sing some songs and drink some wine
Do all we can to make the moment last

Refrain: Lets have some fun, now let's have
        some fun
Let's have some fun, now let's have some
        fun...woo ha

We will dance all night till there's some light
If the band still plays then I guess we'll just
Have to sing some songs and dance some
        more
Even if of the wine there is no more

Refrain

It has been great to see you again
We had some fun that is not a doubt
We did sing some songs and dance and drink
It will not be long till we do it again

Refrain

18

A Secret Revealed

In the early part of the next day, Zar called a meeting. Zar, Jyres, Elonda, Vurth, Lalatco, and Leah were all in attendance. Zar thanked them for coming and started the meeting. "We must decide what is to be done next," he stated. Vurth immediately asked what the options were. "I was getting to them, my dear dwarf," Zar replied. "First of all, let's talk about the gate. If it is opened, a terrible power will be unleashed. What that is I cannot say, but we must not let Meslar open it. As we found in the library, to open the gate he will need the key, which brings us to our decision. We can search for the key and try to keep it safe ourselves. Or we could leave the key, hoping Meslar does not know where it is, and we go after him. Or we could wait for him at the gate, or we could do nothing." Zar leaned forward on his knees, waiting for a response.

Jyres was the first to speak. "Well, we can't do nothing, so that option can be thrown out." Everyone else shook their head in agreement.

"What are the chances he knows where the key is?" asked Lalatco.

Zar shrugged. "I am not sure. He may believe that it is in a castle, as that is my thought as well. So if it was me, I would start looking at the oldest castle first. I doubt he knows all of the castles and their history. There are a lot of castles' remnants on this side of the mountains, but he would find it eventually, and he may have already started looking."

Vurth's deep voice was the next to be heard. "He could find the key at any given time, and I say it is too great a risk to leave it, if we know where to find it." Most everyone shook their heads in agreement.

Zar sighed. "I do not disagree, Vurth, but my thought is only a guess. If I took a guess based on my knowledge of this world's history, I would search the oldest human castle I can think of. It is in ruins now and was once called Stone Heights."

Elonda did not look as though she liked the idea. "What if we attacked Meslar instead? We have a good number of soldiers. I doubt that Meslar does."

Zar nodded. "That is another option. He won't have soldiers, but he may have creatures under his power like he did when he attacked us with the orcs and goblins. Nor do we know where he is."

Jyres contemplated the ideas, trying to figure out what would be best.

"Well, we have already decided that we have to do something, and I don't like the idea of waiting for him at the gate. I say we either attack him in an effort to kill him, or we find the key and keep it safe."

Zar agreed that those sounded like the two best options. He then added, "However, it will not be easy to kill my son."

Everyone there gasped; they had no idea. No one had heard Meslar and Zar's conversation during the last battle. All this time they had been traveling with Meslar's father. Jyres did not know what to say, nor did anyone else.

After an uncomfortable silence, Zar continued, "He is very powerful. He will not be easily defeated, with or without an army to support him."

"Shall we vote?" asked Jyres.

"No" was the quick reply from Zar. "You are the one who will stop Meslar, so you shall decide."

Jyres asked for everyone's opinion, and there was not a strong case for either option.

"Well, we will attack Meslar then. Let us end this now." Later, when everyone was packing up camp, Jyres approached Zar. "I am sorry, but Meslar must be dealt with."

"No need to apologize." The old man smiled. "It is not your fault my son is power hungry. It had been a long time since I had seen him last." His smile quickly faded as Zar remembered the last time he had talked to his son. "Right before the great battle, I decided he should help lead everyone across the mountains. He was very mad at me. He wanted to stay and fight. I of course did not want him to die in battle, though now it looks like it may have been for the best. I was selfish in making that decision."

Jyres spoke up. "You cannot blame yourself for the path Meslar has taken. If he really wanted to fight, he would have. His choices have brought us here, not yours."

Zar gave the faintest of smiles. "Or my decision to send him away made him so bitter, he cannot think rationally."

Jyres looked at Zar straight in the eye. "I promise he will have a chance to redeem himself. We will not kill him without talking to him." Zar merely patted Jyres on the shoulder and went to ready his horse.

Before long, everyone was ready to march. There were ten horses, but most people would have to travel on foot. Zar, Jyres, and Elonda were at the front on horses, while Vurth, Leah, Lalatco, and a few others were on horses but spread out among the group. The only problem was that they did not know where to search for Meslar. It was decided that four elves would be sent on horseback to scout out the area in all directions, looking for any sign of Meslar. The rest of the group continued to march toward the southwest.

Elonda and Jyres talked a lot as they traveled, and she quickly grew fond of him. Jyres enjoyed the conversations but was completely unaware of her feelings. Zar would often chuckle to himself when Elonda would drop a hint and Jyres would completely miss it.

The next night, one scout reported back that there was no sign of Meslar. The night after that, however, a second scout returned with a gargoyle accompanying him. This gargoyle had a small knowledge of the basic language and was able to report that a single knight had been seen traveling this way some days before. The gargoyles had returned to track him the night after they had seen him but were unable to locate him. Zar and Jyres thanked the gargoyle for the report and continued in that direction.

The other scouts caught up the next day and had nothing to report. The company grew very hopeful that the one knight spotted would have been Demorous and that he was on his way to reunite with his comrades, confirming they were heading in the right direction.

Elonda and Jyres continued to talk with each other, and Lalatco and Leah were happy to see that. Lalatco and Leah's relationship had continued to grow, and the two were inseparable. Every chance they got they were talking to each other and walking their horses so close to each other no one would have been able to get between them if they tried.

Almost a week since the group started marching southwest and their question about whether it was Demorous the gargoyles had seen was still unanswered. The small army was traveling through very swampy land and came to a little hill. Jyres, Lalatco, and Elonda quickly climbed the small hill, leaving their horses at the bottom. What Jyres saw shattered the confidence he had had in this mission. The three saw a castle that was not too far away. The still-standing castle was surrounded by a lake and more swampland. Flying around the castle were many gargoyles, and camped around the castle and in the surrounding swamplands were thars, even more thars than the army of dwarves and elves.

As Jyres looked down on the area, he took a deep breath. Although they were too far away to see if Demorous, the knights, or Meslar was around, the number of thars scared Jyres.

"This must be the other gargoyle clan Gargan had talked about," said Jyres.

"If that is the case, and a Knight of Enchantment did go this way, Meslar could be in that castle." Lalatco sighed.

"All those creatures around the castle would probably support that thought," said Elonda.

Another meeting by Zar and the others took place as the army set up camp and patrols. Although the swamp was not the best place to be, it was not nearly as cold there as on the trip. Winter was certainly now at its worst, and although it was cold, the swamp seemed warm compared to their last week of travel.

Thanks to the quick look over the hill, they guessed that Bram, the gargoyle Gargan had warned them about, was the leader of the castle; and for some reason, thars were now surrounding the outside.

"Even if we assume Meslar is here, I do not think attacking Meslar is even possible now," said Jyres.

"That is probably true, but it would still be possible if we attacked while the gargoyles were stone, during the day." Lalatco looked around the small circle of people watching for responses.

"I like the way you think, elf," responded Vurth with a tone that indicated he was ready for battle.

"First, we would need a better idea of what we are up against before we can even plan an attack." Leah sighed. "We don't even know for sure that Meslar is in there."

Zar shook his head in agreement. "A scouting mission must be made to see what is really going on."

"I will go," volunteered the always-eager dwarf.

Zar laughed and said, "Sorry, Vurth, but this kind of mission is more suited for a nimble and quiet elf." Zar knew that there would be many elves in the group that would be willing to go on the mission, but it was decided that Lalatco would be the one to go. Flick was also chosen to accompany him.

"In the meantime," continued Zar, "I will have to try and conceal us from the unwanted searching eyes of gargoyles." After the meeting, Zar went and stood in the middle of the camp. He closed he eyes and concentrated, focusing on the power deep within; and with a few well-recited words, he cast his spell of concealment.

The next morning, Lalatco made ready to go. He ensured he had all his knives; he also attached some rope to his belt and filled his canteen at a nearby stream. Leah was helping him prepare and had tears in her eyes as she hugged him.

"Do not worry. I will return to you," Lalatco said with a soothing voice. He kissed her and gave her one more hug before turning to the hill. Jyres and Flick were at the top of the hill waiting for him.

"Best of luck to both of you," said Jyres who clasped hands with Lalatco and tapped Flick on the head. Jyres watched as the two descended the hill into the fog and mist of the morning.

Jyres returned to camp and found Zar and Vurth relaxing and smoking pipes next to each other. The two of them looked quite comfortable for being so close to one hundred thars, and possibly a crazy wizard as well. Jyres joined them and took a seat on a log.

"Hi there, lad, nice of you to join us." Vurth smiled and blew a smoke circle out of his pipe. "We were just talking about Zar's son and wishing he was on our side."

Jyres's expression did not hide the fact that the statement shocked him.

Zar smiled and simply said, "My son has become a fine wizard and leader."

If only he were not so evil, Jyres thought to himself.

19

The Lone Scout

Lalatco and Flick traveled on foot through the mist. Flick would dash to a hidden area with his lightning speed and make sure things were safe, and then Lalatco would follow quickly and quietly. They were not too close to the castle yet, but they were being extra careful. It was a good thing too, because as Lalatco peeked out from behind a tree, he spotted two of those long-fanged creatures, thars. The fog was still plenty thick, and Flick and Lalatco easily slipped past the creatures unnoticed. By the time the morning fog had lifted from the area, Lalatco and Flick had snuck past many thars, and they were getting close to the castle.

Lalatco, sitting just on the edge of the lake, now had a good view of the castle. He could see the castle gate and only one way to get to it. There was a bridge that went over the lake and led to the castle gate. He could also tell from where he was that it was heavily guarded by thars. Lalatco was stuck with the decision of trying to sneak in through a heavily guarded front gate or heading around the lake toward the back of the castle, hoping to find another way in. That, of course, would take time; but he did not have many options. Lalatco sent Flick back to camp to report what they had seen and that Lalatco was going to try to find a different way in.

Lalatco continued around the lake to the northeast. He went cautiously at first, but after not seeing any thars, he quickened his pace. As he moved across the swampy terrain, he kept his eyes constantly moving from side to side, always on the lookout. By the time midday had arrived, he had traveled a good distance around the lake; and in another arc or two, he would be at the back side of the castle.

Later in the day, Lalatco was on the northern side of the castle, the lake still between himself and the castle. He knew he would need to find a way across the lake, but he also knew the gargoyles would soon be awake, and that would make everything more difficult. With only a few thars in sight, he was safe for the time being and sat down to rest and think. He watched as a big fish jumped out of the lake and landed again with a splash. If he were a fish, he could cross the lake, no problem; strangely that gave him an idea.

Lalatco saw a huge tree sticking out of the shallow water close to where he was sitting. Many of the tree's roots were in the air, out of the lake and swampy terrain. Lalatco easily hid himself in the roots of the tree. Although he got a little wet and very cold, he was well hidden among the tree's roots. The sun went down, and the gargoyles awoke.

As the night lingered on, Lalatco could often see a gargoyle glide over the area, well above him. Only if a creature walked right up to the tree could someone have seen Lalatco. Fearing that he was getting too cold and his clothes too wet, he took off his outer garments and hung them over a root. He made sure the clothes were hidden but out of the water as well. To stay warm, Lalatco kept as much of his body in the water as possible, for the water was surprisingly much warmer than the frigid air. Had Lalatco not been fortunate of that temperature difference, he would have indeed been in trouble. For his clothes, although warm, would have been useless soaked with water. He was lucky to be able to sit comfortably on the lake bed as the lake was shallow.

Lalatco did one other thing as he waited for the night to pass. There was waterweed sticking out of the lake near his hiding spot, and he cut off a few of the hollow tough weed shoots. He cut the shoots into different sizes, checked them over, and whittled them when necessary. Confident that his work was satisfactory and he was well hidden, Lalatco closed his eyes and rested.

*****

After Flick had returned with news on Lalatco's progress, Leah found herself looking over to the hill thinking of Lalatco as she ate a few scraps. There was very limited food here in the swamps. Elonda sat on a log near Leah, and it felt like forever to Leah, but not much time had lapsed before Elonda said something.

"Don't worry, Lalatco is very skilled. He will return."

"Do you know him well?" Leah asked.

Surprised that Lalatco had not told Leah of her, Elonda tried to maintain her composure. "We are friends" was all she said. As the two women sat in silence, a patrol reported that four thars were getting close to camp.

Jyres called Vurth and Elonda to him and told them, "Take some warriors and kill the thars. Be careful not to alert any of the others. Make sure you get all four of them."

The afternoon grew late as Vurth and Elonda led twelve warriors to where the thars were sighted. Elonda took the elves with her and hid among the trees. Vurth and the seven dwarves that were along circled to the other side of the four thars. "All right, boys, hit them hard, and force them back. They will run right into a bunch of flying arrows." Vurth smiled after giving the instructions and then with a wink rushed out of hiding, ax in hand.

The thars growled at the dwarves and met them head-on. Vurth was the first to encounter a thar; he ducked under the thar's swinging arms and thrust his ax into the foot of the beast.

The beast growled and kicked Vurth off his foot, the ax still implanted in his foot. The rest of the dwarves came in right behind Vurth, stopping any momentum on the thar's part.

Eight dwarves on four thars would actually be an even battle, but these dwarves were heavily armored and resilient. While one dwarf ran in at the thar near Vurth, Vurth used the opportunity to retrieve his ax. His fellow dwarf almost got squashed as he charged in, but dove out of the way just in time. Working together, Vurth and his friends drove the thars back, toward the waiting elves, who were already taking aim.

Just as one dwarf was sent flying by a thar's punch, Elonda and the elves unleashed their arrows. Each of the thars was caught by surprise and as a result had two or three arrows in them before they could even find the new attackers. Elonda and the five elves now charged in swords drawn.

Elonda jumped over a thar's kick and sliced it across the stomach. Two dwarves then chopped at the beast's legs with their axes. The thar was able to knock aside one dwarf, but Elonda came in with another slash, and the other dwarf threw his ax into the back of the beast as it fell to the ground. Elonda saw a second thar go down to her right and watched Vurth finish him off as his ax sliced into the creature's neck, ending its life. Blood splattered all over Vurth, who merely shrugged. A third thar soon went down as well, and the fourth started to run looking to escape. But three elves were right on its tail and quickly brought it down.

With the battle over, Elonda scouted around, making sure no other thars had seen or heard them. The elves retrieved any arrows that were still usable, and the dwarves hid the thars' bodies the best way they could. It was not an easy task. Three dwarves had been injured in the fight, but none of the injuries were severe, and they would heal fast. Satisfied, the group returned to camp full of pride for a job well done just before night would fall when the gargoyles would roam the skies.

*****

As the first rays of sun lightened the night into morning, Lalatco was awake and ready. He looked around the area, making sure all was clear. He fastened his belt around his waist, with rope and his canteen hooked on the belt. He also put on his knife bandolier over one shoulder, and it went diagonally across his naked chest and connected on his back. He also grabbed the waterweed shoots he had worked on. Although Lalatco was cold, the sun helped a little, and he was planning on going for a swim, so his clothes would do him no good. He chose to brave the elements with nothing but his undergarment, belt, scimitar, and bandolier.

The fog was even thicker this morning than the last as Lalatco quickly waded into the lake. First, he had to test his plan. He put one end of the waterweed shoot into his mouth and ducked underwater. The shoot worked a little but not as well as he had hoped; the other end stuck out of the water and allowed him to breathe, but he also got a little lake water through the weed. Lalatco assumed there was an unseeable hole in the shoot, tossed it away, and tried one of his other shoots. This one seemed to work very well, and Lalatco was happy his plan would work. He tied a second shoot to his belt just in case and again went underwater, this time swimming toward the castle.

The lake got deeper as he swam, and the shoot continued to work perfectly as an air device, and Lalatco could breathe in and out of it. Lalatco was now halfway across the lake, and no one could see him or took notice of the end of a waterweed shoot moving slowly across the lake.

A little while later, the water started to get shallow again, and Lalatco stayed completely under water and as close to the bottom of the lake as he could. When his belly was touching the bottom, Lalatco slowly popped his eyes out of the water. He had veered a little farther to the left than he wanted to but not too much. He was very close to the back of the castle now, and there were just a few thars wondering about. None of the thars were too close to him at the moment. The fog was still in the air, but not as thick as it was before, and Lalatco knew he had to move before it was all gone.

He waited until the closest thars were not looking his way, and crawled out of the lake, not making a sound. He lay in the long weeds; the weeds tickled and itched his bare skin, as he waited for his opportunity. Then with no thars looking his way, he ran as fast as he could to the wall of the castle. He hugged himself tight against the wall and waited. No alarm was raised, and no thar had seen him yet. He moved along the wall to a spot a little more hidden from view and looked all around him and up the wall.

So far so good, he thought to himself. The cold air and cold stone of the castle wall chilled him to the bone. His heart was racing, but he remained confident. He had done many things in his life and had been trained well. He undid the rope from his belt and quickly tied one of the ends to a knife. He looked up again and saw the underside of an overhang of the castle. He put his arm back and threw the knife toward the overhang, and the strong elven metal pieced the rock and stuck. Lalatco gave the rope a good pull, making sure it was secure before quickly starting up, using his feet on the castle wall to help him climb.

He could feel the knife starting to loosen, and quickened his pace. Lalatco grabbed on to the overhang right as the knife gave way. Lalatco's feet caught the rope, and he was lucky he did. Right under him, there was a thar, the rope dangling right above his head.

Lalatco pulled himself up just a little and peeked over the overhang. He almost lost his grip in pure surprise; right in front of him was a giant gargoyle, stuck in its stone form. He regained his composure and pulled himself up, hiding by the gargoyle. The rope was still hanging between his feet, and as soon as he was seated on the ledge, he started pulling up the rope. Lalatco stared at the thar as he pulled the rope up. To him his heart seemed to sound like a drum as he pulled up the rope as fast as he could. The thar seemed to make a movement to look up, and Lalatco got back from the ledge as the last of the rope came up.

Quickly, Lalatco put away his rope and knife and surveyed his surroundings. This gargoyle was working as a great place to hide, and many of them could be seen along the top of the castle. The tops of the castle's four walls were lined with gargoyles, and a small tower was on each corner of the castle. The castle's middle section rose up to even height with the walls, but another tower rose up then from the middle section and was higher than the castle walls. Lalatco also could tell that the back castle wall connected to the midsection of the castle, but the other walls did not. Lalatco realized then that there was a courtyard between the castle gate and the castle's center.

Staying very low as he ran from gargoyle to gargoyle, Lalatco checked to see if anyone one was around each time before running to hide behind the next gargoyle. Remembering what Gargan has said, that gargoyles can wake if needed from their dormant state, he made sure to make no noise and not to touch any gargoyle. It quickly became obvious that gargoyles were indeed the inhabitants of this castle, and no other creatures were.

Lalatco reached one of the corners of the castle, finding the small watchtower empty. He let out a breath he didn't know he was holding and shivered his body, now going numb to the cold. He now had a better view of the courtyard from this position and saw three small figures moving about the courtyard, one more on the wall above the gate, and another on the ground next to the gate.

Assuming these figures were Meslar and the knights, Lalatco knew there could only be five more because three of the knights were captured. Lalatco could not see any of the others and descended the tower's stone stairs toward the courtyard. He cautiously looked around as he exited the tower onto the courtyard. He stayed tight to the wall of the inner castle and moved along it, which took him closer to the figures in the courtyard.

The castle started in the exact middle of the four walls and steadily grew wider and taller. He dared to get a little closer because he saw a door leading into the main structure. Without making a sound, he ducked into the entryway. Cautiously, he headed toward the start of the castle. He saw no one and came up to the inner gate of the castle. Just a few steps on the other side of the inner gate were Meslar and two knights. Lalatco pressed his ear against the wall, and his acute elven hearing could make out most of what was being said.

"You have offered them things you cannot give them," Lalatco recognized it as Demorous's voice.

"It will not be a problem. The thars will follow me until they realize I am lying, and that will not be until after I have ultimate power and I kill them." There was silence for a while after Meslar had spoken, and Lalatco wished he had heard more of the conversation. The other knight spoke up a little while later.

"What about these gargoyles? What is your plan for them?"

"They are powerful allies to be sure," said Meslar, "and they would be even worse enemies. Bram and I have had the same goal of unlocking the power the gate holds, and I am hoping that after all this, we will find a mutual agreement."

Lalatco could not hear the next few things Meslar had said, because he was distracted by the sound of wrestling metal behind him. He instinctively ducked, and he did in the nick of time as a knight's sword struck the wall above Lalatco's head. The Silver Shadow had snuck up behind him and had almost lived up to his name. Lalatco took off running the way he came, and the knight was close behind, yelling, "Intruder!" Lalatco was able to stay just out of reach of the knight's sword and dove out of the entryway he had come in.

Lalatco drew his scimitar from his belt as he rolled on to his feet and ran.

Demorous was laughing to himself watching the half-naked elf run from the Silver Shadow. Meslar chanted something and unleashed a fireball at Lalatco, who dove into the stairwell as the fireball exploded on the tower's wall. The Silver Shadow was right on top of him then, and their two blades clanged on each other time and again as Lalatco backed up the steps. Lalatco slipped a small knife from his bandolier and threw it with his free hand, and the knife pierced through the armor and dug into the knight's lower leg. The Silver Shadow hit the steps hard and rolled down a couple more, making it hard for Demorous and Meslar to pursue.

Lalatco raced up the steps and exited the tower, and as soon as he had, an arrow flew past him, barely missing his head. The knight on top of the gate, Sigmon, continued firing arrows as Lalatco ran along the wall. Demorous and Meslar reached the top of the stairs and charged after Lalatco. Lalatco saw more than a few thars on the outside of the wall he was on. He knew the lake was his only chance. Getting as much of a running start as possible, he ran and jumped as far as he could. A sweep from Demorous's sword just missed him when he jumped.

Meslar watched as the elf flew through the air. Surprised, he realized that the elf was going to make it to the lake. Meslar quickly sent a bolt of energy after him, which struck the elf as he splashed into the lake. Meslar yelled for the thars to find the elf.

Lalatco struck the water hard, but struck the lake's floor even harder. The jump was far enough to get him into the lake, but he had jumped from such a height that his momentum still brought him to the lake's floor. His legs buckled when he hit the lake's floor, and he collapsed into the lake. The painful energy bolt's effects were also lessened by the water, but Lalatco could still certainly feel it. What pained him the most, though, was his right leg.

Lalatco swam as hard as he could, holding his breath and getting deeper into the lake. He struggled to remain conscious as he undid a waterweed shoot from his belt. He continued to swim underwater and used the shoot to breathe. Lalatco struggled against the pain in his leg as he swam to the other side of the lake. His swimming slowed and his pain grew and he fought to stay alert. Slowly the water started to get shallower. Lalatco could no longer bear the pain; his leg was burning severely. His foot touched the bottom and he heaved himself forward and all went black.

20

Worry

Leah started to grow very worried for Lalatco as the morning started to go by. It would soon be a day and a half since he had left, and he still had not returned. Yes, Flick had returned yesterday with some news about Lalatco trying to find a way into the castle, but Leah's concern had grown and grown. Quietly she snuck out of camp and over the hill. Quickly she traveled across the swampy terrain, keeping her eyes open for thars. She went from tree to tree, and before she knew it, she was approaching the lake.

Leah looked out from behind a tree and gasped. There she saw three thars approaching a figure in the weeds on the edge of the lake. Leah panicked; she could not tell if it was Lalatco or not, but who else could it be? Quietly she armed her bow with an arrow and let it fly. The arrow hit the closest thar right in the neck. Leah quickly fired a second arrow, hitting the thar again in almost exactly the same spot, and it struggled to stay on its feet. The other two thars charged her, and she let loose two more arrows before drawing her sword and retreating a few steps. The thars continued their charge as arrows hit their chests.

Rolling, Leah avoided a thar's swinging arm and blocked the club of the second thar with her sword as she came up on one knee. She kept her sword moving, swinging it all around her, keeping the thars at bay as she stood up. To her surprise, in came the thar she had shot in the neck. She charged it head-on, and diving between its legs, she was able to slice them both with her sword, and with the arrows still protruding from its neck, the beast fell to the ground. The other thars were quick to attack, and she failed to roll completely out of the way as the unarmed thar swung his claws. Leah received a gash on her back, and her sword came around, giving the thar a gash of its own.

Lalatco, who had been unconscious for the better part of an arc, had gotten quite lucky. His thrust as he went unconscious had gotten him close to shore, his head just peeking out of the water and saving his life. To Lalatco's surprise when he woke up, he was neither dead nor captured; and as he turned, he saw Leah battling with two thars. He could not believe his eyes. What was she doing out here? While doing his best to stay quiet, and not scream out in pain because of his injuries, he crawled the rest of the way out of the lake. He propped himself up on his good leg and drew a knife. He realized he was still very dizzy as he tried to aim. He let the knife fly, and it struck a thar in the back of its leg.

Leah blocked a swinging club and saw the other thar roar and reach down to the knife in his leg. Leah took the opportunity and plunged her sword into the beast's belly; removing it, she blocked another swing of the other thar's club just in time. The hit would have rendered her unconscious for sure; it took all the strength she had to deflect the club and hang on to the sword. Quickly she leaped out of the way as the dead thar crashed to the ground in front of her. The last thar came at her more ferocious now, and a hard swing of its club sent her sword flying into the air toward Lalatco, who used what strength he had to crawl toward it.

Leah desperately kept dodging the thar's attacks, trying to get to her sword. Then she was knocked to the ground by the thar's free hand. The thar roared as he lifted his club high in the air, about to deal a final blow. But Lalatco had reached Leah's sword and threw it to her as the thar's club started to come down. Leah caught the sword and rolled just in time, the club coming so close it tore her shirt. Leah jumped in the air and plunged the sword into the chest of the thar. The thar staggered and fell hard to the ground.

Leah, still full of adrenaline, retrieved her sword and Lalatco's knife and sliced the neck of one still-breathing thar. She then ran to Lalatco lying almost naked on the ground and breathing hard. Leah helped him up, and he put his weight on his good leg. She gave him a big hug, and she heard a whispered "Thank you" from Lalatco.

The two hid behind a tree, and following instructions from Lalatco, she retrieved his clothes and helped him get dressed. He was an awful shape: frozen, injured, and struggling with consciousness. She then looked back to the lake and saw a thar come upon the dead ones. He roared a loud angry roar, and a few more thars could be seen coming. Leah supported Lalatco whose right leg seemed useless as they tried to go from tree to tree and stay unnoticed. Not daring to look back to see if they were being followed, Lalatco tried to go as fast as he could, wincing anytime his right foot touched the ground. Leah spotted an elf on patrol and called to him. Leah and the elf quickly carried Lalatco back to camp, and the sun was now high in the sky.

Two elves, with experience in treating injuries, quickly discovered Lalatco had broken his leg. Lalatco drifted in and out of consciousness as the two elves put bandages and some of Jyres's healing salve on his cuts and made a wooden brace for his broken leg. The elves did what they could for Lalatco and hoped his leg would mend well. Leah's back was also tended to, the salve helping ease the pain the thar's claws had caused.

Leah told the others what had happened and was afraid that they would be found because thars had seen their dead companions. Vurth had an idea and quickly got his dwarves to work. The dwarves gathered their tools and started to dig a tunnel underneath the camp. Digging in the swampy terrain was the easy part, but creating a tunnel where the walls were strong was the challenge. While the dwarves were working, Jyres and the others were busy hiding any hints of a camp. Zar even found a dense patch of trees to hide the horses.

The dwarves were very skilled at building tunnels, and just as the day turned into night, the warriors filed into the underground tunnel. The whole group, minus Zar and a few others who stayed hidden with the horses, fit tightly into the dark tunnel. Inside the tunnel, it was very dark and claustrophobic, but that did not bother the dwarves. They were at home in the dark tunnels. Jyres was at first very uncomfortable, but when his eyes adjusted to the dark, he could see a little. He noticed the beautiful Elonda was the one brushing against his back. This put him at ease, and he felt better about the situation.

Zar saw many gargoyles take flight, and he assumed they were looking for the ones who killed the thars and snuck into their castle. Zar cast a spell of camouflage on himself, the elves with him, and the horses, adding to the cover the trees were giving them. Having the small group to protect was much easier and less taxing on his energy then protecting the whole group had been the previous nights. With what was sure to be numerous enemies out looking for them, he appreciated the dwarf's idea of a tunnel. Time and time again, a gargoyle passed over them, but none could see them. Many gargoyles also glided over the camp but could not see the tunnel the dwarves had built, or any sign that there was a campsite.

Everyone in the tunnel stayed very quiet during the night for fear that an enemy would happen to walk past as they sat uncomfortably in the tunnel. Jyres tried to rest his head against the wall of the tunnel, but it was rocky and slimy. Elonda, already sitting shoulder to shoulder with him, pulled him closer; and he rested his head on her shoulder and drifted off to sleep.

Jyres awoke to many sounds of wrestling around him. Scouts had checked the area and deemed it safe to exit the tunnel. Everyone was beginning to exit the tunnel and creating quite a ruckus. Elonda smiled at Jyres as he lifted his head; he returned the smile and let out a yawn. As the last of the army filed out of the tunnel, Elonda's and Jyres's eyes locked. Jyres quickly looked away, embarrassed. Elonda gave his shoulder a nudge with hers, and they both laughed. Elonda gave him a quick kiss on the cheek, and a feeling of warmth and happiness rushed over Jyres. They both looked at each other, not sure what to say. Then a voice broke the silence.

"Well, what do we got here." Vurth laughed. Elonda, embarrassed, looked down, and Jyres tried to stammer out some words, but it was mostly incoherent. Vurth chuckled some more and said, "You two are needed for a meeting, and Lalatco has recovered enough strength now to tell his tale."

Jyres, Zar, Elonda, Vurth, and Leah listened as Lalatco told his tale. After he was through, Vurth laughed heartily and said, "A naked elf running around a castle would have been a humorous sight."

Lalatco's mission had produced some valuable information, including the fact that Meslar and Bram were working together to unlock the power of the gate. Also, that Meslar had promised the thars something and probably cast a spell along with that to get them to protect the castle.

Jyres pondered the information before speaking. "If we attack now while it is still early morning, we can complete our task before the gargoyles awake."

Leah was not so sure. She sighed and said, "There are too many thars around. You won't make it to the castle in time, if at all. And remember, gargoyles have the ability to awaken if needed to. Isn't that what Gargan told you?"

"Yes, I guess that is a possibility. I do not know how much it takes to awaken them from their slumber. As far as the thars go, perhaps we could draw them out and sneak in behind them," commented Jyres.

"Yes," exclaimed Vurth, "a distraction! Send an army to the west and draw the attention of all the thars, and send a smaller group in to take the castle and Meslar."

Jyres saw many heads nodding in agreement and said, "We must act quickly, while the day is young."

21

Time to Act

Vurth and Leah led a force of forty warriors out to the west. They led the force trying to make it look like they were moving to go around the lake. As soon as Meslar noticed the army, he ordered Demorous to gather the thars and organize an attack on the army. It seemed the diversion may work. Soon enough, Demorous had an army of thars coming out to meet Vurth's army.

Vurth and Leah, who were both riding on horses, stopped the marching company and checked the formation. Vurth had positioned the dwarves along the front and sides, with the elves in the middle. Vurth knew that this way the elves would be able to fire many an arrow before having to reinforce the front lines.

*****

Jyres, Elonda, Zar, four dwarves, and four elves were already slowly moving toward the castle. Lalatco had begged to go along even though he knew he would be of little use with a broken leg, but Jyres and Elonda had forced him to stay behind at camp with Flick and a few elves. As the small group went along their way, they saw a knight gather the thars and head out to meet Vurth's army. The plan had worked; almost all the thars had cleared out of the area, leaving it unguarded for the small group of eleven to get to the castle without conflict.

Before long, the group was near the land bridge that crossed the lake to the front gate. There were a handful of thars in the area, and Jyres spotted one knight above the gate. Jyres turned toward the group. "Well, here we are. Let us end this right now." Elonda gave him an encouraging nod, and with that, Jyres drew his sword and let out a yell as he charged the bridge.

Elonda was right alongside Jyres as they charged at the first thar. Each of them sliced its legs with their swords and avoided the thar's swinging club and kept on running. The dwarves quickly overwhelmed the thar as the elves and Zar followed Jyres and Elonda. They started to cross the land bridge, and Elonda pulled Jyres to the ground, an arrow just missing him. Two elves returned fire at Lemont who was on the wall above the gate, as the other two elves and Zar ran past the fallen pair and intercepted three fast-approaching thars. The thars put up a good fight, but they were soon defeated when the dwarves caught up and joined the fight. The small group continued to cross the land bridge on their way to the gate.

Lemont continued to fire arrows, but two of the elves kept him pinned down as the rest of the group reached the gate. The strong wooden gate would not budge, and "Now what?" Jyres asked. Elonda quickly started to climb the wall, the agile elf finding footholds and handholds as she climbed. Another elf, Silvan, tried to follow but could not match Elonda's speed. As Elonda started to near the top, the knight on the wall spotted her. With incredible quickness, she flung herself on top of the wall and raced down the steps. Lemont started to follow, but an arrow found its way in between his armor, striking the knight in the arm just below the elbow.

Elonda was met at the bottom of the stairs by a second knight, the Silver Shadow, and Jyres and the others could hear their swords clang against each other again and again. The two were at a stalemate, but then Lemont joined the fight, and it was two against one. Elonda fought hard, blocking a thrust from one knight and a slice from the other. She tried desperately to stay out of the middle of them. The two knights started to push her back from the gate. Elonda was very skilled, but fighting two knights would be hard for even the most skilled swordsman. Their swords continued to clang, and Elonda continued to get pushed back. But out of the corner of her eye, she saw Silvan, who had followed her up the wall and run down the stairs and to the gate.

*****

Demorous had managed to get the thars in somewhat of a formation. He was at the head and stopped their march just out of bow range from Vurth's position. Demorous looked over the opposing warriors; he had them beat in numbers, that was for sure. Perhaps his army was almost double the size. A confident smile came across his face. This would be an easy victory. He turned to his force behind him and yelled in a loud voice, "Show yourselves worthy today, and Meslar will reward you beyond your dreams!" A few roars were heard from the thars. They used very deep growls to communicate with each other, but Demorous was confident that most could understand the basic language. "Today you start a great history for your race! Never have you been united as you are now! Show yourselves and Meslar how powerful you can be!" That got a huge roar from his army, and Demorous yelled, "Now march!"

Vurth watched as the thars started their march toward him and his army. Vurth was impressed that Demorous had gotten them into a somewhat tight formation. Even as they marched, they stayed in close formation. Vurth turned his horse to face his warriors. He urged his horse to a trot, crossing back and forth in front of the formation as he talked.

"Are we afraid of dirty, smelly, dumb thars?" yelled Vurth.

A loud "No!" resounded from the warriors.

"Are you ready to do your part to save our lands from the insane Meslar?"

"Yes!" came the response even louder than the first.

"Then let's hack them down and send them running. They will regret this day for years to come." The warriors, elven and dwarves alike, all cheered so loud Lalatco heard their war cries back at camp.

Vurth dismounted from his horse and joined the front line; an elf mounted the now-vacant saddle and went to the left flank. Leah was on a horse on the right flank of the formation. Vurth could tell the enemy force had picked up a little speed and were now about fifty yards away. Vurth yelled, "Ready, aim…fire!"

A good twenty arrows were loosed from the elven bows behind Vurth and his dwarven front lines. Vurth shouted, "Aim!" again just as the first arrows were hitting the marching thars. "Fire!" followed shortly after, and twenty more arrows leaped into the air. Many thars went down after the second barrage of arrows hit their first lines.

"Charge!" yelled Demorous from the middle of the enemy lines.

Vurth answered with "Fire at will!" and arrows filled the sky. The elves were known to be able to aim and fire arrows faster than any other race, and this group of elves was living up to the reputation. They were firing arrows at a rapid pace with pinpoint accuracy. Leah was no slouch with a bow either, firing almost as fast and just as deadly. Although they were still outnumbered, Leah and the elves had evened the odds considerably with their accurate shooting.

The first thars plowed into the army's front lines, even knocking a few dwarves over. "Hold the line!" yelled Vurth as his ax claimed his first kill of the day. Elves filled in where dwarves fell, and the front line held against the thars. Soon, however, the thars attacked the sides of the formation as well. Vurth yelled at the top of his lungs as he ducked under a swinging thar's arm, "Don't let them circle us!" A chop of his ax and a thar lost his arm; Vurth's attacks were relentless, not letting one thar get past him.

Leah had seen the danger Vurth had announced as well. If they were circled by the thars, it would all be over. As the thars charged at them, she put away her bow and drew her sword. Just before the thars struck the right flank, she urged her horse right at them. Trusting her horse's strength and will, she wove in and out of the thars, hacking and slashing, while narrowly avoiding the thar's clubs and claws. Many of the thars went after Leah and forgot about the dwarves and elves. Leah's smile grew as she heard Demorous yelling for the thars to remain where they were. The right flank was easily defended as Leah galloped among the enemies, foiling their tight lines.

Vurth's army continued to fight to a standstill with the thars. Vurth and his dwarves were a tough group of fighters. Although many had taken hits, it took a lot to make one of these dwarves stay on the ground. As the battle raged on, Vurth realized the left flank was going to fold soon. If that happened, it would be tough to hold their ground. Vurth hoped their distraction had been long enough and started yelling out orders as he dodged a thar's claws.

Leah who had returned to the front lines had held her flank well, and now it was time for the retreat. She heard Vurth's voice loud and clear and yelled the order to her side of the formation.

It was amazing how well and efficient the unit worked together. Vurth had done well in the short time he had had to explain what orders he would use. Those not in the thick of the battle gathered up their fallen comrades and started toward the right flank. Vurth left his post and with a battle cry ran into the thar's left flank, taking two of them down without even blinking. With another yell by Leah, the formation had completed the change. The right flank became the front line. The warriors charged in with Vurth and demolished the left flank of the thars. The wounded, or worse ones, were quickly filed out behind the wall Vurth and the others had created.

Demorous was very impressed how well the opposing army changed formation and ensured their escape route. Demorous had stayed back out of the action but now charged ahead a little, barking out orders as the opponents started a full retreat away from the thars.

*****

Elonda ducked under a slashing sword and blocked a second, then Lemont's sword came around, again knocking Elonda's sword from her hand, and a punch from the Silver Shadow knocked her to the ground.

The gate started to creak as Silvan turned the crank to open the gate. The knights heard the sound and turned to see Silvan. Realizing that they had been distracted made the knights furious; both Lemont and the Silver Shadow raised their swords to deliver a devastating blow to Elonda. Elonda waited until the last possible moment then kicked her legs up and to the sides. She kicked the sides of the swords as they plunged to the ground. The sword on the right just missed her, pinning her to the ground through her clothes. The sword on her left gave her a small cut on the side as it also pinned her clothes to the ground. Amazingly though, her kicks had misdirected the knights' swords just enough.

After what seemed like an eternity, the gate was finally high enough for Jyres to squeeze through. Pain and fear grabbed hold of him when he saw the knights standing over Elonda. He ran as fast as he could toward them, throwing all caution to the wind. He watched as Lemont turned to face him and pulled out a knife, leaving his sword to keep Elonda trapped. He saw the Silver Shadow draw his knife and stand over Elonda.

Elonda was not able to move, pinned by the two swords. She watched as the knight raised his knife and heard Jyres scream, "No!" as the knight thrust it down at her chest. Jyres had jumped past Lemont as he screamed, the knight slashing at him with his knife.

Elonda saw her life flash before her eyes but never felt the knife plunge into her chest. Jyres had saved her, tackling the Silver Shadow just in time and receiving a knife wound in the process. Jyres found himself thrown aside as the Silver Shadow attempted to regain his feet; the two knights retreated in a hurry then, as they saw more of their enemies coming to Jyres's aid. Lemont and the Silver Shadow pulled their swords free and ran to the inner castle and shut the door before the others could get to them.

Jyres got onto his knees before he realized he was bleeding. He slipped back to the ground and put his hand over his side where the knife had cut him. His hand was quickly becoming red, and Jyres started to panic, but then Elonda was by his side. His breathing became steady again, his panic calmed, as he looked at Elonda kneeling beside him.

Silvan threw Elonda his bag as the small group started to look for a way inside the inner castle. Elonda rummaged through the bag and pulled out some rolled-up cloth. Unraveling it a little, she removed Jyres's hand gently. "Don't worry. It doesn't look too bad." She smiled at him and could tell he was a little shaken up over the wound. "It is not so deep that it should cause you to worry," Elonda said as she applied a little pressure and secured the cloth to the wound.

Jyres winced at the pain but nodded his head in thanks.

"You saved my life," she said, looking at Jyres in the eyes and holding his attention. "Thank you. I owe you one."

"It was nothing." Jyres tried to sound confident and nonchalant in his reply.

"It wasn't nothing. It was brave and—" Before she could finish, Jyres kissed her.

Inside the castle, Meslar and the four knights were considering their options. They quickly realized there were only two: hold off the small group either until night and the gargoyles awoke or until the thars won the battle outside or, the other option, make a run for the horses.

Before the attackers found a way into the castle, Meslar and his knights were heading to the top. There they could get on the castle wall and follow it until they were close to the area where the horses were. They reached the top and the castle wall, and although they were a little ways ahead, the attackers had split up to find them. As Meslar and the knights started moving on top of the castle wall, Jyres, breathing hard, and two dwarves appeared at the door leading out onto the wall. After catching their breath for a brief second, Jyres and the two dwarves continued chasing after their enemies.

Meslar and his knights continued their run along the wall toward the back-left corner watchtower. Stone gargoyles could be seen on the wall and uppermost parts of the castle as Jyres and Tagro kept their pace, the other dwarf following behind. Jyres was thankful the creatures were stone at the moment, but he also knew that would change for sure in a few arcs' time or at any time if disturbed enough. As Jyres and Tagro reached the halfway point, they could see that the knights and Meslar would soon be at the watchtower.

Jyres saw Zar and the others racing across the courtyard, then his eyes fell upon the stables. "They are heading to the horses. Hurry!" Tagro could not keep up with Jyres as he somehow quickened his already-fast pace considering the knife wound he had received. Meslar and the knights disappeared through the doorway of the watchtower as Jyres sped on.

He slowed down as he came to the doorway, but not fast enough. Sigmon's sword came swinging at Jyres whose only choice was to fall to the ground to avoid being decapitated. Jyres hit the ground hard and rolled into the tower's stone wall even harder. He had no time to decide if he was hurt again; Sigmon's sword was swinging at him a second time. This time it barely missed him as he rolled away. He sprang to his feet and jumped over a third swing of the knight's sword. Jyres pulled out his own sword to block another attack, this one from Digmon who had also waited for him. But Digmon had come out from the doorway just as the slow Tagro charged into the action, testing Sigmon's defenses.

As the battle raged on the wall, Meslar, Lemont, and the Silver Shadow reached the bottom of the tower and the courtyard. Meslar noticed Zar and the attackers running across the courtyard and knew this was no time for stealth. Meslar knew there were only six horses, and that would at least even the odds if he got there first. It soon became apparent that they would get there first, and they did, but not by much. Meslar, Lemont, and the Silver Shadow saddled themselves, each on a horse, as their enemies bore down on them.

Swords clashed, and horses panicked as the fight started. It was short lived, however, and Meslar and the two knights were off on their horses. Two dwarves uselessly ran after them as Zar, Elonda, and two elves tried to calm the remaining horses. After calming down the horses, Zar saddled a horse, as did one of the elves, and they finally got going after Meslar as well.

Elonda, who had saddled the last horse, was struggling with a decision. She saw Jyres in battle at the top of the wall with the sun getting lower and lower. She also saw Meslar racing to the gate, which was still only half open. As she stared wondering where Meslar thought he was going with the gate not open far enough, she saw him raise his staff and usher some sort of a hazy light from it. The light hit the gate as they thundered at it at full speed. After a second, the gate started to open, the magic haze forcing it to rise up. Elonda had made her decision. Her horse turned and accelerated toward the tower and Jyres.

*****

Vurth's army continued the retreat. Vurth's retreat plan had worked well. Leah's well-guarded flank became the way out, and Vurth and some stubborn dwarves slowed down the chasers. As the army came close to the camp, Vurth knew what happened in the next few moments would be the key to survival. Vurth's army poured over the hill and into camp, the thars close behind.

Vurth saw one dwarf struggling as he carried an injured comrade up the hill. Vurth charged down the hill, taking a thar out at the knees with one swing of the ax. Vurth stuck one arm under the shoulder of the injured dwarf, and the three of them started up the hill. As the three dwarves crested the hill with thars' hungry swings just barely missing, a smile came across Vurth's face.

The thar army followed the elves and dwarves down the hill, and as they reached the bottom, there were sounds of crashing and snapping, and thars' agonizing roars soon followed. Lalatco and the few elves left behind had been busy. Using part of the tunnel that was created the night before, strategically placed pit traps had been set up. The dwarves and elves, knowing how to spot them, did not set them off. At the bottom of the pits were sharpened sticks that acted as spears.

The traps were actually even more effective than Vurth had hoped. Thars who had fallen in the traps were roaring in agony, and their fellow creatures were no longer so quick to join the battle. The thars not only saw but heard how bad their fellows in the pits were hurt, and quite a few of them had fallen in the pits. Just like that, the thars were scattering, and Meslar had lost his power and control over them.

*****

Zar urged his horse on but could not make up any ground. Demorous, retreating from the lost battle, had now joined Meslar and the two other knights who were riding away. With no hope of catching up, Zar and the others gave up the chase.

Back in the castle, the battle up on the wall continued. The other dwarf, who had been following Jyres and Tagro, joined in the battle with the two knights. The knights were working hard and started to back down the stairs of the tower. Little did they know who was coming up the stairs; Elonda came at them sword swinging, and the knights were stuck in a narrow staircase with nowhere to go. Soon Sigmon's and Digmon's swords were knocked away, and their opponents' swords were pointed at them. The knights put up their hands and surrendered. None of them saw a nearby gargoyle's eyes flick open.

As everybody returned to camp, the sun was starting to set. Jyres was glad to see that Vurth and the others had done well. But the group was saddened as well, for a few dwarves and elves had lost their lives. Many were injured, but everyone would heal in time. It just made Jyres mad that the lives lost were for almost nothing because only two knights were caught and not Meslar. The group all huddled close together, as Zar used another spell to hide the group.

Later on that night when the group was sleeping, Elonda woke up to loud growling. One growl would answer another. Elonda woke up Jyres, and the two of them carefully crawled toward the noises. They crawled and hid under a couple of bushes. Not too far away from them, gargoyles were standing all around, and in the middle were Gargan and another gargoyle. This gargoyle was huge, even a little bigger than Gargan. He skin was colored purple. Jyres noticed he also had a medallion around his neck, similar in color but a different shape than the one that adorned Gargan's neck. They were speaking to each other in their own language, and neither Elonda nor Jyres had any idea what they were saying. Although the language of the gargoyles had sounded like growling from far away, up close it sounded totally different. It was nothing like the deep, hard growls of the thars. It still sounded rough compared to the basic language, but different sounds and pitches were distinguishable.

As the conversation continued, Jyres could tell it was getting more intense. Then Gargan said something that silenced the huge purple gargoyle. Neither gargoyle said anything for a long time. Then after a few words by each creature, the purple-skinned gargoyle turned and walked away. Some of the other gargoyles around turned and followed him.

Gargan and a few of his gargoyle friends waited until the opposing gargoyles had dispersed from the area and then walked in the direction of Elonda and Jyres. Gargan, knowing they were there, waved at them and came over to greet them.

"Who was that?" Jyres asked.

"That was Bram, a gargoyle who is hard to reason with," was the answer from Gargan. "He is the leader of another clan of gargoyles, though I don't believe he is worthy of such a title. We are in need of a conversation."

22

Another Trip

With the group gathered, Gargan began with saying, "It is clear that Bram and Meslar are working together." His low distinguishable voice was set in a serious tone.

"Bram was here looking for you. He could tell something was restricting his sight of this area and knew that you attacked Meslar today. I was glad to be here before he investigated further. He will not take action against you with us here. He knows neither of our clans could afford an all-out war, and as you can see, I have many of my clan with me. But he did ask us to leave immediately or he will test our resolve."

The group offered them their thanks and listened intently to the gargoyle.

"I know what this human you call Meslar is trying to do, and I know it must not be allowed to be done. Zar knows what has been written and says you, Jyres, will be the one to stop him. So I have been doing everything I can to keep you safe. Although I don't know what would happen if he succeeded, the stories that have been passed down speak of the serious danger the gate has locked away. Believe me, friends, you don't want Meslar to succeed in opening the gate. Now with Meslar and Bram working together, I believe a path has been opened for Meslar to accomplish what he wants."

After a short pause, Gargan shared more of the conversation he had with Bram with the group. "Although Bram did not share much with me, I believe I know him well enough to understand his purpose. Somehow Bram knows where the key for the gate is, and that is how this partnership has now become dangerous. Meslar must have convinced Bram that he was the one and only one to be able to open the gate."

"How would he have done that in such short time?" asked Jyres.

"I don't believe it was a short time," said Zar. "He must have been planning this for a while. Meslar didn't come by this castle by chance. Somehow they had already been in communication."

"Well, how do you like that?" said the veteran dwarf in an exasperated voice. "That is concerning if they have been in this together all along."

"I could not say for sure if they have been in contact," said Gargan with much thought in his voice. "I know they have flown far and wide out from their castle, but impossible it becomes to track all of their gargoyles and their movements."

"What about the captured knights? Certainly they must know something," suggested Leah.

"Vurth and I questioned them." Elonda was shaking her head in frustration. "They either are not afraid of us and refuse to give up information or truly know little of their master's plans."

"Bram wouldn't share much either, and what he did share we can't trust. But Meslar must have promised Bram something substantial for Bram to work with him and be willing to give up the location of the key." Gargan growled in frustration after saying this.

"So can we assume Meslar and three of his knights are on their way to where they think the key is? If so, that does not allow us much time," stated Jyres.

"I don't think we can assume anything," said Lalatco.

"What about Bram? What is he going to do, Gargan?" asked Jyres.

"I am not sure. Either he did not know or he would not tell me. Bram's clan and my clan have never seen eye to eye since Bram became their leader. I do believe they are working together, but I would not be surprised if both Meslar's and Bram's end goal is to be the sole person who benefits from the opening of that gate, which means it is hard to predict either's actions."

Zar spoke next. "I want to go after Meslar by myself. He is my son, and I want one more chance to face him. As Jyres had said earlier, he should be given one last chance to change his course." No one replied or said anything to contradict his thinking. Zar saddled a horse, and Flick got on behind him. "I will follow their tracks the best I can, as that can be relied on more than anyone's guess of direction. I trust the rest of you to make the decisions you perceive as right. But I must confront my son." Then Zar gave a wave and a nod as they rode away, and that was that.

The others continued the discussion, and it was soon decided by the group that they would split up. They did not have a clear picture and wanted to try to plan for multiple scenarios. Vurth would take his dwarves and start heading toward the gate. Gargan said his clan knew of its location and mentioned that it was easy to find and that Bram's clan would know of it as well. He described to Vurth in detail on how to get there.

The other group would head off to the ruins of the Castle Stone Heights, the castle that Zar had suggested to look for the key. Hopefully find it, and keep it safe. Gargan said that he and his gargoyles would try to keep an eye on Bram and his clan in an effort to stay ahead of their plans.

The gargoyles stayed with the group that night as extra protection from Bram and his gargoyles. Jyres and the others tried to get some needed rest. Jyres took the time to think more than he did to rest. It surprised him how much Bram knew about the situation. He wondered how old he was and how he knew the key's location. Bram and Gargan could not have been alive when it was hidden, could they? These questions filled Jyres's mind. Jyres hoped everything he was going through was worth it. He wondered what it was that drove people like Meslar to do such things. After a while he realized the power was the answer to that question. Why did some need it? Why did some need to control others? Jyres figured those questions would never be answered.

As the two groups got ready for their journey the next morning, they cleaned up camp with sleeping gargoyles watching. Vurth and Jyres approached each other, and surprisingly, Vurth swallowed Jyres up in a big hug. Then "See you soon" was all he said. Within a quarter of an arc after that, both groups were heading off in their different directions. They left with the comfort that the friendly gargoyles would be keeping an eye out for their enemies during the long nights.

Elonda and Jyres rode horses at the front of their group as Lalatco and Leah rode toward the back. Both couples talked a lot to each other as they rode. Leah was full of concern for Lalatco as he recovered from his leg injury, but he was on the mend and would be better in time. However, Jyres's focus was elsewhere. Ever since he had kissed Elonda on the battlefield, he talked with her constantly, hoping to discover she had the same feelings for him as he now did for her.

The group covered a lot of ground in the first day, and they found a nice spot to make camp that night. It was a small valley nestled in between a couple of hills. Five individuals were assigned to keep watch, and the people on watch would change every two arcs. As Jyres was taking his turn at one of the watch posts, some movement in the shadows caught his eye. He continued to watch and spotted several small shapes moving about. He could not make out what it was and quietly crept over to the nearest watchman. Jyres knew Silvan would have better vision than he did.

Once Jyres was by the elf, he pointed the figures out to Silvan. The elf recognized them as wolves and said there were probably seven to ten of them. The pack of wolves gradually got close to the camp, so Jyres roused a few more elves that took up defensive positions and readied their bows. Whether the wolves sensed something was wrong or smelled something they did not like, Jyres did not know, but the wolves retreated into the distance.

The rest of the night was uneventful, and the group was moving with the rise of the sun. Their progress was slower this day, however; a hard snowstorm hit. The ground was soon covered in snow, and the group worked hard to get through snowdrifts of three feet in some places.

The group camped for the second night, but this time the always-joyful elves were not content to stay quiet. They broke out into songs, many of which Lalatco led. The elves were all in good moods as if nothing was wrong and they were not in the process of a challenging quest.

Jyres and Elonda sat next to each other as the elves entertained. A camp with all elves was different than a camp of dwarves and elves. The dwarves sometimes did not like the singsong lifestyles of the elves, unless, of course, spirits of the vine were involved. Then the dwarves were the loudest ones. Leah, the only other person around that was not an elf, came over to sit by Jyres and Elonda.

Leah watched Lalatco intently, smiling at him all the while, his hair stark white in the night and reflecting the snow. The elves ended the night with a song sung in elvish, Lalatco leading the group again. The song was beautiful, and Elonda translated it for Jyres and Leah. Lalatco and a select few sang the verses, and the rest of the elves responded.

> Long ago in a faraway place
> Alahadra was the greatest of his race
> He was an elf, yes, he was!
>
> There was a great battle long ago
> Alahadra was there to fight his great foe
> The foe was a dragon, yes, it was!

The dragon was meanest of all
To destroy the elves was the dragon's goal
That was his goal, yes, it was!

Just when all seemed to be lost
Alahadra stuck his mightiest of blows
The dragon went down, yes, it did!

Alahadra's blade pierced the heart
The dragon's spirit would soon depart
It asked for help, yes, it did!

Alahadra and the dragon dealt
Forever defend the elves was the deal
The dragon agreed, yes, it did!

Alahadra cast his greatest spell
The dragon was saved that is well known
The dragon was saved, yes, it was

In the sky the dragon still flies
And Alahadra's memory will never die
Alahadra the elf, Alahadra the elf

23

The Search for the Key

On the fourth day of their trip, their destination came into view. What once must have been a great castle now was a pitiful sight. The group reached the ruins by nightfall. Rocks and boulders were everywhere the group looked, and remnants of the castle wall and its towers still stood in some places. Some of the group kept watch as others searched what remained of the castle.

After a short time of searching, Leah found a passage that went down under the castle. Leah led the way; Jyres, Elonda, and three other elves were not far behind. There was a winding staircase of stone, and with each step, it got darker. Elonda sent an elf back to start a fire and bring a torch. Once two torches were brought back to Elonda, they started down the staircase again. Those still aboveground prepared camp for the night.

After what seemed like an eternity, the six adventurers reached the bottom of the staircase. The light from the torches started to penetrate the darkness, and the group saw an oval expanse with a small ledge going around it. The wall around the expanse had small rooms cut out of the stone. Jyres guessed this used to be the dungeon of the castle. Then the light reached the ceiling, and the adventurers saw hundreds of bats hung there. Some, startled by the light, screeched and dropped from their perch, flying past the intruders.

The six individuals looked around and searched the small rooms for the key. They could not find the key or any another entrances or exits. So with only one option left, Jyres tossed a torch down the pit. Eventually it did hit the bottom and illuminated a little of the area. Leah was the first to volunteer, and they quickly tied some rope around her waist and started to ease her down into the pit. Leah used her feet to keep her steady so she would not spin or bump into the wall as she was lowered down. When she had reached the bottom, Leah grabbed the torch off the ground and untied herself from the rope. Leah looked around using the light from the torch, but all she saw were the walls and the floor of the pit.

Leah started to inspect the walls more carefully. She had gotten about halfway around the pit when she thought she had heard some noises from above. Thinking nothing of it, she continued her work until something caught her eye. A closer look revealed a small hole in the wall. She brought her torch closer and saw a small object in the hole. Quickly she reached in and freed the object. As she studied the small shield-shaped object, she heard another noise. This time she looked up, and she did just in time to see a huge gargoyle floating down. Unsure of the allegiances of the gargoyle, Leah stuffed the object into her pocket and ran to the rope. She pulled on it, and to her despair, all of the rope fell on top of her.

The gargoyle landed with a crunch. Based on how he had been described to her, she recognized him as the one Gargan referred to as Bram. Bram's intimidating form froze Leah. Bram took a couple of steps forward, a smug look on his face. Leah finally got herself to move, just before it was too late. Her free hand quickly drew her sword, and she tossed her torch right at the purple gargoyle.

Bram was taken by surprise and was slow to bat the torch away. Leah maneuvered away from the gargoyle whose shoulder was burned by the torch. Bram turned to face Leah as the torch fell to the ground and went out.

Gargoyles could see very well in the dark, but even Bram could not see in the darkness that enveloped him. Bram listened for any sound, but Leah remained perfectly still. Both warriors now had to rely on their other senses besides sight. Going as quietly as humanly possible, Leah made her way back to the rope, listening closely all the while. Bram had not even moved; one step from him and the whole ground would shake. He was simply waiting. Leah felt the rope with her hands and ever so carefully set her sword down, pulled out her knife, and tied it on one end of the rope. It was not easy to do in pitch dark, but she got it after a few tries.

Leah held the knife in one hand and the coiled rope in the other. Blindly she threw the knife as far and as high as she could. She heard the knife hit home into the wall of the pit, but she had no idea where or how high. Bram heard it as well, and he leaped toward the sound. Leah heard him as he landed to her left on the wall, his claws digging into the stone. Quietly and slowly Leah followed the slack in the rope until she was right under where the knife had anchored into the wall.

Leah waited a few moments before pulling on the rope to make sure the knife held in place, and it did. She only hoped it was high enough. As she started to climb, using both the rope and the wall, she knew she was being too loud. She heard and felt what was like an explosion as Bram hit the wall not far from her, his claws digging into the rock and holding him there. She knew he had to be close to him and dared not move. She tried to scream a moment later, but for some reason, no sound left her body as a giant hand grabbed the back of her coat and yanked her off the wall. Leah desperately hung on the rope with one hand as Bram held her. Bram moved his claws across her body, looking for anything she might have. He felt an object in her pocket and tore at her jacket. He plucked out the object.

Then Leah was falling for a moment as Bram let go, and she clenched the rope with both hands as the momentum slammed her back against the wall. The knife gave way, and she was falling again, for more than a moment this time, and a scream escaped her lips as she fell to the ground. Then no sound or thought came to Leah as she lay on the bottom of the pit.

*****

The gargoyles had taken the elves setting up camp completely by surprise, dropping in among them and keeping the elves from sending any warning or organizing any defense. In the dungeon, Jyres, Elonda, and the three elves did a little better than the elves camped above them; but against the six powerful gargoyles that came into the dungeon, there was not much they could do. The gargoyles had not killed anyone, however; they had everyone under guard with hands bound. Well, except for one.

Thankfully, Jyres thought, Silvan had somehow crept away out of the dimly lit area. Although Jyres was tied up and helpless, he knew Silvan was waiting for the right moment to free his friends. Then Jyres and Elonda looked at each other in desperation as a scream came forth from the abyss and then was immediately silenced. Jyres swallowed hard as he saw Bram emerge from the abyss. The huge creature was examining something in his hand as he walked over to the other gargoyles. They all started to leave, when Jyres shouted after them, "Why are you doing this?" Bram turned around at the bottom of the staircase and didn't say a word. He merely stared back and smiled.

The one torch still lit and close to Jyres started to die away as Silvan who had managed to stay hidden emerged from a cell in the wall. He ran to his captured companions and untied them. Jyres and Elonda ran to the edge of the pit and the torch they had struggled to hold on to life. The other three elves ran up the stairs to check on the others.

"Leah!" Jyres yelled but got no response. Jyres took a calming breath and tried to think. He did not have any more rope and could not climb down the pit without any tools. Unless, he thought, Jyres ran over to the spot where Bram had climbed out of the pit. Just as he had hoped, the gargoyle had left many holes with his claws. Jyres quickly began his descent using the claw indentations whenever he could as hand and footholds. He made good progress but had a long way to go, and the torch above him had just gone out. He slipped a couple of times in the dark and almost fell once, his task becoming very hard.

Finally a few of the elves returned from the camp with news that no one had been hurt and they brought fresh torches. One was tossed down to Jyres who made a nice one-handed catch. He held the torch below him and could see Leah lying on the ground. "I see her," he called to the others above the pit. He dropped the torch safety away from Leah, and it hit the ground and fizzled before giving off its full light.

The new light helped Jyres a lot, and he made it to the floor quickly. Jyres ran over to Leah. "Leah, are you okay?" He shook her shoulder a little bit as well, but Leah did not respond to either his voice or his touch. He put his cheek as close to her mouth as he could; he could feel very faintly a little breath.

Thankfully she was breathing, shallow, but breathing nonetheless. Jyres clapped his hands as loud as he could next to her ears but got no response. Jyres pondered what else he could do, but then he heard a small whimper. He looked down to see Leah's eyes open. She tried to move.

"Don't move. You could be hurt badly. How do you feel?" Jyres asked as he looked her over to see if he could see anything wrong with her.

"I ache" was all she said. Jyres ran his hand along her back and arms and legs, hoping not to find anything obviously out of place.

Leah moaned a little as she sat up. "I feel like I was run over by a dragon," said Leah as she stretched and moved her arms and legs.

Jyres was thankful she had not broken anything but wondered how many more bumps and bruises he and his friends could take.

Once everyone was back outside the castle, they decided to camp there one more night. From what Leah had told them about her encounter with Bram, they had to assume that Bram now had the key and would be heading to the gate—the same place this group would now be heading.

Lalatco, still slowed by one leg, hobbled over to attend to Leah. The two fell asleep in each other's arms. Jyres smiled at the sight and found his eyes roaming the area for Elonda. She stood at the edge of the campsite, looking into the sky.

"Another exciting night," Jyres said as he approached. Elonda smiled, but the smile quickly faded away. Jyres put one arm around her and held her close. Both stood in silence, in awe of the task they now faced. The key was in their enemy's possession, and they had a head start toward the location Jyres and his friends all feared. It was inevitable now; one way or another, this adventure was coming to an end.

A moment later, a gargoyle swooped down and landed in the camp. It was a friend of Gargan's, and after a while, they learned that Gargan had tried to warn them of the attack but could not get there in time. Now Gargan and the other gargoyles were trying to track Bram and his force, trying to confirm their destination.

24

Zar's Chase

Zar had ridden his horse hard. Flick and he had been able to make up some ground. They had lost the tracks of the knights on a few occasions, but Zar had used a spell here or there to help guide them. On the fifth day since they had started riding, Zar could now see Meslar and his three knights. The knights made camp as Meslar dug the end of his staff into the ground. He closed his eyes and mouthed some words. Zar and Flick took the opportunity to get closer. They moved behind a snow-covered tree. Meslar's staff started to glow; and the ground started to shake as a beam of purple light came out of the gem in the staff, down the staff, and ran along the ground and into a nearby cave. Curious, Zar watched and decided to wait to make his move. Some time went by, and nothing happened, and Zar really started to wonder what Meslar was doing. A few moments later, however, orcs and goblins began filing out of the cave.

Zar knew the cave would probably extend under the nearby mountains, and this was just one exit of the green creatures' lairs. He continued to watch the scene as more and more orcs and goblins came out to stand next to Meslar and the other creatures who had already exited the cave.

Finally, no more orcs or goblins exited the cave, but the ones who had were all mesmerized by Meslar's staff and had fallen under his spell. Meslar was visibly weaker, and he almost fell but held on to his staff to keep himself upright. "You will serve me," Zar heard him say to his creatures. The orcs and goblins started to chant to their new leader. Meslar now had an army of hundreds. Zar knew he had to stop him here, before the army was loosed on the army of the new world.

Zar casually stepped out from his hiding spot and into the throng of creatures. All the creatures drew their blades and growled at the new intruder. "Father, don't you ever give up," came Meslar's tired voice, followed by an "Attack!" It was Zar's turn to do some spell casting; he threw his arms up into the air and spoke some words from deep within himself, and a wave of energy ushered forth, freezing time and space.

Only Zar, Meslar, and Flick could move, talk, or even know what was happening. Impressed, Meslar smiled and started to raise his staff.

"Still using that staff. How long ago was it you started using that?" Puzzled by his father's conversational tone, Meslar lowered his staff. "I remember that day very well. I gave it to you to help you focus your energy. I would have thought you had advanced beyond that now. You need that staff to stay focused on your spell casting and to focus your power. How in the world do you think you will be powerful enough to harness whatever is in that gate?"

"That is the whole point, is it not, Father, to get more power."

"Do you know the prophecy?" Zar asked.

"I have it right here."

"You have half of it."

Before Meslar could respond, Zar spoke the other half of the prophecy from the book he had read in the library.

"That being said, it is not a power that should be unlocked. Powerful would a man be if he could harness it. But none can. They are uncontrollable. That is why the key has been hidden. Well hidden. May it never be found, and the gate never opened."

"You lie!" Meslar yelled back.

"Your prophecy is ripped on the bottom, is it not?"

Meslar did not respond; so what if it was true? He would be powerful enough. What did his old man know about power?

"You want the power for yourself, don't you, Father? You can't have it. It is mine to take."

"Meslar, listen to me. Continue this path, and it will lead to death."

"You are right, but not my death—it will be yours!"

Meslar pointed his staff and called out his words of power in a loud voice, but from out of nowhere came Flick. Like a lightning bolt, he flashed from his spot and ran up Meslar's leg and bit his arm. A huge ball of flame came forth from Meslar's staff as he swung an arm at Flick. Flick was long gone, and his action had caused the staff to move more than enough, and the ball of flame missed Zar and cooked a few frozen goblins.

Space and time were reestablished, and Zar and Flick fled the scene, knowing hundreds of creatures would not be far behind. Once Zar and Flick reached the horse, they had no problem outrunning the disgusting creatures, who soon gave up on the pursuit. The rest of the day Zar then spent following Meslar but stayed far enough back to avoid being noticed.

The next day, Zar had gotten a little too close to some of Meslar's army. Six goblins came after him. Zar wasn't worried in the least, as he waited for them. As they came near, he started a spell. Then the ground in front of him started to crack. The goblins were about to strike, and the ground broke open just in front of Zar. Four of the goblins could not react in time and fell into the fissure. The two remaining goblins decided to turn and run, but it was too late. Zar used two rocks as missiles and used his power to send them into the heads of the retreating creatures.

Two days of following Meslar and his army brought Zar to where he knew his chase would end: the gate. He looked down upon the gate from a cliff, and what a sight it was. A hawk landed suddenly on a nearby tree. Zar walked up to the bird and offered it his arm. The hawk walked across his arm to perch on his shoulder. Using a soothing voice with a hint of magic, he gave the bird a message and a destination. The hawk flew up into the sky and disappeared high above the clouds.

Zar could not believe what had happened to his son. His mind went back to many years before when he had first started training his son. Where had he gone wrong? If his mother had not gone ill, would she have helped? What was it that turned him? More and more questions that he could not answer filled Zar's thoughts. He sighed to himself, resigned to the fact that his son was lost to him.

25

Dwarven March

Vurth and his dwarves had been marching for three days now. They were about to make camp for the night, but a scout had reported that four thars were not too far away. Vurth decided they would take care of them before they became a problem. He split his force into two, wanting to attack from two sides.

Vurth led the charge of one group, and as the two groups attacked, the thars panicked. They growled and tried to run, but it was over quickly.

The thars had been mulling around a cave, so Vurth sent in some dwarves to check it out. Before long, the all-clear came back, and they set up camp in the cave. While setting up camp, two dwarves searched the backs of the caves, using torches to help. The dwarves wanted to check the cave again to make sure they were alone. To their astonishment, they found a tunnel. Vurth was called for, and before long, he was in the entrance of the tunnel.

"Sure would be nice to travel underground for a while. The tunnel seems to go in the same direction we were going." A smile came across the old dwarf's face. "Sure would be nice," he said again.

As Vurth was eating, scouts reported back that the first parts of the tunnel seemed safe and still ran in the same direction. Vurth spread the word around camp that the group would travel underground for the next couple of days.

Dwarves are very comfortable in caves, tunnels, and the like. In fact, some are even more comfortable underground than above. So the next morning when the group started into the tunnel, they seemed reenergized, and the group moved quickly through the tunnel. Within a few arcs, the dwarves had traveled rather far and came to a point where the tunnel intersected another. Two dwarves were sent down each tunnel to investigate while the others rested.

Once news arrived that they should continue in the same tunnel, the dwarves were off again. Vurth had a great sense of direction, even when underground; and although the tunnels took a few turns here and there, he was confident they were heading the direction Gargan had told them to go. After a few more arcs, Vurth and his dwarves came to a point of many intersecting tunnels. Vurth moved the group back a little ways and sent a few dwarves to investigate. The other dwarves got a needed rest.

Tagro was one of the dwarves sent to investigate one of the many tunnels. Tagro had been in his tunnel for a little while already. The tunnel was very large, and Tagro tried to stay close to the wall on one side. His tunnel seemed to continue to descend, and he decided that this tunnel would not be of any use. He was about to turn around, but he noticed that up ahead, the tunnel seemed to open into a big room.

Tagro continued down the tunnel and into the "room." The young dwarf fell down on the ground in astonishment. There right in front of him was a huge bear. The bear was even larger than the thars they had dealt with and one of the largest creatures he had ever seen. Tagro didn't know it at the time, but this bear was one of the race known as Black Donosin. Many tales have been told of them. Some even said there was a time that the Black Donosin Bears could speak. The bear let out a roar, and Tagro was up in a hurry. He yelled in terror as he raced up the tunnel. The beast was right behind him.

*****

All the dwarven scouts had reported back except for Tagro. It took a while to try to establish which direction all the different tunnels were going. The tunnel they were in now had started to turn a little too much to the west and started to descend more, which was one thing Vurth did not want to do. Vurth decided to choose a tunnel that seemed to angle up slightly and possibly would go back to the east a little.

Vurth was getting worried about Tagro though and was about to send some dwarves after him. But Vurth and others soon heard screams and roars, and Vurth barked out commands telling the warriors to ready their weapons. Vurth watched as Tagro emerged from the tunnel running as fast as he could. Then roars spilled out of the tunnel followed by a black bear, at least four times the size of Tagro.

After a split second of shock, Vurth ordered the retreat down the chosen tunnel. All the dwarves fled down the tunnel, Vurth and Tagro the last ones in the line. The beast followed, just barely fitting into the tunnel, which was a little smaller than the last.

Tagro and Vurth looked at each other, both realizing the same thing. They could not let this beast attack their kin. The two turned and charged the powerful beast. Vurth thought he could see a smile come across the black bear's face, and he rolled to the right as the bear swatted at him.

Tagro took the opportunity to race around the bear. The dwarf hacked at the bear's back and drew some blood, also black, as the bear spun around and swung a big paw sending Tagro to the ground. The beast backed out of the tunnel, and Vurth followed it, avoiding the swipes from the bear.

In the small area, Tagro and Vurth circled the beast, which licked his lips. The area was too small for the donosin to move too much, and that is what probably saved the two dwarves. They were able to stay away from the bear because the bear could not move as fast in the cramped entryway to the tunnels. The dwarves hacked with their axes and dodged the donosin as they circled around it.

Hoping they had given the other dwarves enough time, they ran for the tunnel, but the bear swung around quickly, and it blocked the tunnel entrance. The dwarves were forced down a different tunnel, and the bear followed, running on all fours.

Tagro and Vurth glanced at each other as they ran, and Vurth yelled at his son, "I would bet my beard that we are battling a donosin!"

Tagro's face was one of utter surprise as he realized what his father was saying. Black Donosin Bears were thought to be extinct. Even before the great war, donosins were rare.

Both father and son allowed for big smiles to appear on their faces. They were battling a Black Donosin Bear and loving every moment of it. Never in his wildest dreams had Tagro thought he would battle such a beast. He knew by himself he would already have been dead, but with his father by his side, they could at least survive long enough to enjoy the thrill.

Tagro almost got his leg clawed off, the beast just missing him. Vurth looked back and saw the beast was about to pounce. Vurth thought he saw something, and he took a chance, pulling on Tagro as he dove to the right. They dove through a small opening in the tunnel just as the form of the black beast pounced, its big form landing where the dwarves had just been moments before.

The two dwarves were quickly crawling through the opening to the other side. Father and son rose to their feet and looked backed through the small opening to see a bear's face staring back. They looked at each other in disbelief and started down their new tunnel. It did not take too long to join up with the other dwarves, and Tagro and Vurth shared their run-in with the black bear, their voices full of excitement and wonder and telling the story as only a dwarf could.

The next arcs felt uneventful after what they had experienced. After what Vurth surmised would have been about two days of choosing tunnels and only minor skirmishes with creatures, he decided it was time they try to head back up to the surface. Eventually, the group found a tunnel that led up to the surface. The dwarves followed the tunnel, and as they did so, some light started to fade some of the darkness.

Vurth led the dwarves out of the tunnels and into the sunlight, which looked as though it would soon disappear. The group started traveling north and sent out scouts in all different directions. The scouts were looking for any sign of the gate. One such scout found more than a sign—he found the gate.

The scout crouched on a cliff behind a boulder looking out over the land. He saw a magnificent sight. There stood a gate of fire. No metal or stone of any kind could be seen. But fire was everywhere, forming a gate. The middle of the gate was arched at the top, and bars of fire ran vertical over the length of the gate. The fiery gate itself stood tall, wide, and intimidating. Around the gate was a ring of fire. Only the gate and the ring were consumed with fire. The land around it remained untouched. However, there was no accumulation of snow. Even the land between the ring and the gate showed a few signs of life. There was no discernable reason for the gate. Either side of the gate was just dry ground with patches of growth, so going through the gate it seemed to the scout would just bring you to the other side. The scout reported everything he had seen to Vurth and the other dwarves.

The dwarves had made camp for the night, and soon all the scouts had returned. Vurth had trouble sleeping that night. He knew tomorrow he would march his dwarves right up to the gate. He did not know how long they would camp there, nor did he know if Jyres and the elves had succeeded in getting the key. All he knew was his job: to get to the gate and defend it.

The next day, the army of dwarves prepared themselves for the march. It had gotten mighty cold, and the snow was blowing. The stubborn dwarves marched against the cold and the snow. They were in good spirits, knowing by nightfall they would reach their journey's end. The good spirits did not last, however, for as the dwarves came in view of the magnificent sight of the gate, hundreds of orcs and goblins were camped in front of it.

The sun seemed to fall out of the sky as it darkened, as did Vurth's heart seem to fall out of his chest. Because as his dwarves approached, he could see Meslar on horseback in the back of the camp. Vurth looked over the scene. This whole group of creatures had moved into the area in the last day or so. None had been here when his scout first saw the area. His mind was racing, trying to think of the possibilities that would allow Meslar to be here but not Zar or Jyres and the elves.

Vurth knew he had made a mistake; he marched right in assuming the area was the same as it was the night before. Now he had no tactical advantage, and he had twenty dwarves against hundreds of enemies. It was too late to try to make it to the high ground. It was all over. The orcs and goblins started their approach.

26

The Final Battle

The creatures were getting closer, and the dwarves knew this was it. The odds were stacked against them, and this time there were no hidden traps for the enemies. Vurth yelled to his men to make ready and then followed it with "It has been a pleasure fighting with the likes of you, men. Let's see how many of these disgusting creatures we can take with us." Vurth had a flashback to a similar circumstance when he and a few others were waiting on a hill to be slaughtered by goblins, but a dragon had saved them. Not even realizing it, Vurth looked up into the sky. To his absolute amazement, he saw two giant figures flying like an elven arrow down from the sky.

The two dragons landed to shouts of joy from the dwarves and screams of agony from goblins that cushioned the dragons' landings. Vurth let out a battle cry and barked out orders to defend the dragons' flanks. The dragons let out waves of fire from their giant maws as the creatures attacked. The dwarves hacked away as the first wave came at them; and the dragons clawed, bit, and inflamed the orcs and goblins.

Zar looked on from his hiding spot as a hawk gave a squawk and flew by him. Zar smiled; he had done his job. The hawk's message had reached the dragons just in time. Zar was glad they had finally fully joined the fight against Meslar. He just wished it would not have taken so long. Then again, he thought to himself, the dragons were wise creatures; and they may have known it was all going to come down to something like this the whole time and were saving their strength. Who was he to question such amazing creatures?

Vurth, the dwarves, and the dragons defended the first wave of enemies brilliantly. Not one dwarf could be seen on the ground, though their cuts and bruises were many. Even the dragons showed signs of wounds. Vurth took a deep breath, preparing for the second wave that was sure to come. Then in the sky came some gargoyles. To Vurth's dismay, they landed on the side of the enemy. Bram's force had now joined the battle, but Gargan's was not far behind. They landed among the dwarves.

Gargan patted Vurth on the back as they watched Bram approach Meslar. "He has the key and has been able to avoid confrontation with us," Gargan said, anger clearly heard in his voice.

Then the group was in battle again. This time the orcs and goblins, and now gargoyles, came on in full force, knocking Vurth's and Gargan's forces back. Steel met steel, and claw met claw as the fighting raged. Vurth deflected an orc's thrust and reversed his ax and chopped the head of the orc right off. Then he spun to block a goblin's sword, but Tagro had already sent the creature to the ground. Father and son nodded to each other and worked together slaying creature after creature.

Gargan and his gargoyles were just as impressive as the two dwarves. Their claws were deadly, and Gargan himself was untouchable. He sent goblin and orc alike flying back the way they came. Bram's forces though were also now in the battle. Many gargoyles were in duels with each other, as was Gargan now as a big orange gargoyle attacked him.

The battle continued on, but Vurth and his friends were starting to be pushed back by the overwhelming odds. The two dragons were showing signs of tiring, the dragons being the real reason why anyone else was still alive. A dragon's tail flew over Vurth and Tagro and sent the two enemy gargoyles they were fighting flying into orcs and goblins. Two goblins then slipped inside the dragon's defenses and hacked away at the creature's belly. The dragon cried in pain before closing its mouth around the goblins, swallowing both the goblins whole.

Then from out of nowhere arrows flew into the enemy horde. Jyres's group had arrived. The elves sent a second and third arrow volley away before their first arrows had even hit their marks. The group had snuck onto the rocky cliffs over-looking the battlefield, everyone except Jyres and Elonda. Elonda led Jyres in and out from behind the rocks at the bottom of the cliffs. Their hope, to reach the enemies' back lines and stop Meslar before it was too late.

Even this small group of elves could be deadly, as they sent arrow after arrow into the enemies' army, thinning their ranks with each shot. Bram led the retaliation. He and some of his gargoyles took to the air and closed in on the elves. The elves got off a few more shots before the gargoyles were on them. Bram landed and with one strong punch sent one elf off the cliff, ending his life.

The elves took a couple of casualties before forming up behind Lalatco and Leah. Both of them were still injured, but both of them were ready to take on Bram and his followers. A loud roar erupted out of Bram as they charged, and a mighty blast of wind came from behind Leah and Lalatco, slowing the creatures' charge. Lalatco did not have to look to know that Zar was behind them.

A gargoyle charged in right at Lalatco and Leah who both sidestepped the charge and sliced it as the creature went by. The gargoyles' tough skin was all the armor they needed against the sharp blades. Lalatco quickly discovered this was not going to be an easy battle. Lalatco ducked under a punch and put another scratch on the gargoyle, his scimitar barely piercing the skin. All around Lalatco the elves were experiencing the same thing, and the gargoyles pushed the elves back.

Zar stood at the back of the elven army. He too saw what was happening and was in the middle of a spell. It was a spell he had not cast in a long time, and he had to be very careful he got it right. After a few more moments, he looked up at the elves, and all their blades were aglow with a bright red. Zar smiled; his Piercing Power spell had worked.

Lalatco and Leah saw their blades start to glow a bright red. Lalatco guessed right away what that meant. Leah and he both rolled forward under the swinging claws of their enemies, his supported leg screaming with pain the whole time. Simultaneously they rolled to their feet behind their attackers and plunged their blades into the backs of the gargoyles. The glowing blades pierced the gargoyles' skin and sent the enemy to the ground. Zar had evened the odds.

*****

As the battle continued on, Elonda and Jyres snuck to the back lines. They saw Meslar approach the ring of fire, but a dozen or so orcs stood in their way. Jyres watched as Meslar took his first step inside the ring of fire. With a scream that could scare even the mightiest of soldiers, Jyres charged. Elonda was just a step behind. Jyres blocked the first orc's wild swing, moving right on to the second orc; he plunged his sword into its belly. Elonda finished off the first.

In almost the same fashion, Jyres and Elonda killed two more. Jyres cut the legs out from another as he blocked a different orc's swing. Elonda's sword movements were just amazing as she slew two orcs without even a thought. Jyres killed another, and his path was clear. He took off like a ruptured duck, reaching the ring as quick as he could have. Elonda, however, was left with five orcs to deal with.

*****

The elves had accomplished one thing though: their arrow barrage had done the trick. It had ended the enemies' charge and caused them to regroup. Vurth and Tagro looked at each and laughed. Both were bloodied beyond belief, and both were happy for the short break. The break was very short, however, for the enemy army quickly regrouped and started another attack.

Vurth quickly yelled out orders to his army. He knew their enemies would bring at them everything they had this time. The dwarves and gargoyles responded right away to his orders. Everyone got in as tight to each other as they could. The dragons were in the middle. On the dragons' right were Vurth and Tagro, and on the dragons' left was Gargan. Vurth hoped they could more effectively use the dragons' power and keep them safe with everyone tight together.

As the enemy army charged, Vurth saw that this time Demorous, the Silver Shadow, and Lemont led the enemy forces. Vurth let out a loud battle cry, and Gargan followed it with one of his own. The two dragons then let out roars so loud that Vurth thought for sure the ground had shaken. The enemy army ran full steam ahead, and flames were the first thing they met, claws and axes second.

The army on the cliff had fared okay; they had taken some losses but had cut some of the gargoyles down as well. Lalatco and Leah urged the group on, knowing they had to help their friends down in the valley, but the gargoyles were tough fighters, and whenever they gained ground or Zar cast a spell, the gargoyles would soon make the ground back up. Both Vurth's and Lalatco's armies would soon be in trouble.

*****

As Jyres stepped inside the ring of fire, somehow untouched by the flames, his vision became blurred. All he could see were flames around him. He pushed on, then he saw his village being attacked; it seemed so long ago now. He pushed on. Then he saw Lalatco, Leah, and Vurth, all fighting and all in trouble. He stopped; he had to help them. He saw Lalatco fall to the ground, but Jyres took another step, and then another. But then he saw Elonda who he had left to battle five orcs, and it stopped him in his tracks. He watched as she was overmatched and struck to the ground, and an orc sent in his killing blow.

Jyres tried to scream, but no words came out. He fell to his knees, the fire growing all around him, looking to consume him. Then a voice came to him. He did not know whose voice it was or how he heard it. All he heard was "It's not real. Continue on." And miraculously he did. He got up and almost ran. Then all of a sudden everything was clear. He saw Meslar at the gate. He saw him pulling the key out of his pocket. Then Jyres was at the gate next to Meslar. Lightning fast, he drew his sword as Meslar reached the key toward the lock. The key fit in its place, and Jyres swung his sword, his sword hacking Meslar's arm off at the elbow. Jyres pivoted on his foot and turned his body, keeping the momentum of the sword going as he turned. Without hesitation, he plunged the sword into Meslar's chest. Meslar had a look of confusion on his face as his body fell onto the ground.

Jyres turned to see the gate start to open. Not even thinking of the flames, he flung himself at the gate, trying to grab the key as he did so. Jyres wrenched the key from its spot as his body slammed into a gate that felt more of metal than it did of fire, and he fell hard on the ground. Something leaped out of the gate, as the gate slammed shut. A creature stood before Jyres, in human shape, but some sort of gelatinous form. The creature smiled and reached down for Jyres's throat. But Jyres felt a wave of energy come over him as the creature's hand hit what seemed like an invisible shield around Jyres. The creature swung and swung his arms but could not reach Jyres. Confused, the creature retreated into the distance.

Jyres looked back to the battlefield. What was left of the orcs and goblins retreated, shrieking as they did so. With Meslar's death, the creatures' minds were free, and none of them wanted to continue the battle against the resilient army. Jyres also watched as Bram and his gargoyles took flight and left the battlefield, arrows following them in the sky as they did so.

Looking down at Meslar's lifeless body, Jyres let out a sigh. Jyres had killed Meslar, but not in time. Something had escaped from the gate. Jyres wondered if all this had been for naught, if whatever escaped from the gate would be even worse than anything Meslar was. His thoughts dwelled on that as he left the area of the gate. The whole thing was too much. Whose voice had he heard? How did he not burn up? How did he slam into a gate that was pure flames? And where did the creature escape from?

Zar met Jyres as he walked toward the dwarves and dragons, where everyone seemed to be congregating. Jyres was the first to speak. "Zar, we failed. Something got out of the gate."

Zar smiled. "We did not fail. You have saved us. One creature escaped, yes, but there could have been many more. You did well, Jyres, you did well."

Jyres watched as Zar approached the ring of fire and his dead son. He stopped right outside the ring and looked over at Meslar's body. Meslar's body started to disintegrate into the air, and Zar watched sadly but reverently as the last of Meslar's body disappeared. He assumed the mere power of Meslar and the gate caused the body to disintegrate. Very tired, and using the last of his strength, he cast one more spell; and Meslar's staff rose from the ground and moved toward his outstretched hand.

Jyres approached the group and noticed that Demorous and the Silver Shadow had been disarmed of their weapons and were in the middle of the group. As he walked, he passed a knight lying on the ground, lifeless. Lemont had not survived the battle. Jyres walked into the group gathered, and he clearly saw obvious looks of confusion on the faces of the knights.

"Look," said Demorous, "I have no idea what is going on. I don't know how we got here or where we are. All I remember is…" Demorous stopped talking then, as if he did not remember anything. Jyres, remembering a conversation he and Lalatco had, guessed what had happened and responded to him.

"Do you remember Meslar?"

"Yes, actually, that is all I can recall. I see him and nothing else." The Silver Shadow nodded his head in agreement.

"Their minds have been controlled for so long they don't even remember who they are," commented Jyres to those gathered around. "Let them do as they please," said Jyres, who got a surprised look from Vurth. Unaffected, Jyres continued, "Knights, I suggest you stick with us, however, and have some people fill you in on all that has happened since Meslar has dominated your mind. A long time that has been, but lucky for you, we have a long trip home."

Jyres now looked over who was all gathered around. He had already seen Vurth, bruised but not beaten, and he had seen Zar. He continued to scan the area looking for Lalatco, Leah, and Elonda. He spotted Lalatco and Leah, both in rough shape, but both with smiles on their faces. A few more moments and Jyres started to become nervous; no sign of Elonda. Had the orcs bested her? Jyres was about to look over in that direction when he saw her, right next to his good friend Gargan. Jyres went over to greet both of them.

Overall, the battle had been a success. Some dwarves and elves had died, and a few gargoyles would be returned to their castle, most likely never to leave their stone form again. But Meslar too had died, and many orcs and goblins. The most important result was that only one creature escaped when Zar said there could have been many. Still, Jyres wondered what that one creature would now do.

The whole group started to help collect their dead companions. It was a sad day, for over half of the group that Vurth and Elonda had led across the mountains had died. Each body was put in its own grave, and a stone was put in the middle of the area. On the stone, Zar used magic to inscribe the words "To those who fought bravely and gave their lives so that the world would not be thrown into chaos and their families destroyed, we thank you." Gargan and his clan collected those of his kin saying that they would be returned to the castle to join their brother who unfortunately had not overcome his injuries from the previous battle with Meslar.

After that was done, the group all headed home together. During this long trip, the group continued to talk to the knights who were slowly starting to recall certain things about themselves. Zar and Jyres talked often. Jyres asked Zar at one point, "So was it your voice I heard when the fire was about to consume me?"

Zar just smiled and shook his head no, but Jyres knew that it was.

"And the energy shield so the creature could not harm me, I know that was you. Don't even try to deny that one."

Zar laughed out loud and said yes, that was him.

Epilogue

A few weeks after everyone had returned home, the dragons hosted a party in the valley. Everyone was invited, including the reunited knights. The valley was filled with creatures. Dwarves, elves, human, gargoyles, and even Ogla the Orc were there.

Everyone exchanged tales, and food was prepared by some of Malick's best cooks. Although no tables were set up, there was still an organization to where all the people were seated. Jyres was in the front and center along with Zar and the dragons.

The food and wine were soon served, and shortly after that, people started calling for a speech from Jyres. As Jyres stood up to oblige the crowd, he took in the mass of those who were looking at him. His heart started to thud a little faster in his chest; he wasn't confident enough for a speech like this. Then he took a deep breath. His mind quickly recalled some of the adventures he had come through to get to this point, and his heartbeat started to slow. Then in the loudest voice he could muster, he started his speech.

"It is right for you to throw a party and right for you to lavish on your guests' food of no comparison. And it is great to toast to someone with the fruit of the vine. But this is not all done to honor one man. This is done to honor everyone and anyone who in any way helped with the battle against Meslar. I could not have even come close to defeating Meslar without the help of many. Yes, we should be throwing a party, but it should be to honor Vurth and the dwarves. Never have I fought beside such brave and determined fighters." At this, a hearty cheer went up from the crowd, and Jyres paused until it died down. "Oh, and by all means serve this great food, but not in honor of me, but in honor of the elves, whose arrows killed more creatures than I care to count on that battlefield." Again, cheers went up before he continued, "And please raise your glasses high and toast, but don't toast me, toast to those that saved my life more than a few times. Toast to Gargan and his friends for always knowing when I was in need of their help, toast to Lalatco, brave enough to cross the mountains with me and brave enough to take on a castle by himself. Drink to Leah and Flick, our first friends we met on the other side and the two who led us to Zar. After you finish, fill up your glasses again for another toast, this one to Elonda. Elonda is the one who saved me from wolves and led me to Meslar in the final battle. And, friends, raise your glasses high to Zar. Zar helped me when I needed it the most, when all was about to be lost. And finally, raise your glasses to the two creatures that changed the tide of that final battle, to our hosts, the dragons."

Once Jyres had finished his speech, the whole crowd erupted in cheers and applause. Everyone hooted and howled; and finally when the crowd had quieted down, and finished eating, dessert was served.

After the celebration, there was a meeting, and many were in attendance. The two dragons were there along with Malick, Elonda, Lalatco, Jyres, Vurth, Demorous, Zar, Leah, Ogla, and Gargan. The point of the meeting was to talk about important issues, such as the week of peace, the nations on the other side of the mountains, and the future of Alhazar and Tomackus.

All sorts of ideas were discussed, and many opinions were voiced. It was decided that the week of peace would be no more, and a king and an army would be appointed to rule "the land." It took a long time for the group to finally decide that "the land" would include any land on either side of the mountains. Gargan and Zar had a hand in persuading the rest of the group to that conclusion. Zar and Gargan also agreed to sit down with an elf from Malick's family who would draw a map of the entire land, or nation.

As the group continued their discussions, they agreed roads would have to be built and monitored, especially one that would follow the mountain pass. A few other important things were mentioned as well, including Castle Mystic or the Valley of the Dragons as possible spots for the king to reside. Finally, toward the end of the meeting, the key to the gate was brought up and what should be done with it. After many attempts to destroy the key, which all proved useless, the key was handed back to Jyres. Once he had it in his possession again, everyone agreed it would stay there for the time being.

Those at the meeting were sent back to their people and asked to come up with nominations for the positions of king, advisor, and captain of the guard. They were also asked to come up with ideas for keeping the key safe.

Jyres and Leah returned with the elves to their home, and they enjoyed their time with the elves. They both were introduced to more elves than they could remember, and all of their needs were cared for by their hosts.

One morning, Lalatco and Jyres presented themselves to Malick.

"Welcome, friends, to what do I owe the pleasure of your visit?"

In response, Jyres came forward and got down on one knee in front of the king, his sword in its sheath lying across his arms. "I bring back to you the sword which you had bestowed upon me. It has yet again proven itself worthy of its inscription." Jyres laid the sword at the feet of the king.

"Rise," said the king, and Jyres did. "Proud has my family been for you to carry this sword. Glad we are to have both it and you returned to us."

Jyres offered one more bow, as did Lalatco, before they took their leave of the king.

*****

Things really could not have gone much better, thought Bram, who was standing in his private area of the castle. All of his planning had turned out rather well. He was somewhat surprised at the ease of which Meslar was able to approach the gate. Meslar had guaranteed him that he would be able to, and he had lived up to his part of the bargain. Bram had promised the key, and he had delivered that as well. The interesting part of the bargain was that both he and Meslar would have wanted complete control over any power that the gate held.

Bram left the inner part of his castle and climbed to the top of the front gate and took in the view of the area. He grinned as he saw five gargoyles returning in a hurry from their recon mission. His wide grin stayed on his face as he continued his train of thought. Jyres had done him a favor; he had eliminated Meslar from the equation. Now with Meslar out of the way, the power was his to take, and that power appeared to be in the shape of a creature. Only one creature escaped from wherever the mystical gate kept them, but that was a problem that Bram would soon rectify.

After the battle was over, Bram and his gargoyles had watched and observed the creature who had escaped from the gate. Not much had been learned about the creature, however, and Bram wanted to know more.

The five gargoyles who had just returned landed by Bram.

"Report," said Bram sternly in the language of the gargoyles.

"We have found it. It is still on its own and seems to be exploring."

"Show me," said Bram, and all six gargoyles took flight.

As the creature was walking through the jungle, the very same jungle where Lalatco and Jyres had met Leah, Bram and five other gargoyles jumped out and encircled the creature.

The creature seemed to be unaffected, his facial features hard to distinguish in his gelatinous body. Bram spoke first, using the basic language. "So you have escaped. The stories speak of ultimate power, no offense, but it does not seem that the gate has provided such."

The creature gave some sort of a laughing noise before replying in a garbled form of basic. "I am...only...one...more... would you...see power."

Bram eyed the creature, wondering what secrets or powers it contained. "What will you do now? Your whole race is trapped behind, or should I say in, some magical gate?" he finally responded.

"What...would you...do?"

"Well, I guess I would do anything I could to free them," Bram growled.

"As is...my mind...set" was the quick response.

Assuming the conversation was over, the creature started to walk out of the circle of gargoyles. As it did so, Bram started talking again. "Do you have any idea how you are going to do it?"

The creature stopped and turned around, a look of confusion somewhat visible on the odd-looking creature. "I can help you," continued Bram. "I know what you need to get and who you need to get it from."

"Why...would you...help?"

"The stories tell me whatever is in that gate has ultimate power, and you are what came out of that gate, and I want ultimate power." Bram could not help but let out a loud chuckle. "I am sure we could reach some sort of an agreement." A smile came across the big gargoyle's face.

*****

Two weeks had gone by since the last meeting, and now everyone from anywhere was invited to the Valley of the Dragons to hear the nominations for the positions that would lead the new land. Esmeralda was in the center of the valley and used her loud powerful voice to recite the nominations.

"The following names have been nominated for the position of king of the land: Vurth, Malick, and Crimson. The name who gets the loudest cheer will be our new king. The first name, Vurth." After saying the name, the crowd responded with cheers, the loudest coming from the dwarves. Malick's name was read next, and many cheers were heard not only from the elves but from some others as well. The cheers were much louder for Malick than for Vurth. Esmeralda then said Crimson's name, and the cheers were again louder than the ones for Vurth, but not as loud as they were for Malick.

After a moment or two had passed, the dragon's voice was heard over the many conversations taking place in the large crowd. "I present to you your new king, King Malick." Malick stepped forward from the crowd, as they cheered loudly for their new king. Malick spoke a few words about prosperity and peace before returning to the crowd.

The same process was done for both the position of captain of the guard and advisor to the king. Vurth, Demorous, and Gargan were nominated for the position of captain; and the cheers for Vurth far outweighed the other two. Vurth was then appointed captain of the guard. The position of advisor had many nominations, and Zar received by far the most cheers. Zar, however, respectfully declined, saying he was too old for such an endeavor. It was decided that the spot of advisor to the king would go to Esmeralda.

After the crowd had dispersed, King Malick, Captain Vurth, and Esmeralda called Jyres and Lalatco to come by them. Just to the small group of four, the king said, "Finally, we are to appoint two people who are to be in charge of the safety of the key. So, my captain and advisor, I give you Lalatco and Jyres, the keepers of the key!"

Acknowledgements

I tip my cap to everyone at Covenant Books for helping make this dream a reality. Thank you to Joshua Vick for his encouragement and advice throughout this process. A special thank you to my wife, children and extended family who have supported me in this new adventure. Finally, thank you to everyone who read The Prophecy of the Gate. I hope you enjoyed it!

About the Author

The Prophecy of the Gate is B. J. Vanderhoof's debut novel. His love for fantasy and science fiction inspired him to begin writing. When he is not writing, Vanderhoof is working at a YMCA as a program executive. He enjoys playing board games, watching movies, reading, and spending time with family. Vanderhoof lives with his wife and three children in Appleton, Wisconsin. He plans on continuing to write, and you can follow him on Medium or on Twitter @BJV_TheYGuy.

Visit his website at https://bjvanderhoof.com